FROM MY COLD DEAD HANDS

HILLY BARMBY

www.bloodhoundbooks.com

Print ISBN 978-1-5040-7268-7

PROLOGUE

The train to Victoria was packed. Pushing others aside, I fought to get on and grab a seat. They might grumble, but what did they know? *Hide in plain sight.*

Hunkered into my seat by the window, I pulled my cap low over my eyes and tucked my hair into my hoodie. Someone landed with a thump next to me, almost causing me to scream. My mind a supernova on steroids. Bright lights spiralled at the corner of my vision. *Keep it in.* Keep the *howl* welling inside of me in. But no, I was all right. For now.

Tilting my head, I scanned around me. There were too many witnesses here, but then, when had witnesses ever been a deterrent? *Never.*

As the train jolted out of Brighton station and the city melted away into the countryside, *that* terrible image overlaid what was in front of me. It was as if I were seeing it afresh, over and over again. So much blood. How could there be that much blood? My legs wouldn't stop shaking, adrenaline and exhaustion vying for possession of my body.

Waiting at the door as the train slowed into Victoria, I stayed in the middle of the crowd surging for the gates. My hand trembled as I punched in my ticket. Don't look back. *Don't show your face.*

I forced myself to walk. Although my body was set to flee, to race, I couldn't risk that. *Don't look back.* Except I couldn't help myself. One quick glance over my shoulder. A smokescreen of unknown people behind me. My breathing ragged, I hugged my arms around myself, clinging to the bag strung across my shoulder. I'd chucked the one I'd previously owned into a bin in Brighton station. This new one was my lifeline.

Walking up Victoria Street, the buildings on either side loomed above me, stealing my light, my air. So close now, so very close. At any moment, I expected a voice behind me, a hand to grab me, pain and then terror. Left down Buckingham Gate, tears blinding me. Where was it? St. James' Court Hotel. Red building? There it was. Speeding up, all I could see was red: red brick, red blood.

Oh, fuck! I'd made a terrible mistake. The entrance to the hotel was on the other side of the road. How had I got that so wrong? *Disorientated, head full of things I didn't ever want to see, too many tears.*

I spotted the doorman, all suited and booted with his peaked cap, standing under the ever-so-fancy arch. Rummaging in the bag, I grabbed hold of the hotel key. *This will save me.* I can't stop myself. I run, run toward that sanctuary, the tears streaming down my face.

'Help me! *Please, help me!*' The cry ripped from my throat.

The doorman raised a hand. Yes, he recognised me, but there was a strange look on his face. His mouth moved, made shapes, though I couldn't hear the words, as the white noise in my head blocked it out.

'*Help me!*' I was shrieking now, and then I saw it.

Something vast and black came at me from the side, and it didn't stop, *couldn't stop,* and then the impact sent me into the

2

air. Spinning like a thrown dolly, I smacked against the tarmac, knowing there was pain but not feeling it yet. Shouts and cries came as if from a distance. A dark shape lunged over me. Had I been caught?

I watched my hand open, that precious hotel key skidding away from me. No, no, *no*!

Help me.

1

THE HOSPITAL

'Cassie.'

The doctor stands at the foot of the bed. I've been conscious for nearly a day now, but I don't feel awake. Panic tugs at me, insistent. Who am I? I don't recognise anything, least of all myself. I want to scream until I burst all the blood vessels in my eyes. Maybe I'll wake up then.

'Cassie?' he says again.

Staring for a moment out of the window, the bright light from outside is dimmed by blinds. I don't remember the sun. In my head, it's grey, damp and dreary. Is that what happens after a "trauma"? Your mind loses its light?

The room is private, shiny and clean, with crisp white sheets and plump pillows. It's full of flowers from well-wishers that are names on pretty cards only, with no recollection of faces to fit them. I sniff and regret it. The air is redolent with their perfume, cloying and heavy from the hundreds of roses and lilies overflowing vases, vying for space on the bedside table and window ledge.

'Am I in a flower shop?' It doesn't sound like my voice.

'We're in the Piedmont hospital in Atlanta.'

'But you told me I was in an accident in London.'

'That's true, but the moment we could, we brought you home.'

I look around. 'I thought flowers weren't allowed in hospitals anymore.'

The doctor clears his throat a couple of times. 'Well, yes, but your father insisted.'

'My father can overrule hospital regulations?'

'They are only recommendations, really.' He clears his throat again. 'Your father is highly regarded here, and if he wanted you to wake up to flowers, then that's fine by us.'

I read between the lines. My father is someone that they don't want to piss off, except what sort of man that is, I can't guess. Fear snags me as if I'm leaning back into a transparent thorn-riddled bush.

In that voice all doctors use, I'm told that my family will be here soon to visit me; my father, my husband, my son and daughter, all of whom I have no memories of. They say, maybe when I see my husband Nick, it might jolt something in me, like using jump leads to start a car or paddles on a stopped heart. But my heart feels as if I've already snorted a gram or two of some illegal substance. It's beating so fast that they have to give me something to calm me down. *It's okay*, they say; I'm bound to be anxious, only normal after all.

I think it's more than that. The word "children" means nothing, a big cavity inside of me where, I presume, they used to reside. "Father" equals a dull throbbing fear, like an old bruise that is no longer really painful, but you know it's still there. Yet when I think of the word "husband", I feel a jolt all right, sharp and shiny and piercingly bright. It's like there's a plastic bag over my head, and I'm gasping in my last few breaths. They haven't mentioned my mother, although I know she's the beacon in the dark that keeps the monsters away. And the monsters are real. But I can't remember why.

'I hope my father knows whether I suffer from hay fever or not, because my eyes are itching something rotten.' I say, trying to make light of it.

I'm worried that if I cry now, I'll never stop. I tweak a tissue from a box on the table by the bed and dab gingerly at my eyes.

'I'm sure he's taken all that into consideration,' the doctor says, patting the end of the bed where two lumps show my feet. At least I hope they're my feet. I haven't found the courage to ask if any more tangible bits are missing, other than the deep void of space in my head. More shock, and I might disappear completely.

'Remember,' says the doctor, 'Your name is Cassandra Barber-Davenport, and you're from the state of Georgia.'

'I'm in America then?' I ask, realising it's a pretty stupid thing to say.

'The United States, yes.' He smiles brightly at me. I'm nearly blinded by his perfect, dazzling white teeth. His skin is a strange orange colour, which offsets the glow of his teeth and white coat nicely. He looks a bit *stretched*, as if he might tear when he sneezes.

Where the hell is Georgia? Down south maybe, hazard a guess here.

'Oh. That's nice.'

What does he expect me to say? How do I ask what kind of life I have? Am I rich? Am I poor? Am I trailer trash? I know I'm white. I feel in my gut, somehow, that money has not crossed my path. But I do seem to have many friends judging by the flowers, and someone is paying for this room, although I really hope it isn't me.

'So, you know where you are now?'

'We've covered that. The United States of America,' I say. I wonder if I'm expected to salute or sing the anthem.

'Good. And you're American too, aren't you?'

'Seemingly so.'

'It's just that, I'm rather perplexed as to why you're speaking with a British accent? Can you explain that?'

'What? Am I?'

I think for a second.

Yes, I can hear his accent, yet I can't hear my own.

'I have no idea, but then that's the whole point, isn't it? I have no idea about anything, do I?' I say.

'It will get better. I think it's about time you looked at yourself in a mirror. You have to consider the fact that you don't normally look like this, but try to see beyond. Try to see "you" if you can.'

He holds a small mirror up to my face.

Is he kidding me? I mean, of course, I don't *usually* have a massive bandage around my head. My jaw is held together by bolts like Frankenstein's hideous sister and a zip-like set of staples is zigzagging across the left-hand section of my strategically shaved skull. I gaze at what's left of my face that I can see. Well, maybe I *normally* have eyes redder than the devil's and bags under them so big they would hold a couple of frozen chickens. How would I know? I hope I don't have the green and yellow bruises, although there's something horribly familiar about that. Of all the things about me, that's what is the most recognisable.

This doesn't bode well.

I put the mirror down.

'Your family have asked to see you. What shall I say?' he asks.

My family. *Oh, dear God.* 'Tomorrow?'

'I'll let them know. They'll be so excited. Take your time. I'll be back in a bit.'

As he leaves, I can hear his solid shoes *squeak* on the green linoleum floor as if he's trodden on a mouse.

The door slides shut.

I pull the thin hospital bed covers up over my mouth and scream into them.

2

THE FAMILY

'How are we today, Cassie?'

I blink. Considering I only saw the doctor yesterday, what does he expect me to say? I'm so much better, that I think I could sail the Atlantic single-handed? Preferably with one arm tied behind my back and wearing a pirate's patch, just to make it all the more challenging?

'Oh, same old, same old.'

I'd dearly like to ask him how he'd feel if the only reason he knew his own name was because someone had told him what it was. And the name "Cassie"? Not even repeating it a hundred times that first night of consciousness had made it feel like mine.

I have "retrograde" amnesia. I can remember this because, although I have lost my ability to recall memories, I can still encode new ones. I remember general knowledge rather than specifics. I can tell you boring stuff quite happily. I just can't remember any "autobiographical episodes" apart from taking a London black taxi on, head to windscreen.

The doctor says the amnesia is usually temporary, and complete memory *usually* comes back after a patient is treated by exposing them to triggers like family, friends and their environment. But what if it doesn't?

The doctor taps my chart, bringing me back. 'Cassie, your father has asked to be allowed in first. Is that okay with you?'

'My father?' I feel all the moisture in my mouth dry up as if I've eaten a handful of ash. 'Are they all here?'

I glance at the door. I mustn't scream anymore, or they might transfer me to a psychiatric ward.

'Can I let him in?'

'Yeah, all right.'

I'm lying. I don't want him to come in, except it's too late to say "no". What will he be like? Something in my gut curdles. I long to creep under the bed, but that won't save me; it never had.

'Now be prepared,' says the doctor. 'It will be difficult on both sides. All of you have to have patience. Things like this often sort themselves out in their own time. Mostly all it needs is a trigger, and it'll come flooding back.'

Do I want it to come "flooding back", or will I find I'll drown in it? Father, husband, *terror*.

'I'll do my best.'

Is there a hint of sarcasm in my voice? Bloody hell! I'm about to meet a bunch of strange people, some of whom apparently, I gave *birth* to, probably argued with, cried with and who I must love unconditionally. You know what? I don't have the faintest idea what colour their hair is, or whether their eyes are light green, like mine.

'Take a deep breath,' he says, 'and smile.'

He opens the door, and I hear it whisper on its well-oiled hinges as if it's taking a deep breath instead of me.

A tall and distinguished-looking man walks into the room. Snow-white hair that's been cut military short. His shirt and trousers are casual but ironed, and they don't look cheap. Eyes the colour of recycled glass, just like mine. My father. I pull the covers up tight around my neck.

He holds a shaking hand across his mouth.

'Cassie, baby-girl.' He says, as he crosses the room and reaches out for me, 'I've been here every day until you woke up. Then the doc recommended us to leave you to recover for a bit, get your bearings. I'm so sorry this has happened to you.'

He sounds normal, caring even. What was I expecting? A filthy beast with crazy eyes and huge brutish hands? I have to remember that I've had a colossal whack on my head, and my brains must be like scrambled eggs being cooked in a microwave. Look at him. Why would I ever hide from him? Though the allure of the space under the bed is still calling to me.

'Dad?' It sounds strange to me as if I haven't spoken this word for a long time. 'They told you about–' I can't seem to say the word.

He strokes a piece of hair away from my eyes. It feels like someone has thrown a handful of salt into them. They sting, and I feel wetness on my cheeks.

'Dad? Yeah, I like that.' His voice is deep, resonant, like a Shakespearian actor with an American accent. 'It's okay now. Dad's here. We all thought we'd lost you, Cassie. Praise be to the Lord for your safe return. He is ever bountiful.'

Hallelujah, I think. Praise be! If he's so bountiful, why couldn't he have included all of me, not just the "squishy" outer bits? Would I rather have a part missing in exchange for my memories? Maybe, if it was only a toe or a finger, but not an eye or a nose. Can you barter with God over something like this?

'My poor, sweet girl.'

He looks like a movie star. Is this man really my father? And he loves me, doesn't he? I can trust him, can't I? But somehow, I know I never have done.

'What happened?' My mouth feels like someone has shoved

a wad of cotton wool in it. 'I have empty space in my head, and it's terrifying.'

'You were in England, a business meeting, and as you were coming back to your hotel, you were involved in a terrible accident. They treated you in a British hospital for three weeks. The moment we knew it was okay to move you, we brought you back here so you could get proper medical care.' He wipes his eyes. 'You gave us quite a scare there, baby-girl.'

'I don't remember anything. At all.' I suppose what I'm trying to say is, I don't remember *you*.

I want him to hold me in his arms as if I were a small child again and let me sob out my fear and frustration on his broad shoulder. My dad is here, and it's going to be *right as rain*. It's weird though. I want this so badly, but I pull from his grasp. He is still a *stranger*, sitting on the edge of my bed, holding my hand. And the fear is still there, coiled like a sleeping serpent in my gut.

'Cassie. You'll be fine. The doc has told us that it's like a switch, and when it's flicked on again, all your memories will return. You'll be back to your old self in no time.'

'What's my "old-self" like?'

Do I want to know?

He laughs. It's rich and throaty, and I smile back at him. It hurts, but I can't help it, as his laugh is contagious. And I really need to laugh right now. The sound blows my fear away like dandelion seeds in a summer breeze.

'You're a wonderful daughter, an exemplary mom, and you are universally loved by everyone who has ever met you. Haven't you taken note of all the flowers? There are more at home because we just couldn't fit them all in your room without it turning into a flower store.' He leans forward and gently kisses my exposed cheek. 'Mom's really sorry she's not here. She sends her love and she'll see you when she gets back from her campaigning. She just couldn't get away. That huge bouquet is from her.' He gestures at a whopping bunch of blood-red roses. I glimpse a weighty, gold wedding band on his finger.

'Mum?' So, I do have a mother too, except now my heart is in a vice, being squeezed and there's a weight pressing down with giant hands on my chest. I long to cry. Where is she? Busy campaigning? Against nuclear war? Wearing fur? Strangled dolphins caught in tuna nets? Too busy to visit her nearly dead daughter? Where is my mum?

'I'll look forward to it.' I think I might hurl the roses out into the corridor if I can't get the window open, but then I feel a surge of emotion. What is it? Guilt? My mum's too busy doing something good for the world to visit. *Grow up,* I tell myself. I cough, feeling the shame creeping hotly up my neck, but I still wonder why she isn't here with me instead of this man I don't know. I want my mum.

'Send her my love.'

'I have to go. We're in the middle of a billion-dollar deal, and you know what that's like.'

'A billion dollars? Of course, I do.'

My dad pats my hand, and before I can ask what the family does that involves billions of dollars, he says, 'I suppose I'd better not monopolise you too much. Nick and the kids are waiting outside. Shall I ask them to come in?'

I nod, as I can't risk my voice. He gets up, and the bedsprings *boing*. He opens the door and turns slightly.

'I'll be back later, baby-girl.' He pauses at the door. 'Oh, by the way, a young man came in a couple of days ago to see you. I told him you weren't taking visitors yet.'

'Do you know who he was?'

'No, I didn't recognise him, but then you've got so many friends it's not surprising. He said he'd meet up with you soon. In fact, he said you could count on it.'

He sweeps his hand to show the people standing clumped outside that have been given permission to enter. I watch as my father leaves, and I see their shadows. I hear my father's voice, except now it's like he's growling. I can't make out individual words, yet there's a menacing vibe to the sound.

The shadows start to move. They're coming closer, crawling into the room. *I'm a wonderful daughter and an exemplary mum.* I can live with that, but I still feel as if I've swallowed a couple of live ferrets that are fighting to get back out. I wonder if I'll make it to the bathroom in case they manage it.

I don't know what to expect. My children are here. Should I call them "darling"? Hold out my arms to them? Will they run, sobbing, to be engulfed against my warm, motherly breast? Like hell! How can I have two teenage kids? They tell me I'm thirty-eight. Well, that's obviously wrong. I know I can't be. Married with kids. It doesn't feel right.

The machine by the bed has multicoloured squiggles and numbers undulating across the screen. The numbers in red speed up.

Three people move slowly into the room as if they're walking through tar, their feet sticking. A man, dark hair, eyes nearly as red as mine, and that's saying something. Maybe he's been crying? Either that or he's a heroin addict, which might be more like it.

Then I look at the other two. A girl. Lithe, slim, attractive, fierce-looking. Backcombed black hair, a tattoo curling across one bare shoulder and climbing up her neck. A piercing through her nose and one spiky looking one below her rosebud lips. Ferocious black-ringed eyes glare at me. Is this wild beast mine? Did she come out kicking and screaming? A whelp of the devil?

And the boy? Even prettier than his sister. Neat, well turned out, takes care of his appearance. Did he play with dolls as a boy? Am I stereotyping my own son on sight? What was I expecting?

I feel as if they've somehow guzzled all the air and left none for me. I want to call out to my dad as he tugs the door closed behind him. *Don't leave me alone with them.*

I try to smile, except if I look in the mirror now, would it appear more like pain? *Mum has not only got a massive bump on the head but now it seems like her appendix has just burst.* Is that what they're thinking?

'Hello?' I hear my voice, and it sounds like an old person's, cracked and with a tremulous waiver. I find I can't swallow; the spit gets stuck in my throat. I start to choke. Air feels as if it's being sucked in through the eye of a needle.

The man in front of me, the man who must be my husband Nick, and at whom I can barely look, seems to leap across the room. I hear water being poured, but it hurts to turn my head. A glass is pushed up against my mouth. It stings, and I whimper.

'Gently now,' he whispers, his breath soft against my ear. I *slurp*, although now my lips don't work as they should, and water sloshes down the front of my gown, staining it a darker blue. I grab at the glass, but I touch his hand where he's holding it, feel the skin, the tendons raised, and the hairs on his knuckles. I jerk and pull away.

'Cassie!' He practically throws the glass back on the table.

I wrench my head round to look into his eyes. I want to see the man I'm afraid of, but his eyes are scrunched closed as if I've smacked him hard across his cheek.

'Hi, Mom!'

I tear my gaze from his face, swivel painfully and try to focus. Yes, it's the girl. What's her name now? I feel as if my head is about to "pop" like the lid of a jam jar, just proving it hasn't been tampered with. Well, my lid has undoubtedly been tampered with.

Lucy? Is she called Lucy? I open my mouth, but the words hover below the bolts through my jaw, unable to get past them. I make no sound as I stare at her, this girl who is my daughter. What can I say? *Who the hell are you?*

She steps forward, one step, that's all. She's in lace-up ankle boots and a frilly black dress covered in grinning skulls and red roses that would be welcome at a Halloween party. Leather bracelets adorned with silver spikes weigh down her thin wrists, the sort that pit-bull owners use as dog collars.

'Lucy?' I hope I've not called her by the wrong name. My voice is hoarse, probably from all the screaming. I don't know what to do. I hold out my arms to her, but it's as if she's being dragged across the squeaky floor by forty wild horses, resisting every tortuous step. She bends down and brushes a near kiss somewhere left of my vision. In fact, it sounds more like a "hiss". Her back and shoulders roll away, a practised movement, like a cat that won't ever be stroked. She coils from my still open arms.

'I just want to say...' but she stops. I can see emotions rolling across her pretty, painted face, but I'm not sure what they are. She starts again. 'Mom? I'm glad you didn't die.' She dabs at her eyes, the black is so smudged anyway, but I think she might be crying. Now that's a strange thing to say, like somehow, she might have been glad *if I had died*? What a disconcerting thought.

'So am I!' It's a croak.

'Mom.' The boy, George, doesn't move for a moment, and then he's across the room. He reaches out, his long fingers flutter near my face but don't touch me. 'This is so *fucked up.*'

'*George!*' There is outrage in the man's voice. And pain, *old pain* as if he exudes it like sweat. I don't recognise it, his tone, its timbre, his natural inflexions, or the accent. 'There's no need for obscenities!'

I disagree. I believe this is the perfect time for obscenities, and the more, the merrier! I can think of quite a few to get us going. I sneak a peek at this man, my husband. The man whom I presumably produced these two children with. A man who must have seen me naked. Did I shag him senseless? Did I enjoy it? Think of England?

I really need them all to go away, leave me alone. Has the room got smaller? The walls seem to be a lot closer than they were a few minutes ago. And they are still gulping down all my air. The bastards! Leave me alone. *Go away.*

I drag in a breath like I'm sucking on my last cigarette before the firing squad cocks and aims.

'Damn right!' I focus on the boy. Nineteen? Have I really got a nineteen-year-old son? I only feel about twenty myself. Dear God! Help me. I recognise that stance, defiant, needy, *hurting.* Something in his eyes too. Is this my son?

'*What* did you say?' Lucy snaps my attention back. She turns from me to her father, who I still can't look at properly.

'I'm sorry–' but I don't get to finish, not that I know what I am going to say.

'Didn't you hear?' There is such a layering of emotion in those few words, 'George said it's so *fucked* up!'

I don't need her to shout at me.

'I'm not deaf. I'm injured.' I feel the heat rising up to burn my cheeks as if I've stuffed a handful of bird's eye chillies down my throat. I don't want to cry, lose control. It's always worse if you do. Please don't cry.

'Fucked up!' She springs across the room. I fear she'll bounce on the bed, and the bolts holding me together will fly out.

'*I know,*' I roar back at her. '*It's right royally fucked up!*'

'Oh, man!' George spreads his hands wide. 'You're not making it up, are you? You really can't remember anything?'

'And you're putting on that British accent again.' Lucy spits her chewing gum in the general direction of the bin. It misses, although she makes no move to clean it up. 'Why are you doing that?'

'Lucy!' Her father is pleading. 'Pick up the gum.'

'Whatever!' She dances over and scrapes the offending gobbet off the floor, flicks again and "scores".

Do I do a *Mexican wave* to celebrate?

'You haven't answered my question. Why are you still talking like a stupid Brit? I mean, you come back each time acting like you're more British than the actual Brits. Why do you do this?'

'It's really annoying, Mom,' says George. 'We know you love the royal family and all the English shit, but you're not one of them.'

I push on the panic button. 'How the hell should I know why? Which part of *amnesiac* has bypassed you?' I want the orange-hued doctor to ask them politely to leave, and if that fails, to throw them all bodily out of the room.

Nick saves the day. Good for him. 'I think your mom has had enough. We'll come back when she's ready. You remember what the doc told us. Small steps. Go on now. I'll be out in a minute. I just want a word with your mom.'

The kids leave without a kiss or even a wave in my direction. I don't know how to feel. Nick stands by the bed but not too close. 'Cassie? We're so glad to have you home.'

'You mean some of me, don't you?' I push back into the pillow. If he hits me, there's no place to go. *Yellow, green bruises.*

'Honey,' his voice is soft, 'when the police called, I thought you were dead. But you're here, and you're alive. That's more than I could've ever hoped for. It was touch and go for a while, Cassie. We thought we'd lost you.'

'I've lost me.'

'Oh honey,' he reaches out, and I recoil from him.

'*Don't touch me.*' The words rasp out before I think them through, some forgotten reflex. He whips his hand back like he's just touched burning coals. Burning coals...

... I'm peeling potatoes. The sink is grimy with soil and last night's grease from the washing up. Her back is to me, but I can smell cigarettes and the wonderful tang of the coal, where she's stoking the fire in the grate. We'll have a hot bath tonight in the old tin tub.

'You're such a mynah bird,' she says.

'Do miner birds have to wear little helmets with tiny lamps on when they're down the pit?' I ask her in a northern English accent. I tweak some potato skin out of the peeler. The blade is blunt so it's more like scraping than peeling. My fingernails are filthy.

'Eh?' she says. Her head turns. I only see curls of dark hair. She taps her cigarette, and an inch of ash falls on the chequered black and white kitchen lino, although the white is more a dull yellow now. There are splits in it where she's dragged out the old washing machine to wiggle the pipes at the back, hoping to get it working again. As she says, it's no fun washing sheets in the bath.

'What are you on about, sweetheart?' She straightens up and rubs the small of her back, round and round in little circles. It must be playing her up. Her old *war injury*, as she calls it. She always makes light of it, but it's where he shoved her down a flight of concrete steps because she "spoke back to him". Her back's always given her pain since then.

'When the miners took them miner birds down the pit with them, did they have to wear helmets and all?' I can nearly see her face.

'Mynah birds? Down the pits?'

'Yeah, you know. They talk, don't they? Didn't they warn the miners when the walls were going to fall in on them or something?'

'No, love. That's canaries. When the pretty little things stopped singing and fell off their perches in the cages with their feet in the air, that's what told the miners to leg it quick.'

'Then why are the other birds called miner birds?'

'That's mynah birds, with a letter "y", silly, and they mimic you. They're only copying your words. They sound like they're talking, but they're not really.'

I see her shoulders start to shake. She's laughing, and I know the great snorts that will follow. She always sounds like someone emptying a full sink. 'Those birds are like Craig. He sounds like he's talking, but he's just managed to string words together all in a row. The silly sod!' That makes me laugh as well, except I'm laughing with her; I wouldn't ever laugh about *him*...

'I've just had some sort of flashback,' I catch my breath, but already the images are fading faster than I can hold onto them, their colours and shapes dripping like melted wax in my mind. I know what I saw was important, yet it's slipped away, and then it's gone, like a wisp of dawn mist burned off by the heat of an early morning summer's day. But instead of being warm, I feel cold and hollow, as if I've lost something extraordinary.

'That's good, Cassie.' Nick yanks something out of his pocket. It's a silver necklace with a pendant dangling from the thin chain. 'If you're having sudden memories like that, then it means the healing process has begun. You'll be back to your old self in no time.' The chain slides through his fingers and loops onto the bed covers. 'For when you remember.' He looks back over his shoulder as he gets to the door. 'Oh, by the way. I like what you've done with your hair. It's more... natural.'

The door shuts. I know I shouldn't, but I'm like a scream junkie. I pull the cover up around my mouth and shriek until my throat knots. I hear a faint "clink" as the necklace lands on the floor.

What kind of mother am I? What kind of mother wants her children removed from her sick room and her husband handcuffed to a seven-foot bruiser of a policeman? I don't think that went too well. My maternal instincts seem to have hidden under the bed without me. Will they understand? I mean, it's not like the kids are a couple of cute, tail-wagging puppies; they're complex young adults that have years of a relationship that I have no comprehension of. And their reaction seemed a bit obtuse, considering I was only recently very close to "shuffling off my mortal coil". They also didn't come across as the affectionate types, no tear-stained faces of joy at seeing me alive, no running into my waiting arms. Maybe we're just not the *hug* and *kiss* type of family.

As I finally drift off to sleep, I can see them on a shore facing me in the distance. Their faces are indistinct, blurred as if I've already forgotten what they look like. The water separating us is very still. I crunch my toes into the sand, and the softly lapping waves lick at my feet. There is a subtle movement. I peer closer. Suddenly, I see a dark shadow gliding in the depths, and the tip of a dorsal fin breaks the surface. I stumble back, although now there are jagged rocks behind me, and there's no place I can go.

3

HOME SWEET HOME

W e drive through Atlanta. All I remember are tall
buildings and glass, too much noise – human noise – as
well as the wailing of sirens. All the deafening sounds of a city,
but now blocked out by the softest hiss of a window closing.
There is a lot of green outside, more so than I would've
expected, and a wide variety of trees and shrubs. As we start to
leave the city centre, I see what I believe to be old-style
buildings, from the days of *Gone with the Wind*. Do people still
live in such places, or are they only full of dust and memories?

I'm in the back seat of a silver limo. I'm not sure, but I think
we own it. My dad is lounging on the plush leather seat opposite
me. I glance through the dividing window over his shoulder, see
the driver's eyes staring at me, reflected in the mirror. He's
wearing a smart dark-grey uniform with a peaked cap. He's
black, with a dash of a young Denzel Washington about him.

'Would you like the air-con on, ma'am?'

'Yeah, great.' I thought air-con meant you wound the bloody
window down, not pressed a button and smooth, cool air
whooshed over you. It's early August and the height of the
summer. It is so hot outside; I swear you could barbecue a few

23

shrimps on the car's bonnet. 'I'm sorry to ask, but what's your name?'

'Tyreese, ma'am.'

'Right. I'll try not to forget again.'

He does an imperceptible nod, except his eyes crinkle as if he's perplexed.

Out of the city, we're passing rolling hills studded with trees. It reminds me of a beautiful patchwork quilt, lovingly sewn from squares of rich green and yellow silk. The trees look as if they have all been knitted from wool. I want to reach out and touch them.

Tyreese now seems to be looking more at me than the road. There's something in his eyes like he's searching? Is he also trying to find "the old me"? Do I usually joke around with him, ask after his grandparents' health, and know the names of every member of his family? I smile tentatively at him, and his eyes snap forward. Oh God, he didn't think I was trying to flirt with him, did he? I'm old enough to be his mother, and what a truly ghastly thought that is. I still can't believe I'm old enough to be *anyone's* mother. Or maybe I've never met him before this?

'This is Madison.' Dad points out the window as we slide through a small town. 'It was once cited as the most cultured and aristocratic town on the stagecoach route from Charlestown to New Orleans.'

It certainly is pretty. There are restaurants and an ice cream shop and conservative-looking stores with conservative-looking people looking purposefully through their glinting windows. There must be a roaring trade in window cleaners here. I spot a candy store, and I have a craving for something peppermint. Can I ask if we can stop? But no, that'd mean I'd have to get out, be seen by the populace in general, some of whom might know me, and I'm not prepared for that yet.

'We were lucky.' Dad sighs loudly. 'The South believed that

twisted idealist Sherman would burn his way through us like he did with nearby states. He was persuaded to pass us by, thanks be to God, or all these mighty fine buildings would have been destroyed. He'd have devastated our heritage, and we would have had nothing to pass onto our children.'

'You sound like you were there.' I wonder if he's noticed that I'm putting on the accent. Or hopefully, he's noticing that I haven't got one anymore. It comes quite easily to me. Like a mynah bird.

'We still are, baby-girl. We still are.'

Has he understood what I've just said? Because if he does, what does he mean? In the mirror, I see Tyreese's face; watch a muscle twitch under his eye. He keeps on driving, staring at the road, but his jaw clenches tightly.

Dad smiles at me, and it's like a movie spotlight has been switched on. I practically burn from the intensity of his gaze.

'We'll have you back to your old self in no time, Cassie. Hey, I reckon the moment you see the house, it'll all come rushing back.'

'Here's hoping,' I say.

I turn to peer out of the window. It feels like we are stationary, on a film set, the passing scenery merely projected on a screen. If I open the door now, could I step out? My hand creeps toward the door handle.

'You okay?' Dad has his own hand held out. 'Not going to do anything... silly, are you?' There's something in his eyes. Is it a warning that I might hurt myself or that *he* might hurt *me?* I pull back sharply.

'The doc said–' He keeps his hand outstretched to block the door. '–that you might be disorientated.' His eyes seem to have changed colour. Anger darkens them to wine-bottle green. And after that comes the violence. I know that. Cringing back in my seat, I wait, ready to protect what's left of my head with my arms, raise my legs to ward off blows to my stomach, but he absently scratches his chin and stares out of the window, leaning back into his seat slowly, as if he's deflating like a punctured balloon.

There is silence for a long time. I wonder where these feelings are coming from as I surreptitiously peer at my dad from under my lashes. How can the quiet, contained man in front of me be the crazed creature in my head? Has my mind been damaged beyond repair by my accident?

The car starts to slow down, and the indicator light is on.

'Home.' Dad laughs and pats my knee. I flinch.

'Oh, I'm sorry if I hurt you.'

'No, that's fine.' *But it's not, is it.* If I keep repeating the word "dad", I seem to be okay, as if that word is different from "father" somehow. Dad is not scary, but "father" has connotations that make me shiver deep inside as if I've caught a chill.

I watch out of the tinted window as we drive lazily up a gravelled driveway between sculptured gardens. The grassy areas look as if a manicurist has been down on her knees with a little set of nail clippers to ensure the lawns are all perfect. Bugger me! How could I ever forget this?

As we curl around the final bend, I see the house. My parents' house. *My house.* This is where I used to live as a kid, and this is where I now still live. It seems when I met Nick and succumbed to the bonds of matrimony, I simply persuaded him to move in with us. We glide to a stop, and I stare up at the place.

'Wowee!'

Dad is facing me, smiling widely as we park under some roofed whatsit he calls a *porte-cochère.* How wonderfully pretentious is that! There are two other cars already parked. One is a four-wheel-drive Land Rover, splattered with mud, and the other looks remarkably like the sort of car James Bond would drive. Can I drive? I must be able to, mustn't I? Could one of these be mine? Oh, I can feel greed like a randy little dog locked up in a kennel full of bitches in heat. *I want one!*

'Don't tell me you still can't remember this?' Dad opens the door before Tyreese can untangle himself from the seatbelt, and I nearly fall out.

I'm dressed in a gaudy pink and purple tunic which Dad brought from home. A make-up artist and a hairdresser came to my bedside at the hospital to make me look like my usual self. Or so they tell me. When I looked in the mirror, I must admit I felt more shocked than when I'd seen myself that first day. The bandages and bolts have been removed, and the bruises and the swelling have gone down. But they seemed to have replaced them with a ton of foundation, light blue eyeshadow, eyeliner, blusher and thick, sticky lipstick. Did I really put this much make-up on? And I don't even want to think about what they've done with my hair. I know they're trying to cover up the nasty looking stitches and stubble across my skull, though I think they might have got a little carried away. Bouffant is possibly the word I'm looking for. Enough hair spray that I feel I could probably kill someone with my back-combed lacquered fringe alone. Death by lethal hair-do. Is this really me?

'Welcome home, baby-girl.'

'You are kidding me, aren't you?'

It has an air of faded elegance about it. A large flag hangs limply from its pole, stationed right outside in a circular lawn. I can see it is coloured red, white and blue, yet it seems to be different from the typical American flag. The front of the building has shrubs hiding a broad set of stairs leading to the double front door and so many columns that it's like looking at some ancient Greek amphitheatre. It's got a hint of soft green in the white paint. Darker green accents the window frames and their tall thin shutters, of which I can count at least twenty. The upper floor has a walk-around balcony, so every room can access it. How many rooms has this place got?

I have a memory, a flash of black walls, some sort of damp that had a life of its own. A running joke that it is an alien lifeform living in our house. We were frightened we'd catch something nasty from it. Is that here? It's certainly humid enough. I feel sweat start to trickle down my ribs, and I worry that I have great sweaty patches under my arms. How attractive.

'Come on, baby-girl. Let me help you.' Dad gives me his elbow, and I cling onto his forearm, feeling his wiry grey hair under my gripping fingers. There's nothing physically wrong with me, although I've been told that it'll take a few weeks to get my full strength back after so long lying down. The doctor says I might experience headaches and nausea, especially if I get stressed, although he thinks it'll calm down as I start to recognise things. I've been doing my physio exercises religiously, but even this short walk has made my legs feel like they're made from rubber. I'm frightened I'll fall, but my dad is strong. He holds me up.

'Nearly there, my precious.'

I limp through the door into dim coolness. As my eyes adjust, I realise that this magnificent room is only the bloody *foyer*. My heels click on the marble floor, and I worry that I might skid and humiliate myself by falling over and showing my red lacy thong that is currently riding up into places I didn't know existed. If I usually wear thongs, you'd think I'd be used to them, yet I would prefer the "hold it all in" big knickers that became trendy after watching *Bridget Jones*. I'm unused to these high heels, too, and I go careering across the floor like it's my first time ice skating. The shoes fit me like, well, shoes, I suppose, except I don't know how to walk in them. Why isn't this second nature to me, like riding a pushbike, something you never forget? Why do I feel like a fish out of water?

Light is gently diffused through two stories of windows. To the right of me, a door opens into a formal dining room with a crazy looking arched ceiling. It is the sort of space you expect political dignitaries and Hollywood A-listers to be in, nibbling at caviar on toast and gobbling gold-foiled chocolates, sloshing it all down with gallons of champagne. The walls are a soft, moss green colour. A massive, dark wood, spindly-legged table and matching chairs dominate the space. It's been dressed beautifully. Light sparkles off the cut-glass wine glasses and glows on the highly polished cutlery. Offsetting the colour scheme nicely, fresh flowers of orange and yellow add a heavy note of pungency, but remind me too much of my recently vacated hospital bed. I back out quickly.

'Are people coming for dinner?' I feel a little queasy, not wanting to have to meet, greet, and, God forbid, talk to anyone.

'It's always like that. Your mom likes to be prepared, and she likes things to look good.'

I wouldn't want to be the one who has to keep all this stuff dust free. Does my mum do that? In amongst all that campaigning? I pull my gaze away, and to my left is a library. I hobble over and stick my nose in. All the walls are covered in bookcases jammed to overflowing. I sniff. Now that's more like it. I can smell age and wisdom, leather and old paper, maybe even the ink?

'Oh! I can't wait to get in here.' I itch to touch these precious tomes, to lose myself in their worlds, but I'm startled when my dad tugs me away.

'The library, Cassie? I've never seen you with a book in your hand. Why, I remember you saying you'd rather eat Caesar's droppings than read a book.'

It's like he's just clobbered me over the head with a flat shovel. I don't like reading? No way!

'Who is Caesar?'

'Caesar is your oldest and most loyal friend. Of all of us, I thought you'd remember him.' His eyebrows scrunch together, and deep furrows crease his forehead. I tear through the fuzz in my head, uprooting and rifling about for anything to make him smile. I can't bear it if he turns on me like a feral dog. Caesar? Caesar? Droppings?

'He's my rabbit?'

His eyebrows pop up. 'I don't think you won the Georgia Women's Equestrian Hunter-Jumper event seven years running by riding on a rabbit.'

'I've got a horse?'

I shudder involuntarily. They scare me. I know that. Too big, too lumbering with massive bodies and horrible, twitching flanks, far too many great big, chomping teeth and let's not forget the bits forged and nailed and ready to kick.

'A donkey ate my jumper!' *Where did that come from?* I can't seem to stop, 'I ended up with my arm down its throat right up to my elbow.'

'You did? I don't remember that.'

'Mum was there. She whacked the donkey on its nose until it let me go. She didn't know whether to laugh or cry.'

'Mom was there? She never told me.'

'It was a long time ago. I was very little.'

'That explains it then... But Cassie?'

I look up and see his eyes are crinkling at the edges. 'You're remembering stuff. That's a great sign.'

I grin at him. It hurts as if I might have split some bit that'd only just managed to heal.

'Come on,' he holds out his hand, 'we're nearly at the family room.'

Straight ahead of us is a massive room by anyone's standards. It has double banks of windows that fill the room with light. The walls are painted a sweet yellow that reflects the sunshine back at us. Two fat, squidgy, brown leather sofas face a simple but gorgeous white marble fireplace. The light shines off the dark, polished hardwood floorboards and a soft-green, woven rug fronts the fire. A simple white ceiling fan hangs over one of the sofas, suspended above in the incredibly high ceiling recesses. Dad flicks a switch, and I hear it start to whir. A wave of hot air passes over me like the lightest kiss from a lover.

'I'll fix us a drink. Champagne okay with you?' He walks to a large, chestnut-coloured unit behind the sofa. 'I have a bottle chilling. Or, I can call Dolores to fix you what you'd like, if you'd prefer?' There are decanters and cut-glass tumblers and a bucket of ice. How there is still ice in there is beyond me.

'Can I just have a tonic? Sorry, who is Dolores?'

'Our maid.' He frowns and I worry that I have offended him. 'Come on, Cassie. You're allowed a glass this time. Let me celebrate having you back from the dead?'

'Champagne it is, then.' It takes a moment to digest the fact that not only do we have a driver, but we now have a maid. Have we got a butler and a cook living downstairs somewhere too? What kind of world have I woken up in? But that probably accounts for the ice.

I think about the horse. 'It's weird, but I can't believe I've got a horse. I'm ninety-nine per cent sure that I can't ride.'

He snorts with laughter. 'You're one of the sharpest and most competitive riders in the state. I bet it'll come back the moment you see Caesar.'

I lower myself into one of the sofas that quite frankly should be in a Hollywood film. It rises up to envelop me in comfort. Maybe that's it. I've accidentally stumbled onto the set of *Dallas*, hence the eighties hairstyle and god-awful clothes. I believe I should have more taste than this, and I hope that Dad merely grabbed the first thing that came to hand. My outfit doesn't seem to fit with the casual splendour and elegance of my surroundings.

I push into the soft array of cushions, lean back, and look around for the cat. I think about what Dad said to me at the hospital.

'I think it's best for all of you if you come back home with me first until you get organised.'

'Okay. If Nick and the, er, children are all right with that?' I didn't want him to see how relieved I was. How I didn't want to have to face the scary daughter, the gay son and the psycho husband.

'Nick says he'll have the kids at the lodge by the lake for a few days while you get settled in here.'

'That's great.' We have a lodge by a lake? I'm struggling to take it all in.

I pat the space on the sofa. 'Dad? Where's the cat?'

'What's that, sweetie?' I can hear *clinks* and *sloshing* noises behind me.

I bob up and look about. 'The cat? Where's the cat?'

He comes over with two champagne flutes in his hand. He bends down and hands me one. 'What's that about a cat?'

'Where is she?'

'We don't have a cat. You're allergic, remember? Oh, I'm sorry, I didn't mean to say that.' He lowers himself carefully into the seat next to me, as if his joints are aching. 'Anyway, you loathe cats. You're a dog person, through and through.'

I can remember the cat arching under my tousling fingers, scratching her under the chin, calmed by her rumbled purring from so deep inside of her. I know she doesn't purr for everyone. There are some she'd dearly like to claw and hiss and snarl at...

Now I have an image in my head, matted fur, blood around her muzzle, eyes glazed, no breath, no breath...

The glass slips and smashes into pieces on the floor, spilling golden liquid that dribbles through the cracks in the boards.

'Oh, I'm so sorry.' I pull my arm over my head, defensive, waiting for the blows to fall on me, protecting my face.

'Cassie!' Dad pulls me into his arms. 'Baby-girl, it's okay. Daddy's got you. Don't flinch like that; it's only me. Nothing is going to hurt you now you're home. Tell me what's going on.'

'He killed the cat!' I hear the fear and anger in my voice. *'He strangled it.'*

'Who did?' There's horror in his voice.

'Craig.'

'Who is Craig?'

I can hear the words in my head. Craig is mum's boyfriend. My stepfather. *What the hell?*

He asks again. 'Who is Craig? I don't like the idea of someone killing a cat.' He pulls from me, and his eyes have a yellow sheen that must be a reflection from the walls, but it's as if I'm looking into the eyes of a wolf.

I realise I can't say what I'm thinking in case I'm mauled by him. I have to come up with something else, something believable.

'No, no. I'm getting all muddled up. I think he was a kid at school, someone who was said to have killed a cat. I don't know why, but it suddenly came into my head. You wouldn't believe what I sometimes remember, and it makes no sense. I'm sorry if that shocked you. I didn't mean to blurt that out.'

'Well, the doc said you'd probably experience weird flashbacks that are from different times of your life. I'm not sure how that explains it. Especially as you went to a young women's academy.' He draws in a deep breath. 'Maybe it was one of the handymen or something, but why anyone would do that to a cat is beyond me. Still, it's still good news that you're remembering more, even if it is, as you say, a little unnerving.'

I want to smack myself in the face, like that'll help me in my present condition. It's not half as *unnerving* as what I was going to say.

4

DISAMBIGUATION

I must have dozed. When I shudder awake, I know I'm alone in the room. How long have I been out? The light has changed, it's dimmer, and instead of sunshine streaming through the windows, there are shadows on the walls. The sun has moved around the side of the house. I scratch at the edges of the adhesive bandages. Itching means healing, or does it mean infection? I'll know if my head swells up and pops like a ripe tomato.

Over in the corner is a white-painted cabinet cluttered with picture frames. I haul myself out of the sofa, but it doesn't let me go easily. There are so many faces peering out at me, some grinning gap-toothed, some smiling shyly, others looking what I can only term as incredibly belligerent. I presume that's me on a big black and tan horse, both of us looking down our long noses, except I look different. Can't tell which one of us is more "horsey". Nick is there. In one photo, he's looking at me in such a way, as if I am the only woman in the world. *Was it like that once, then? What happened?* The children grow up from frame to frame, and I can see the metamorphosis from cuddly, open-faced kids into surly, snarling teenagers.

There is a photo of Dad. He's much younger and so handsome. In the next photo, he is with a striking blonde woman...

'Cassie?'

I turn at the sound of his voice. 'I'm awake.'

He's standing, framed in the doorway. 'I've got Dolores to make us an early supper. We can have it in the kitchen if you like, less formal than the dining room. Then, I expect you want a long hot bath and to get into your own bed.'

'You took the words right out of my mouth.'

'She's cooking your favourite. Bacon mac and cheese with hash browns. I know it's more of a breakfast thing, but I thought it might be comforting?'

'Great. What's mac, by the way?'

He looks at me as if I'd just said that we didn't land on the moon and that it's all a conspiracy theory.

'Macaroni cheese. You've practically lived off it since you were a little girl.'

'Really?' I try to envision that, but I get a picture of falafel in my head. Is this what it's going to be like? Someone says the word "white", and I see black?

'Dad, I've got so many questions, but I can't ask them all.'

'Why don't you write a list, get them in the order of importance, and we'll tackle them one by one. How does that sound?'

He lets me lean on him, and we shuffle into the spacious kitchen. The countertops are grey-flecked granite, and all the cabinets are stained a deep cherry red. I see the back of a woman beyond the large island, set with tall seats, that dominates the kitchen's centre. She is stirring a pan on the hob.

'*Mum!*' It comes out as a shriek. I stumble toward her, arms raking the air. 'Mum, mum?'

'She's not your mom!' My father pulls me back. There is

anger spreading across his face like a nasty rash. 'That's Dolores, our maid.' He looks like he's grinding his teeth together. 'Our Latina maid!'

I yank my arm away from his grasp. I turn to look at the woman, but tears have blurred my vision. 'But she looks like her.'

'Are you out of your mind?' He shakes me by the shoulders. 'Your mom is tall and blonde and white!'

I hear her voice then, her accent. There's a quaver in it. 'I am sorry, Señor Davenport. Should I leave now?' I think I've frightened her as much as my dad.

'Go run Madam Davenport's bath.' It's like he has to spit the words out between his gritted teeth.

'Yes, Señor.'

She hurries past me, eyes lowered. She's smaller than me with a softer, rounder figure. Her eyebrows are thick and arched and very black, as is her hair coiled into a bun beneath her starched, white cap. She cannot be my mother, can she? I shake my head.

'Where the hell did that come from?' I can hear the emotions fighting in his voice. He's furious, although he doesn't want to show it. The wolf is leashed and muzzled, but for how long?

'I don't know.' I feel the tears dripping off my nose, my chin, onto the slate flooring beneath my feet.

He pushes me toward one of the high stools tucked by the island. I'm beginning to shake from deep within, and it's spreading outwards. My breath is juddering out of me.

'Sit down.'

He switches off the hob, ladles gunky yellow stuff into two bowls he fishes out of the cupboard above the oven. Crispy brown things are put on a plate. The hash browns and bacon? One bowl clatters by my elbow, a spoon closely follows it. I look at the thick sludge inside the bowl. The plate of crispy brown things is laid between us.

'Eat.' He slaps the counter as he scrapes a stool closer to the top. 'Eat. It's your favourite.'

I've upset him. What will he do? Punch me or take off his belt with the hard, sharp buckle? I stuff the food down, but mostly it gets stuck in my throat. I really need that glass of champagne now. My hands are trembling so badly I can barely use the spoon to eat. I can hear him chewing each mouthful, can hear each tortuous swallow.

'I'm sorry, baby-girl.' He stops eating. 'I really am. It was such a shocking thing to say, and I overreacted. You're all mixed and muddled up. I need to keep this in mind. It's just now you're home; I kinda thought it would all go back to normal.'

'I don't think', I start to hiccup, and it breaks the tension. 'I don't think normal will come into it for a while.' I drag in great shuddery, shaky breaths. In what I believed was a flashback at the hospital, my mum had dark hair. What the hell is happening to me? I remember the woman in the photo with Dad. She is tall and blonde. If that woman is my mother, then who is the other one?

'I think you're right. You need to drink a glass of water from the other side.' He fills a glass and hands it to me. I try to drink, hanging over the glass, except all I do is hiccup each time I lower my head, and water sloshes across the countertop, so I give up and drink the water instead.

I look up at him. 'May I be excused?'

He laughs loudly at that. 'Since when have I ever excused you, young lady? You've always done exactly what you wanted. More's the pity.' He shakes his head. 'Hell, I won't go there now.'

I stand up, and my legs feel like they're made from putty. I might crumple in on myself and end up a boneless mess on the kitchen floor.

'Need help?'

'Sorry, just feeling a bit wobbly. It's all so pathetic. I don't even know where my room is.'

He puts a strong arm around me, and we inch our way up an elegant curved stairway to the second floor. A door is open, and I can hear noises coming from within.

'This is your room. I hope you get a good night's sleep. I'll see you in the breakfast room tomorrow at about eight.'

'I'll start writing that list.'

'You do that.' He kisses me on my brow. 'Goodnight, baby-girl. Sweet dreams.'

So, this is my bedroom. I wait expectantly for the memories to come rushing back, yet it remains a room I've never seen before. The four-poster bed is out of an historical romance novel. It's the sort of bed where the hero throws the quivering heroine bodily onto it, ripping his shirt open to reveal a nicely tanned six-pack and a strong set of biceps. The dark wood frame is encapsulated in sheer frilly nets, pulled back with lacy ties. The bed is suffocating under mounds of cushions and embroidered pillows. The windows are tall and elegantly thin, with internal, white-painted shutters. A massive gilt-framed mirror, with enough curly bits and fat cherubs to impress Marie-Antoinette, is hanging on the wall at the head end of the bed. All the furniture is dark hardwood, probably stained oak or walnut.

I remember something. Out of my pocket, I pull the necklace that Nick gave to me in the hospital. Do I throw it away or leave it out? There's a writing desk in one corner. It's got fancy paper edged with gold and with the initials C. B. D. in the corner and an assortment of expensive-looking pens. Well, they're not going to be a packet of ballpoints, now, are they?

Holding the necklace by the thin chain, I take a last look at it. A locket in the shape of a heart, but I haven't opened it yet. A small drawer in the centre of the desk is sticking out. It's empty, so I place the necklace in there.

Peeking off the top of the wardrobe, that I suspect masquerades under the name of an armoire, are several grubby, boggle-eyed teddies. They look like they haven't been cuddled in a while, and I feel the urge to pull each one down and kiss it, but then I spot a large doll with a painted face. She's in a bonnet. It's one of those Victorian ones with a china head and arms and eyelids that move. I'm convinced I've seen a movie where they come to life and, tottering across the bedspread, knife you as you drag yourself from sleep, leaving only the image of their glazed eyes as you die. I pull a wooden chest over from the end of the bed, stand on it and push her back into the dust and the cobwebs.

'Go away!' There is no way I can sleep with that horrible thing staring at me.

'Madam Davenport?'

I jump off the chest as if I'd been caught thrusting unpaid for sweets into my pockets by an irate shopkeeper.

'Yes?' I can feel the heat prickling up my neck.

'Your bath is ready, madam. I have put ylang-ylang in and lit the scented candles. I hope this is to your satisfaction?'

'Thank you, Dolores.' I close my eyes for a second. What must she think of me? 'I'd just like to say that I'm sorry about... earlier. I'm not feeling myself right now.'

She looks at me strangely and nods, except I can't decipher what it could mean. Is she angry with me? She hauls the chest back to its original position.

'Will that be all, madam, or do you need me for anything else?'

I'm confused. What else can she possibly do? Scrub my back? Clip my toenails? I blink rapidly. I don't want to know.

'Dolores, how long have you been here?'

'Twenty-five years, madam.'

I nearly fall over at that. I'd made the assumption that Dolores called me "madam" because she was new here.

'Why on earth do you call me madam?'

'Until you were married, you were Miss Cassie and then when you married Mr Barber, you ordered me to call you Madam Barber-Davenport. Then you told me to call you Madam Davenport.'

'Ordered you?'

'Yes, Madam Davenport.' She keeps her eyes cast down. I know the rug is pretty sumptuous to look at with all its ostentatious swirls and patterns, but I feel it is more than that. She's subservient, afraid to look me in the eyes. Does she think she's not my equal because she works for my family? What does that say about my family? And more importantly, about me?

'What exactly do you do?'

'I am your maid. I take care of all your needs.'

'But what does that mean?'

She frowns. I'm not making it easy for her. 'I do everything you ask of me. Without question.'

'And what does that mean?'

'I am your servant.' She shuffles her feet. She's wearing flat and comfortable-looking black shoes. Her dress is knee-length and simple, with no extraneous ruffles or buttons or cinched-in bits. A working dress. She is indeed a servant.

'May I go now, madam?'

'Thanks, Dolores. And please, can you call me Cassie?'

Her head raises, and she stares at me. Tiny frown lines crinkle across her brow, and I can see... *Now what can I see?* Wonder? Can I see wonder in her lovely, deep brown eyes?

'If you wish. But perhaps it would be better if you asked your father first if it is appropriate? I don't want to do anything that he doesn't like.'

'Yeah, okay.' I take it that she's frightened of pissing him off, too. She bobs some sort of curtsy and then can't get out of the room fast enough.

My head is beginning to feel like it's packed full of unshelled walnuts. I wander into the bathroom. Hollywood stage set here I come. There are enough lotions and potions in the bathroom cabinet to keep all of the women in Atlanta in shiny hair and moisturised skin. There are names on these bottles that I've only ever seen in glossy magazines whilst waiting for the dreaded root canal at the dentist.

The claw-footed bath is so deep I think I might drown, and I peer around for the life jacket or at least a rubber duck. Bubbles reflect the light from the fat church candles dotted around the edge. The tap is on the side of the bath, so you don't bash your head on it as you relax. The scent from the bubble bath vies with the scented candles. I can live with that. A tiled shower area with a seat (I suppose in case the effort of standing is too much) is at the back. A massive extended vanity unit covered in tea lights runs along one wall. A comb and brush with what look like ivory handles are neatly placed on it with a folding box of make-up. I rifle through, feeling like a thief, unwinding a lipstick and dabbing it on my lips. The colour looks wrong on me, and I wipe it off with a paper tissue from a box. A dressing table and chair, draped with a soft white towelling bathrobe, is to one side. The ceiling lights have been dimmed. I look behind me, but there's no one there. I strip off my clothes as fast as I can and slide into the bath, feeling my skin tighten.

Right. I know the questions I need to ask. What does Dad do? In other words, what has paid for all this magnificence? What is "Mom" campaigning for? What do I do? Apart from ride a dirty great big ferocious-looking horse? Why was I in the UK, and why the hell am I speaking with a British accent if I'm obviously not British? I must try to always mimic their accent until it becomes my own, as it'll make it easier for all of us.

Why am I so frightened of Nick? He seemed genuinely upset, but is that real? Is my son George gay? If he is, I wonder if he has a boyfriend? And if I've met him?

Why does Lucy give me the impression she doesn't particularly like me? Have we fallen out over something, and if so, what is it? Or have I just forgotten the horrors of bringing up teenagers? This is probably normal. I might even be lucky, come to think about it. She could be a meth addict who is selling our old family jewels on the black market. Or worse?

The bubbles dissipate as the bathwater cools. How long have I been dozing here? The tea lights have all burnt out, and the room is dimmer, now only lit by the larger candles. Shadows undulate in the corners like living things. I haul myself out quickly and yank the bathrobe about my shoulders. It smells lovely and is so soft that I feel like I'm now wrapped in summer clouds, which push the shadows back. I peep into my room, but there's no one in there apart from the teddies with outstretched paws and the silent accusation from the pushed over dolly.

I'm not going to be bullied by a scary Victorian doll.

I notice a set of shelving on the wall opposite the windows, where stacks of rosettes and trophies are piled up. First in *this* event and first in *that* event and loads of golden rearing horses on cups with my name and various dates engraved on the bases. There are more photos. Caesar jumping over a pole in a field. Caesar jumping over another pole in a different field. Lots of fields and lots of jumping. The woman astride him is concentrating hard. They work as a team. She's got blonde hair that is curled like a character from *Charlie's Angels*. I look again and realise that I'm looking at me. I have blonde hair in every photo. That was what was so different in the pictures in the family room. I thought it was the clothes, and then I remember what Nick said in the hospital, 'I like what you've done with your hair. It's more natural.'

I tug a strand of my hair free and stare at it. Dark brown.

And then, Caesar? A giant black and brown horse. No, I still have an image of a rabbit that is more real than the photos, medals and gilded trophies in front of me. His name was Flopsy. He was all brown and camouflaged but not so camouflaged that he didn't end up in the pot. Craig thought it was such a laugh when he told us *afterwards* what we'd just eaten. *Oh God!* Is that a memory? But of what? And when?

I run to the bathroom and only just make it in time.

5

OUR FURRY FRIENDS

There is a bedside clock with green glowing neon numbers that have been winking maliciously at me since about four this morning. Time is a funny thing. Early morning is notorious for when your thoughts go into hyper-drive, you can't stop, and every second lasts a hundred times longer than it should. *Who the bloody hell is this Craig bloke?* He seems to be stuck in my head, and if he's some crazy figment of my amnesiac brain, then I've conjured up someone pretty nasty. And if he's a real memory that keeps catapulting to the surface, then I can't ask Dad now, can I? I must do something to take my poor old befuddled mind off it. He can't be mum's boyfriend, can he? But then, what do I know? Maybe she's been having an affair, and I found out about it before the accident. But something inside of me tells me I've known him for, like, forever. Stepfather? How could that be? Should I say something to Dad? Is it any of my business? What a nightmare.

Switching on the light, I creep to the closet. It's the size of an aircraft hangar. Surely I'll find something more stylish than the clown costume that Dad picked out for me? I pull clothes out and lay them on the bed. There are shirts embroidered with motifs of horses and rifles and such like. The garish dresses with their ruffles, frills and bows look like they've come from some terrible eighties catalogue. They're all the wrong length. Some have big, floppy material flowers stitched to them or wide belts with giant gold buckles and great dangling bits of this and that that. I swear there's even one with a lampshade stuck on it. That's not even the worst bit. If I didn't know better, I'd say I had a variety of real fur coats at the back of the closet. I should delicately enquire if the neighbours' Alsatians are all accounted for, either that or one is made from wolf skin, thick and hairy and still vaguely kicking. A few leopards will be feeling chilly, as well as a number of beavers. I seem to have a rabbit skin jacket. Is this where poor Flopsy ended up? I can't see for a moment. I touch the soft fur.

'I'm sorry.' I never meant to eat him, but I was starving. I hate Craig so much. What the hell? Craig again? I want to bash my head on something hard, to see if I can shake some sense into it.

I wipe my eyes. The shoe storage reveals equal horrors, full of high-heeled, glittering shoes. Are these really mine? And as for all these *bloody* great wedge things, they've been covered in most of the known cat family. They really look like they're made from fur, real bits of actual animals. How many species have I got in here? How many cats have been skinned so I can have spotty shoes? I shut the doors quietly.

I need a paper bag as I'm hyperventilating, even though I know they've proved it doesn't help. Crawling back onto the bed, it's a relief to yank the quilt over my head. If I scream now, will they hear me? Can I risk it? I know I need it like a fix. How silently can a person scream? I want to sleep, but will I dream? I feel like Alice as she falls into the rabbit hole, except I'm not following a white rabbit with a pocket watch; I'm chasing a brown rabbit that tastes so good. *Please, I don't want to dream.*

I'm gripping the bedcovers. I try to relax my fingers enough to be able to prise them off and rub them to get the circulation going. Dim light is filtering through the white-painted shutters. I pull them open to reveal French doors that lead onto a balcony. I open them and step out. A green leather chaise longue is set to my right on the widely planked deck, and a small wooden table with two simple cane chairs is to my left. On the table is a glass hurricane lamp with a lumpy melted candle. My skin is sticky as I let the early morning air tickle over me.

I lean on the balustrade. A deep bank of purple cloud lies heavily over a wedge of lightest blue sky. Although the sun hasn't risen yet, I watch as the sky turns through pink and orange and glowers red. Red sky at night, shepherds' delight, red sky in the morning, shepherds' warning. Does it rain here? The clouds slowly dissipate. The land in front of me comes into focus, and the colours brighten. I peer around the corner and realise the balcony is wraparound, with other doors that open up onto it. I creep back into my room as I don't wish to disturb anyone, but the sunrise has helped my mood. I long to sneak downstairs and slip into the Olympic-sized pool that I've just glimpsed at the side of the house. Is that ours too? I need to wash away these thoughts swirling in my head like angry hornets stuck in a bottle, except what if the house is alarmed and I set it off? Would the S.W.A.T. team turn up with guns raised? Gun raised...

... The hand has long, deep-red-painted nails and a glittery watch at the wrist, although the red doesn't stop there, it's splashed everywhere, as if the bottle of polish has been shaken with the lid off....

Quarter to eight, give or take a few laborious seconds, I'm startled by the door hissing open. I'm trying to shake off the terrible image that is in my head. What the hell was that last vision? Red in the morning, warning, warning...

'Good morning, Madam Davenport.' Dolores hooks the door open further with her foot and swings into the room, a large tray held in front of her. A silver pot wobbles precariously, with a cup and saucer.

'Good morning, Dolores. Remember it's Cassie now.'

Again, she looks at me strangely, like she thinks I might bite her or something. What kind of relationship do we have?

'I know this sounds stupid, but what day is it? I think I've lost track.'

'It's Friday. Your coffee, madam.' The tray has fold-out legs, and she deftly swings them out and places the tray on the bed, straddling my midriff. Embarrassment wells up. I hope that she is doing this because I'm still supposedly an invalid. She pours, and the smell of strong black coffee is overpowering. More to the point, where is the milk and sugar?

I turn my head away before I gag. 'Oh, I'm really sorry. I don't think I can face a coffee right now.' Especially after the night I've had.

'I will take it back to the kitchen, madam.'

'I'm sorry if I've put you out.'

Her head bobs up, and she frowns. 'Of course not, Madam Davenport, you can never "put me out". Is there anything I can get you instead?' She refolds the tray and lifts it easily from the bed.

'Is there juice in the kitchen?'

'Orange, pineapple, mango and orange, and I think we have red grape. Shall I bring a glass up to you?'

'No, no. I'll get it as I go to the breakfast room. Dad told me to meet him there at eight, so I'd better not be late.'

'As you wish.' She curtsies again and backs out of the room. 'The pull-cord at the side of the bed rings in the kitchen, so if you think of anything, you can pull it, and I'll come as fast as I can.'

'Thanks.' *Who is this woman who is literally at my beck and call?*

As she departs, I scramble from the bed and call after her, 'Dolores? Where is the breakfast room?'

She turns carefully and gives me directions. *I must try to get a map of this place, so I don't get lost.*

My choice of clothes is limited. I drag on a pair of jeans that are too big on the hips and too narrow and short in the leg, and a baggy sweatshirt with some unrecognisable emblem on it.

Following the directions, I find Dad reading a paper in a sunlit room, overlooking the grounds that roll away to a wooded thicket in the distance. From the haze outside, it looks like it's going to be a hot day.

'There's more coffee in the pot.' He looks up and twitches the paper down as I enter. 'Sleep okay?'

'Sure. Great.'

'Any more memories?'

I keep my back to him. 'No, not yet.' *How can I tell him what I've glimpsed?* None of it makes sense.

'They'll come in due time.'

I'd slugged down a glass of mango and orange juice as I passed the kitchen and feel my stomach can now handle a real coffee. There's milk, and sugar, and I ladle it into the flowered cup.

'Milk and sugar, Cassie? You normally have it black?'

'Do I? Well, today I'd like it sweet and milky.'

'Whatever you want. I'm having country fried steak and

eggs for breakfast. Sets a man up for the day. As you had bacon mac and cheese yesterday, perhaps you'd like to join me? Dolores can make it in a bit once we've had a chat?'

The coffee makes my head spin as if I'd just climbed off a carousel. Sitting down at the table, I nod. 'Sounds good.' Although something about that doesn't sit right with me. Fried steak for breakfast? Where's the fruit compote and yogurt?

'Dad? Can I ask you my first question?'

'Fire away.'

'Right.' I clear my throat. 'What do you do? I mean, how did all this', I wave my hands expansively, 'come about?'

His eyes narrow slightly. 'Peaches.'

'Peaches?'

He nods. 'And pecan nuts. We tried for the three "p"s, but the peanuts just didn't want to grow for us.'

'Your money comes from peaches and pecans?'

'That's why it's named "The Peach State" because it's so sweet. I started small, but God was good to me, and my business flourished.'

'Yep, I think we're doing all right.'

'Your Mom helped me build this up from next to nothing. God bless the sweet woman.'

'That's my second question. What is Mu... Mom campaigning about?'

'Well, honey. She's a member of the SSW, and she's been going from State to State, I must say tirelessly, to instil their virtues to those who need to know.'

'Sorry, what is the SSW?'

'It's so hard when you ask questions like this. It's her heart and soul. The Sisterhood of Southern Women. All those women who come into the world with the blood of a confederate soldier coursing through their veins.'

'Oh! And what do they campaign about?'

'The furtherance of the true history of the South. They ensure future generations understand the incredible richness of their heritage, a heritage steeped in honour and glory.'

I don't want to be the "party-pooper" by reminding him that as far as my shaky history goes, we, the Confederates, lost the war and that it was over their, I mean *our,* right to keep slaves, other living people as our property.

'Er, what exactly do they advocate?'

'Your mom can tell you better, though it's along the lines that they don't consider the cause which their soldier ancestors held so dear to be lost or forgotten.'

'Uh, huh.' I can feel little speckles of cold, like tiny, icy-footed mice chasing each other over my skin. How many ways are there of interpreting that? I must've misunderstood what he said.

He continues, 'She's speaking at the Memorial Service at Grace's Episcopal Church on Sunday morning and then she'll be home. We'll miss attending church this Sunday unless you want to go?'

I shake my head vigorously, then regret it as it hurts.

'No, didn't think so. You don't want to be seen in your current state, do you? We can go the week after if you're feeling up for it. I'm sure God can let us off one week, but after that, we can't let God down, now can we?'

'No, of course not.'

Am I religious then? This hadn't occurred to me to ask in my brief time awake since the accident. Why not? I nearly died, didn't I? Why didn't I turn to God or at least wonder where he might be?

A thought crosses my mind. 'Am I a member of this Sisterhood?'

He laughs so loudly that he's practically bent double. 'With your heritage, you can't but help be. Heck baby-girl, you're practically a confederate soldier.'

I turn toward the window. From here, I can see the pool and the decked areas, with tastefully placed stone urns trailing bougainvillea and marigolds. If I could, I'd jump into it right now, fully clothed and let the cool water close over my head and blot out the world. There's a white cabana, with a long table and chairs protected from the sun. This is my life, so why do I feel as if I've stolen it?

'I'm sorry, Dad. I really can't help asking stupid questions.'

'No offence taken. I can't even begin to comprehend what it must be like to have all your memories wiped. To have no true recollection of who you really are.'

'It's like I'm wearing a stranger's skin and looking through a stranger's eyes. It's terrifying.'

'I know it must be so hard, baby-girl. I really do. Remember that stranger will be gone soon.'

'I hope she goes soon.' I feel fidgety. My chair scrapes across the tiles and sets my teeth on edge as I stand. I go to lean against the window frame.

'Cassie? I know this will be difficult, but we need to have this conversation sooner rather than later.' He smooths the wrinkles out of the paper in front of him.

'Which conversation is that?' I turn to him.

'About the kids. Well, more Lucy than George. You were going to try to get to grips with it all before you went away. Obviously, I'm not sure how far you got.' His eyes are searching my face.

'What do I have to get sorted?'

'They've got to know they can't keep on behaving the way they do, saying the stuff they do. It isn't right, and as their mother, you have to be the one to lay down the rules.'

'How are they behaving? What are they doing?' Is there any

possible way I can duck out of this conversation and just go and hide somewhere? I don't want to deal with anything at all.

'I know they're your kids but trust me, somehow their heads have been filled with hateful and degenerate lies. This has to be stopped, Cassie. You know the impact on our family if word ever got out that they believe such terrible stuff. Like I said, it comes more from Lucy, but she leads George on. Now he's at college, he's less influenced by her, although he sure has his moments, too.'

'What do they believe? I don't understand.' My head is pounding like someone is playing drums on the inside of my skull. 'I thought you said I was an exemplary mom?'

'You are. This filth doesn't come from our side of the family.'

'It's Nick then? Has he been saying things to them?'

'I don't want to drive more of a wedge between you, but he has never held our views on life, our moral beliefs and our devotion to God.'

Ah, so there is a "wedge" then. I'm not imagining that part. 'Is he a non-believer?'

'I wish it were that clear cut. Nick believes, but not what we do, and he's passed that onto your children.'

'They're good kids, I'm sure of it. I'll do whatever it takes to protect them.'

'I know you will.'

I take a risk. 'I'm frightened of him, of Nick, except I don't know why.'

'I can surely understand that. The man has not treated you right since the sorry day you laid eyes on him. At least you can remember that.'

'Why did I marry him?'

'You were always an impetuous girl. The more I said "no", the more you were going to do what you wanted.'

'I was obviously an idiot. I hope I've grown up since then.'

'You've made me the proudest father in the whole United States.'

I shake off the word "father" and hear only the word "proud".

I have to ask. 'Does Nick hit me?'

'If that man ever hit you, I'd blow his brains out. You know that. Are you telling me he has?' His hands are bunched, white-knuckled.

I take a quick step back. 'No. I'm so mixed up I don't know up from down or black from white. But you're sure you've never seen me with bruises or... anything?'

'Never. Only when Caesar bucked you off the day you got him. Boy, did you deal with that. No, Nick may be many things, but I don't think that abusive husband is one of them. For a start, like I said, he'd know I would kill him if he did, and the man's a coward.' He takes a deep breath, and his mouth is set hard. 'Not such a coward that he allows your kids to do and say stuff that would make you sick to your stomach.'

'Are my kids really that bad?' Tears are prickling at the corners of my eyes. 'You make me feel like I've failed them.'

'I know you must think I'm stabbing you in the back, but the answer is "yes". In a way, I'm glad you can't remember, yet you still have to deal with it all.'

'Maybe that's why I can't remember. What can I do?'

'Talk to them. Let them see the error of their ways, be a candle in the dark for them, a guiding light to lead them safely home.'

'But I don't know who I am. I feel lost, and I don't know if I can even lead myself home.'

'They need their mom, wherever she may be. I know you'll come back to us soon, Cassie. I know that.'

'And *my* mom? When will she be home? I miss her so much.'

'She'll be here as soon as she can. She misses you too, but she's gotta continue the good fight, you know?'

'Yeah, of course, she has.' *But what exactly is "the good fight"? From the bits I'm piecing together, do I really want to know? And how do I tackle the kids?*

He taps a fingernail rhythmically on the glass pane. 'Be careful. Lucy will try to manipulate you and work you. For such a youngster, she's pretty proficient at it.'

'She's just a kid, Dad. Isn't that what they do?' I feel insanely protective of my own "baby-girl". 'Are you sure you're not overreacting? Maybe it's a generational thing.'

He stares at me as if I'd said I'd found maggots in a jar of his favourite peanut butter.

'Trust me,' he forces the words out, 'it's more than a generational *thing*. They are spitting on hundreds of years of their own precious heritage. It's disgusting.'

What are my kids like? Can I save them from themselves and from Nick? I don't even know how to protect myself.

I close my eyes and let out a breath. 'I'll do my best, but I don't feel prepared for all this. Quite frankly, I'm shocked.'

'Cassie, it's okay.' He leans in and pats my cheek. I am forgiven for my doubt. 'We'll get them back into the fold one way or another. We know that Jesus watches out for the lost sheep, the troubled souls, and he welcomes them back when they repent of their wicked ways.'

I rest my forehead against the coolness of the window. 'Tell me what to do.'

'Like I said, talk to them.'

There is a chiming sound. I turn. 'Is that the doorbell?'

'Who's here at this time?' Dad looks annoyed.

We start to move toward the front of the house, but Dolores intercepts us.

'It's Nick,' she says. 'He's asked to speak to Madam Davenport.'

I take a step backward.

'I'll deal with him.' Dad pushes me into the dining room. 'Wait for me in there. I won't be long.' He strides off. Anger exudes from the set of his shoulders to the clenched fists.

I sneak to the window, but it's in the wrong position to see anything. Taking a deep breath, I slink to a room that overlooks the driveway. I hunker down like a *peeping Tom*, so I can just see over the sill. Dad is remonstrating with Nick, pointing back along the road. His mouth is moving, and I can see he is baring his teeth as if snarling. He is obviously threatening Nick, who is standing rigidly, waiting, and when Dad has seemingly run out of steam, he also points toward the house. He glances over Dad's shoulder, and I can hear shouted sounds but not words. I think Nick can see me peering, so I dodge behind the curtain, cheeks burning. Did he see me? I feel like I've been caught doing a bad thing, and I will be punished. Dare I risk another look? By the time I tweak the curtain back, Nick is nowhere to be seen, and I can hear Dad's footsteps.

I go to the door and peer out. 'What did he want?' I ask him.

'He said he wanted to speak to you, but I told him you weren't ready for that yet.'

'Thanks.' I rest my head against the frame. Things are swirling beyond my reach, things I see briefly but can't catch hold of. 'I don't feel well.'

'Maybe,' says Dad, 'this is too much too soon. Leave it for a while.' He comes to my shoulder and pats it. 'Okay, changing the subject then. We've still got the morning, so how about we go down and visit Caesar? See how the old fella is doing without his Mistress?'

'Okay.' I say.

Deep down, I really, *really* want to run away.

6

CAESAR

We approach the stable. It's not just one stable; it's a whole block of them.

'We own quite a few racehorses and a few "hunter-jumpers".' Dad waves at a paddock nearby, dotted with fences and other obstacles.

'What are hunter-jumpers?' I have this weird picture in my head.

'Hunters are horses that have what we call "form" as they jump over fences. By that, we mean consistency, a steady and controlled ride with the correct distance of strides between the jumps. Jumpers clear fences and the form isn't supposed to be as important, but trust me, it is.'

He makes some funny moves with his legs, and I hope he isn't having a stroke or something.

But then he laughs. 'One of our sayings is, "loose knees makes for substandard jumping". I mean, yes, the main goal is to clear the obstacles and get around the course fast, but we all agree, if you can do that beautifully, then that's always a bonus, isn't it?'

'I did all that? I jumped over those?' The fences in the

paddock look unbelievably high, and they're in the distance. I believe they will be of mammoth proportions if I get up close to one.

'Those are nothing compared to what you jump in the events. Those are for little kids. Now you trained in our arena behind the stable block. Come on, I'll show you after you've seen the big fella. I'm sure the moment you see him, you'll want to climb straight on him. It'll be like riding a bike. You'll be fine.'

The place has got that earthy, horse dung and straw smell, with a trace of oil. We walk in, and it's cool inside. A movement startles me, but it's only Tyreese.

'Sorry, Mrs Davenport, I didn't mean to make you jump. I was mucking out Caesar.'

'So you're our driver and the guy who runs the stables?'

Dad clears his throat. 'He's one of our grooms. A stable boy.' He jerks his chin toward the end of the stable. 'Tyreese, go and clear out Juno.'

If you throw a bucket of freezing water over someone who is not suspecting it, that's what Tyreese looks like at that moment. He picks up a shovel, tosses it into a wheelbarrow and rolls it down to another closed stable door. He leads a horse out and locks it in a stable opposite. It's light brown, with four white socks.

A massive head appears over the stall, and I take a step back. 'And that must be Caesar?'

His head bobs, and he snorts at me. I can feel his breath on my face. It smells like hay. 'How big is he?' He looks like he must be at least ten feet high. Did I need a ladder to get on him?

'He's a seventeen-hand bay, and he's one of the best, possibly even the best hunter-jumper in the region. His breed is Holsteiner. He cost more than forty thousand dollars.'

'Forty thousand? Is any horse worth that?' I notice his big black eyes are fringed with light hairs, but the tips of his ears are black. The heavy black mane and forelock are a contrast against his rich orange coat. He is a stunning-looking beast but still, *forty thousand dollars?*

'Oh, he is. Trust me.' He reaches out and pats Caesar on his great hairy nose. Caesar's ears flip forward, and even with my very limited experience I realise what this means. There is an obvious familiarity between them.

'Dad? Can I have a moment alone with him? I just want to get a feel for him, if that's okay?'

'Sure, honey. I'll be in the arena.' He strides off and disappears through an exit at the end of the building.

'Hello, Caesar.' I stare into his eyes, though there's nothing familiar except the sensation of fear. He snorts again, and I can see a little of the whites of his eyes. His ears go back.

'Do you know me?' I reach up to touch him, but he rears, and I hear the thump of a hoof on the wooden panels that separate us. I stumble backward. Then Tyreese is there, speaking soft words to the horse, but it has a calming effect on me, too.

'I don't know him, and he doesn't know me either.' I slump down on a bale of straw, belatedly aware of how sharp and itchy it is. 'Ouch.'

'Sure he knows you. It's just that I think he can feel that you don't know him. They pick up on that.'

'That I'm terrified of him, you mean.'

'Are you? Really?'

'Hell, *yes!* I was hoping I could get closer, but he knows I've never seen him before in my life. I know I haven't. He's a giant, scary beast. I'll never be able to do this.'

'It's second nature to you. The moment you are on him, it'll all come back.'

'Like wearing high heels? That certainly didn't come back.'

'I can't say anything about that, ma'am.' He smiles shyly. 'But I'm sure it'll all work out.'

'I'd better go find Dad.'

As I struggle to rise, he tentatively holds out his hand to haul me up.

'Thanks.'

'You're welcome.'

I take a last look at Caesar, my supposed best friend and my trusty steed. He sweeps sideways and kicks the stable door so hard, a bucket that is hanging on a nail clatters to the floor.

'Same to you,' I say.

The "Arena", as it's called, is beyond the stable block. It's a covered area, and it's full of jumps so tall that you'd need to be riding a winged horse to fly over them.

'If I ever really jumped over these, then we'd better re-name Caesar as Pegasus.'

Dad is leaning over the fence. 'Caesar suits him just as well. There is only one Caesar, after all.' He turns to look at me. I can see the question in his eyes.

'I don't think I'll ride him yet.'

'Take your time, but I know that'll it be okay.'

'That's what Tyreese just told me.'

I can see Dad's eyes narrow as if I'd said something I shouldn't. He doesn't elaborate. We walk back through the garden, bordered by tall, well-pruned mature shrubs. A bird is singing somewhere in the distance, but its song is alien to me.

My room is still the same. The wardrobe door is open. Staring at the jumble inside, I make a decision. I don't think I can live with all these "dead" clothes. I'd feel like I was wrapped in death, and as for the other revolting examples of my previous taste, I think a trip to the local charity shop is called for. A thrift store visit. But whom can I ask to help me? Dolores? Would it be a terrible blunder to ask a servant for some advice? What about Lucy? Okay, so she's in some sort of trouble but wouldn't this be a good time to try to talk to her? Build bridges. Surely she'd be the one to help her mum get out of the eighties?

I find Dolores in the laundry room to the rear of the kitchen, where she's unrolling sheets from the industrial-sized dryer.

'Dolores? How can I get hold of Lucy?'

The sheets are coiled around her shoulders like a hungry boa constrictor about to start squeezing.

'You could phone or text her. Her number should be on your cell phone.'

'I have no idea where my phone is.'

'Then you could ask your father if he's got her number? Or simply drive down to the lodge and see her in person. It's the summer vacation, so she should be still there.'

'Can I drive?'

'Yes, madam. The Aston Martin is your car. It's parked out the front.' A muscle twitches in her cheek, and she clamps her teeth tight.

It takes a moment for her words to trickle through to the functioning part of my brain. *Oh my God!* I own the "Bond" car! Yippee! I have to stop myself before I do a victory dance and moonwalk across the shiny linoleum floor, but then I hit an impasse. Something deep inside tells me not to get behind the wheel.

'I don't want to risk driving, so what are my options?'

She half blinks, like Morse Code, and I know there is a message in that tiny movement, but I don't have the tools to decipher it.

'Ask Tyreese to run you over to the lodge. The drive through the woods is beautiful. After all, that's one of his jobs.'

'Dolores, you know us all pretty well. Do you think Lucy would come shopping with me? I get the feeling that I'm not at the top of her popularity list.'

'Possibly not, but if she says no, what have you lost?'

'True. Can you tell me why we don't get on?'

'You seem to have some differences of opinion. Most parents and children do. We all have our crosses to bear.'

'Do you have kids?'

'Two. My daughter drowned in the bath after having an epileptic fit, and my husband has disowned my son as he is not the son he prayed for.'

'Oh. I'm so sorry to hear that. You are true to your name then.'

'What do you mean?'

'Dolores means 'sorrows' in Spanish, doesn't it?'

'How do you know that?'

'*Ah-ha! Puedo hablar un poco de Español.*' (I can speak a little Spanish)

'Since when did you learn to speak Spanish?' Dolores asks, warmth draining from her face.

'I don't know. It popped out before I thought about it.'

'*Puedes entender algo más? Sabes lo que estoy diciendo?*' (Can you understand anything more? Do you know what I'm saying?')

'*Sí, claro.*' (Yes, sure)

'This is very strange, madam. You cannot and would not speak a word of Spanish before your accident. So how come you can now?'

'Probably the same reason I can remember a rabbit called Flopsy and not a great big flaming horse called Caesar. It seems a head trauma can make you feel like you're someone else entirely.'

'I can understand that, but can it allow you to do something you've never done before, like speak another language you don't know?'

'Well, let's just say if Caesar is anything to go by, I'm not going to risk getting behind the wheel of my lovely little car in case I find driving is something I've forgotten.'

Tyreese lives in a long, low building at the side of the house. It's the old servant's quarters, or should I say, slaves? I stop walking because I find the thought that my family might once have owned another human being as a piece of property really disconcerting. Truth is, I find it vomit-inducing. This is yet another question I have to ask someone and hope I don't get a slap for it. Probably Dad has got Lucy's number, but I'd prefer to speak to her face to face. I need to see her face.

There's deep purple bougainvillea climbing sturdily up a wooden frame by the door, which is slightly ajar. Soft voices drift out, one deep and the other musical, a voice with laughter in it.

'Hello?' I tap lightly on the door. Is Tyreese even working?

The voices stop abruptly, and there's movement, a scraping of a chair leg across the floor. Tyreese appears at the door, pulling a T-shirt down over a well-muscled torso.

'Mrs Davenport. How may I help you?' His eyes flick sideways. 'Would you like me to saddle Caesar for you?'

'No, it's not that. I'm really sorry to bother you, but I wondered if you could drive me to the lodge sometime. I'd like to speak to Lucy.'

'Lucy?' His pupils dilate.

'You know, my daughter.'

'Yes, right.' But he doesn't move. He's transfixed as if I'm a rattlesnake about to strike.

'It doesn't have to be right now. I mean, I'm not even sure if you're working today. Are you?'

'It is Friday, and I'm on my lunch break, but I've nearly finished, so I can drive you over there.'

'Are you sure? I don't need to go right now.'

'Can you give me ten minutes, and I'll meet you by the cars.' It's weird how I get the feeling that he's blocking the door. Does he think it'd bother me to know he had a "lady friend" round? Do we have house rules about stuff like this? Is it like being on campus and trying to sneak a date into your room? Sometimes it's all too confusing and complicated.

7

THE LODGE

There's another car parked at a skewed angle under the porte-cochère. A small Fiat in the softest ice blue. It's the sort of car that should be whizzing around Rome, like a bumper car, beep-beeping and avoiding hitting other vehicles by a hair's breadth. Whose is it? I wish it was mine, but then I spot the Aston Martin, and my stomach does a cartwheel. It's so yummy that I long to lick it.

A movement makes me jump. It's Tyreese, except now he's back in his uniform, the cap pulled low over his dark eyes.

'You don't have to wear the uniform for me.' I don't feel comfortable with this.

'The uniform is part of the job.' He opens the back door of the Land Rover. Initially, I'm disappointed, as I was hoping we'd be driving the Aston Martin, then I look closely at this other car. It's a smoky grey colour, like an early winter's morning just before the sun rises.

'I'd prefer to sit in the front, if you don't mind?'

'Normally, you'd be in the back but it's entirely up to you.' As I clamber in, I smell leather, see the dark walnut wood veneer dashboard, all lit up and winking in myriad colours like the controls on the Starship Enterprise. No expense spared here.

The engine starts with a soft purr, and we roll out from the cool shadows into the glare of a hot summer's day. It's as if we're not on the ground at all but gliding at least a foot above. There's no bump and rattle of the chassis, no jarring jolts that make you bite your tongue or clack your teeth together, just a whisper of sound like we're driving on clouds.

Sliding off the main Carl Sanders highway, we start up a forest road and follow a sign to the Apalachee Woods Trail that leads to Oconee lake. This is the first time I've been outside the house. It feels so good. I stare around me as we drive, as the countryside here is spectacular. Leaves rustle invitingly above us as if the trees are chatting. Snatches of deep blue sky can be spied through the ever-moving green haze.

'Can we drive with the windows open? I glance sideways at Tyreese. 'I want to feel real air on my face.' The windows hiss down, and I dangle my arm out, watching shadows flit across my elbow. When there are patches of sunlight, the heat from the sun makes my skin prickle.

Something sparkles in the corner of my eye as we swing around a wide curve. A large white car is hurtling toward us at speed, and it's on our side of the road. I have no idea where it came from. I could swear it wasn't on the road a moment ago.

'Jesus!' I can hear the panic in Tyreese's voice, 'Get over your side of the road, you stupid *douchebag!*' He wrenches the wheel around as both cars are passing side by side. Things slow down, and I can hear the squeal of metal on metal, the weight and force of the other car shunts us across the road. Tyreese is wrestling with the wheel, but now I'm looking through the darkened tinted window of the other car, which is wound down just a little bit. There's movement. I hear a voice. It rasps something, although I can't make out the words. The sound makes me feel as if I've been electrocuted. A coldness raises the hair from my scalp, and *it's like tiny bolts of electricity* shoot out of my fingertips. My breath whooshes into me, but I don't let it out until bright spots dance before my eyes.

'Holy crap! Hang on,' shouts Tyreese.

As the air explodes out of me, I realise we're skidding rather elegantly toward a gully at the edge of the road. I instinctively brace my feet against the dashboard and grip onto the door handle. There's no screech of tyres like in the movies, but a deep scrunching gravelly sound like a giant clearing its throat. Tyreese pumps the brakes, and we slew across the road. I think we're teetering on the edge as there's a weird kind of rocking movement. But at least we've stopped. I crane my neck to turn around, hampered by my seat belt.

'The shit's just kept on going.' My stomach is doing somersaults like it's signed up for cheerleading and wants to impress the judges. I unlock my belt and hang out the window, gulping in air and hoping I don't throw up down the side of the car.

'Are you okay, Mrs Davenport? That was pretty close.'

'Yeah, I'm okay.'

'Didn't catch the license plate, did you?' Tyreese has opened his door and is peering down. 'I think it was a Chevrolet truck of some sort, but you kinda don't register stuff when it's driving right at you.'

'Not a chance. Where the hell did he come from?' I somehow have put a gender on our mystery driver.

'I don't know, but I need you to get out and stand away from the car. We're right on the edge, and if the car tips, we'll be in there.' He nods at the ditch. Water gurgles, threading past the tall entwined reeds.

'Can't we call someone?' I look back along the road, but there's no sign of the truck.

'That'll be a helluva wait, and then they'll only do the same, so we might as well risk it. It's a Land Rover, so it's built to do a lot of manoeuvring. I think it'll be fine, but just in case?'

I clamber from my seat. The camber of the section of road we're now perched on means it's difficult to extricate myself, and I flounder around like a flatfish in a bucket.

I watch as Tyreese revs the engine and inches his way back up onto the solid flat asphalt of the road. The Land Rover is now purring, but it's been injured. I run my finger along a deep scratch that has torn the paint from along the passenger side.

'Any closer, and the truck would've been in my lap.' My hands are bloodless and clammy, even in the summer heat. Like they're two dead pieces of fish where my hands should be. I wipe them on my jeans.

Tyreese stops the engine. 'Do you want me to call the police?'

'And tell them what? That some idiot forgot what side of the road they were meant to be on? It's probably a foreign tourist, or maybe he nodded off at the wheel and is as shaken as we are.'

'He should've stopped. He didn't know that we weren't injured or stuck out here.'

I notice that Tyreese has also made the assumption that it was a man driving. 'Are you sure you're okay?' I can see unease in his eyes.

I nod. 'You mean considering I've only just come out of hospital from the last road accident I was in? Yeah, I think I'm fine.' I finger again at the scratch. White paint from the truck has now overlaid the grey like a hint of dawn. I can still hear the voice in my head. Cold and hard, like an axe blade, something unforgiving. How could I construe that from a passing sound that must've only been a second or two at most? I'm not sure if I will keep my breakfast down, but I don't want to worry Tyreese.

We wait a few more minutes, then there's nothing else to do

but get back into the car. Tyreese drives off slowly, checking in his mirrors and scanning ahead.

'I don't think there's anyone else going to ram us off the road today. We can't be that unlucky, can we?' I resist the urge to look behind us again.

Tyreese grunts.

I stare out the window. 'Is that the lake?' It slips away, and the trees close in about us once more. I need to concentrate on something else.

'Lake Oconee. It's Georgia's second-largest lake. You can go fishing, hunting and horseback riding here and there are golf courses, boating and picnic areas. It's a cool place to go.' There's a tight edge to his voice like he's reeling in a weighty fish that's fighting back.

'Blimey, something for everyone. How close is the lodge to the lake?'

'About as close as you can get, short of paddles.'

A parting in the trees ahead of us suddenly reveals the lodge. Tall with a steep pointed roof and a stacked chimney. It's painted a muted duck-egg blue. A wrap-around covered deck encircles the house, sections of it screened. It looks like you can get to it from every room, so this must be a local design style. There's furniture dotted about outside, I suppose ready for that early morning cup of coffee while you watch the sun come up over the lake, which is only about fifty feet down a gentle slope. Talk about lakeside views! I remember when estate agents told you that the property you were about to view had a sea view. But in reality, that meant you had to stand on a box and peer out of a window at an oblique angle to see a dot of blue in the distance between the rooftops.

Tyreese unclips his seat belt and sprints round to my door. A car is driving up fast behind, and I have a momentary image of it crashing into the back of us. But it's not the Chevrolet.

Twisting around, I recognise the little blue car, and Lucy is uncurling out of it.

'Lucy!' I take a step toward her. 'I didn't realise that was your car. I must have missed you at Dad's.' Didn't Tyreese know it was her vehicle? It could've saved us the journey. Maybe it's a new car, and he didn't recognise it?

'Yeah,' Lucy ignores Tyreese, which I consider to be a bit rude. 'I spoke to Dolores, and she said you were looking for me. I shouted, but you drove off before you saw me.'

There's no "how are you" or "good to see you".

'Lucy? Did you pass a white Chevrolet truck when you were driving here?'

'Hell yeah. Whoever was behind the wheel was really gunning it. Nearly hit me.'

'Well, it drove us off into a ditch.'

I see Lucy's eyes flick at Tyreese. 'Are you okay?'

'We're fine, although the Land Rover's going to need a paint job.'

'It actually *hit* you?'

'Scraped us up. We're a bit shaken but not hurt.'

Tyreese coughs politely. 'Mrs Davenport, do you want me to wait for you, or shall I come back later when you're ready?'

'That depends on Lucy. Can you give me a few minutes?'

He nods and goes to stand by a brick-built campfire further down near the edge of the lake.

Lucy says nothing. Her face is entirely blank, a china mask like the ghastly Victorian doll.

Best to get it over with. 'I don't mean to offend you–'

'Hmph!'

It's a noise I'm not sure of. Does it mean, "You always do, so why bother saying that?" I plough on, waving my hands up and down.

'Well, you see, it's like this.' But I stop. How can I not offend her by saying that I hate every scrap of her mother's wardrobe?

'What's it like?'

I take a deep breath. 'My clothes are the most revolting things I've ever seen. I'm sorry if that might upset you, as you know me as your mom who actually wears such stuff, but unfortunately, in my present condition, I wouldn't want to be buried in any of it, let alone be seen alive in it. It's all truly awful.'

Her face is a picture-perfect moment of shock. Where is a camera when you need it most? I'm tempted to push her pretty mouth closed with my finger, as it is currently hanging open, but I'm aware she might bite it off.

'You hate all your clothes?'

'And all the utterly ridiculous shoes.'

'But you think they're the epitome of elegance.'

'I'm obviously a completely tasteless idiot then. I know I was alive in the eighties, but I don't want to live through them again.'

'Really? Is it possible that I'm hearing this from your mouth?' Her eyes are greener today as if they're sucking in extra colour from the leaves above us. 'So if you no longer like what you've got, what do you want?'

'Have I got any money?' My palms are itching, which I seem to remember usually denotes that I have to hand money over to someone else.

'Are you kidding? You've got a black Amex card. Or go to a store where your credit is good and put it on a tab. That would be all of them in this area. No one would ever turn the great Madam Davenport down.'

Her words "the great Madam Davenport" are said in such a sarcastic tone that I'm not sure how to react. I wish I knew how bad our relationship was and what caused it in the first place.

'I wondered if you might help me choose some new clothes?' I ask her.

'Me? You'd go shopping with me?'

'Why not? Aren't mothers and daughters meant to do stuff like that?'

'You stopped shopping with me when I refused to wear the clothes you bought me. You cut off my allowance, and I've been buying my own clothes ever since. That was over three years ago.'

'So how did I want you to look, and please don't say like a "mini-me".'

'Oh, yes. I'm nearly twenty-one, and I wanted to look like a kid, not a middle-aged Southern lady with chronic aspirations.'

'I don't want to look like that either. I was thinking of jeans, skinny black jumpers and plain T-shirts, nice boots and maybe a simple black dress. How does that sound?' I tug at the off-red sweatshirt and baggy ill-cut jeans. 'I'd really like to get out of these.'

She points at the symbol on the front of my sweatshirt. 'Do you know what that is?'

'Haven't a clue.'

'It's the Confederate flag.'

'They have a flag?' I squint down at the emblem. 'I thought we were all under the old red, white and blue.'

'Not here we're not. It's the symbol of your beliefs. Maybe you should look up what that flag represents.'

'Could you enlighten me?'

Lucy places her hands on her hips. 'I've been trying to enlighten you for years.'

'I don't understand.'

'That's always been the problem.'

'Do I take it that you won't be coming shopping with me then?'

'I haven't decided yet,' she says. 'I don't know who you are now. You seem different, though what happens if all your memories come back again? What about when you return to being you?'

'Is that such a bad thing? Can't we take this as a fresh start? Let whatever has happened in the past remain there.'

'I'd like to think that can happen, except I don't trust you. You might not remember all the things you've said to me, but I do. I don't think you can ever know how much you've hurt us all.'

'I'm sorry about that, and you're right.' I motion around me. 'I don't. You're all strangers to me. This whole life isn't mine. I'm floundering around, and I'm lost. Lost to all you lot and lost to myself. I don't remember any of you.' My throat closes. I'm having trouble getting air in. Maybe I'm asthmatic, and I'll put us all out of our misery by dying out here by her feet. I drop to my knees, wheezing, sucking in those pitiful molecules of oxygen. Maybe the shock of nearly dying again has just hit home.

I hear Lucy call out. 'Oh shit! Quick, Tyreese, get her in the house.'

Many arms haul me upright, hang onto me under my armpits and around my waist, and I totter forward, guided by their movements. I'm lowered into something soft and scarily red-hued, and a glass of water is put gently into my hand. It takes a while until I can see out of my eyes again.

'Cassie?' Nick pushes in through an open doorway. He hasn't shaved for a while, and dark growth shadows his face. 'Dear God, are you okay?'

I bob my head once. Behind him, I can see light-coloured cupboards, a speckled breakfast marble bar and a pillar-box-red food blender. There's an old-fashioned olive-green coffee pot and a section of the most oversized, shiniest silver fridge freezer

I've ever seen in my life, the rest of it obscured by the doorframe. It looks like a galley kitchen, but maybe it opens up around the corner out of sight. The whole place swims in colour, and I have difficulty focusing.

Nick hovers in the doorway as if he's unwilling to step any closer to me. Has Dad warned him away from me even here? 'Tyreese said you had some sort of attack. And he mentioned an accident? What can I do?'

'I'm fine now.' There's conflict inside my mind. My dad says Nick has never thumped me, yet I know I've been hit. Repeatedly. My head is spinning. Afraid of father but not of dad. Who the hell is Craig? Afraid of husband. Afraid of husband but is that Nick? And there's a shadow of someone else. Someone I don't ever want to remember. I'm terrified of this other shadow, even more so than of Craig.

'Mom?' Lucy perches on the arm of the sofa and bends down to stare at me. She's clutching a bottle of cola. The glass is misted and condensation dribbles from under her hot hand. When did she get that? I can see the true colour of her eyes now, green with tiny flecks of gold and a dark blue ring around the outside of her iris. Beautiful eyes. 'I heard you went to visit Caesar. How did that go?'

I don't know how to answer, so I look about the room. Brightly coloured Moroccan goatskin lamps are on cabinets overflowing with books. *So, someone here reads.*

'I'm terrified of Caesar,' I say quietly. 'He's huge, and I don't believe I have ever been able to control an animal like that.'

Nick goes to stand by a sideboard that is also crammed with books and CDs. I wonder what we all used to listen to. *Did we listen together?*

Nick says, 'They say it's like riding a bike, once you've learnt you never forget how to do it. I'm sure the moment you're on him, it'll feel natural, like always.' There's an indefinable sadness in his voice.

Lucy shuffles on the sofa arm, creeping a little closer. 'Can't you remember anything?'

'I'm having funny little flashbacks, except I haven't been able to piece them together yet. You know, I remember the lamps,' I point at one. 'We heard a funny sound one night just after we'd bought one home from a market trader. We didn't have a clue what it was, but it sounded bizarre. When we switched on the light, we found the cat chewing on the lamp. And when we looked to see how much damage she'd done, we found the lamp still had hair on it.'

Ugh!' Lucy squirms. 'That's really gross.'

I see a movement, and I realise that Nick has inched closer. 'You hate cats, Cassie. You're allergic. How can you remember a cat?'

'I remember the cat distinctly. Her name was Chintzy. It was like she was made from bits and bobs of bargain-basement material; like a badly made patchwork cat.'

Lucy puts the cola bottle on a small round table with a rather garish tablecloth on it. 'Good to see you remember a fictitious cat before us. And by the way, who is "we"?'

'I think I saw mum, but I'm not sure, and I loved that cat–'

'You mean "Mom", don't you?' Lucy grabs the bottle again and upends it. I see the fizzy brown liquid sloshing into her mouth. 'I'm intrigued. Why were you talking with a British accent when we came to see you? And you've just said "mum" not "mom".'

'I don't know. Mu...' I correct myself, 'Mom said I was like a mynah bird, with a 'y', I might add.' I laugh, although it hurts my sore mouth and neck.

Lucy stares at me like I've gone bananas. 'Grandma said that?'

'I think so, but then some of the things I remember don't seem to fit in with all this.' I wave my hands around.

'Grandma hates all this kind of stuff.' Lucy also flutters her hand around the room. 'And maybe I should point out the fact we have a dog and have only ever had a dog. Do you know what her name is?'

'I don't know of any dog.'

There's a rattling of claws on the wooden floorboards, and a white and liver-spotted Springer Spaniel rounds the corner from the other side of the room. Has she been listening for her cue? Enter dog stage left? She looks at me with her huge brown eyes and sniffs, and then her tail is wagging. She rams her head between my knees and snuffles. That's probably why I don't like dogs that much, as they always either sniff your bits or hump your leg. Cats are too aloof to stoop to such antics to get attention. Or maybe they have more self-control and only resort to lying on your entire face when they think it's time you should be up to get them breakfast.

Nick laughs. 'Well, there's someone who recognises you.'

'So, what is *her* name?' I scratch her on the nose and across her head and down her side until her back leg twitches.

'Molly.' Lucy runs her fingers through her hair, which is hanging loose over her shoulders. 'Dad. You're going to find this hysterical. Mom has asked me to go shopping with her. It seems she's finally realised that she needs an update.'

Nick cocks his head to one side and stares at me as if trying to see into my brain, my thoughts. 'I think that'd be marvellous for the both of you.'

He's a good-looking man. Taller than me, which is saying something as I'm a touch "lanky" and mostly men speak to my nostrils. His eyes are green but not like mine. They are luminous, like a cat's, and have deep speckles of gold in them. Dark hair, quite long, more pirate than hippy. Even in the T-shirt, I can see he's fit. If I didn't hate him so much, I'd be more than happy to make the "beast with two backs". How strange. It's the first time I've dared to look at him, and now I'm staring, and he's staring back.

'Oh, I'm s-s-sorry.'

'For what?'

'For staring.'

Never look him in the eye; he thinks it's defiance, which always gets you a clout around the head. Like any wild beast, they don't like you looking them in the eye for too long. It's a challenge, and you get what's coming to you and what's coming hurts.

Levering myself off the blood-red sofa, I nod out the door. 'I've left Tyreese hanging about outside, so I should probably get going.' I edge past Nick, who steps away from me.

Lucy raises one eyebrow. 'That's a first.'

I stop. 'What do you mean?'

'You've never worried about leaving him hanging about before.'

'Well, now I do.' I leap through the door and head to the car. I don't look back. I listen for his heavy footsteps and the rough hand, but it doesn't come.

Lucy's voice floats out, disembodied behind me. 'Curiouser and curiouser.' She finishes her cola with a *slurp*.

8

BABY BEELZEBUB

Tyreese drives in silence. The fact I'm in the front seat seems to unnerve him. He's astute enough to keep quiet. I lay my head back against the seat and close my eyes, although I can still see the sun dappling light and shade over my eyelids...

... She's got her head in her hands. I know she's trying not to cry, but I can see her shoulders shaking. The piece of paper in her hand is like the albatross in 'The Ancient Mariner'. It weighs her down. A bill that, yet again, we can't pay. Men in uniforms came to switch off the supply this morning. Mum did her best, but they weren't having any of it.

'It's colder than the fridge in here.' I stick my hands under my armpits, but that barely warms them, as my sweater is so threadbare.

'Maybe it's our lucky day,' she says, 'considering it packed in weeks ago. At least the milk won't go off.'

'We don't have any milk either.'

'I know, sweetheart, I'm so sorry.'

It's beginning to get dark outside. I don't want to be in the flat in the dark. I hear things I don't want to hear, and in the morning, the bruises aren't the only things I wonder about. I want to ask about the marks, but she hides them when she sees me looking.

'Won't he help us?'

I know I'm a kid, but I don't understand how he can eat everything in the flat, drink and smoke himself doubly stupid, do things to my mum that leaves horrible bruises but leave us with no electricity or gas. And I'm so hungry; it's like my belly is fused to my knobbly backbone. I wonder if I dare steal anything from the corner shop again, except I think they're watching me now.

'Him?' There is such hate in her voice. 'Help us? Wake up, love!' She wipes her face roughly, though her face remains hidden. 'The only thing *he* loves is himself. He'd happily bleed us dry and leave us to fester in the gutter.'

'Can't we run again?' But I know the answer. Even the women's refuge couldn't save us. If they can't, who can? No one. We have to protect ourselves, although I am too young to work out what we must do, and she's so tired and ill. Last time, he grabbed me when I went to the totally secret school that Social Services had sent me to. He may be thick as pig-shit, but he knew enough that she'd follow wherever he dragged me. It's my fault we're back here again.

I hunt for stub ends of candles and a lighter. At least I'm bound to find one of those, the amount of stuff he smokes, and I don't mean cigarettes...

I wake with a jolt.

'Oh, God!' I wipe the sweat from my forehead and see my hands are trembling violently. 'I think I nodded off there.'

'Are you alright?' I can hear the concern in Tyreese's voice. 'It sounded like you were having a nightmare.'

'I was, but it didn't feel like a dream. It felt real.' Yes, the anger and hate were overwhelming. Residual emotions are still swirling in my gut, and my scalp feels like I've rubbed an ice cube over my head. 'I keep getting these glimpses of things that are really horrible, except I don't know if they are real or not. This time it was more like a hallucination.' Again, it's all slipping out of reach, like a mackerel darting into the depths of the sea, a flash of rainbow scales, and then deep darkness closes around it, and it's gone.

'Bad dreams can be pretty strong. They can leave you shaken up.'

'I know, but this is different somehow. I can't explain it. I'm seeing people and situations that aren't anything to do with here.'

'We're almost back at the house. Perhaps you need to talk some more with your doctor. Surely he can explain what could be happening?'

'Maybe he'll tell me I died in London, and now I've come back as someone else.'

I register the look of shock on Tyreese's face. *'What?'*

'Sorry. That was a joke.' I'm still staring at his face. 'A bad taste joke in hindsight.'

'No shit,' he mumbles.

We turn into the driveway. I can see the house in the distance behind a row of squat trees. Seeing it anew is strange. I know it, and yet I don't know it. Recognition is seriously lacking. Dropped at the carport, I make my way in and get lost trying to find the downstairs bathroom.

Dad is standing by the table in the kitchen. He's tapping on the window. The view is over the pool and the decking. No clouds sully the deep-blue sky, and the water looks like polished azure glass, so still and smooth I believe I can walk on it.

He looks over his shoulder at me as I make a ham, cheese and mayonnaise sandwich. 'I saw you go off with Tyreese this afternoon. Dolores told me you'd gone to talk to Lucy. How did that go?'

'Not particularly well. I'm waiting to find out. I asked her to go shopping with me, you know, some mother and daughter time?'

'She said, yes?'

'She said maybe.'

'Well, that's a start. Did you see Nick?'

'Briefly.'

'How was that?'

'Strange. He kept his distance if that's what you mean. You did warn him off me, didn't you?'

'For your own good. You can't deal with him and sort yourself out at the same time.'

I nod. 'What's really peculiar is that I had memories of the cat again. If I didn't know better, I'd say I'm going mad.' I laugh, but even in my ears, it sounds shrill and nervous. The way that Tyreese stared at me as I walked off said it all. I should never have said that because the idea is now stuck in my head.

'Don't you go down that route, Cassie. You're not mad, just disorientated. I know your memories will return, and then you'll be back to normal.'

'Oh, we had an accident while we were driving over to the lodge–'

'An accident? Did Tyreese crash the car because if he did–'

'No, no. Some guy in a white Chevy came at us on our side of the road. In fact, if it hadn't been for Tyreese, I'd probably be back in the hospital, or worse.'

'My God, what happened?' Dad tugs me into his arms and speaks into my hair. 'Don't frighten me, Cassie. I've already almost lost you, and I surely don't want to experience that again.'

I mumble into his shoulder. 'Tyreese got us out of the way. A pretty nifty bit of driving, although the car got scratched down the side.'

'Down the passenger side?'

'Yeah.'

'Hell-fire, Cassie. You called the police, didn't you?'

'Well, no.'

'Why in Heaven's name didn't you?'

'Because we weren't injured, and he was long gone before we thought about it. We were too busy trying not to end up tipped in a ditch.' I smile up at him. 'You should give Tyreese a bonus.'

'Hmph.' Dad smiles back at me. 'Maybe, I will. And I don't think I'll let you out of my sight for a while. You're too accident-prone for my liking.' He taps the window again. 'Well, if you're really feeling okay, I think it's about time you got back on Caesar. It's just like riding a bike; you never forget how.'

'I kind of think I have,' If anyone mentions "riding a bloody bike" again, I'm going to rip out their lungs with my bare hands. And what about accident-prone? Surely being on the back of a whopping great big horse might not be the way to go right now?

'It'll do you a world of good,' says Dad.

'Have we got time?' I'm really hoping we haven't.

'It doesn't get dark until just gone nine. We've got plenty of time. And anyway, you used to ride at night in the arena as it's got stadium lights.'

'Wow, I must have been dedicated.' I lick my fingers clean, but I notice my hands are shaking.

'You were beyond dedicated. I've already asked Dolores to lay out your riding gear. It should be on your bed by now.' He *shooshes* me away like I'm a silly chicken. 'Go on.'

When I return, I find him pulling on his own riding boots. I tweak at the bum on my well-worn jodhpurs, amazed and horrified at how they can inch up into places they really shouldn't. The helmet that's tight under my chin seems scant protection, but at least there's something between my head and the ground, which I feel might soon be coming at me a lot faster than I would like.

Tyreese has led Caesar into a nearby field. Out of his box, I'd expect him to be smaller, dwarfed by the sky and the field, except the closer I get to him, the more he looms over me. His ears are nearly flat, and he tosses his head so the reins jingle. He obviously still doesn't like me, and the feeling is mutual. Tyreese pulls the reins tighter and nods. 'I'll help you up if you want me to, Mrs Davenport.'

'Go on now, Cassie.' Dad smiles at me. 'You can do this.'

My legs are wobbly with fear. I hook my foot into the stirrup, and then suddenly, I'm flung up into the air and only manage by sheer luck not to pitch bodily over the other side of him. I grapple with the saddle and grab hold of a bit of mane. Caesar doesn't like this much, and he sidesteps. My right foot is now dangling. I struggle to slip it into the stirrup, which is now bouncing against his round belly.

'Woah, there Caesar,' says Tyreese. 'There's a good boy.'

He rubs the horse's soft nose, and I get my foot where it should be. He hands me the reins, and I fumble about with them. Am I meant to hold them tight and yank his head right back or let them hang around his neck like a leather thong? I kind of do both, and he jerks around. My foot bangs into his side, and this must be a signal or something because he rears up a little on his hind legs, and then he's off like a bleeding rocket! I'm bouncing up and down, my arse slapping that hard old saddle and my arms wrapped tightly around his neck in a rictus. I don't think a crowbar could break my hold on him. I can smell him, a thick heavy horsey scent. My legs are flapping like a bad-tempered goose, and each kick only spurs Caesar on. Now I can hear voices calling behind me. I crane over my shoulder. The change in movement nearly throws me off, but it's enough to realise that Dad and Tyreese are waving and shouting. What did Dad say earlier about 'loose knees'? *Holy crap!*

We've hurtled out of the field and are going like the clappers down a gravelly lane toward buildings. I recognise the stables. I force my head up, then belatedly realise that isn't a good move either. I only just duck in time as we sweep under the doorframe and come to a skidding halt outside of his box. I'm practically sitting on his nose by now, but he calmly throws back his head and takes a big bite from a suspended hay bale. I half fall off him and then get out of his way. He turns his head and peers at me while still munching and crunching, shaking his head a few times for good measure.

I'm not a mind reader, yet I can hear what he's thinking; 'Don't try that again, or else.'

'Dog food!' I stick my tongue out at him.

Tyreese puffs in first. 'Are you all right?' He bends over and rubs at his side.

I wipe at my eyes. 'I think we can all categorically conclude that I can't ride. What do you say?'

He looks a little shifty. 'You lacked a certain finesse.'

'Really? And let me tell you, if anyone mentions bikes again, I will do them serious damage.'

'I think I've got the message.'

'Tell my father as well, will you.'

'You'll have to tell him that yourself.'

Up the lane is a figure, walking slowly. I feel a surge of guilt. My dad might be young-looking and sprightly, but he's still in his sixties and running after his hopeless daughter might not have been good for his health. I hurry toward him.

'I'm so sorry. It's not there, at least not where I can access it.'

His laugh is wheezy. 'Well, you certainly didn't look your best out there. Maybe another day?'

I don't want to crush his hopes, but I can't see myself climbing back on Caesar's big old bony back any day soon. 'Maybe.' That's not a lie. 'These jodhpurs don't do anyone any favours.' I tug them down.

'You have a lovely figure. Like your mother.' He stumbles, and I catch hold of his elbow. 'Sorry, not looking where I was going.' He looks at me intently with such a strange expression. 'Come on. I need a coffee after all this excitement.'

'I know you're disappointed, Dad.'

'The doc said it will take time, and I mustn't push you too hard. This was just a little too soon.' He reaches out and pulls me into a hug. His scent isn't that different from Caesar's.

9

IS THIS REALLY ME?

E ven though I felt shattered, I think I backstroked around my enormous bed about a hundred times last night. First, I was star-shaped, then curled in a foetal ball, then diagonal across one side and then the other.

... 'If anything happens to me,' says Mum, 'you need to get to this Post Office Box at Victoria station.' She hands me a key with a plastic label.

'What do you mean, if anything happens to you? What might happen to you?'

'Apart from the no. 38 bus to Hackney, I meant acts of God or whatever. Listen to me. This is important. Don't lose this key; it's the only one I've got left. The box has got stuff in it that you need to know. No matter what, you've got to get to it and read what's inside.'

'Why don't you tell me now?'

'Because I'm a coward.'

'Mum, you're one of the strongest, bravest people I know.' I can't comprehend why she should say such a terrible thing. 'You're not a coward.'

'Oh, sweetheart, in this case, I am.' She reaches out and cups my face. 'I'm so sorry for what I've done.'

She walks quickly away from me before I can ask her more, and I'm left feeling that the world has shifted under my feet. Instead of ground, there is now quicksand that is already sucking me down. What could possibly be in that Post Office Box?

The bedclothes are squished down the back of the headboard. Half the cushions are strewn across the floor so far; I must have been using them as frilly throw toys in the night. Was that a dream or a memory? Victoria station? Something in a Post Office Box? Maybe I'm re-hashing some dumb show I saw as a kid on TV? That would explain the disparity between my reality and these visions?

There is a gentle tap on the door, and it slides open. Dolores enters but this time, there is a glass of juice along with the coffee pot.

'Good morning, Madam Davenport,' she says, glancing around the room.

'I had a bad night.' I struggle to pull the covers out from where the headboard is hanging onto them. 'I don't know if you heard, but I tried to ride Caesar yesterday.'

'Was it a success?' Her face is serious, not even a hint of a smirk. If she saw me, she must have laughed her socks off. I'm sure I would have if I was her.

'Not exactly. He bolted for his stable, and I couldn't do a thing about it. I think my dad will be upset, but I never want to go anywhere near the brute again. He doesn't like me, and I really don't like him.'

'I find that hard to believe. That horse is your life. He is your, how do you say, your *everything.*'

'Not anymore.'

Dolores unclips the legs of the small tray table and places it over my midriff.

The picture on the cup comes into focus, and I stifle a snigger.

'Is this a joke?'

Princess Diana and Charles. An image of their engagement, she in a blue dress, her head tilted shyly, a bit of a stoop, so she doesn't look taller than him. He's a bit stiff and slightly glazed but no more than most of the royals. And let's not forget a world of surprise to follow. *Poor bitch!*

'This is your favourite cup. You have it every morning, without fail. You adore the royal family.'

Dolores places the coffee pot on a mat on the bedside table and hands me the cup, which rattles slightly in the saucer. The coffee slops over the side.

'Oh, I'm terribly sorry, madam.'

'No worries. I wasn't holding on to it properly. Listen, do I always have black coffee? Because I have this idea I usually start the day with a mug of tea. With milk and two sugars and not a royal in sight.'

'Never, madam. You only ever have black coffee and then a cigarette to clear your head.'

'*I smoke?*' More coffee slops. 'No, no, no! This isn't right. *I'd never smoke.* I know that much about me.'

I struggle to disentangle myself from the tray and the bedclothes that have wound about me like an amorous anaconda.

'Madam?' Dolores places the tray on the chest at the foot of the bed. Then opens the drawer in the bedside cabinet. There are loads of pieces of paper, but beneath it, I can see the pack, already opened and a lighter with a Union Jack on it. Who am I? A groan slips out, and I place my head in my hands.

'This is not me,' I mumble through my fingers. 'None of this is right, Dolores. I don't know how to explain this. All the things I've seen and been told about have nothing to do with me. It's like they're to do with someone else entirely.'

'If you will forgive me, madam, I agree that you are not acting like your normal self. At all.'

'First off, please stop calling me "madam", I find it really creepy and second, have I gone mad?'

'I certainly hope so.' She bobs a curtsey and sprints from the room.

I pull open the drawer and crush the pack of cigarettes, then return it to the drawer. I want a reminder that this is something that I will never do. Pushing open the doors to the balcony, I sit for a while on the chaise longue and drink my juice, which is grapefruit and beautifully acidic. The colours have changed, are sharper, more defined. It will be hot today. The pool is a welcome thought but do I have a swimming costume? At least one that I will be happy to wear.

There are many places to scrabble through, but my search finds a black one-piece suit with turquoise stripes down the sides. I lock the door in the bathroom and try it on. It's flattering with high legs and padding that pushes my boobs up into nice pert mounds. At last, I've found something that is acceptable. I also find a phone in a bureau drawer and a charger. I'm intrigued as to whether it holds any secrets, so I put it on to charge.

I'm not expecting the phone to ring, as it's more of a plaything at present. It's an iPhone, and I can't get over how beautiful it is. I'm back in the world of technology and feel connected, even if it's only to cyberspace. I'm wondering if I've got a computer somewhere, but I haven't discovered its whereabouts yet. I hope I have a posh laptop of some sort.

'Hello?'

'It's Lucy. I've been thinking about what you said yesterday. Okay. I'll come out with you. I think this could be interesting. We can drive up to Atlanta this afternoon, do a bit of retail therapy and then eat out. I know it's Saturday, so we'll just have to use our elbows. How does that sound?'

To say the least, I'm flabbergasted to get a call from her, and of course, there's no nice preamble, just straight to the point.

'I don't have any money,' I say, 'and I can't borrow from you. I never thought we might go today.'

'Don't worry, Dad has given me his card. I'll drive us. Be ready by about two-thirty, and I'll pick you up in the carport.' The phone goes dead. Not even a "goodbye" or "see you later".

Rummaging through the inside of my scary closet has not revealed many clothes that I feel comfortable in. Having found an electric razor, I run it up and down my furry parts like an Italian lover. Now, I feel confident to wear a cotton, navy coloured, A-line skirt circa 1970 that might be back in fashion, and a light blue strappy top, which is only acceptable when I cut off the garland of floppy flowers with a set of nail scissors. I try out the peep-toe shoes, and they fit, although the leather is tight. I bash them against the bedpost and knead the backs to soften the leather. I can manage in them if we aren't expected to walk too far.

It's only just gone ten when I feel ready, but now I've got hours to waste. I wiggle myself into the swimsuit and wrap the bathrobe around me. My bare feet pad silently down the polished stairs, and there seems to be no one around as I slip out the doors that lead to the pool. The glare off the water makes my eyes ache, so my next find must be sunglasses. I look around.

There is no one near, so I drop the robe on one of the rattan chairs and step down onto the first step. It's not what I was expecting. No ripping the breath from your lungs because it's so cold, no goosebumps erupting over your entire body that leads to a great deal of teeth chattering and shaking and the necessary ten lengths to get your frozen blood circulating again. Maybe I remember swimming in the winter here, but I can't even envision winter right now. I slide in deeper and let the tepid water flow over my skin, see the distorted reflections in the ripples, my hair floating out, and then I push myself under and rise again at the edge of the pool. *I can swim then.* Closing my eyes, I can see dapples of colour through my eyelids, and the sounds become more distinct.

Bugs are making strange droning sounds that bring the heat to life, and a bird calls in a nearby tree while another calls back in the distance. The whistles, chirruping and buzzing continue as I plough up and down through the shimmering water. My stomach rumbles and pulls me back to now. What time is it? I clamber from the pool and use the bathrobe to dry myself. Where is my watch? I realise I've never seen one, except I must have one, surely?

Hurrying inside, I pluck a piece of cheese from the fridge and an apple off the side in the kitchen. I'm halfway through tugging up the skirt when the phone rings again.

'Where are you?'

'Sorry, I lost track of time.' I skid down the stairs and through the lobby, stopping only to check if Dad is around. I don't want to talk to him right now.

Lucy's car is compact and has a pleasant smell.

'So where are we going?' I eye her long, baggy cotton trousers and halter neck top. Is she always in black? Her hair has been scraped into a tight bun with chopsticks threaded through it.

'A place called Lenox Square Mall. It's supposedly, according to all the adverts you see on the TV, the ultimate in luxurious shopping, dining and entertaining destinations. I don't really care about all that. I just like the place.' She laughs, and it catches me by surprise. There's something familiar about it, but I can't remember her laughing when she's been with me before. It's warm and soft, more of a cuddly chuckle.

'You know, they call it "the Beverly Hills of the East", she says. 'They seem to think that just by stepping into the place, you will automatically be *fabulous, darling!*'

'And are you?'

'Only if you're rich. Not everyone can shop till they drop in Giorgio Armani and Versace, now can they?'

'Is that where we're going?'

'Do you want to go there?'

I shake my head. 'Not particularly. Do I normally shop in places like that, because I can't understand why my clothes are so hideous if I do? It seems to me that the tasteful gene must have missed a generation and passed straight to you.'

'That's funny considering you always call me "grungy". Anyway, to answer your question, you have your own designers that come to the house. They charge an awful lot and make you look like The Duchess of York, who, by the way, is also one of your favourite royals.'

'The Duchess of York? You mean Fergie? Dear God, that explains a lot then. Life is getting weirder and weirder.'

'You can say that again.'

'Is there anywhere else that does nice stuff that won't make me look like a trussed-up chicken?'

'There's a store I like there when I've got a bit of cash. I think the new "you" will like it. They've got the classics, but they've also got trendy clothes. I think we can find something suitable that will look classy but not make it look like you're trying too hard.'

'I'd like that,' I say.

Lucy knows her way around Atlanta, and we park easily and are in the mall before I've even realised we'd arrived. Navigating like a seasoned sailor through treacherous waters, she leads me to a shop that is definitely more my style, or at least the style I'd like to have. The clothes are simple but with a touch of luxury, and the mannequins make you ache to buy every scrap of clothing and accessories on them.

'I thought we'd start with jeans first,' she says. 'Get our priorities right.'

There is the distinct feeling that this is a test. If I pass this one, we might get further, but if I fail, all doors and hatches will be slammed shut and sod any dinner later. We might be falling back onto instant soup in a cup.

I choose a couple of pairs of jeans, one bootleg and the other long and skinny. As I emerge to show her the skinny pair, I discover her sitting on a large, squishy sofa with a bored husband, waiting for his wife I'd just seen with an armload of clothes. He knows he's here for the duration. Lucy cocks her head like Nick did back at the lodge.

'What do you think?' I twirl for her, but it is the husband who answers.

'Get them. They look good.' He winks at me. 'Do you think you could ask my lovely wife to hurry up?'

'Lucy?'

'I agree with him.' She nods at the man next to her.

They both seem to like the next pair too. We migrate to the dress rail. I pick a simple, black sheath dress, cinched in at the bust and slightly above the knee. There's something scratchy under my arm. The price tag, a beautiful and artful rectangle of card, has got caught. As I untangle it, I peer at the price.

'Dear God!' I gape at Lucy, aware that my mouth is now open like hers was earlier. 'This is over three hundred and fifty dollars!'

'So? That's nothing compared to what you normally pay.'

'I've never paid anything like this in my life. I know I haven't.'

'No, because it usually has another zero on the end of it.'

'Can we afford this?'

'You really have lost it, haven't you? This is peanuts. You told me you wanted to dress down, so here we are, dressing down. How about some T-shirts and maybe a jacket? Oh, and let's not forget some shoes and a bag.'

One chunky, Italian tweed jacket, with oversized buttons and three-quarter length sleeves. *Ker-ching* at five hundred and seventy-eight dollars. Two dresses and two pairs of jeans that come in at a neat seven hundred and fifty. Plus, a couple of T-shirts and a lovely long black V-neck sweater. The shoes are classy and stylish even if they are a bit high for me, so I compensate with simple, black, shell-toe ballet shoes made from Italian suede, with patent trim.

Lucy uncurls from the chair she's been waiting patiently in and comes to adjust the length of the strap on the bag I'm looking at, 'So, your hair is now natural, with no backcombing or lacquer. I can't see much make-up, and your entire clothes sense has had a major shift. To the better, I might add. What am I to make of all this?'

'This feels like me. Now.' I wave the bags and packages around. 'Not the price tag but definitely the style. Maybe everyone needs a big crack on the skull once in a while.'

10

CARDAMON HILL

W e're hurtling down Interstate 75 near downtown Atlanta. I changed into the bootleg jeans, the black sweater and the new flat shoes back at the store. I feel like I'm beginning to find myself, but what will this evening bring?

'What's this place like?' I ask. 'Have you been there before?'

'Cardamon Hill. Yeah, I've been there a few times. It's Indian cuisine from the Kerala region with a more modern take. The chef uses gentler spices, lots of coconut and blends European, Indian and other Asian cooking techniques. I love it there. It's very laid back.'

'Do I like Indian food?'

'We're about to find out.'

Although the outside area isn't that salubrious, the inside is a shock. Was I expecting mauve flock wallpaper and heavily patterned carpets, with faded posters of the Taj Majal? Is that what I'm used to? But here the rooms are partitioned, the floor a bizarre combination of coloured wood, the walls either plainly painted or with sections of gold and chocolate patterned paper. There is not a jot of flock in sight. The chairs are high backed with brown embroidered upholstery, and every table is simple dark wood.

'Good evening, ladies.' A small dark man, with bright eyes like shiny pieces of coal bobs toward us and waves his hand to show us into the restaurant. 'Welcome to the Cardamon Hill. Our chef Kiran Nair will be preparing your food tonight.'

Lucy does a stage whisper that probably most of the diners can hear. 'Kiran Nair is just the best. What she does with chicken thighs, coconut oil and curry leaves makes me nearly glad I live in Atlanta. I bet in no time, we'll have to book a couple of months in advance to get a table.'

We are ushered gently to a small table that faces an incredible carved and sculptured wooden door, hanging like a painting, next to a tall, thin wooden-framed mirror. In front of the mirror is a waist-high urn with trimmed branches of some unidentifiable tree. Menus are handed to us.

The waiter hovers. 'Can I get you anything to drink?'

Lucy nods. 'Mom, I'm having a small glass of red.'

'Fine, but I don't normally drink–'

The look of shock and then incredulity on Lucy's face is disquieting.

I chew on my lip, a nervous tick I have. 'I somehow thought I didn't, but your look says otherwise.'

'Yeah, and then some. Have a glass with me or not; it's all the same to me.'

I swallow and look up at the waiter, who is patiently waiting. 'I'll have the same.'

The man slides off silently like he's wearing slippers. Glancing at the menu, I have no idea what to choose.

'Can you recommend anything?' I ask Lucy.

'All of it. I think I've worked my way up and down the menu. Let's see, depending on if you're dieting, there are seasonal fruit salads. They're drizzled with the most sublime lime and cardamom dressing and topped with spicy shrimp.'

'I'm already dribbling. But if I'm not dieting?'

'The duck and plantain croquettes with dried figs simmered in tea and cinnamon bark are to die for.'

'What are you going to have?'

Two bottles of chilled spring water in tastefully designed glass bottles are set in the middle of the table, together with two square-shaped tumblers that are so highly polished they positively gleam.

'Thank you.' I look up at the waiter and smile. 'Sorry Lucy, what are you ordering?'

For a moment, she watches me. The waiter has again slip-slipped off across the shiny floor as if he's ice-skating. 'It's a toss-up between the braised short ribs served in a roasted coconut sauce,' she reads from the menu, 'or the fish rubbed with a mild spice paste, roasted in a banana leaf and served with a load of side dishes. A tricky decision.'

I look at the prices and wonder if it would be sheer greed to ask for the whole menu to be served *and make it snappy!*

'Right,' She cracks the menu shut, and that seems to be the signal for the beady-eyed waiter to return, 'the short ribs have won out.'

I have to make a choice. 'The duck for me.' The menus are whisked from our hands, and two glasses of red wine are placed in front of us. I raise one. 'A toast, I think. To... understanding and reconciliation.'

Lucy bobs her head once. 'And to open minds and change.'

The wine is spicy with hints of vanilla and oak tannin. Yes, I must like red wine. Now I wish we'd ordered the bottle, but Lucy is driving, and I don't want to be drunk if she's sober. Maybe I do drink then. My head is spinning, although it can't be due to that one mouthful of wine.

One of those silences settles over us like we're enveloped in a warm, wet blanket and can't struggle out of it. I know I shouldn't ask, yet it pops out of my mouth regardless, like I just couldn't keep it in any longer.

'Lucy, why don't we get on?'

She slumps down in her chair and twirls the wine in her glass. It coats the surface and leaves a dark red pattern. 'I don't want to talk about that. It might lead us back to where we always go.'

'Where's that?'

'Arguing, screaming, incriminations.'

'That good, eh? So, how are we going to play this then?'

'I ask you questions, and you answer them.'

'That easy?'

'That easy.' She stares at me. 'Are you a Republican or a Democrat?'

'Which one's which again?'

'Don't you know?'

'I get muddled.'

'Republicans are considered on the right end of the political spectrum while Democrats are on the left.'

'And that means?'

'I personally believe that the right is generally pro-religion, anti-bureaucracy, pro-military, pro-business and pro-personal responsibility. They advocate pulling yourself up by your bootstraps. Work hard and obey God, and all will be good. The left says that everyone pays taxes to equalise society; the government should solve problems and should be counted on to help people who can't take care of themselves. They are more liberal, usually more educated and open-minded and a little more realistic.'

I nod at her. 'Are you saying you can't be a well-educated Republican? Or that they can't be open-minded or help their fellow man? Or you can't be a Democrat who believes in God?'

'Like I said,' Lucy raises an eyebrow, 'this is a massive generalisation that simplifies it for you.'

'So possibly not that black and white?' I see her flinch. 'Who gets your vote?'

'I'd like to believe that I'm open-minded and I hate the military and its agenda. Work it out.'

'Which one am I then? Normally.'

'Normally, everything that's the opposite to me, except you're not normal at the moment, are you. Okay, which one sounds the best to you today, now, here in this restaurant?'

'I'd have to say the one that has a government that helps the more vulnerable people in its society.'

'That'll be Democrat. How did you feel about Obama? A black man in the White House.'

'I thought it was brilliant. I mean, nobody needed another Bush, did they. No one can be as stupid as Bush.' I laugh.

Her eyes are luminous. This time I can see the tips of her teeth through a smile. 'You know Grandpa said the Confederate flag should be hoisted high and proud as it proclaims a glorious heritage. Don't you agree with him?'

'I really haven't a clue. My history is a little shabby concerning such things.' I rub at my nose.

She persists, and I realise that this is important by the tone of her voice. 'But a black man as the President. Who'd have thought it?' There's a strange glint in her eyes.

'Good for him. I must admit I never believed it would happen in my lifetime. I'm glad I've seen it. He's an eloquent man, and that wife of his is a marvel, didn't she win it for him?'

'Seemingly so. Funny, isn't it. Obama being awarded the Nobel Peace Prize simply for not being George W. Bush.'

'Surely there's more to it than that?'

'Maybe he'll actually earn it. He eliminated Osama bin Laden and even though he added three-quarters of a trillion dollars to the national debt, he ordered the drawing up of plans for the kind of health care reforms that we've been dreaming of for years. It nearly sank him, giving the good ol' Republican boys the ammo they needed. They forget to mention that "Obamacare",' she waves her fingers in the air, 'extended health coverage to thirty million poorer Americans than ever before.'

'Then he would have got my vote.'

'Really? Did you vote for him?'

'I have no idea, as I can't remember, but I'm sure I did.'

She makes a strange snorting sound at the back of her throat and shakes her head slightly.

'Oh,' she says quietly, 'I'm sure you didn't.'

'Why do you say that, Lucy?' My beloved daughter is beginning to annoy me.

She twiddles the napkin as if nervous. Or angry. 'Really? You care about poor Americans?'

'I hope I do. I'm sorry, but why are we talking about Obama? He's not President anymore. This next guy might just make Bush seem like the better option after all.'

Again she snorts. 'This next guy will get us all nuked! Or start another civil war.'

'Then if nothing else,' I stare across the table at her, 'on that we are agreed.'

The head waiter approaches our table. 'Are you ready to be served?'

'Great,' I say, 'I can't wait.' We need to be distracted from the turn in the conversation, especially as I don't get what she's trying to winkle out of me.

He clicks his fingers, and large wooden platters are hurried to our table filled with food of the most amazing colours. Rich tangerine oranges and bright lime greens, warm ochre yellows and fiery chilli reds, with sides of burnt and bubbled naan breads. Wafts of the most tantalising smells drift up, and my mouth waters.

'Mmm,' I say, 'this is wonderful. I can see why you like it here. Do you often come here with someone?'

'What's that supposed to mean? Are you asking if I have a boyfriend?'

'That wasn't my intention. I wondered if you came with your dad, or grandpa or grandma or maybe George. I wasn't fishing into your private life.'

'Oh. I sometimes come with Dad, but mostly it's with friends from college.'

'Have I met any of them?' I dig my fork into my duck and balance a bit of plantain and a slice of fig on top. The flavours explode in my mouth.

'Some. You weren't impressed.'

'Why not?' Although I long to shovel it all down like a ravenous dog, I slow down so I can savour each mouthful.

'Because most of them are not what you expect my friends to be.'

'I'm sorry about that.' I wonder why I might not like them. Is it because they're all drug-dealing pimps with bad-boy, gangster rap attitudes? How can I steer us away from this subject? What could possibly be a good topic of conversation that won't cause either one of us a meltdown? But she gets there first.

'Do you...' she pauses, looking for the right words, I suppose, 'do you think that one race is superior to another?'

'What, you mean like the Germans and their endless "Vorsprung durch Technik"?' I sip my wine. 'You have to admit that German technology is pretty good, so it's not exactly boasting, is it?'

'No, I mean totally superior in every way, morally, intellectually, socially.' I can now see where this might be leading. The bowls on my platter are being scraped. Even though there wasn't a great deal of food, I feel full up. Maybe because I didn't stuff it down as if I was starving, my body had time to catch up.

'Do *you*?' I reply, but I don't really want to know her answer. Lucy has also finished, and I wonder if we'll order a dessert and coffee.

'I thought I was asking the questions, Mom. Do you believe that all men were created equal?'

'If you're born into wealth, your life will be infinitely different from being born into abject poverty. That is where the inequality lies.' I peer over my shoulder for the waiter. 'Are we having anything else?'

'Amazing.' She frowns and looks down at the table, which has a smear of sauce on it. She wipes it off with her napkin.

'What about the idea that students who identify as LGBTQIA+ must undergo "conversion" therapy, which aims to use counselling and religious teaching to convert someone who is homosexual. How do you feel about that?'

'That's terrible. Are you talking about kids being brainwashed by religious fanatics? Look, Lucy, I don't really understand what this is all about. Your grandfather warned me... we had differences of opinion.'

'Warned you? I bet he did.'

'He's worried about you and George.'

'Leave George out of it. Come on, Mom. Being gay is a sin against God, isn't it? Don't you think that gay people are "touched by the devil" and should be *taught* the error of their ways?'

'Lucy, I don't mean to judge you, but these things you believe aren't right.'

'I believe? You are kidding me, right? They're all your

beliefs, Mom. Oh, man. You must've had one helluva bang on the head for you to turn all you hold dear completely around.'

What the hell is she saying? I'm having trouble breathing. The chair falls backward and crashes to the floor as I stand. 'I'm not having this, Lucy. We're going to pay up and get home. I'm not going to let you do this to me.'

'Do what, Mom?'

'Try to pin your awful ideas on me; make me think they're mine. I know I have never, ever advocated any such stuff.' I turn to pick up the chair.

'Who are you now?' Her voice is barely a whisper. 'Where is your God?'

Tears are coursing down her face, and she's wiping them away with her fingertips. People are staring, and I can hear the soft shoe shuffle of the head waiter coming our way.

'Not who you are insinuating I am.' I know there are couples close by eavesdropping, earwigging like fine-tuned radar. There's nothing like a bit of a ruckus, a smidgeon of malcontent to get the average diner's attention away from their own boring conversations. This is probably not the time to point out a certain glaring fact, except I can't help it.

'I don't believe in God.'

Heads swivel, and there are repeated intakes of breath like an audience queued for a particular response. I hear whispers, 'She said she doesn't believe in God! What an awful woman.'

I know that I've prayed and prayed, and my prayers have always gone unanswered. If God is out there, he isn't listening to *me*. I'd like to come back here to sample some more marvellous cooking and try a pudding but maybe shouting at the exclusive set of diners to "mind their own sodding business" is not the way to go.

It's a long and uncomfortably silent journey home. I try to occupy myself, but the road is mostly dead straight, with only direction signs and billboards to look at. What's beyond the edge of the road is an ink-swirled impenetrable darkness.

The wing mirror flashes at me every so often. Car headlights from behind us are reflected in its tiny surface, but then it blazes like a rectangular torch.

'Hey!' Lucy thumps the wheel. *'Douchebag!'*

'What's the matter?'

'Just some asshole shining his headlights on full. They're blinding me.'

I twist to see through the back window. The lights are glaring, and I wave. Whoever is driving can see me clearly like a cut-out silhouette. The beams suddenly shift sideways, and as the vehicle roars by us, I recognise it. It's a white Chevy with tinted windows.

Before I can say anything, Lucy has blared her horn and given the driver the benefit of her middle finger. 'Looks like the same shit who ran you off the road.'

I can see that she's thought through her words as her expression changes. 'Sorry, what a stupid thing to say. There's no way it can be, and anyway, there are tons of white Chevies round here.'

'I know.' But something is left hanging in the air between us.

As I climb stiffly from the car, Lucy turns to me. 'Look up what the design on that sweatshirt you were wearing actually means. Then get back to me.'

I think about the emblem on my sweatshirt and what Lucy said. I find it hanging over the end of the bed. A stars and bars flag, surrounded by a laurel wreath with a bow holding it together with the dates 1861 to 1865. There's some sort of insignia or letters, though it's hard to make out. SSW? I type it into my iPhone, and a website pops up. The Sisterhood of Southern Women and it's their emblem. Lucy said it was the Confederate flag. Is this mine, or have I borrowed it from Mom? I retype in "Confederate flag" and am shocked by the many different responses. It seems that it is no accident that Confederate symbols have been the mainstay of white supremacist organisations, from the Ku Klux Klan to the skinheads. I gather from my reading that they did not appropriate the Confederate battle flag simply because it was pretty. They picked it because it was the flag of a nation dedicated to their ideals, "that the negro is not equal to the white man". According to the Southerners who still use the Confederate flag, it represents heritage, not hate, except it's a heritage that has exploited and debased millions of other human beings. As one person writes, 'Why should we celebrate this?'

Why indeed? And more to the point, what is this thing doing in my wardrobe?

11

PLAYING WITH GUNS

I don't feel like I've slept properly as the night was filled with billowing things just outside the curtains of my bed. I pulled them closed last night, but maybe this was a bad idea as all my thoughts crowded around and whispered to me from outside. I shower quickly, drag on what I was wearing last night and manage to get to the kitchen before Dolores can come up with Charlie and Di.

'Good morning, Dolores. Have we got any tea?'

There is an opened box of English breakfast leaves by the kettle, which is rumbling to a boil.

'Yes, madam.'

'Don't worry, I can do it. Please call me Cassie.'

'Okay. May I say, *Cassie,* that you look different this morning.'

'Different better?'

'Different. More natural.' She shrugs her shoulders. 'Did you enjoy your trip with Lucy?'

'It was interesting, to say the least. I seem to be finding out all sorts of things about myself, and the more I discover, the more confused I feel.'

'I'm sorry to hear that, yet one bit of information may be the key to unlock your memories.'

'I know, but it feels really painful right now. Sorry, do you mind if I hunt around for stuff, you know, get orientated so I can fend for myself?'

'I thought it was my job to fend for you.'

'I think it's time things changed a little around here.'

'Please be careful, Cassie. Change is not something that is welcomed here. *Poco a poco, entiendes?*'

'*Sí, lo entiendo.*'

'Hey, baby-girl, there you are.'

Dad walks into the kitchen, and I feel a cold tickle skitter down my back. How much has he heard? Dolores is now busy filling the coffee pot, her back to the both of us. I walk around the island to the fridge and tweak out the carton of milk, which I slosh into my mug.

'Milk in your tea, Cassie? You surely are an Anglophile.' He doesn't give any indication that he heard us.

'Here is the sugar, madam.' Dolores pushes a lidded pot across the counter and turns to my dad. 'Coffee will be a couple of minutes, Señor Davenport. Would you like it brought to the breakfast room?'

'No, we're both here now. How about some fried steak and eggs? What do you say, Cassie?'

'Have we got any muesli?'

'You're kidding, right? Muesli? I think you mean granola.'

'I suppose this isn't the moment to mention falafel then?' I see Dolores's eyes widen and her lips purse. She's trying not to laugh.

'Are you yanking my chain here?'

'Of course, I am. Who could ever turn down a fried breakfast?'

'Madam, would you like your eggs sunny side up as usual?'

Dad chips in. 'She'll have nothing different, Dolores. She needs conformity whether she wants it right now or not. That is what will help her to regain her memories. Is that understood?'

'Clearly, Señor.' She begins to prepare breakfast with accustomed speed.

Dad sits down at the breakfast bar. 'Heard you went out with Lucy yesterday. How'd that go?'

My mug of tea is suspended by my mouth. *How did it go?* 'Not particularly good. I'm bewildered about the things she said. It didn't end well.'

'I told you she was manipulative.'

'Yes, but she's still my daughter, and something's gone terribly wrong between us. I just wish I knew what had happened to cause all this, so I can set it right.'

'Nick is what happened.'

I see out of the corner of my eye that Dolores twitches. Actually visibly twitches. She clumps around, dishing out the breakfast and then she walks out of the kitchen as if she's offended or something. But by what?

'Yes but,' I swallow, 'surely I must've been there too? What was I doing to let things get this bad?' I rub my head, and it stings. 'I want my memories back, but they seem to be getting further away, the harder I try to remember.'

Dad pulls our plates across the counter. 'They'll come back soon, don't you worry.'

I pull my sleeves up. Dad squints at me.

'You look lovely this morning. New clothes?'

'At least something good came out of yesterday.'

Dad eats with his fork, cutting his food with the side of it and shovelling it in. 'Listen, how about we do a little target shooting after breakfast? We can take some rifles out to the range and just have us some fun. What do you say?'

'We're going to shoot rifles? Are we in the Wild West then?'

I feel a wave of anxiety wash over me like I've stepped into a band of freezing fog. Guns?

'No honey, we're in the Deep South.' He smiles. 'If nothing else, it'll let you get rid of a bit of angst. Blow the heck out of something. Always makes me feel better when I'm having a down day.' He glances toward where Dolores just exited. Did he notice her behaviour too? Does he know what it meant?

He puts his arm around my waist as I stand up. A part of me wants to run, to hide, but another part longs to feel loved and cherished, and I don't want that sensation to go away. Now there is warmth enveloping me. I wait and try not to move even one muscle in case I push him from me. But he stays by my side.

Staring out the window, there are glitters of light rippling across the surface of the pool.

Finally, he pulls apart from me, and it's like someone has blocked the light. It's cold again. 'I'll get the rifles as they're under lock and key. Go across the decking by the pool and cut through via that gate at the end. The gun range is behind that little copse of hazel over there.' He points, and I follow the end of his finger.

My hair is standing on end. I think of the goldfish I bagged at the fairground, swimming dazedly in circles in a tiny, clear plastic bag, and a small, red-haired, potbellied plastic troll with beady black eyes. I had to give the fish to a neighbour, as it didn't stand a chance with us. I stop and clutch at the counter. If this is a memory, it's a start and maybe I have to remember my childhood first and work up from there? But why didn't the goldfish stand a chance with us? I shake my head and slip out of the French windows, and still, some part of me can only wonder that I have such a luxurious swimming pool in my garden.

This type of amnesia really seems to regress certain things but leave others bright and shiny. The gate bangs shut behind me. I recoil in fear as if someone is coming at me with a knife. I remind myself it's only a noise, and my poor old head must be really sensitive after the accident. I look around, so where are the targets?

I don't hear Dad as he walks up behind me. I jump again when I hear his voice.

'Just look at these babies.'

He holds out two guns that look kind of girly to me, but what do I know.

'This one is an Uberti 1874 Sharps Extra Deluxe Rifle, one of the best long-range rifles in the world. Somewhere inside of you is a place that can remember its model number, how many grooves it's got, the fact that its frame is case-hardened, and it has a tang mounted Creedmore sight and pewter forend cap.'

'Are you reading that from a manual?'

'Ha, ha. I know my stuff, and you do too. It's a beautiful gun, baby-girl, and it's yours.' He hands it to me. I lift it in my hand, although I don't expect it to be that light.

'How much does this cost?' Even I know that something like this must cost a pretty penny.

'That'll set you back about three thousand dollars.'

'*Oh!* A mere snip, then.' Where are the money trees, these sweet peaches that have enabled us to be so extravagant? Can you pluck hundred dollar bills off as you pass by? Thousand-dollar bills? What comes after that? Can you get a million-dollar bill? Hard to cash, maybe, but I'd like to have one in my hand for a moment.

His gun is also narrow looking, slim line. 'What's your one then?'

'This one is a Winchester. It's a Theodore Roosevelt Safari Custom Grade. It's got a twenty-four-inch barrel, and the stock is made from walnut.' He shows me the barrel and what he points out is the "stock". Deep engravings of African big game writhe over the polished walnut, and the sunshine glints off little gold inlaid embellishments.

'They're beautiful.' I balance my one lightly across my open palm.

'It's only eight pounds,' says Dad. 'A suitable gun for a lady, I think. I suppose you won't remember this, but we got them as part of a limited number of two-gun sets. Both you and your mom have the matching pair.' A big grin splits his face. 'Hell, they even threw in a copy of Teddy's famous book called African Game trails.'

'Oh, what Teddy Roosevelt? He wrote a book?'

'He knew his stuff.'

'Have you read it? Have I?'

'Not likely. I think it's termed one of those "coffee-table" books.' He raises the gun to his shoulder and aims it across the field. Targets come into focus where I hadn't noticed them before. Proper bullseyes.

'They're still set at fifty yards, so if you want, I can call Tyreese to go reset them to maybe about twenty-five. Only if you promise me to put the gun down first. You haven't got the safety on. I'd hate for you to accidentally shoot one of us.'

'Hell yes. Fifty yards? I don't think I can hit something that far away' The gun is lowered carefully in case I shoot my foot instead. I need to find out where the safety is pretty quick. 'Why call Tyreese? Can't we move them ourselves?'

'I do wonder what we pay the boy for?' He sighs loudly. 'I'll go move them or we might be here all day'

'I'll do it. I need a bit of exercise.' I drag the two targets closer. There's a feeling in my stomach like I'm on a pitching ship, and goosebumps skitter across my skin.

Dad picks up his gun. 'You can either stand or kneel if you feel that makes you steadier. Follow what I do carefully.'

Watching everything he does like a hungry bird of prey, I twizzle this bit, lock that bit and finally, raise it to my shoulder.

'Hold it more like this,' he says, showing me how. I can see through the sights, and the target looks big enough to crash a bus into. I take my eye away, and it's still pretty small. A barely seen movement catches my eye. I pull the rifle up and focus through the crosshairs. There's something in the far stand of trees. Small branches twitch by one particular tree, but nothing else in the area is moving. I wait, holding my breath, so I don't wobble. As I think I'm imagining things, a figure steps partially from behind the tree. He's indistinct, more of a hazy man-shaped outline, but a bad feeling creeps from my gut.

'Dad? There's a bloke in the trees over there.'

'A bloke? You mean a man?' He steps to my side. 'Where?'

I nod as I don't want to alert the man by pointing in his direction. I see a glint of sunshine reflecting off something. His glasses? Has he got binoculars? *Is he watching us?*

My dad stares through his own sights, and I can see the gun moving deliberately, scanning the trees ahead of us. 'If there was someone there, I can't see him now.'

'Do you know who it could be?'

'Normally, I'd say it was the groundsman, but as it's Sunday, I don't know. They don't usually work on the Sabbath.'

'I think he had binoculars.'

'There's a golf course across the way. Maybe it's someone who has lost their ball? Or a kid who's hoping to make a quick buck by finding all the balls lost by others on the course. Selling them back to the club can be quite lucrative.'

'Okay. But I don't like the thought of someone watching us.'

'Hey, baby-girl. Are we that important that someone is now spying on us? Have we got the President coming over for supper?' He chuckles throatily. 'Even so, I'll call security to check it out. Just in case.' He turns his back on me and speaks quietly into his phone. I don't hear the words but I catch the tone. He turns back to me. 'Now, where were we? I'll go first,' Dad raises the gun back to his shoulder, 'so you see how much kick-back you get. Don't go rigid, or you'll bruise.' He fires, and the sound makes me jump. I see a tiny implosion in the centre of his target.

I try to follow his instructions, but my shoulder is jerked back when the gun goes off. Have I hit the mark, or is there now a dead bird or squirrel in a nearby tree? Or possibly a dead man?

'Bullseye, baby-girl.'

Am I good at this, or was that a lucky shot? I want another go to prove that I can do this. I want him to be proud of me. We reload and go again. The target gets moved back to fifty yards and then a hundred yards, but I start to miss after that.

'You're doing fine.' Dad pats me on the shoulder. 'That's some good shooting considering, in theory, you haven't done it before.'

'Except at the fairground.'

'What? Oh, you mean the County Fair? Yeah, you always came home with the best prize. One time, you won a teddy bear that was bigger than you. It's still up in the roof space somewhere.'

'Not a troll?'

'A troll?'

'Never mind.'

He shows me the gun again like it's the most beautiful thing in the world, which I suppose it might be to him. 'The original Sharps rifle was first made in 1848 by Christian Sharp. It's a famous gun. When seven-hundred Comanch warriors attacked thirty buffalo hunters, the hunters retaliated using these guns to wipe them out. A truly glorious day.'

So, thirty buffalo hunters used their technology to kill seven hundred warriors who were only trying to protect their land, their resources. That's terrible. And what about the number of buffalo they slaughtered? In my mind, I glimpse a wasteland of humped and hairy horned beasts and the shouts of men on horseback far away. Could they even see their frightened, dying eyes? Hear their laboured snorts or even comprehend the near extinction of a species? What am I doing with this thing in my hand?

'Dad? Have I ever killed anything? I mean with a gun?'

Dad rolls his eyes. 'Honey? You're one of the best hunters in the state. I remember you saying once that the old natural history cameramen might sit in their little hidey-hole for months to catch a sight of a snow leopard, but you'd do it for years if it meant you could wear it afterwards.'

I see the rabbit fur jacket... I drop the gun.

'Baby-girl?'

I run and keep on running, even when I can hear him calling my name behind me. I'm not Cassie. I can't be this woman. *I can't be!*

I've outrun him, but now I don't know what to expect. Will he be angry with me? Will he morph from a sweet old man into a nightmare creature with fire pouring from his eyes? Fear crashes over me, gushing up my nose and down my throat, half blinding me as I stumble up the stairs to my room. I know I can't lock the door against him. After I wedged the door shut with a chair under the door handle, he took the whole lot off and hit me with the back of his hand so hard, I crashed into the wardrobe and fractured my collar bone. At the hospital, he told the nurse I was "such a clumsy girl".

My head starts to spin when I reach my room and find the door handle still there and the key in the lock. What the hell is happening?

How can I placate him? Will I be able to stop the monster from erupting out of him? Or am I simply going mad? My addled brains from the accident conjuring terrifying scenarios that do not, and have never existed? Why would I ever think this of this loving, caring man?

I find him sitting under the shade of a large, white linen umbrella by the pool. I stand and watch him for a while. He's a distinguished-looking man, elegant even while lounging, yet the ghost in my head is a snarling heavy fisted brute. Are these memories? How can they be? They don't fit with anything I know in my newly acquired world.

I walk over slowly and sit cross-legged on the edge of the pool a few feet away. 'Dad. I'm so sorry about earlier. I got really freaked out by the guns. I don't remember them being in my life at all.'

He leans forward. 'I must admit, I was shocked by your reaction. Never, ever drop a gun like that again. If your mom had seen you do that, she would have fainted out cold! Dearest God, Cassie, didn't you hear how much those guns cost? Didn't I tell you that yours and your mom's were a set? If they get damaged through stupidity and negligence, then that's a crying shame.'

'I was... frightened.'

'I just don't get it, Cassie. You've been shooting since you were nine.'

'Maybe in your world but not in mine. Like I said, I'm really sorry.'

'Alright, but next time, let me know what's going on in that pretty little head of yours. Talking of pretty, aren't you going to return to being blonde?' He tousles my hair. 'After all, they say blondes have more fun?'

This is all so normal. He isn't shouting at me, calling me such names that would make your cheeks blush. He hasn't backhanded me across my face or started to undo his belt to teach me "a valuable lesson". Who is this other dream man in my head? I finger my hair, pulling a strand free of the slicked-back ponytail. It's glossy and dark. That'd take a humongous amount of bleach to change it back and strip all the shine off, and hell, why do I want to be thought of as "stupid"? Blondes may have more fun, but they're also treated like dumb little kids that know sod all by the rest of the populace. Haven't I been called that enough times in my life? Stupid. Worthless. I feel nauseous. Hang on a minute? Who here has called me stupid or worthless? *Who would dare?*

I swallow and shake my head. 'I like it this way. I'm going to leave it for a while.'

I think of the pictures of me in my room, thundering around on old Caesar, and I know I don't want to go back. I'm all smiley teeth and wide eyes. Now I don't feel that is me anymore.

'Okay. It's up to you, but I prefer you blonde, and so does your mom.'

'Please don't pressure me. I have to do things in my own time.'

'Okay.' He crosses his legs, hitching his trousers up from the knee first. 'So, what's the next question on your list?'

That throws me for a moment. 'Um...' I could ask all manner of things, except most of them would make him wonder if I should be sectioned.

'Go ahead.'

Come on, think. What was the next question on the list?

'Oh yeah. What do I do? And why was I in London in the first place? You said a business meeting or something?'

'You've been to England a couple of times recently, but we were never really sure what it was all about.'

'Does anyone know? What about Nick?'

'I asked him, and he said you didn't bother to enlighten him about what you were up to. By the tone of his voice, he was telling the truth. As to what you do, Cassie, you are a Southern lady.'

'And that means?'

'Our motto here is, 'Wisdom, Justice and Moderation'. You took it upon yourself to preach the word to your sisters that the pen may be mightier than the sword, but you should always keep a sword handy in case the pen breaks.'

'And what does that entail?' *Keep the sword handy? Red-painted nails…*

He doesn't get a chance to answer. His phone rings, and he answers it, twisting away to whisper responses. When he turns back, he is smiling. 'That was Mom. She'll be home within the hour. She's just finished speaking at the memorial service, and she's bringing some of our dearest friends back with her. I bet you can't wait to see her, can you?' He pulls me into his arms, and I'm encircled with love. How can I fear this man?

My mum will be here within the hour, and she'll make it all better like mums are supposed to do. I feel like a massive wave has crashed over my head, and I am, after a few moments of dizziness, floating in some soft blue haze. I know I'm crying, but there's nothing I can do. He wipes the tears from my face.

'There, there. You wash your face now and get ready. Remember to brush your hair and put some make-up on. You gotta look your best for your mom.'

An hour may seem like a long time, but it's nothing when you're worrying about what to wear, how to do your hair, what perfume to dab on your wrists and how much make-up to put on. I tug on the cord by the bed, and Dolores comes running to my rescue.

'Everyone says I've changed. Oh, Dolores, what if my mum doesn't like me now?'

Dolores is laying out my new skinny jeans and T-shirt. 'Cassie, calm down. Your mother loves you, and although you may appear different, you are still her little girl. But you must try to be calm, as she doesn't appreciate shows of emotion. She's a very controlled woman. She prides herself on how she appears.'

'What does that mean? She won't allow herself to cry in case it messes her mascara?'

'Exactly. Now let me brush your hair and put it in a bun for you. Your mother will expect that you look your best if her friends are coming to visit.'

She's echoed what my dad said, but why should it matter if my hair is messy or I've forgotten the blusher? Surely the most important thing is that I'm alive? I hope she cries so much on seeing me that her mascara runs down to her chin. The woman in my visions would do that, but who am I about to meet?

12

MOM

I hear the car crunch up the gravel and the sound of voices as the group climb out. I peer through a side window, but the glass is rippled. I can see her distorted figure walk across the driveway, hear her turn the handle, and my breath catches in my throat as she steps in through the doorway.

'Mum?' I can't move. It's like my feet have been licked and stuck to the shiny marble floor of the foyer. Like they're feet-shaped suckers that won't allow me to take a step toward the woman staring at me.

'You're not my mum!' The words fall out of my mouth before I can stop them.

I see her face harden into a mask. And what a face she has. High "Hollywood" cheekbones, alabaster skin, blue eyes the colour of a summer's evening, a full red pout. Her hair is white blonde and gently curled like Marilyn Monroe. She's tall, made taller by the stiletto heels she's wearing. How can she be my mum? I was right; the stylish gene has definitely jumped a generation.

'Hello, Cassie.' She takes a deep breath and smooths down

her jacket. She's in a skirt suit that would blend in perfectly in a war movie from the forties. A phenomenal hourglass figure perfects the look. 'Well, it's good to be home, isn't it?'

'Oh, I'm so sorry. Of course, you're my m... mom. Please forgive me. I'm so confused. Dear God! You look like you've stepped out of the pages of Vogue. Are you really my mother?'

She must spend hours down the gym on top of all that crusading.

A look of surprise is quickly replaced with a smile. 'Cassie. Thank you. Vogue, eh? I like the sound of that. Come here, child.' She holds out her arms, and I stumble into them. She pats me on the back, but there is a gap between us which is more than just air.

My mum is here, and she'll make it all better, won't she? It's then that I realise that other people are crunching over the gravel and pushing in through the door.

'I brought some of our friends with me.' She pulls my face close to hers. 'Cassie, I don't need you to say that I'm not your mother, okay? That wouldn't be good.'

'Of course not. I'm so sorry.' Tears blind me, and I can't see who has come in; they are animated shadows only. I know I shouldn't cry as it just makes it worse, but I have lost all control.

'Aw, how sweet!' A woman's deep drawl, like she's speaking through honey. 'Look, that is such a picture. Poor, poor Cassie, how we've missed you and your wise words these last few weeks.'

I wipe the tears from my eyes and try to focus. A plump woman wearing a cloche type hat with what could be a bit of ostrich caught on top is smiling at me. She's in a tight lavender-coloured suit that does her no favours. Her ankles are swollen, and her shoes look like they're cutting into her feet.

'Cassie,' my mom guides me by my elbow. 'This is Mrs

Radnor. She's the Chair of the Sisterhood. You've known her since you were a little girl.'

'Cassie, darlin'. I can't believe you've lost your memory. It's devastatin' news for all of us.' She does a dramatic sweep of her hand, and some lacy handkerchief has appeared from her copious bosom. She dabs at her eyes.

A man steps forward. 'I'm Bob.' He extends his hand. 'And I dangled you on my lap when you were no higher than this.' His hand cuts through the air at knee level.

Mom laughs. 'This is Senator Robert Raines.'

'I'm so sorry this has happened to you.' He rubs the top of my arm and then pinches my cheek. Is this something he's done a thousand times before without even thinking about it? I take a step backward.

I feel I'm expected to say something. 'It'll all come back in its own time. The doctors are confident.'

Senator Raines is not as old as my dad, but not that far off. He is one of those men who know they are distinguished-looking, with a neat grey sprinkled "musketeer" beard and moustache and light blue eyes. As far as I can ascertain, he still has his own hair, thick and neatly clipped and a fine set of pearly whites.

'Welcome, all of you.' Dad sweeps in, shaking hands and kissing cheeks. He lingers by Mom, and as they brush lips, the electricity between them is so palpable I tingle. How many years have they been together, and they still have that sort of chemistry? Why haven't I got that? If not with Nick, then at least someone else?

My mom's smile is brilliant, like Christmas lights. 'I was thinking that we'll have dinner once we've all had a chance to freshen up. How does that sound? About eight? And that gives me time to have a good chat with Cassie before that.'

'Fine by me,' says the senator, 'I need to rest these weary old bones in a hot tub.' He nods up the stairs. 'Usual room?'

Dad slaps him on the back. 'As if we could ever palm you off with anything else now. You always bagged the best room in the house. Go on, and I'll get Tyreese to bring your bags up.'

My mom wings out her elbow, and I link my arm through hers: mother and daughter. 'I think we'll get Dolores to mix us something delicious and go and sit in the sunroom. Then we can have a little heart-to-heart, can't we?'

'I'd love that.'

We settle in rattan chairs with crisp white linen cushions. Dolores has been ordered to bring us two rum and cokes with ice and a slice of lemon. She arrives with frosted glasses on a small tray and a plateful of canapés.

'We have smoked salmon mousse, peach and prosciutto and watercress.'

She keeps her eyes lowered at all times. Even though I have this idea I shouldn't be drinking, it slides down nicely, and now I want more. I reach for one of the dainty canapés.

'These are delicious.'

My mom is here, and she'll make it all better. But I don't know her. I have never known her. Where is the recognition? Why hasn't it come to me? She's not the woman in my head, as much as Dad is not the man. I don't know what is happening to me. This is horrible! Please let me remember my real life... and not this terrifying other world that seeps from my damaged mind.

Mom pats my hand and sips her drink. 'Tell me everything that has happened so far.'

Where do I start? In the hospital or coming home? Do I mention Nick and the kids? Tell her of all my fears? But I begin to speak, and the words rush out of my mouth until I see her sip her drink. A red imprint is left on the glass...

... She leaves a red lipstick kiss on the mirror as she goes.

'See ya later, alligator.'

Her hair is hidden with a multicoloured scarf and her eyes behind huge sunglasses. She's pulled the collar up around her neck. It's a tan gabardine raincoat. 'So wet and grey here,' she says. 'I don't know how you stand it.'

'This is only an April shower. You ain't seen nothing yet.' I'm trying to make light of it, her going, of her leaving me here in all this *shit* when she's going back to *that*. Some part of me wants to shake her until her eyes roll out across the floor like marbles.

'Maybe I don't want to see it.'

'Are you saying you're not coming back?' I can't bear it if this is the last time. I take a step toward her.

'Why should I?'

'To see me?' She tilts her head, and I hear a chuckle. She's amused, and I hate her for it. She's going to make me beg. She has that power over me.

'I've seen you, haven't I?'

'To see me again.' Now I hate myself. 'Please come back and see me again.'

Who is she?

'Cassie? Cassie, are you all right?' My mom's worried face hovers in front of me, but my eyesight is blurred with that other woman's image still imprinted on the back of my eyes, like a residue. I blink to try to clear them.

'What happened? You were someplace else for a moment there.'

'I saw something, I mean someone. I think I know her. She seems important to me.'

'Did you see her clearly? Can you describe her?'

'No, she was all covered up, like she was hiding.'

'*Was she* hiding, do you think?'

'No...' I close my eyes to see her again. 'No, it's more like a game she's playing.'

'Do you think you like her, this mystery woman? Could it be Marcie?'

'Who is Marcie?'

'Your best friend. Hasn't she called you yet?'

'No.' I try to recapture the feeling I had. Exhilaration, yes, fear, a little and what else? Jealousy? She was teasing me. I want what she has. I want it badly.

'It's hot in here.' I push my fringe away from my face. 'How long have I known Marcie?'

'I'll put the fan on. I don't normally as the hum drives me mad.' She stretches and sways elegantly to flick a switch. A whirring starts above my head. 'As to Marcie, you met at elementary school and have been joined at the hip ever since.'

'Then why hasn't she contacted me?'

'Maybe she's waiting to hear that you're better. You have to realise that as hard as it must be for you, Cassie, it's equally hard on us all too. Try to put yourself in our shoes. You come back from near death, but you come back as a stranger to us. We have our life with you like snapshots in an album, and yet you're completely blank or worse, you seem to have, as far as you've just told me, memories of things that haven't happened and things that don't exist.'

'In other words, you think I'm going nuts?'

She laughs like a peal of heavenly church bells, something that mortals should never hear on this Earth.

'We're not signing the papers on you yet, Cassie. Time heals all things; just don't wait too long about it. I heard about your escapade on Caesar, and I'd like to point out that trials start next month. By all accounts, we do not want a repeat performance. Your Papa was not particularly complementary.'

'I really hope no one filmed me. I'd be getting top hits on YouTube by now.'

Her smile disappears. 'They didn't, did they?' I can see tiny wrinkles spreading out from her upper lip. Crimson lipstick has begun to bleed into the cracks.

'Why would anyone want to film me? I only meant that it must have looked hysterically funny–'

'It's not funny at all, Cassie. You're the best rider in this state, and it would be a disaster if anyone saw you riding like that.'

'I'm sorry. I don't understand why that's such a big thing.'

'Because of who you are. Because you are Cassandra Eleanor Davenport, of the long lineage of Davenport and Bauvier, and we are not people who can be jokes to others. We are the people that the average Joe Schmoe out there look up to. We have exacting standards that must be upheld.'

'No one filmed me, I'm sure of it.' I tentatively touch her arm. 'I've been very rude and talked at you for ages. Tell me what you've been up to.' In other words, I need to get the focus off of me.

My mom is curled like an elegant Persian cat on the cushion.

'Well, we had a wonderful memorial service at Grace's Episcopal Church. The congregation was packed, and we finished the sermon on the lawns. The new president of the Young Confederacy spoke to us, and he is so eloquent. He is going out to actively recruit new members to our cause and get them involved at all levels.'

'Can anyone join?'

'Well, yes, as long as one parent has the blood of a Confederate running in their veins.'

'What if you're adopted?'

'You've answered your own question, no true blood, no admittance.' She leans across between us, and at first, I think she will kiss me, but she only tweaks something from my top. 'I wish you'd been there, Cassie. You'd have loved it. Hundreds of kids pledged to preserve our pure ideals, to honour the memory of our beloved veterans and to study and teach the truths of history.'

Silly me. I thought there was only one truth of history. I know I shouldn't ask, not now, when I'm so happy and nearly feeling like I'm actually home. But the bit of me that won't take "no" for an answer kicks in. 'Remind me what those truths are?'

'This is so strange. It's like talking to you when you were eight again. We aim to act in a manner that will reflect honour upon our noble and patriotic ancestors. We reconcile the "Lost Cause" between the traditional white societies of the South with the defeat of the Confederate States of America. We reconcile why most of the grand old families lost their wealth and power, and we meet old friends and acquire new ones while we gain insight into ideas for advancing our objectives. At Richmond, we keep our heritage alive.'

I can feel her patriotic fervour like a second sun burning my skin.

'And what are our objectives? Just so I know?'

'It's been a long journey, so can we talk about this later? I really need a hot bath and maybe a little nap.'

'Yeah, later.' More tangled threads to weave in and the tapestry forming slowly in my head is not a pleasant one.

Her teeth are perfect, apart from a tiny smudge of red, like she's bitten her tongue and there's blood. 'The main thing is, I'm so glad you're safe back home where you belong.'

I slide my arm through hers, and we head upstairs. She tucks my hair behind my ears when we get to the landing.

'At eight then?' I say. 'Is it formal or casual?'

'It's a party, so dress up.' She snorts. 'We don't want to be outshone by Mrs Radnor, now do we?'

'Not in this lifetime.'

13

IGNORANT

I cool down by having a cold shower, rinsing my hair and massaging my scalp to wake me up.

I need to focus. What am I going to wear? The black sheath dress is sweet, but I pull out the second dress I chose at the store. It has block stripes of deep fuchsia and bright orange. A gathered skirt flares out from the waist, and it's cut deep at the back. My new strappy shoes with gold dots on ochre suede seem to fit, although I need some other adornment. I'd already gone quickly through the bureau drawers when I was looking for clean knickers. I remember the velvet boxes in a drawer to my right. Opening one, my jaw metaphorically crashes to the floor. If those are diamonds, genuine diamonds, then I must be loaded. Lucy wasn't kidding, was she? I finger the necklace like a thief and even hold the earrings up to my lobes. A bright pink centre dazzles when you get them in a particular light. My heart is thumping as if I'm accompanying a big old brass band. Are these really mine? I put them back into their velvet bed and take another box. By the time I've chosen a simple gold chain with a tear-shaped pendant and matching earrings, I realise the clock hands have been whizzing around. It's five past eight. I squirt perfume in my general direction and then start to run, hoping I haven't mixed up the Chanel No. 5 with the bathroom freshener.

There's no dignified entrance as I hurtle into the dining room and gasp: 'I'm so sorry I'm late.'

'Hell, little girl,' Senator Raines is puffing on a cigar. Blue smoke hangs heavy about his shoulders like a mink stole, 'you ain't late, you're early.'

At first glance, there's only him in the room, and I feel foolish. 'Oh. Right. Shall I go away again and return in a bit?'

'Come and have a drink. I think you need it.' I notice a man stood stiffly to attention in the corner of the room and then it's like he's been wound up and set free. He pours me a glass of champagne and hands it to me, then returns to wait in the corner. I think of that old wives' tale that champagne doesn't make you drunk. I know I need to be cautious.

'Thanks,' I nod.

Senator Raine's eyes travel from my head down slowly to my feet. 'Hmm, well, I'd just like to say that you're looking mighty fine. There's something different about you, and I don't mean just your hair.'

'I'm getting that a lot recently.'

Dad arrives next. 'Bob. Cassie.' He also stops and stares at me. 'Never seen this before.'

'My shopping date with Lucy.'

'She has good taste.' Senator Raines nods and blows a smoke ring.

Why do men of a certain age feel the need to smoke cigars? They're really quite overpowering, and your breath stinks afterwards. Is he married? Does his wife put up with ashtray breath? Or is he having an affair with Mrs Radnor? Are there deep secrets to be unravelled, or is this just the product of a feverish mind? How do you ask questions that you are supposed to know? And I find it irritating that they naturally assumed that Lucy picked out my dress for me.

'I chose it.' I'm about to top up my glass when the man, presumably a butler, is ahead of me. I watch as the liquid froths to the top of the glass. He's in a butler's uniform, so I presume he has been hired in for the evening to attend to our needs and wants.

Mrs Radnor bustles in, her heaving bosom barely contained in a tight cocktail dress. When you have skin the colour of old winter apples, perhaps wearing lemon yellow chiffon is not the way to go. She looks like she's died, but someone forgot to tell her. And even with my seemingly appalling taste, I know you shouldn't team that particular yellow with the yellow shoes she's chosen. Maybe she's colour blind, and I wish I was too.

Relying on my mom to keep the family end up is easy. Twirling into the room in a red silk dress that accentuates her tiny waist and perfect skin, she nearly takes my breath away. Or that might be the amount of perfume vying for attention in the room. Perhaps I misread Senator Raines, and this is his defence system against the reek of so much expensive scent.

'Champagne, my darling?' Dad motions at the butler, who materialises at mom's side with a filled glass. I watch as my mom takes it. Her every movement is elegant. She exudes sophistication in the same way as the rest of us sweat.

'A toast.' She raises her glass. 'To the return of our beloved daughter, Cassie.'

'Here, here.' Senator Raines stubs out the cigar. 'And to the rest of her safe return.'

'Here's to Cassie.' Mrs Radnor is dabbing at her eyes. I'm mesmerised by the amount of cleavage that is on show. A knotted pearl necklace dangles provocatively in the deep cleft. 'You look exquisite. Quite modern, I should say.'

Hallelujah, for that!

There are small bowls and plates on the table. I see the canapés from earlier and a few different varieties. Salmon and horseradish, goat's cheese and a red berry jam that I think might be cranberries. Along with light crackers, slices of cucumber and radish, there is a silver platter of oysters. Do I like oysters? Maybe this is not the time to discover I have a seafood allergy. I'm not sure where to start and I don't want to ruin my appetite. The butler tops up our glasses when they get too low, but that means I'm beginning to lose count of what I've drunk. Dad sighs heavily. 'I really thought that we'd take back Congress and the White House in 2012. I know this is a conversation that we've had many times, yet it's one close to your heart, Cassie.'

The senator pulls out a chair. 'Ladies? Do you mind?' He sits down. 'I agree. We thought they were in denial. Turns out it was us.' He suddenly grins like a little boy. 'But boy, can we celebrate now.'

Mrs Radnor dabs at her eyes. 'I can't believe that decent Americans voted that man back in twice. It's utterly outrageous. At least it can't happen again. But as you say, now we can celebrate.'

Dear God, either she's emotionally unbalanced and hey, who am I to say anything about that or she's also got chronic hay fever. Maybe I should take all the flowers outside?

Mom sits down to the senator's left, so I take a chair on her other side. 'I just can't wait for this administration to really get their teeth into sorting this country out. And it's so good to see he's surrounded himself with *our* type of people.'

I hear the emphasis and wonder what she means. 'Mom? I'm sorry, but what are *your* sort of people?'

'Why rich people, my darling. Billionaires, millionaires, investment bankers and venture capitalists, Wall Street insiders and family fortune heirs, educated at the best schools in the land. The new treasurer, what is his name now?'

'Mnuchin.' Dad laughs. 'Sounds a bit like munchkin to me.'

Everyone laughs except me.

'Yes, that's him.' Mom continues. 'He has proposed tax changes that will greatly benefit people like us.'

I don't think I can hide the sarcasm in my voice. 'You mean us and other rich people?'

'Exactly.'

'And what about all the poorer families in the US?'

Dad looks perplexed. 'Why should we care about them?'

I wave my hands around. As if this helps. 'Because we should. We should be enforcing a decent minimum wage and ensuring all Americans have access to affordable health care.'

'Baby-girl,' Dad scratches at his nose and looks down at the pristine white table cloth, 'I do believe that bump on your head has befuddled your brains a little. Obamacare has already been rolled back, and all Americans should have private health insurance.'

'But millions can't afford it. So what happens to them?'

Senator Raines drawls, 'I guess there'll be fewer people sponging off the state.'

'And,' says Dad, 'let's not forget what Pudzer stated, that a higher minimum wage would hurt workers by forcing many of their workplaces to close down. You see, Cassie, we know what's best for the less fortunate.'

I close my eyes for a second. 'Otherwise, God forbid, big businesses might have to take a cut in their massive profits.'

Dad frowns. 'What's got into you, Cassie? You, yourself, are a benefactor of this very process, so I think you can climb off that big ol' horse of yours now.'

I bite into my lip. There are so many words swirling in my head but not many I dare say in this so-called polite society. Does being very, very rich then preclude you from empathy?

Why do I feel like I've been on the other side of this conversation? Oh yeah. My befuddled brain!

Mrs Radnor clears her throat delicately. She is embarrassed. She obviously wishes to change the subject. 'I can't believe that Pamela Ramsey Taylor and her children received all those death threats.'

'Disgraceful!' says Mom. 'After all, what she said was the truth, plain and simple.'

Dad nods. 'We all know the truth is not something these liberals want to hear.' The word liberal is spat out like it had stung his mouth.

I know I should shut-up and hang my head low, except I still have to ask: 'I'm sorry? Who are you talking about?'

'That poor woman,' says Mrs Radnor, 'who merely said it would be so refreshing to have, now how did she put it? Oh, something like a beautiful, refined First Lady in the White House. I mean, who could take offence at that?'

It's like a bright light in my head. I remember this. It's there, the memory. 'Wasn't that the woman who also went on to say she was tired of seeing an ape in heels?' I say the last bit clearly, slowly. Had they all forgotten that part?

'Exactly,' says Senator Raines.

I take a deep breath. 'She was talking about Michelle Obama.' I wait.

'And?'

'She likened Michelle Obama to an ape.'

'It was merely a little joke, darling.' Mom tilts her head at me.

'No,' says Dad, 'I think the best quote was Carl Paladino, who said, "I'd like her to return to being a male let loose in Zimbabwe to live in a cave with Maxie, the gorilla". Now that was funny.'

They chuckle, white teeth showing, eyes crinkling, nods of approbation.

I can't believe what I've just heard. 'That's about as racist as you can get.' Heat spreads up my neck to burn my cheeks. Who are these people? My family.

Dad stops laughing. 'Racist? It's a statement of fact. You know that, Cassie.' Before I can answer, Dad, interjects, 'That woman is working class and by her own admission a descendent of slaves. I mean, she freely admits this. You know she overstepped her role as First Lady with her public support of gay marriage and her alliance with Hillary and her agenda.'

'Well–' I try to say something, though it's like a spark has ignited something highly flammable in the room. It metaphorically *fizzes* and *pops*.

Mrs Radnor prods at the table. 'As we all know, AIDS is God's way of dealing with homosexuals.'

'What?' I can't be heard over my dad.

'Look at who he appointed as the attorney general. You couldn't have asked for a better man than Barr. He's argued for an increase in the United States incarceration rate, and he's been an influential advocate for tougher criminal policies.'

'Well,' drawled Senator Raines, 'I still liked old Sessions. He was my kind of guy. I mean, look at his position on all that gay rights baloney, not to mention abortion rights. As if it's a right! He's a hard-liner on immigration–'

'Come on, Bob,' said Dad, 'now we have Barr; we'll see him do right by real Americans.'

'Aren't all Americans real Americans then?' I manage to get the words out.

'Not all of them. I sincerely hope you get your memories back soon, baby-girl. I don't understand this new version of you.'

'He's a pro-lifer, Cassie,' Mrs Radnor says, smiling. 'Thank God we finally have a man in power who reveres all life like we do and will punish these women and their cohorts, who willingly murder unborn innocents.'

I'm having trouble keeping up. 'But surely the right to an abortion,' all eyes turn to me, 'is the sole right of the woman?' I remember some of the things Lucy said to me in the restaurant. 'If you're in a stable relationship, then yes, discuss it with your partner, but if a woman has been left high and dry by the man, or worse, has been raped, then that must be her decision if she ' wants to bring a child into the world. Do the men in this scenario have no responsibility then? Why is it always the women who are punished and the men let off? It's not like we have a shortage of unwanted kids.' There's a flash in my head: a cold hard bed and someone's hands on me where they shouldn't be. I shudder involuntarily. *Oh, God! Please don't let that be real!*

'What are you saying?' Mom stares at me as if I'd just sworn something foul across the table. 'You know we are pro-life and always have been. All of us.'

'Maybe all of you, but from where I'm sitting, that doesn't include me.'

'It used to... before.' Dad sounds angry, and his eyes have that terrible "wolf" yellow glow. 'Now you sound like one of those weak-assed Civil Rights activists.'

I need to back-pedal, or I'll disappear into the vortex that's spiralling around me.

'I'm... I'm out of my depth here. I don't mean to offend anyone, especially not you, and I'm having difficulty taking everything in right now.'

'We understand, sweetie.' Mrs Radnor leans over to pat my hand. 'We do.'

'Come on, Cassie.' Senator Raines tops up my glass. 'You're all mixed and muddled up right now. I can see you're confused but trust me, sweetheart, you do feel the same way as the rest of us. You'll remember this in time.'

'But hopefully not too much time,' says Mom. 'Maybe you need to eat something. Your blood sugar might have dropped.' She stands up. 'I'll ring for dinner.' She pulls on a cord a couple of times. A faint *tinkle* can be heard a distance away.

'Dear Lord,' continues my mom, 'our most beloved nation has been brainwashed and lied to for so long it's going to be a haul to get ourselves out of the mess that Obama's left.'

'Look at the threat he posed to us.' Dad's tapping is getting more insistent. 'We believe in the right to bear arms, and they were even suggesting that not only are we not allowed to have weapons to protect ourselves, but they were also even thinking of disarming the police. And we wonder why America has such law-and-order problems with thinking like that. It makes you wonder, doesn't it?'

The senator continues. 'It's an American's responsibility to be armed. It's our constitutional right. We should be more like Virgin in Utah.'

I venture a comment. 'What are the virgins in Utah like then?' I can see I've possibly said something wrong by their startled looks.

'For a start,' says Dad, 'Virgin is a place, and secondly, what Bob meant was every resident in Utah is expected to carry a gun.'

It's all too much now. This bit I understand, though some part of me wishes I didn't. I know I come from a culture where guns are everyday things, like a compact and lipstick, but I'm frightened of them, with good reason. How many people have died from a lethal dose of foundation or lip-gloss?

Mom shakes her head. 'You remember that debacle when the Brit Piers Morgan tried to step in? Who the hell did he think he was, coming into our country and throwing his weight around like he's somebody special? Trying to take our rights from us. They should have deported him like Alex Jones suggested.'

'Don't we have,' I say, and all their eyes are on me again, 'the greatest amount of deaths in high schools by kids getting hold of guns and ammo like they're just candy in a candy store and then shooting loads of people?' I swallow loudly. 'Mostly innocent kids?'

'I'm sorry,' Mom is looking at me, 'what exactly are you saying?'

'I'm saying that America seems to allow easy access to kids to be able to buy dirty great big assault rifles–'

'Semi-automatic firearms, Cassie. You know that automatic ones are banned.'

'That's the point. They can still get hold of semi-automatic rifles, I mean firearms, and mow down lots of people in seconds. How is that right?'

'Are you advocating gun control?' Senator Raines is leaning forward, and he doesn't look happy. 'Any initiative to limit access to weapons is an attack on our constitutional rights to own guns. You know that more than all of us here.'

Mrs Radnor fans her face. 'I understand what you're saying, Cassie. We all do.' She looks agitated. 'But we will not allow law-abiding gun owners to be blamed for the acts of criminals and madmen.'

'We need,' Dad points at me, 'we need more guns, not less. If we arm everyone that should be armed, then crime goes down.'

'I'm only saying,' I know I'm digging a big hole here, and I'm likely to topple or possibly be pushed into it, 'that in most other countries, people and especially kids can't walk into a store and buy a gun that can kill loads of other people in the blink of an eye.'

'The Second Amendment,' says Bob, 'is to keep our children safe, especially after all these tragedies. As I just said, you, of all people, know we have our range days where the children are introduced to guns so that they will be prepared to protect themselves. They all go through firearm safety training courses. We educate young people and encourage the safe use of firearms.'

'Doesn't that mean,' I say, 'that you end up training everyone on how to use a gun accurately and lethally?' Sweat beads my upper lip, and I wipe it off with the napkin. 'Wasn't there a case where a nine-year-old shot her shooting instructor dead? Right there on the range? Using some great big gun?'

'It was an Uzi, and yes, maybe a submachine gun for a kid so young wasn't the wisest course for this particular range.' Dad taps the table again, and I find it unnerving. 'Nonetheless, I don't think you know what you're talking about at the moment. You sound like a child who is trying to talk to adults. I would suggest that until you can speak to us like an adult, Cassie, you keep quiet.'

My mouth resolutely snaps shut. I hope it will unclamp when the food arrives, but I feel so useless and inconsequential. I obviously have no witty barb of a comment to add, no profound retort that will make them all nod with me and suck on their teeth. Dad says I know nothing of what they are talking about. The bits I think I've understood have unnerved me, but even more unnerving is that they all seem to think that I agree with them. Used to agree with them. I'm glad when Dolores arrives with the first course on a wheeled trolley. Two smartly dressed young women accompany her.

'Seared foie gras, apple, toast and honey,' she declares, before the women place a small plate in front of us all and then leave silently. What's on it is tiny but delicious.

'Mmm, absolutely mouth-watering as usual. Dolores is a

catch, you must admit.' Mrs Radnor either does not see or ignores the look my mother flashes at her, but I see it.

'We had the caterers in. Dolores is merely the waitress.'

Conversation switches to the excellence of the ingredients. After a suitable period of time the women return and remove the plates. It is all practiced and does not interrupt the flow of conversation. They are practically invisible. The champagne bottles are swapped for white wine as the second course arrives. The butler, with a white cloth over his arm, changes glasses and pours us drinks.

Dolores waits while again the food is placed in front of us, before the waitresses slip quietly out the door.

'Pasture-raised lamb, broccoli, mint and peppercorn,' says Dolores, then she too, leaves on silent feet.

'Excellent lamb Margaret.' Mrs Radnor waves her fork and simpers.

Margaret? My God! I didn't even know her first name. Come to think of it, what is my dad's first name? Call it too much wine, but my head spins for a moment.

'The pasture-raised lamb is from the White Oak Pastures. It operates its farm as a living ecosystem. The meat is just divine, isn't it?'

I baulk. The lamb is pink, bordering on bloody and my knife hovers over the meat.

'Am I vegetarian?' I blurt.

'Not in a million years,' huffs my mom. 'In fact, I do believe that you'd gnaw its little leg off while it was still jumping round the field.'

'Oh. Right.' I still can't get the idea out of my head but I saw into the flesh and punch the meat down. Finally, we now have a plate of leek, pistachio, mint and a drizzle of chilli put in front of us. All these dishes are tiny but exquisite. The butler has been quietly going around the room topping up glasses, and now they are a different shape and red-hued. I definitely prefer the red stuff, and it slips down ever so nicely, thank you very much.

The dessert is lemon souffle with sesame and chilli. Even though each portion of food served so far has been small, I don't feel hungry. Neither do I feel stuffed. I know this must be my life, but it's like the first time I have experienced anything like this. Mrs Radnor is in full flow about the economy once again, and I don't mean to, but I tune out until I hear my name.

'Cassie?' She's swivelled to speak to me. Her magnificent breasts jiggle as she takes a deep breath, and I can't help but look down. It's hard to concentrate with them both wobbling around like a couple of pink blancmanges...

... I'm very little, about six or seven, and I'm at the school Christmas party. I'm sitting alone as no one wants to sit by the fleabag kid. I've wolfed down the tiny plate of dry turkey, crunchy roast potatoes, wizened parsnips and soggy yellow sprouts. Pudding is pink blancmange in a plastic bowl, but it's not soft and gooey like my mum makes. It has about a three-inch skin on it, and I hate skin on stuff. Anyway, I haven't eaten this much food in ages, so my stomach is stretched to bursting point. I push the bowl away, but a figure soon looms above me. It's Santa, all red and puffed up with a cushion stuffed down his poorly fitting trousers, a scraggly false beard and a big black belt. I'm scared of the belt and rear away from him.

'Ho, ho ho,' he says, except there's no joy in his voice. 'Why haven't you eaten your dessert, little girl?'

'I don't like the skin. It makes me sick.'

'Well, you know what makes me sick?' He bends over and leers into my face. He has the same whiskey breath as Craig, so I know this won't be good. 'What makes me sick is when kids

FROM MY COLD DEAD HANDS

don't eat what's put in front of them.' He stands unsteadily and pulls my bowl back in front of me. 'Eat this. You don't know how lucky you are. There are starving kids out there who'd give their right arm to have this.'

'It'll make me sick.'

'Eat it.'

I push in mouthful after mouthful, and then I throw up over his dirty black boots.

I hate Santa...

I push this vision from my mind, as I can't fathom where it has come from. But it was so painfully real, so clear, even down to the reek of the vomit across his boots. Why would I be the "fleabag" kid? I wipe at my eyes but I can still see his face, twisted in disgust...

I realise that Mrs Radnor is saying something to me again.

'I can't wait for you to come back out with us campaigning. You're such an eloquent speaker, so much fervour and passion.'

'Oh, right?' *Why am I seeing such things in my head? How could that be anything to do with me?*

'The way you endear yourself to the women of our great state is legendary. I wish I could speak the way you do.'

Struggling to focus, I say, 'I can't imagine talking about anything important to anyone. Not after what Dad has just said to me.'

Dad stirs. 'I'm sorry, Cassie. You're not your normal self, and I shouldn't have gone off at you like that. As Mrs Radnor said, you are a real inspiration to us all.'

'What do I speak about?'

'Why,' enthuses Mrs Radnor, 'how it is the job of women to take care of their families. That women can be strong. As strong as our most esteemed men folk. You cry out to them that as concerned citizens, they can fulfil their duties and responsibilities as Americans.'

'That sounds good to me.'

Do I really do that? Stand up in front of people and admonish the women to be strong? Have I found that strength in me?

'Why Cassie Davenport,' says Senator Raines, 'I'm sure your Ma and Pa are mighty proud of you.' He raises his glass to me, and I feel heat spread up my neck. There's a possibility I might have drunk too much, and as the butler sidles up to me, I finally cover my glass. But it might be a bit too late.

'Thank you.' I nod. 'I do hope you'll excuse me, as I really need to find my bed. It's been a pleasure to meet you all, and I'll see you in the morning.' I push from the table, and they all politely stand up. I hope I don't trip over as I make my way to the door, but the butler is ahead of me, and it swings open.

'Goodnight, madam,' he says. He has a British accent.

'Goodnight,' I say and start to cry.

14

NICE BUNS

Dad is holding a coffee mug. He's leaning against the doorframe leading out to the pool area. It's late morning as the night has been turbulent, filled with half images and fugues, and I only managed to drift into a fitful sleep as the sky started to lighten. I'm trying to dislodge all the comments I heard last night from my over-active mind, except it is worrying at them like a terrier in a barn of trapped rats.

He turns to me, and he has a look that I can't decipher. 'How are you feeling this morning? You certainly drank a lot last night.'

'I know. I'm sorry, but it was all a bit too much and that butler bloke kept topping me up, so I lost track of how much I drank.'

'That butler *bloke*? Is this another word you've picked up in England?'

'Probably.'

'Yeah, well, try not to make a habit of drinking so much. You do have this, er, propensity to drink a lot on occasions, Cassie. You won't remember this, but the last time caused the family a whole heap of trouble.'

'What did I do?' My head hurts, and there's a dead mouse stuck to my tongue that no amount of toothpaste and mouthwash can seem to shift.

He sighs very loudly. 'This isn't the time to go over all that, but be careful. Now, on a lighter note, how do you feel about a little barbecue around the pool this afternoon?'

'That sounds brilliant.' I hesitate. 'Will Nick and the kids be there? What about Senator Raines and Mrs Radnor?'

'Mom and Mrs Radnor have driven to Atlanta to visit one of their Sisterhood divisions. They said to give you their love, and they'll be back as soon as they can. Bob has elected to have a few days off and stay with us if that's all right with you? I took the liberty of extending the invitation for this afternoon. You know him well, Cassie and I thought it might be good for you to talk to someone who is, well, outside the family. I haven't invited Nick and the kids, as I still don't think you're ready yet. A splash around the pool, though, a glass of wine, and you'll feel peachy.' He coughs, before saying, 'And I do mean *one* glass of wine.'

'I think I've got the message.' I put my mug down on the wide windowsill. 'Bob's a Senator? That's really important, isn't it?'

'Only to him!' Dad laughs. 'Just kidding. We've known Bob for years. He's like your favourite uncle or, as I'm sure he'd prefer, your sophisticated older cousin.'

'Yeah? I'll bet. I mean, should I call him sir or senator or what?'

'You call him Bob like you've always done. You like him. A lot.'

'What time?'

'About four. We'll get the barbecue fired up in the yard and get the drinks cooled.'

I hesitate. 'Dad? Have I got a bank account? I wondered if I could catch up with, you know, stuff?'

'You should be able to access your account on your laptop. You're notoriously bad at writing all your passwords and numbers down on paper and squirrelling them somewhere. I warned you enough times how dangerous this is, but maybe this time, it's all worked out for the better.'

'Do you know where I keep these bits of paper?'

'This may sound kind of weird, but they're all stuffed in the skirts of that Victorian doll of yours.'

'Ugh, gross! And more importantly, where is the laptop?'

'You have a study next door to your room. You can either access it via the hallway or the balcony. I think it's best to try it all out first and see if you do things by rote. You never know; you might remember bits. I'm going to play a round of golf with Bob, so if you need help with anything, we'll be back for the barbecue.'

I half run up the stairs but feel quite exhausted by the time I'm clinging to the top rail. The doll glares at me as I haul her down and ransack her undergarments, but there are folded pieces of paper with a tiny scrawl covering them. My handwriting looks strange. I trot back out and fumble with the handle to my study. Is this now where I will start to piece my shards of life back into something I can recognise?

There are childish pictures tacked to the white wall, but they're signed with my name. Where are the drawings done by my kids? The laptop sits on a suitably expensive and ergonomic desk, and there are more of the ubiquitous photos of Caesar and myself. What strikes me first is there are no family portraits here, nothing of Nick and the kids, Mom and Dad. Only that bloody horse.

Smoothing out the crumpled paper, I read through each section. There's an expensive looking red ballpoint pen in a holder, along with fountain pens and other writing paraphernalia. I circle and number what I think are the most important ones. Yes, all my bank account details are here. I shake my head. Lucky I didn't chuck the doll in the bin or out the window. I key in all the log-in names and passwords and wait for it to register. It comes up on my screen. I scan through, but it takes a moment for the actual figure to filter through. I stare at the number of dollars that I have in my bank account. I wonder if it'd be ironic if I suddenly had a heart attack at the exact moment I discover that I'm a multimillionaire?

How much? Fuck me!

I minimise the screen and look over my shoulder. Has anyone seen this? Does Dad know I have so much wonga that I can probably buy a small island off the coast of Jamaica? I calm my breathing, then I have another look. Hell, I'm *rich!* Woo-hoo!

Money comes in, but I look closely at what goes out. There's been a series of large withdrawals over the last ten months, although even that has hardly dented the amount in there. Backtracking many pages reveals that I'm a stingy bitch. Not a charity in sight. How can I have this much money rolling in and not donate a penny to Cancer Research? Or the Women's Refuge? I will get it sorted. There seems to be an anomaly. I am paying for three iPhones, not one. They all have a different number, so I fish the one I have out and match it up. But why do I have another two? I probably have a back-up in case I drop one down the toilet or get pissed and go swimming in my clothes. But where are they now? I dial the other numbers to find one goes straight to voicemail.

'Er, hello? This is Cassie Davenport, and if you get this message, please can you call me back. It's urgent. My number is...' I read it from my list.

The other phone is answered immediately. I can hear breathing, but the person on the other end doesn't say anything. It sounds like a man.

'Hello?'

Still nothing but the breathing quickens.

'Sorry, but this seems to be my phone. Did you find it or something?'

Breathing and then a laugh. The phone goes dead, except I'm left shaking and disorientated. Why didn't he answer? And there's more. I know that laugh. I know it like I know my own. It's a laugh that has only ever meant violence and death. What the hell is happening? Who was the man on the other end of the line? How can I find out? And more to the point, do I want to? There are spangles of bright, white light as if a disco ball is spinning at the edge of my vision. I know that laugh.

It takes me a long time to calm down, as I try to rationalise this feeling. I have to change to be ready for the barbeque but it's like I'm wading through honey. Glancing repeatedly at the clock, I make sure I'm not early to the barbeque, but as before, Senator Raines is already there. Dad is nowhere to be seen.

'Cassie, my little darlin'.' Bob places his hands on my shoulder, his fingers trace down my neck and across my collarbone as if this is what he always does. He leans in to kiss me, but I twist my head and the kiss lands on my cheek. If I hadn't, I would've had a "smacker" right on the lips. Is that how the Southern gentry greet each other then? Kisses for married ladies on the lips? I squirm from under his embrace.

'I didn't really get a chance to say this last night, but you've had a bad time of it, and now we're all praising God for your safe return to us.'

'Yep, praise God.' If only they knew the half of it. I try not to think about the man on the end of my phone. How did he get it? I must know him, surely? Just the thought of him makes me queasy.

I spot Dad striding toward us from the other side of the pool. 'Good, we're all here.'

Dolores is standing at the end of the table. Initially, I think she's been invited, then I notice she's still in her uniform. Dad clicks his fingers, and Dolores snaps into action like an automated doll that has been wound up and let go. She pulls a wine bottle from a silver bucket of ice and pours a thimble-sized slosh into a tall-stemmed wine glass.

'Your wine, madam.' She hands it to me. It's barely a mouthful, and I wonder how I'll make it last for longer than a minute. I sip at my wine and eye the bottle. How I can get another glass in without them noticing?

Dad is in a gaudy set of swimming shorts with a Hawaiian theme, all palm trees and coconuts. 'It's hot enough for the steaks to griddle themselves.' He wades down the circular steps of the pool, and I hear him sigh as he immerses himself. 'This is heaven.'

'If you can't beat them, join them.' Bob pulls off his crisp, white linen shirt. His deeply tanned chest is covered in tiny white curls of hair, but some part of me suspects he is holding his stomach in. He's wearing khaki shorts with large pockets. As he jumps in, they fill with air like emergency airbags, and he floats around the pool. I laugh but then cover my mouth.

'Ho, ho. Find that funny, young lady?'

'Well, it is.' Have I already gone too far? The sun is in my eyes, and everything is pale like I'm wrapped in white gauze. I can feel the heat tighten my skin as if *I'm* under the grill and not the waiting steaks. This man is supposedly a long-standing friend. I want to be able to laugh, to have fun and to feel that it's allowed, that I'm good enough to be loved and cherished, yet I can't seem to let go of the feeling in my gut that something's not right.

My dad is thrashing up to the deep end, sending bow waves crashing into the sides of the pool.

'Come on, Cassie. What ya waitin' for?' Bob throws a handful of water over me. Quite frankly, these two old men, splashing about like children in the pool, give me the collywobbles. 'Get that dress off and come in. You must be cooking out there.'

There's something in the way that he's looking at me that I find disconcerting. It's like the dress is already off, and he's mentally eyeing up my naked skin. I don't know how to get out of this situation without offending someone. So, I wriggle out of the summer dress at the edge of the pool and dive in. I found the dress hanging off a hook on my bedroom door. I surface close to him, and he lunges across the pool and pushes my head under. I flail around, and then I hear "burbling" sounds above me. I splutter as I break the surface and push my dripping fringe away from my face.

'Ouch, you're hurting me.' I pull from him, but his fingers are tangled in my hair. A creeping panic slides over me.

'I'm sorry,' Bob rubs water from his own face, 'I completely forgot about your injuries. Please forgive me for being an old fool who still believes he's thirty.'

'That's okay, but can you let me go now.' The moment he releases me, I scoot across the pool and clamber up the steps, though he's right behind me. His hands reach out and sort of bump me up.

'Need a helping hand there, darlin'?'

Not where his hands are now. Confusion and embarrassment overwhelm me like I've fallen into a pit of low-level poisonous gas. I'm finding it hard to breathe. What is he doing?

'I don't know about you guys,' Dad is also heading for the steps, 'but I'm about ready for that cow.' He doesn't seem to notice the impropriety of the senator's actions. Is this normal then? *Is this what we do?*

'Hungry, Cassie?' Bob grins at me as he hauls himself out of the water. 'I could eat the whole cow, hooves and all and leave nothing but the "moo".'

I don't feel safe enough to leave the dress off. I pick it up and wrench it down over my wet skin, but it sticks and gets rolled up.

I hear Bob laugh behind me. 'Need a hand with that?' He yanks and tugs, and the dress inches over my hips. He gives it one last wrench, and his hand brushes my inner thigh. I jump away from him as if he's stung me. Was that on purpose?

I feel chilled, even though the day is practically nuclear hot, and I head quickly for the long table under the cabana. It's already laid out for us: big white plates, serrated steak knives and an assortment of sauce-pots and bottles. I pick one up. Orange-soda-flavoured barbecue sauce. Orange soda?

'I do believe that the barbecue is nicely glowing.' Bob throws a few tons of red and bloody meat onto the ribbed griddle. I thought Dad had been joking, but nearly a whole cow is searing, and I wonder whom we are catering for? It's a state-of-the-art gizmo that does all singing and all dancing stuff, short of eating the food for you.

I need to get back to some semblance of normal, but instead, I think about a comment from last night that troubles me, although I might be putting my size-six foot in it again. 'So, Bob. What's your viewpoint on guns? Do you *really* believe it's our constitutional right to be armed?'

'From my cold, dead hands.'

'What does that mean?'

'It's the AGA's slogan. "I'll give you my gun when you pry it from my cold, dead hands." Charlton Heston epitomised it in his speech when he was President of the AGA. That man knew what he was talking about.'

'Okay, that sounds pretty scary, but I like Charlton Heston.

I mean, he was great in *Planet of the Apes*. I'm sorry, but what does AGA stand for again?'

'American Gun Association. We're all members, and I do mean all of us.' He nods, and I realise he means me too. 'I have an M16 in my living room and a handgun under my pillow. So what do you think my view on guns is?'

'Come on, that can't be true. An M16?' *Maybe I should've kept my mouth shut?*

'I'm not joking, darlin'. They're already at the gate. I'm not waiting for *others* to come and savage me and mine in my own home. No, siree.'

'*Who* is coming to savage you?'

'You know the answer to that, don't you.' This is said as a statement of fact, but if I do know the answer, I've entirely forgotten.

Dolores appears from inside the kitchen with a jug. She pours a tall glass and hands it to me. The ice clinks, and there's a sprig of mint in it. 'It's such a hot day; I thought Madam Davenport might like a glass of freshly made lemonade.'

'Thank you,' I whisper. Dolores does a sort of "wink" at me.

Bob beckons to me. 'Come on, Cassie, help me here.'

I'm sure I can still feel him on my skin like an imprint, but I push this aside. He was only trying to help me. I can't contemplate what it might mean if it was something else. I take a swig of my drink and then realise what the wink from Dolores meant. There is a hefty slug of some "devil" liquor in it. *Hallelujah!*

'You can put the buns on there.' Bob points to the appropriate place on the griddle, and then I feel his hand on the small of my back. I lean forward to prise the buns from the bag when his hand slides down a bit. 'Talking of nice buns...'

I was right then. What should I do? I swivel to look him in the eye. 'I don't know what you think you're doing, but whatever it is, I don't appreciate it. In case you missed this, I'm a married lady with kids. A Southern lady, no less.'

'Like that ever bothered you before.' There's a tone in his drawl that leaves me shaking. He grins and flips the steaks. They hiss on the hot griddle. I can feel another kind of heat like I've pressed my cheeks onto the burning coal surface.

Oh, *dear God!*

Am I having an affair with this awful, smarmy, jumped-up little man? And more to the point, does my dad know? Was this set up? My dad's words come back to me: "You know him well".

'I'm just going to powder my nose.' I could kick myself, but I couldn't think of anything else to say apart from *I'm just going to throw up, hope you don't mind.* I walk past the table and then backtrack to grab the jug of lemonade. Hell, I need some more of this stuff. I don't look back, but I know they're both staring at me.

I skid into the kitchen. 'Dolores?' I'm hissing so she realises there's something wrong. 'Where are you?'

'Here, madam.' She is pulling a dessert from the fridge that looks like it is made from cream with added cream.

'Am I having an affair with Senator Raines?'

She nearly drops the cream concoction. 'Do you really want to know?'

'Whatever gave you that idea?' Lucy materialises from behind the fridge door as if she'd just climbed out of it. By the tone in her voice, frosty doesn't even cover it. 'Oh, let's see. Maybe it's the way he paws at your ass?'

'I'll take that as a "yes" then, shall I?' I put both hands over my eyes, but they can't blot out the horrible image playing out in my mind, involving large gilt mirrors and hairy bums. 'How long?'

Lucy sticks her finger into the dessert and then licks off the cream. 'Maybe a year now.'

Dolores tuts and then smooths over the indent with a knife. '*Carida*, I've told you not to do that.'

I sit down at the island. 'Does Nick know?'

'We've been living at the lodge for months. Since you were fighting so much here, you both thought it was for the best if you separated for a while.'

'Then none of you live here with us?'

'We have our own rooms here and come and go as we please.'

'Do you know what's happened between Nick and me?'

'He found out you were having an affair.'

'With the senator?'

'I don't know if it was the senator. I thought it was someone else.'

'Then he's the one leaving me?'

'As far as I can tell, yes, but I think you were trying to defend your honour by inferring that he had an affair first.'

'Did he?'

'Dad isn't that kind of man. He still loves you, the stupid shit, but hey, love is blind, or so I've been told.'

'Why am I doing this? Senator Raines is nearly as old as my father.' I cling to the breakfast bar, afraid that if I let go, I'll crumple in a heap on the floor.

'It's the prestige. A senator's mistress? Isn't that something that every woman aspires to, and if she can then become his wife, well, all the better.'

'You are joking, aren't you? You're saying I'm not even in love with him?'

'I would say you are in love with his power.'

Dolores is making shushing noises and swatting at invisible flies, but it's too late for discretion now.

I ignore her. 'And my dad knows?'

Lucy turns to Dolores, who is now looking out of the

window, a hand hovering over her mouth. 'Dolores, does Grandpa know?'

'Oh!' She bites at her bottom lip. 'I shouldn't say anything. It's not my place.'

'Tell her.' Lucy lounges across the counter, one thin strap of her vest flops down her arm. I can see another tattoo, one word, 'Equality'. 'Go on. Tell her.'

'Your father instigated it.'

'Why?'

'This is not my business to tell you.'

'I'm drowning here, Dolores!' I say. 'Throw me a rope, please.'

Her hands flutter with anxiety, like they're small caged birds. 'I don't know if you will thank me.'

'Just tell me.'

'When you married Nick, your father did everything in his power to stop you. But you were always a headstrong little girl. Nick, though, he's the son of a middle-class tradesman that has come from outside, and that's a different thing entirely. No class, no true heritage.'

'Is my father really that shallow? Am I?'

'He is really that proud. And as for you, only you can answer that.'

Lucy dances over to me in that lithe, gymnastic way she has. 'Did you look up that flag? The one on your sweatshirt?'

'Yes, I did.'

'And what did you discover?'

'That there's something not right in my world.'

She cocks her finger like a gun and makes a "clicking" sound. 'You've got it.'

'Okay, I'm going to go back out and get through this without, hopefully, offending anyone. Dolores, please keep this lemonade topped up. I'm going to need it. Lucy, are you coming out?'

'I wasn't invited.'

'I'm inviting you.'

'In case you didn't realise, I'm not welcome. It's a wonder they let me through the gates, but then...' she trails off.

'I'd really appreciate it if I could speak to you later.'

'If I'm still here.'

15

SHADOWS

B ed is welcome tonight. I pull the covers up and close my eyes tightly. I wish my performance could've been filmed as I think I would have won an Oscar with the many ploys I used to avoid Senator Bob and his wandering hands, even to the point of feigning heatstroke and leaving the barbecue early.

I'm beginning to have my doubts. If I've managed to get all this wrong so far, maybe I've done Nick a dishonour? Perhaps I'm the monster, and he's the one who has been wronged? Lucy did not make an appearance, so she wasn't here to visit me. I have a feeling in my gut that she was here to see Dolores. *Carida*. Dearest. Is Dolores the woman who brought my daughter up? Where was I? Off riding that bloody awful horse? What did she say the other day about Caesar being my "everything"? Did she mean that he came above everyone, including my children? Whatever was in that lemonade has now, coupled with stress and nausea, made my head pound like I'm at a thrash metal concert standing by the speakers in the mosh pit.

My hair is standing on end. But that's probably because someone is standing at the end of my bed. I didn't think I'd slept at all, but now a figure has emerged by the chest at the foot of the bed, silhouetted through the gauzy curtains against the light seeping through the shuttered windows.

I shrink back into the bedclothes, feeling like I've just been tasered, my breath coming in ragged little pants. There's something horribly awry with the shadow that's being cast, and I realise that there's seems to be another "thing" standing up. There's a man with a massive erection creeping up on me. *Oh, hell! What do I do?* I fumble around me for a weapon. I grab the nearest thing, which is a photo frame of Caesar and lunge through the curtains.

'Take that!' I do my best to bash my assailant on his head, hoping that it'll be enough to give me a fighting chance against him, except now I can see his face.

'Bob?'

'What the hell are you doing?' He rubs at his skull.

I yank the covers back up around me. 'What do you mean, what the hell am *I* doing? *You're* the one sneaking around my room. What on Earth do you think *you're* doing? You scared the shit out of me!'

'I thought that's what you wanted, that it was on as usual.'

'I don't even know you. I find this extraordinary. I'm an amnesiac, which means I can't remember anything, and I certainly don't remember you. How *dare* you think you can just pick up where we might or might not have left off. You're a bloody stranger, mate, so get out of my room before I call the police!'

'Hell, I love it when you're mad. Cassie, you're so hot and sexy...' He's reaching for me as if my words have whizzed over his head and bypassed his ears completely.

'Unless you want another lump to match the one you've got, I suggest that you leave my room right now.' Can I run from my room without him catching me? What would happen if I scream? He's a bloody senator, for God's sake. Who would they believe, especially if we were having an affair?

'Oh Cassie,' his breathing is speeding up and becoming a little laboured. 'I know you've been hungering for me like I've been hungering for you. Oh, I'm such a bad boy, go on, whip me, bite me, get your fingernails in, hit me again—'

So I do. Hard.

'*Ouch!* What did you do that for?' His voice is petulant, like a small boy.

'You told me to. Now find the door and get out.'

There's something dark on the tips of his fingers as he rubs at the new lump. Is it blood?

'You can be such a bitch, Cassie. When you get your memory back, you'll come crawling to me and trust me, I won't have forgotten this.'

'Nor will I.' I wave the picture frame at him as he flops off the bed and lurches across the floor. It's not a pretty sight, but I run to wedge a chair up against the door and bolt the window from the inside.

I watch the horrible green neon beast tell me the time oh-so-slowly, and I listen for noises and watch for shapes that shouldn't be there. I have the feeling that I'm one of them. That *I* shouldn't be there. But sleep finds me eventually, and I wish it hadn't.

… My beloved doesn't know that I'm trying to give myself a chance to get away from him. A friend has forewarned me that he's just got out from being banged up for burgling some poor sod's house in the estate. I have to do as much as I can to escape. We've been together for a few months, although now I'm beginning to realise something. He doesn't like my friends and throws jealous rages if I mention a guy's name to him. Even if I'm out with girlfriends, he can turn up suddenly to check on me.

'Better watch him,' says my friend. 'He's a bad'un. He'll have you up the duff quicker than a rat up a drainpipe to get a flat off the council. And then more to keep you in your place while he's off shagging all the tarts in town.'

'Charming!'

But I know she's right. I have to get away from him before he gets a hold on me like Craig did to my mum. As to kids, I make sure I have that arm implant every three years. Some men tamper with your contraceptive pills, or you might forget one night, but not me. There'll be no kids for him. I wouldn't put a child through what happened to me... And then it hits me. I'm the same as my mum. He's just another Craig.

I'm packing my few belongings, but he comes home early from the building firm where he sporadically works. It's almost as if he's got a sixth sense in that handsome Neanderthal head of his.

'Where *the fuck* are you off to?'

'I'm going to visit a friend.'

'What friend might that be?' He's moving closer. I see his hands are twitching, and there's a set to his shoulders that means violence is close. I can't run past him as he's blocking the door.

'Just a friend. You don't own me. I can leave when I please–' His fist smashes into my face, and then he hits me repeatedly in my belly.

'Your fancy man won't want you with a face like that, now will he?' His ring rips across the side of my head and tears off skin and hair. The pain is terrible. I see something bloody fly across the room, and my mouth is shredded. The rage on his face is pure horror to me.

When we get to the hospital, he is all solicitous concern.

'You're a clumsy girl, ain't yer?' He shrugs at the nurse. 'What can you do?' He puts a comforting arm around my shoulders and smiles so sweetly at me. *I want to kill him!* What have I done? Will I always be "here" with men like them? Is that my fate, then? I know now that I can't escape him, just like Mum couldn't run from Craig. The nurse is stony-faced, seen it all before, but until I say something, she's powerless. He threatened to rip me open with a Swiss army knife if I opened my "big fat gob". He'd leave my carcass under the pier. They'd never find him. He's got connections.

16

SPEAKING IN TONGUES

I wake up, and the sheet is sopping wet. I'm drenched in sweat like awful cologne. What was that all about? I don't mean to, but I start to rock in the bed. I lower my head, and a terrible keening sound leaks out of me. I knew a dog with the worst skin complaint I'd ever seen in my life. He always walked on three legs, as the fourth one incessantly scratched at the horrible mass of flakes and sores. He should have been put down, but the owners didn't care. He made a noise like I was making now. Maybe I need to be put down. I stuff the covers into my mouth.

My phone beeps. I expect it to be a message from Lucy, but all it says is: *Hello sugar, haven't forgotten me, have you?*

The number is the one from my other phone, the one I called. Has that come from the man with the laugh? I don't know what to make of the text. But then, I don't remember any of my old life. I try to shake it from my mind like a dog coming out of a dunking.

I'm sitting up in the bed, waiting, when Dolores knocks lightly and pokes her head around the door. 'I have your tea and a glass of juice. I've also got some toast and conserve.'

'You must be a mind reader. I think I possibly drank too much of that rather marvellous lemonade. What was in it?'

'An Italian liquor that you love called limoncello. I hope you haven't got too much of a heavy head?'

'It seems to be a recurring theme in the morning at the moment.'

She places the tray across my midriff again.

'Did you sleep well, Cassie?'

I look up sharply. But I can't detect any sign that she knows what went on last night.

'Could have been better. I must admit, I feel like I've just completed a triathlon and swum the English Channel, there and back.'

'*English Channel?* Ah, maybe you need a little bit more rest? Shall I come back later?'

'No, thanks. Sleep isn't helping either. I'm having bad dreams.'

'I can't begin to imagine what it must be like to not know who you are.'

'Someone thought they still knew. I had a visitor last night, and it didn't go well.'

Her lips twitch at the corners. 'Someone who might now be nursing a sore head?'

'He had an encounter with Caesar.' I wave at the slightly dented silver frame. 'He was under the impression that I would fall into his open arms, but he didn't seem to understand that I have no idea who he is. Is he angry?'

'He doesn't seem to be in the best of moods.'

'Well, at least I don't have to see him again.'

'You'll be seeing him on Sunday when you go to church with your family.'

'You've got to be kidding me! I feel like I've fallen into an alternate reality. I want the pool and the big house from this new life, but I'd like to trade in the affair and the rather dodgy sounding parts of it. I don't want to be that woman.'

'When you have lost your identity,' her voice is hesitant, 'sometimes it must be hard to come to terms with who you really are.'

'So, I'm a gaudy, eighties throwback with zero taste? And I think I'm a bit of a bitch. Is that about it?'

She puts her hand over her mouth. 'No. You are the woman every woman in this state wishes to be.' She's covering the lie.

'Have you seen what's in there?'

Thrusting the table back at her, I clamber off the bed and wrench open the wardrobe doors. 'I mean, look at this stuff.' I finger a dress, tweak out a pantsuit, an embroidered shirt. 'It's like there are the remains of a zoo lurking in the closet. I wouldn't be seen dead in any of this. How can this *dross* be mine?'

'Dross?'

'Crap! Utter shite!' I wave at the miles of clothes stretching back into the bowels of the house. 'These shoes could snap an ankle as soon as look at it, and as for these *bloody* great wedge things, they look like they've been covered with the pelt of every known cat species. Dear God, even the sneakers are leopard skinned.'

'It is said that you have great taste.'

'I like cats, but I prefer them alive. You know, there is only one pair of half-decent shoes in here, which look like they've never been worn.' I wave a pair of black peep-toed shoes with kitten heels. 'Is this fur real? Please tell me I've got it wrong, and this is all fake?'

'Of course, it is real fur, Cassie. Your father shot all these animals for you. You have both travelled extensively to do so.'

'*What?*' My voice has reached its limits, and I'm reduced to a small "squeak". *Have I sucked in a mouthful of helium?*

'He's a hunter, and so are you.'

It takes a moment for my poor, stupefied brain to process what she's said. She's staring at me intently. 'Of course, I am. I only have to think of the most abhorrent thing in the world to me, and guess what? That's me!' I slide to the floor.

'Cassie?' She helps me up, and I end up sitting on the chest. My head is so tightly packed with feelings; I need a new and bigger skull. And it hurts.

'I want to go home.'

'You are home.' She pats my shoulder, and I start to cry. 'Oh, Cassie. I don't know what to believe. You are indeed not the woman I have known for twenty-five years.'

'Really? Why, in particular?'

'My lady never says "thank you". She only demands, not asks, and she never swears except with Marcie when she thinks no one is around. Southern ladies do not swear in public.'

'Fuck that!' I start to laugh. 'Can a head trauma turn you into someone else entirely?'

'There are cases, or so I've heard.'

'Does the old "you" come back?'

'Maybe, but then I suppose you can choose who you want to be.'

'Do you want the old me back, Dolores?'

'I've had this job for a long time. I've known you for a long time. I never want the old "you" back but then what's so funny is that you already know that.' She stands and stares down at me. 'Your father is waiting in the breakfast room. You need to be prepared, I think.'

'Prepared for what?'

I'm left with that disconcerting thought when I enter the breakfast room. The view out of the window looks the same, except now it's like I've climbed out of the rabbit hole and my world has changed forever.

'Bob left early this morning.' Dad waits, but I pretend I'm looking out of the window, so I don't catch his eye. What does he expect me to say? Has he got a couple of horns on each side of his head, the old devil? Will I get arrested for bludgeoning a senator?

Dad frowns heavily. 'Did something happen last night?'

'Nope.' At least that is truthful in its way.

'Really sorry, but I kinda forgot to give this to you.' Dad hands me another phone. 'You had this on you when you had the accident. It came with you with all your effects, and it's suddenly started beeping. After the accident, I put it on charge in my study as I was hoping there might be something on it to help us work out what happened to you. It got dented in the accident, so I wasn't even sure that it was still working. We can transfer all the data on it over to the one you're currently using if you want to?'

I finger the crack on the back of the iPhone that is part of the evidence of my life pre-trauma.

'This might be the key.'

'Then see if there's anything on it. Maybe there's a message or a text.'

Alone in my study, I sit at my desk and decide to search through the text messages. There are seven of them ranging over about ten months, and reading them sends a shiver racing down my back like someone has dropped an ice cube down my sweater.

· · ·

Can't believe this is all real. Had a fantastic time. Don't worry, will be back a.s.a.p. C x

Have to go to London first but will come down after. Buy wine. C x

Stop worrying, didn't mean anything by it. C x

It was just a bit of fun. I'm sorry. Don't leave messages like that, or I won't come back. You wouldn't want that now, would you?' C x

Baby-girl, you made your bed, so you'd better lie in it. Are we having fun yet? C x

I was only joking. I really wouldn't do that to you. Cross my heart. C x

I'm coming for you. C x

Who is 'C'? I presume he's texting from England, so I must've been meeting him there when I was on my so-called business trips. There's a threatening quality to these few words that even the phone's flat, noncommittal face can't hide. He was coming for me? The question is, did he find me?

I can't help myself. I chew the sides off all my fingernails until I draw blood. There's a conclusion to this line of thinking that I don't want to face. If I was running across that road, was I running from someone? Was it an accident, or was I pushed? Have I got a lover in England, one who might be jealous, or mad, or mad and jealous? Have I got my very own "bunny boiler"? And more to the point, does he know where I live, and can he get to me? My thoughts are swirling. I don't even want to contemplate the man on the other phone or whoever was in the white Chevy. Could it be the same man?

I sit panting on the bed, although I haven't moved since opening the text box. My head's pounding and my heart is thumping as if I've completed a 100-metre sprint. I come to another conclusion. I'm the mad one. There's no other possible explanation. I do not have a psycho stalker nutter on my tail, but I have a head trauma, which might account for all delusions. I reread the messages and look for less hidden meanings. 'C' is someone I know, could even be a girl, and we've been having a good time but had a bit of a falling out. Yeah, that's it. I lent her my best top, and she snagged it. That sounds better, doesn't it? Apart from he, she or it is coming for me. I switch the phone off and hide it under my pillow. I've noticed there are two saved voicemails, although I can't access them, so the phone must have been damaged in the accident. I'll get it fixed and then see if I can listen to them. Should I tell Dad? I don't want to worry him, but maybe I should be the one to be worried. I look down, and I've drawn a face on the Post-it notepad. She's beautiful. I didn't realise I could draw like this. Who is she?

I find my way to what's termed the "music room".

There's no sign of any instruments, nor an iPod or portable speaker dock. I'm fingering through the CDs that are stacked in a robust, oak double-fronted rack. Tucked on the lower shelf of the sideboard, I discover old vinyl albums. A lifetime's worth of music. They range through the seventies, and I calculate that Dad must have been in his early twenties then. That's when music can mean the most, can touch your soul. These round pieces of plastic chronicle someone's life. There's Fleetwood Mac's *Rumours*, a bit of Manilow, the ubiquitous Carpenters and Streisand, a whole gamut of Neils, but they all seem to be middle of the road, easy listening.

But I can see other albums in my head, hear the chest vibrating *thump* as the beat smacks out of the speakers. Where is *Led Zep IV* and Bowie's *The Rise and Fall of Ziggy Stardust and the Spiders from Mars?* I pull them all out, scattering them on the floor and search for Floyd. I know it must be here somewhere because it's deep inside of me. *The Dark Side of the Moon.* That was what I was brought up on. And *London Calling*, punk songs screamed out by Joe Strummer. This is my childhood.

I hear Dad coming down the hall. I scrabble around to put all the albums back neatly on their shelf before he comes in. I feel as if I've been where I shouldn't have, like a light-fingered thief.

He smiles as he enters the room. 'Did you find anything on that phone?'

'There were some texts...' Should I show him? Would he come to the same conclusion as I did, or would he dismiss them?

'Do you know who from?'

'They only left their initial, not a full name.' *I need my memories back right now!*

'So that means you know them. What initial was it?'

'It was 'C'.'

'Who do you know whose name begins with a 'C'? Apart from yourself?'

I gaze for a moment at the floorboards, noting their grain and how polished they are. Apart from "me", the only other person is a fictitious nightmare in my mind, and I can't say "Craig" now can I? 'I'm not sure.'

'Hey baby-girl,' Dad points at the albums. 'You looking for songs?'

'I thought there might be something here that I'd remember, stuff that might trigger a memory.'

'And has it?'

'Is this all you have? I mean, do you have other albums elsewhere, because I remember different music to this.'

'Like what?' He settles in a soft armchair that moulds to his shape.

'Bob Dylan? The Boss? And what about Black Sabbath?'

'What? Black Sabbath? We don't listen to filth like that. What's got into you?' There's anger curling at the edges of his voice like a cobra about to strike, but I plough on, unable to stop the words dropping like lead bricks from my mouth.

'What about Bowie and Pink Floyd? I remember dancing to them with Mom.'

'I don't understand how you can say such things.' He's rising from his seat, hands clenched. 'We have never listened to the ramblings of drug-crazed, lefty spouting, un-godly slackers like these, and your mom has never, as God is my witness, danced to such music. It's a sin to even think such a thing.'

'She thought they were brilliant. We played them all the time when I was little. I remember all the covers.'

'You shut your evil mouth now, Cassie.'

'*I remember!*' He flinches as if I've physically struck him.

'No, no.' He wipes a shaking hand across his eyes. 'I know what this is. Surely I do. It's the kids. That's the sort of thing they play. They taunt you with it, throwing their liberal ideas in your face all the time. They have no love for their church and are un-patriotic and hypocritical. This is why you remember this kind of music. It's what your children play. You've got it all confused in your head.'

'I have? But it felt so real.' I think for a moment. 'Yes, yes, you're right. The woman who's dancing has dark hair, so it can't be Mom, can it.'

'See? It's Lucy, isn't it? She's the one who plays the devil music.'

I nod. 'The devil music.' How come the devil's music sounded so good in my head?

'How about I put on something to calm us both down?'

'Yeah, that'd be great.'

He pulls out an album from the rack and places it carefully on the old turntable, swinging the arm across deftly. Karen Carpenter slides out of it, soulful and doleful. She doesn't make me feel much better, but I smile at Dad, and he seems to be placated. We listen to 'We've only just begun'. I look at the cover. The album is *Close to You*, and it shows Karen and Richard in such a seventies setting that it's like they're in fancy dress. I touch her face in the photo and wonder if either of them knew how it would all turn out.

'How sad to have had so much talent and then die of such a terrible, uncontrollable thing.'

'Everyone has control over their lives, Cassie. Work hard, obey God and life will be good.'

'Do you really believe that's all it takes?'

'That's all it takes.' He pats the top of my head. 'I think I need coffee. I'll tell you, Cassie, sometimes you don't make it easy for me.'

'I don't mean to.'

'I know. But a coffee is waiting for me. Fancy one?'

'That'll be great, thanks. Is it okay if I stay here? I want to sit and listen a bit more if you don't mind.'

'I'll bring one for you.' He stretches like he has a knot in his back. Maybe he's got an "old war wound" too? I'll ask him later as things are getting too confusing right now, and my head feels as if it's been filled with firecrackers. I wriggle back into the soft leather armchair and let the songs drift over me, barely touching me. When the final song concludes, I stir and look down. What shall I play now? Something draws me to the last record on the shelf. I tug out a dusty album that doesn't look like it's seen the light of day for years. I blow the cover clean and wipe it on my jeans, leaving a smear of white. Then I remove the black vinyl disc from its paper envelope and swap it for the Carpenters.

A voice I recognise at last. Joni. I stare down at the cover. Joni Mitchell. Her album *Blue*. Her face bathed in blue light. Joni. Am I crying? I wipe my cheeks, and they are wet. *Oh, God!* I know this so well. This is what I was brought up on. It's like a light bulb has exploded in my mind, there's a searing flash of light, and then the darkness closes in around again. Something has changed.

Joni. I know her.

I hear the mugs as they hit the hardwood floor.

'Dad? Are you all right?' I struggle out of the chair but stop when I see the look on his face. I never realised that old saying "seen a ghost" could be so true, but his face is grey, and there's a vein throbbing at his temple.

'Where did you find that album?' He does nothing to clear up the mess.

'It was the last one on the shelf. Have I done something wrong?'

He sits heavily on the chair next to mine, practically falls into it. I lurch forward and fumble with the button, and for one moment, the volume goes up loud instead of down. I nearly scratch it in my haste to get it off the turntable. Then there's only the sound of his breathing, heavy and laboured.

'I don't understand. Why are you so upset?' I reach to touch his hand.

He covers his mouth, hides the trembling lip and the emotions playing out across his face. This song, or maybe Joni, means as much to him as me.

'It's okay.' His voice is quiet. 'It's passed.'

'What happened?'

'A memory. I haven't heard that song in many years and it kind of brought a few things back.'

'Good things?'

'Things I'd put to the back of my mind for such a long time. It was like it was buried.'

'I just had that too, listening to her, to Joni.' Saying her name makes me feel like someone is patting my back, smoothing my hair, and wiping the tears away with a gentle hand. Why?

'Maybe a memory from your childhood? I don't know. There was a time so long ago I can barely remember that I played this album a lot. I mean over and over. Perhaps you remember that.'

'Why did you stop?'

'It hurt too much.'

'I see. Well, obviously, I don't, but I can understand. Do you want to talk about it?'

He visibly shakes himself. 'No. No, I'm fine. Can I have it please, I don't want to be caught by surprise like that again.' He holds out his hand, and I reluctantly hand it to him, though I feel as if I'm giving a bit of me away. I don't want to let go of her. But I also don't want to let go of him either. He practically staggers from the room, and I follow like a stray dog, wondering if I will get a kick or a pat on the head.

He stops at the bottom of the stairs. 'I'll see you for lunch, Cassie. I'm gonna lie down for a while. I think I've got a migraine coming on.' His feet are slow as they climb. I did this to him. I feel hot salty tears prickle at the corner of my eyes, and my chest tightens against the sobs threatening to erupt out of me. I need to howl like that stray dog, *howl* until all the hurt goes away.

17

TRUTH HURTS

L unch is when we all collide in the kitchen.
'Mom?' She's back, and I didn't know. Now I feel flustered as to what to say. 'Was your meeting successful?' How cold and business-like that sounds.

She air kisses me somewhere near my cheek. 'We had a wonderful time. The drive through the lower hills was delightful. We heard their speakers, and they were so eloquent. One told us that we all have an obligation to perform. She said, like the man in the Bible, we are all given a talent, and it is our duty to do something about it. I thought of you at that exact moment she said that.'

'That's nice,' I say.

'We have to get the old you back soon, Cassie. You are needed on the front line.'

'Dad was going to tell me what I did, but he never got round to it. So what do I do?'

Dad comes in that very second, and he walks over, showing nothing of the emotion from earlier. He pulls the two of us into a firm hug.

'You tell your sisters, the wives, mothers and daughters of

our noble Southern States, that it is their American responsibility to be armed. It is no longer the sole preserve of men to defend their families and neighbours. Every woman now needs to step up and learn to fire a gun. It is their constitutional right to have weapons.'

'*Oh!*' I wrench out of his grasp. 'I advocate that every woman has a gun?' My voice is again sliding up the octaves. 'You are kidding me, right? I mean, I couldn't, ever, ever say that to anyone. Not even in my head!'

Dad looks like I've whacked him across the face with a dead mackerel, and my mom has gone so pale it's as if she's been turned to stone. Maybe I'm the modern incarnation of the *Medusa?*

Dad turns, his face red-hued, and he jabs a finger at me. 'I just don't understand what is happening here. I think we need to get one thing straight, right now, so you come with me.'

'Is this wise when she's acting like this?' Mom has managed to unstick her teeth.

'She has to be shown.'

We walk through the "games" room. It has a full-sized pool table that is big enough to sleep twenty on it. And another fireplace that will keep you warm while you're potting those balls. There's nothing else in there, not even a bar.

He leads me through a door to the left of the stairs. It heads down a few steps and then bends right under the staircase. There's a robust-looking door in front of us, barred with iron hinges and great big studs. It looks out of place like it should be guarding a dungeon. He fishes a key from his pocket; a big, heavy key that must nearly pull your trousers down with the weight of it. Not the sort of key to have about your person every day on a key ring.

'Only family is allowed in here.'

I understand. No Tyreese or Dolores or whoever else looks

after our daily needs.

He turns to me. 'This is our safe room.'

We descend down well-lit concrete stairs, and a metal door bars our way. There is a security system with flashing lights and Dad keys in the correct number, so the door swishes open with a pneumatic hiss. He grunts as he pulls a handle. I hear a generator start up, lights flash and then *ping* on brightly. When we step into the room below, my breath is sucked out of me. I can see an area that must be the full size of the whole house out in front of us. One wall is lined with boxes and cans of imperishable foodstuffs. There are massive plastic water containers, bedding and all manner of survival gear, stoves, gas canisters, tables and seating, areas laid out for sleeping quarters, even chemical toilets. My eyes focus slowly, and on one wall, there are glass-fronted cases, and each case has guns in it. Every kind of gun you could think of.

'Here we go, baby-girl, your favourite room in the house. We can survive down here and protect ourselves for years if need be.' He picks up a smallish handheld gun, and I can feel the world take a big step away. Sparkles of light start at the corners of my eyes, then darkness envelops me.

... He's got a gun in his hand. I hear the retort as I push in through the kitchen door. His back is to me, though he's already starting to turn. On the floor, behind the table, is a leg, twisted at some awful angle. I can see her arm, her wristwatch that catches the light streaming through the kitchen window. She has long painted nails, a deep red colour, the same as the growing pool of blood that is creeping across the lino...

I must be going mad. I must be, mustn't I?

'Dear God in heaven!' Dad is leaning over me, wiping a damp cloth over my face and alternately patting my hand. 'What on God's sweet Earth happened in there? You screamed so much I thought you were dying!'

'I wasn't the one who died. I saw a body lying on the floor. It was real.' I heave in air and clutch at him. 'I was so frightened.'

I hear Dolores run into the room. 'I've phoned for the doctor, Señor Davenport. He is on his way. Is there anything I can do for Miss Cassie?'

'Can I have a cup of tea, please? With two sugars.' I grab the towel and wipe the sweat out of my eyes. 'Oh, that was horrible.'

Mom is standing at the end of the sofa where I'm lying, and she's staring at me with wide eyes. 'Cassie, baby, I don't understand what you saw.'

'Nor do I. Dad, has Nick ever been prosecuted for a crime? Has he ever killed someone?'

'What? No, never. Why on Earth would you ask something like that? Think he got a speeding ticket about ten years ago, but that's about all. Why? Did you see him kill someone? Do I need to call the police as well?'

I tell my parents what I saw.

The doctor from the Piedmont hospital gets here so fast he must have flagged down a passing helicopter.

'What is happening to her?' Dad holds my hand. 'Where are these dreams coming from?'

The doctor is still as orange as ever. 'She is traumatised,' he says. 'Imagine a very young child looking at a huge jigsaw puzzle but not being equipped to put all the pieces back in the correct way to make a recognisable image.'

'Are they real memories?' says Mom. 'She's talking about events none of us have ever experienced.'

'They could be an amalgamation of every memory, and

these include films, what she's seen on TV, what she might have read. The brain is a million times more complex than even our fastest super computer, so when it malfunctions, for whatever reason, the repair job is always going to be equally massive.'

The doctor leans in, and I can smell peppermint. 'Are you frightened by these dreams, Cassie? Or do you think it's more that you expect to be frightened, like when we see a scary movie, we know we should be scared witless, but in reality, we still know it's a film?'

'I'm really, really scared. Even thinking about them makes my heart speed up. They're very real to me.'

'And you think they're to do with Nick?'

'My husband, yes.' This was definitely "husband".

But those other images in my head are of "father". How can I explain that to my dad, now gently holding my hand, that there are two men in my head who terrify me, and supposedly, he's one of them?

But that's just it, isn't it? I have never seen the men's faces clearly in my dreams. It's as if they've been blurred out on TV to protect someone's identity. Is this what my mind is doing, and which of us is it protecting? All I can equate it to is that *sometimes he's my father, and every now and then he morphs into my husband.* There's no rational timeline, and the fear level goes up and down.

The doctor steeples his fingers. 'Have you seen the kids in your dreams?'

'No. Not that I can recall.' Now that's strange. Not once have I seen them.

'I think your brain has gone into overdrive and is simply doing all it can to decipher the puzzle. I don't think you have anything to worry about. I'm absolutely sure you'll wake up, and all your memories will be back.'

After dinner, I sip a glass of cold pinot grigio and stare out of the kitchen window. We eat at the table tucked into an alcove in the kitchen. I don't think any of us feel the need to be in the posh dining room. Not in our current mood. The light is slowly changing from that haze of early evening into the darker Prussian blue of night. Streaks of gold and red are slipping beneath the horizon, though it appears a liquid green above the treetops like they've sunk into a lake.

'Don't you worry, Cassie,' says Mom. 'I know that you'll be fine.'

'Now you're home,' says dad, 'she'll be back to her old self soon enough.'

I stare out of the window...

... She's standing gazing out of the kitchen window, and a shaft of light catches her hair and turns it to spun gold. We're in a basement that looks over our tiny back yard. I've done the best I could in the circumstances. Geraniums in terracotta pots are flowering dark pink and red and tall bamboo is stretching to the light in our walled garden. But it's dying slowly. As am I.

'My, this is so quaint. Back home, we've got acres of land.'

'I can come back with you, can't I?'

'Oh, I'm sure we can arrange something.' She smooths down her dress and scrapes her shoe in distaste, trying to remove something from the sole. I cringe as I realise that it's probably a bit of old dried food from the kitchen floor. I don't always clean up as I should, and this was a surprise visit. I hate it when she does that. It gives me no time to sort myself out. 'I can't just spring it on them all, you know?' she says. 'We have to do this carefully, or people will be hurt, and we don't want that now, do we?'

'No,' I grind the words out between my teeth. 'That would be selfish.'

She strokes a photo that's hanging on the wall by the back door. The sun is at the optimum point where the garden gets some daylight, and a finger of sunshine has lit the frame.

'This is so pretty. Is this your wedding day? What a perfect couple.'

'Haven't you heard a word I've said?'

'I heard. But boy, isn't he just so cute.'

'Would you like to see the cute scars he has given me?'

'I know. He's such a bad boy.'

'Yes, he is. A nasty, foul, vindictive, dangerous bad boy. Please tell me you'll take me back with you.'

'Sure.' She doesn't sound that sure.

'And what about you?' I pull her questing hand from the photo like she's trespassing on private land. 'Are you married? Children?'

'Let's just say, I prefer the married kind. Far less trouble and more gracious, more giving.'

'From what you've told me, do you actually need any more?'

'Oooh, that sounds a little like jealousy to me. Don't be a sourpuss.'

'I have every right to be a sourpuss, as you call it. I have every right to be jealous. Put yourself in my shoes and work out how *you'd* feel.'

'I don't want to be in your shoes, and yes, I'd be mad as hell, but then, I'm not you. I'm me. That's the way the cookie crumbles, dearest one.'

I want everything she's got, and I'll get it any way I can...

18

WHAT A HEROINE

Are these two sides of the same coin? My reality steeped in horror on one face and on the other, the nightmare scenarios of my dreams? There are guns in both worlds, and I presume death. Who did I see lying in their own blood? A memory triggered by that room under the house stuffed with all those guns? I raise my hands. My own nails are naked of colour and uneven.

I sit in my room, staring at nothing, hoping that sense might come through the void if I stop thinking, even for a moment. How could I be a woman who champions women to use guns? It's the polar extreme to how I feel here, deep in my gut, yet it must be true, mustn't it? I've taught children to shoot, and in this twisted world I'm in, it seems I'm a hero and a revered leader, listened to and respected. How strange that I now hate *me*.

What other dark secrets are there to be found out? Should I go searching for them or wait until they creep up behind me like unknown assailants and stab me in the back?

I've made contact, if it can be called that, with Lucy, except now I need to speak to George and find out what he knows. My children seem to be able to reflect me back more realistically than my parents.

'Dad?' I find him in the breakfast room, reading the latest edition of the 'Madison County News' as usual. There are routines that must be followed.

The paper snaps shut. 'Cassie? How are you? I kinda thought you'd be resting still. You know the doc said to take it easy.'

'I know, but I feel restless.' I pour myself a coffee. 'Dad? Do you know where George is at the moment? I didn't see him at the lodge when I was over there.'

'As to why he isn't at home, that's anyone's guess. He's heavily influenced by Lucy, so it's good if he's not around her all the time. He's attending college in Atlanta, and he's living on campus so you could try there.'

'Maybe he's revising for exams or doing research or something?'

Dad raises an eyebrow. 'Maybe. I've got the address here. Are you sure you're up for this, considering what happened yesterday?'

'I'm fine. I've got to get on with living my life and hope it all slots into place soon. I'm sick of living in some dodgy episode of CSI.'

'We should talk about yesterday. It's unsettled your dear sweet mom and I.'

'I know that, but can we leave it for a bit longer? These revelations are too much at the moment.'

His eyebrows scrunch together. 'We can't leave it for too long, Cassie. You've got to get your life back on track and stop acting like some stupid, little girl.'

I cringe at his words. 'I know. I'm sorry.'

'As for George, you need to talk to him. Make sure he knows his place in this family.'

'Do you think George could still be in Atlanta?'

'At the last count he was,' says Dad, 'and I presume he's behaving himself, as I've not heard anything to the contrary.'

'Behaving himself? What's he been up to?' I hope it's only making the locals feel like a right bunch of "hicks" with his super cool suits and tailoring.

'Now, don't you worry about all that. It's in the past. He strayed off the path, but we got it sorted in time. It'd be good for you to speak to him, though. Sort him out. Reinforce our expectations. Why not drive over? The Aston Martin has just come back from the auto repair shop, so it should be fixed now.'

'What do you mean by "fixed". Did something fall off it?' That'd be sacrilege at that price.

'Ah, Cassie. It's from when you had your little "accident". I mean your *first* one.'

'Another one? Do I run out in front of cars all the time?'

'No. You hit a tree down the road. It wasn't your fault, baby-girl.'

'What, did it leap out in front of me then?'

'It did just that, or so you told us.'

'Please tell me I wasn't drunk?'

'It had nothing to do with the champagne you'd drunk at a party that night.'

'So, I was drunk then?'

'Not at all. You told the police that you couldn't walk because you'd been so shocked when the airbag blew up. The sheriff understood immediately. He's a good friend of the family. I've scratched his back a fair few times, and this was payback. Charges weren't pressed.'

'That's awful. I can't believe I'd do such a thing.'

'Well, obviously, you didn't, and I don't want to hear another word on the subject. It was essential that we didn't get our name in the papers at that time. We needed a particular business deal to go through, and that's what led on to the big one.' He clicks his tongue and winks at me. We're conspirators. We have friends in high places that do low things for us.

'What exactly do you do? We're not talking peaches here, are we?'

'Your mom and I are both in the big league, working for the Langdon Corporation. We've brokered some mean deals for those boys.'

'What is the Langdon Corporation?'

'They are the cornerstone of the American way of life. They protect our shores so we can continue to live the American dream.'

Before I can ask any further questions, his phone rings.

'Yes? All right, I'll be there as soon as I can.' He sighs. 'I'm sorry, Cassie. I've got to go. Something's cropped up, and I have to deal with it now.' He brushes a kiss on my cheek and hurries from the room. I'm left wondering a lot of things.

Firstly, I'm sickened to the core of my being that I drove while I was drunk. Even more sickened by the fact that my family connections got me off and deeply relieved that I won't get hanged up in one of those women's prisons I've seen on American shows.

I go to ask Dolores if she can tell me how to get to the university by public transport. She's in the kitchen cooking, and her dark pink apron has a set of oven mitts hanging out the pocket.

'Why don't you drive? The Aston Martin is back from...' She stops and looks uncomfortable.

'Firstly, I don't have any spatial awareness, which means I can get lost inside a shoebox. Secondly, I believe you know why it was in the repair shop. I need to sort that out in my head before I even think of getting behind the wheel.'

'Ask Tyreese to drive you. That *is* his job.' She straightens and rubs the small of her back.

'Dolores, do I get on with my mother?'

'Do you want the truth?'

'Mom tries to paint the picture that we adore each other. Do we?'

'No. You hate each other with a vengeance. Your mother can't allow herself to see that her family isn't perfect. She sees what she wants to see.'

'Is it just mother–daughter rivalry?'

'Rivalry, yes. You fought for years for the sole affection of your father. Neither one of you, as far as I could tell, were able to share.'

'Then she must still hate me?'

'I presume so. Did you manage to speak to Lucy properly when you met her?'

'For a moment, I actually thought we were getting on at the restaurant. Then she told me some terrible stuff, and what was worse, she said they were my beliefs. I don't know what to think anymore. I'm so confused.' I look down and scuff my shoe about. 'I don't think the matter was helped by the revelation about Senator Bob.'

'Do you mind me asking what she told you in the restaurant?'

'She basically said I was a racist, ignorant, prejudiced and narrow-minded idiot.'

'Okay.' Dolores bends down to take a tray of cookies from the oven. I'm tempted to snatch one and run off with it.

'Is that all you're going to say?' Anger and mortification are vying for first place.

'I told you that the two of you have your differences of opinion.'

'Those are her beliefs, aren't they? Isn't that why we don't get on? She's trying to get me to think like she does?' I think that old adage, "clutching at straws", is about perfect here.

'Your daughter is many things, Madam Davenport, but she's not a liar.'

'Are you saying that what she said to me is true?'

'I'm not saying anything, although, maybe, you need to start looking at yourself.'

Is Dolores trying to tell me that I am, indeed, a racist, ignorant, prejudiced and narrow-minded idiot? Seriously? Because she hasn't said anything to the contrary, has she? I don't know what to think about this. I flee from the kitchen without saying another word.

19

GEORGE

I finally find Tyreese mucking out Caesar. By the looks of things, my beloved horse recognises me even less than I recognise him. He kicks the stall again.

'Shut up! Nobody asked you!'

'Mrs Davenport? Can I help you?' Tyreese is trying not to grin.

'Sorry about that. I'm feeling pretty pissed off at the moment. It hasn't been the best few days. I wondered if it was possible for you to drive me over to George's college? I've got the address here.'

'I know it. I've driven there before.'

'Oh, right. Who with?' I wave my hand. 'Sorry, didn't mean to pry.'

'That's okay. I took Lucy and some of her friends.'

'Ah!' Some part of me wonders if Tyreese is getting sucked into the wicked world of Lucy Barber-Davenport? I might be chasing a brown rabbit, but there is a good chance that Lucy is following the white one with a pocket watch. Should I warn Tyreese of the dangers? But he's a grown man, capable of working out what he needs from life all by himself. Anyway, I'm the depraved and immoral one, from all accounts, the one to be avoided. My head is beginning to feel like I have a band of lead bolted across the top of my skull, and it's being slowly tightened. 'No uniform, please. Can we go in the Aston Martin?' I have to sound normal, even if I'm feeling far from it.

'You'd let me drive it?'

'I don't want to drive it myself right now, but I'd love to see what it's like. You have to remember that I've never, to all intents and purposes, been in it.'

His fingers twitch to be allowed to wrap themselves around that wheel, and he can barely contain his excitement. Mind you, nor can I.

If the four-wheel drive is like riding a cloud, this is like being in the mouth of a dragon. As we exit the driveway, I glance up the road. There's a junction at the end. I see a flash of white. A vehicle has streaked across, and horns are blaring loudly. I shake my head.

'Mrs Davenport? Is there something wrong?'

'You know, I think I saw that truck again.'

'What the one that drove us off the road?'

'It can't be, can it. I didn't see it clearly, so I must still be a little jumpy.'

'Listen, Chevies like that are really common around here. Even if it was the same make of car, I can't see that'd be the same driver.'

'No, you're right.'

'Unless you've got a stalker.'

I grab hold of my seat belt. 'What?'

'I meant that as a joke.'

'It's not funny. There are other... things going on. I even thought I saw it when Lucy and I were coming back from the restaurant the other day. Exactly the same, even down to the tinted windows.'

'Are you saying that the lunatic on the road to the lodge might not have been an accident?'

'That sounds pretty mad, doesn't it? No, I'm not saying that, but–' I rub at my eyes. 'Someone has one of my phones. I called it but whoever answered it wouldn't speak to me. They just laughed, and I saw a man watching us when we were out shooting yesterday.'

Tyreese swivels to look at me but then turns back to watch the road. 'If you're worried about anything, then tell your father or go to the police.'

'I can't bother them over weird suppositions and funny feelings. They'd think I was wasting their time. They'd know I've been in a bad accident. They'd blame it on bashed brains.'

'Maybe,' he says, 'but I'd keep your options open. It might be someone you know who thinks he can cash in on your amnesia. You know, take you for a ride.'

'Does everyone know about that?'

'I'm sorry to say, but there was an article about you in the Madison News. It was about how your father brought you home from London and how the hospital was overwhelmed with gifts and flowers from well-wishers.'

'Nice to know I'm liked.' But I see Tyreese's mouth harden into a thin line. Doesn't he like me then? Maybe this is not the time to pursue past relationships.

It takes a while for my nerves to settle. All too soon, we are sliding across the tarmac to park in the spaces for parents. I see admiring glances as the car comes to a standstill. Tyreese leads me to the front office, where we have to check in and get an identity tag.

'I'm here to see George Barber-Davenport. I'm his mother.' I motion at myself. 'Do you know where he is?'

The attendant nods at me. 'I'm sorry, ma'am. Have you any

identification on you? I can't really give out information like this unless you can prove you are who you say you are.'

'I don't think I've got anything on me. Look, I'm definitely his mother. Surely someone can recognise me?'

'I don't know, ma'am. It looks like you've only visited the one time, so I'm not sure if anyone could.'

'Listen,' Tyreese pulls me aside. 'You always used to leave your driver's license in the dashboard compartment. Shall I see if it's there?'

'Can you?' Maybe wearing the pretty high heels today wasn't such a good idea, but I didn't want George to be embarrassed by his fuddy-duddy old mum. So along with the shoes, I'd teamed it with the black dress and the smart black bag.

Tyreese jogs back without even raising a sweat. 'It was in there.' He hands it to me, and I give it to the attendant.

'That's fine. Sorry to inconvenience you, Mrs Barber-Davenport.' He writes an address on a note for me.

'It's nearby.' Tyreese is hanging over my shoulder as he reads the address. I can smell his after-shave. 'We can walk there if you want to? Save having to find another parking space?'

I peer down at my shoes. Blisters, here I come. 'Sure.'

In reality, it is only around the corner, so my shoes don't have time to break me. A large, red-bricked mansion with high leaded windows faces us.

'Apartment 4a.' I search for the buzzer. 'Here it is.'

We wait only a few seconds before a metallic voice answers.

'Yes?' It doesn't sound like George, but then I've only heard him once. I was in a drugged state, and he was swearing at me.

'George?'

'No, this is John. George is still in the shower. Shall I buzz you up?'

'Yes, thanks.'

The door makes a weird sound and clicks open. I hear the

voice ask another question, except the door shuts before he finishes.

I look up at Tyreese. 'Was he asking who we are?' The look on his face is hard to fathom.

'I think so. Look, maybe this isn't such a good idea. Perhaps we should call first, give a little warning so he can, you know, clear up and all.'

'I don't care about stuff like that. I'd just like to see him. I've only met him once, and that wasn't a particularly nice experience.'

We're heading up the stairs. At least I'm heading up, though Tyreese seems to be stuck on the lovely parquet flooring of the lobby.

'I just don't think you should go up there.' His voice is quiet.

'Why not?' Then I see what is happening. George is in the shower. John is opening the door. John and George. George and John. If I've got it wrong and blurt something out, especially as I can hear a door opening above us and the patter of socks, I'll be mortified.

'Hello? Who is it?' A tall slim boy comes to a stumbling halt at the top of the bend in the stairs. He's got "bum fluff" on his chin, and he's in khaki trousers and a red T-shirt with a smiley face on it. But the moment he sees me, his whole demeanour looks like he's had twelve-day-old piss thrown over him.

'Mrs Barber-Davenport?' There's a child's waver of fear in his voice. He backs up the stairs, his socks gripping the edge of each stair, like they're fingers.

'Who is it, John?' I recognise George's voice now.

'Your mother.' I didn't realise you could pack so much pain and misery into two such small words.

'*What?*' It's almost a scream.

'George?' What can I say? 'It's only me. I've popped over to say, well, "hello". Tyreese is with me. Listen, um, darling, if you want to clear up anything, we can come back in a while? I'm not bothered by clutter and whatever. I'd just like to see you.'

'Mom?' George appears and stands by John. 'You look completely different. I nearly didn't recognise you.'

'Hello, George.' I do a stupid little wave with the tips of my fingers. 'And you, John. Can we come back in a bit then? Is there a place we can get a tea or coffee? A Starbucks or whatever?'

'We've got coffee.' George is looking at me like he's never seen me before. I seem to be getting that look a lot recently. 'Tyreese?'

Tyreese shrugs. 'It's up to you, but I think a coffee would be nice.'

'Okay.' He turns, except John is still rooted to the spot. 'Move, John.'

We follow them up and enter a flat. How stupid of me to think it would be a mess. The main room is open plan, with a bespoke kitchen and minimal but expensive-looking furniture. It's all clean, ordered and tasteful. There are only two other doors off the room. One is to the still-steaming bathroom where I can see gleaming chrome fixtures and fittings, and the other to the one bedroom with one king-size bed. I perch on the sofa that's placed under the window. They all seem to be expecting something from me. John dives to the bedroom door and hooks it shut, but he knows that I saw it.

I wave my hands around and look through their magnificent bay window. 'You have a lovely place here. You've got a great view of the park from your window.'

John nods rapidly. 'Thanks. That's one of the reasons we took it.'

Tyreese stirs. 'Hey, how about that coffee?'

John rushes across the room and bangs about behind the

long counter, finding a coffee pot and mugs, all fingers and thumbs.

I cough. 'I'm sorry to be a pain but do you have milk and sugar?'

'Yes,' George frowns. 'But you only drink your coffee black.'

'Not anymore.'

'I had a call from Lucy last night.' George steps closer. 'She said some interesting things.'

'I don't know what happened. I don't know what to believe. Oh, George, Lucy said some dreadful things about me. Are they true?'

'Mom? What do you think is going on here?'

'What do you mean?' I have a fluttering panicky feeling beginning in my stomach as if I've swallowed a few hundred household flies.

'Look around you. John and I. What do you think is going on?' He enunciates every word carefully as if I'm either deaf or thick as pig-shit. A mug drops off the counter in the kitchen and shatters on the terracotta-tiled floor.

'Sorry!' John sounds like a professional soprano.

'Um, well. I don't mean to offend you if I've got it wrong, but I'm making a presumption that you are gay. Both of you. You're a gay couple. You are, aren't you? Gay?'

All three of them are staring at me in such a way that I sincerely hope the floor will open up, and I can leap bodily into the void below.

'And you're okay with that?' George takes another step closer.

'Why shouldn't I be?' Then it hits me like a glass of ice-cold water that has been thrown into my face. 'This is what Lucy was trying to tell me, wasn't it? All those things she said were actually about me.' I rub at my temple. A dull throbbing pain is beginning to build up. 'I presume then from the way you've all reacted to me that I'm usually anti-gay?'

'And then some.' George sits on the sofa, not quite beside me but reasonably close. 'Mom, don't you remember anything?'

'Apparently not.'

'So you don't remember sending me to camp the summer you found out? But not just any old camp, you sent me to the Jesus Camp–'

'Jesus Camp?'

'Yeah. You tried to make sure that no one knew your son was a "homo" and a "dirty queer", but you knew that given enough time, I could be saved from myself. It didn't matter to you what methods they used as long as I would eventually come home "cured".'

'What did they do to you?' My voice is small.

'We're not going into that today. The thing is, homosexuality is not an "illness", nor is it something to be "cured". But this family's attitudes forced me to hide my sexuality, repressing who I am. Grandpa hired detectives to follow me and spy on me when I left for college, and I managed to elude detection because I didn't let myself get close to anyone. I pretended I was someone else. But then I met John, and now things have changed. We moved in here about two weeks ago, but it's only temporary as we hope to be moving out of state soon.'

'I don't think there's anything I can say that could ever make up for what I've done to you.' I start to chew the skin off my bottom lip. 'Sorry seems so lame, but I am truly sorry. What are you going to do now?'

'We're moving to New York. John's got a job lined up, I'm going to get transfer credit for my studies so far and complete my course there.'

'Mrs Barber-Davenport?' John's hands are trembling as he

puts the mugs on the table. 'I'm sorry to say that your family are pretty closed-minded in their attitudes. I kinda think they'd be happy if we regressed back into the dark ages. Atlanta itself is great for the LGBTQIA+ community but we're shit-scared of George's grandpa, considering what he's already done to George. No offence or anything?'

'No offence taken,' I say. 'George? Does your father know you're gay?'

'He's the one paying for the apartment.'

'And Lucy? I presume she knows?'

'She's protected me all my life.'

'From me?'

'From all of you.' George shifts on his seat. 'I mean your side of the family. Lucy said you'd changed. I told her I didn't believe it.'

'Do you now?'

'You're a pretty good actor when it suits you, and you need something. But this...' He opens his hands wide. 'This I can't fathom. What could you possibly gain by pretending to be the complete opposite of who you really are?'

'Listen, in my defence, I don't have any recollections of my old life. I think Lucy must be right. I've had such a blow to my head that it's reset it. Hopefully for the better. The person you all talk about is dead and gone.'

'I just don't understand how this can happen.' George switches on an iPad that is on the main dining room table. 'Maybe there's info online?'

I move to stand at George's shoulder, except he does the same movement that Lucy did in the hospital, the 'don't touch me' cat roll. I can't blame him after what I've done to him. 'What are you looking up? Mental disorders or mind swaps?'

'Head trauma cases. Maybe there's evidence that this has happened elsewhere.'

'You need to know if I'll regress, turn back into the bitch from hell.'

His eyes are a startling blue, but this is the first time he's really looked at me. 'Will you?'

'I hope not.' I add another spoonful of sugar to my coffee, as I need that rush. George finds article after article and speed mumbles his way through them.

I return to the sofa. 'John?' I pat the space next to me, and he comes over like a hypnotised mouse. 'I'm sorry if you've lived in fear. I promise I'll do everything I can to help the both of you.'

'That's something I never thought I'd hear, but I appreciate it.' He leans forward slightly. 'Do you mind if I ask you something?'

'Go ahead.'

'What's it like not to know who you are?'

'You mean, what's it like to and wake up to find you are a totally objectionable person?' I gaze down at my hands lying still in my lap. 'I don't agree with a single thing I've been told about myself. So does that make me mad?' I call over my shoulder. 'Does it, George? Is there anything there that can explain this?'

'No.' He closes the iPad. 'All they seem to say is that head trauma cases can show exaggerated pre-trauma characteristics. But this doesn't fit that supposition.'

I laugh suddenly, and the sound seems to startle all of us. 'Exaggerated pre-trauma characteristics? Sweet Jesus! Like any of us need that!'

'Mom?' George reaches out and nearly touches my cheek. 'Please don't turn back into her.'

'I'll do my best not to.' My stomach gurgles. 'I think it's telling me I'm hungry. How about the rest of you? Lucy took me to a wonderful restaurant called Cardamon Hill.'

'We love it there,' says George. 'It's not too far away.'

'Okay,' I say, 'I feel like eating the rest of the menu. Who's for it? Come on, a show of hands.' I look at each one. When I get to Tyreese, he steps backward.

'I can't go with you. I'm your driver.'

'Well, don't drink then. I'll make it up to you, and we'll pick up a bottle of wine for you on the way home.'

'No, I mean I can't eat with you. I'm in your employ.'

'So what? Not at that time, you won't be. We gave quite a show when we were there, so be prepared if the clientele and staff give us funny looks. But if I'm going to be "that awful woman", I mean to do it in style. I'm quite frankly sick of being a *Southern lady,* and I'm probably going to drink a whole bottle of red all to myself.'

'Way to go, Mom.' George briefly lays his hand on my shoulder.

20

STRAIGHTJACKET, HERE I COME...

The voice on the end of the phone is soft and husky.

'Hey Cee, it's Marcie.'

'I'm sorry, but there's no Cee here.'

'Cassie? It's me, Marcie!'

'Oh. Right.' I'm desperately trawling through the list of friends that Mom and Dad have told me about. And drinking a bottle of wine to myself last night probably wasn't the best idea, although it was great fun at the time. Oh, and let's not forget the myriad tequila slammers and a couple of flaming sambucas!

'Are you there?'

Marcie? *Bloody hell*, she's my best friend.

'Yeah, sorry.' Again there's one of those long pauses. 'Er, how are you?' How lame is that?

'I'm fine. It's you I'm worried about. I phoned your mom, and she said you've been out of hospital a week already. I'm so sorry I've left it this long. Is it okay to come over? Drink us a bottle of cool white wine by the pool? Catch up?'

'That sounds great. What time?' I need a hair-of-the-dog.

'About four. We can swim in the pool to cool off in the heat.'

'I'll be there.' I slap my forehead. Of course, I'll be there. Where else would I be? There's a tightening in my chest as if I've tried to fit myself into a bra that is a size too small. Are there any photos of her snuck in between the pictures of Caesar and me? What does she look like, and will I know her at all?

'Marcie, my parents are going for a spot of retail therapy in Atlanta. They said they'd probably find a hotel for the night, save driving back, in case you wanted to see them?'

'It's you I want to see. Anyway, it'll be nice if we have the old homestead to ourselves, you know?' There's something in her voice, an insinuation, except I haven't got a clue what she might be insinuating. Am I a lesbian? I don't think I can cope with any more revelations about myself.

It's amazing how time doesn't only fly when you're having fun, yet when you want it to go slowly, it whizzes up even faster. Four o'clock comes round, and I'm lurking in the lobby, waiting to hear Marcie's car. My swimsuit is hot and tight under the sundress, and I wonder if I've been a little too hasty. Maybe I should've waited until she was here. She might not want to go swimming, then I'll feel a right berk. The dilemma is, should I lounge, nonchalantly, in the cool shade of the covered terrace by the pool, already sipping a glass of chilled white and reading the magazine I found called Haute Living, extolling a luxury lifestyle to its affluent readers, or be hanging about like I'm desperate and needy. I don't want to leap out on her, but I don't want her to feel that I don't care enough to greet her properly. Part of me is having trouble taking anything seriously any more.

I decide to be proactive, so I fling open the door and wade out into the sunshine toward the woman climbing from her expensive-looking sports car. She also looks expensive, sleek as an otter, with beautiful coiffured hair and a designer outfit. Her hair is bottle blonde but more golden than my mum's. Her heels are breathtakingly high.

'Marcie!'

'Dear God, Cee!' She half trips into my arms and hugs me tightly like she never wants to let go of me. 'I'm so sorry, I was too scared to come over earlier. I didn't know what to expect, and you know me, I expect the worse. I'm such a fucking coward. Can you forgive me?'

She pulls apart from me, and there are little trails of tears running from her eyes. Now that's more like it, proper emotion for once, as I haven't really "felt the love" at all since I've come back from the dead.

'Good thing you didn't. I was rather "Bride of Frankenstein" with all the nuts and bolts and things.'

'Oh my God. I must say you're looking gorgeous now. In fact, you look really different. I never thought I'd ever say this, but dark hair actually really suits you.' She fingers my locks affectionately. There is an ease about her, and I know we must be more like sisters than friends.

'I'm so glad you're here. I've been going bonkers.'

'Bonkers? What a delightful English word. Listen, I've picked up an especially nice couple of bottles of champagne. They're in the chill box in the trunk, along with some snacks. We'll get Tyreese to bring it all to the pool, then it's party time.' She frowns slightly, and I have a moment to take in her face. Her eyes are a startling blue bordering on violet, fringed with dark lashes and heavy brows. There's a quality to her skin as if her foundation has been spray-painted on. She smiles a little crooked smile, although her teeth are perfect and very white. 'I'm presuming you can drink? You're not on any medication that'll kill you if mixed with alcohol?'

'Nope. Listen can't we drag in the chill box ourselves?'

'I suppose, but then what do you pay that gorgeous hunk of a man for?'

'All the other stuff he does.'

'Oh really? You must tell me more.' There's a saucy hint to her voice as she unlocks the boot, and we haul out the blue and white hued box.

'I didn't mean, well, I didn't mean...' I stop, and she laughs, great hooting noises that sound like the mating call of a large wild bird. I can't help but laugh with her.

'Come on, hold your end up properly.' She pulls me around the side of the house, so we get to the pool via a covered walkway that runs along one wall. We drop the box in the shade of the cabana, and she whips off her dress, revealing a black two-piece that accentuates her six-pack stomach and long, lean legs.

'I know I should know, but how many crunches do you have to do to look like that?' I try to hold my gut in.

'Far too many, but you've seen my mother, Cee, and I would rather plunge myself naked into a pit of poisonous snakes than ever turn out like her.'

'Is she fat then?'

'That's funny.' Marcie does her lopsided grin again. 'Ha! She had to have the wall removed in her house to get her out for her gastric bypass. It was so humiliating. You may have forgotten, but I will have this memory ingrained in my brain for all eternity.'

'I know the perfect remedy, get hit on the head by a big black taxi, and all shall be right in the world.' I point at the box. 'Have you got glasses in there?'

'Do bears crap in the woods? Of course there are glasses.' She flips the lid open and fishes out two flutes and a bottle. She shows me the label.

'This is how much I love you. Bollinger blanc de noirs vieilles Françaises 1997.' Ripping off the gold foil, she unwinds it and pops the cork. I hold out two flutes, and she fills them with golden bubbly stuff.

'Okay, how much does this cost?'

'Four hundred dollars.'

'Here's to money.' I raise my glass. 'You know Marcie, I could swear that I've never had money, although I have a bank account that says the opposite. I'm rich, and I love even saying that.'

'So do I.'

We clink glasses, and the champagne tickles my tonsils. Each delicate mouthful is worth every penny. The bottle is soon empty, and Marcie is opening little tins of caviar with foil-wrapped biscuits that probably cost an average person's monthly wage. There are all sorts of lovely things to nibble.

'I feel such a fool having to ask you stuff, Marcie, but you are happily married, aren't you?'

'Married yes. Happily? Well, there's degrees of happiness.' She sucks on the tip of a finger delicately. 'I do love my husband with all my heart, yet sometimes, well, I yearn for a little bit of something different. You know how that feels; eating caviar might be great, but you don't want it every day. It gets boring and a little stale.'

'Okay, if you're not on the caviar, what are you on at the moment?'

'I think I might be on sushi, the dangerous kind where if you eat the wrong bit, you die.'

'Bloody hell, Marcie. What kind of man have you got involved with?'

'Who says it's a man?' She winks at me.

'Oh, right,' I say, feeling my cheeks heat up.

'Ha!' Marcie slaps affectionately at me. 'God, you're easy to tease now. I'm kidding. Girls have never been on the menu.' She grins, and I notice a small piece of black stuff caught in her perfect white teeth. 'My car broke down right out there on the driveway. He was passing, and he offered to fix it, stripping off his shirt and wrenching on this and that underneath the hood. I'll tell you, the view was diverting.'

'Uh-huh. You mean he was tasty?'

'And then some. Well, I had to show him the same hospitality, didn't I?' Marcie licks her lips slowly. 'Hmm, delicious.'

'What? You just invited him in and shagged him?'

'Shagged? Is that an English word for fucked his brains out?'

'Yeah.' I laugh noisily, and she joins me, so we sound like a couple of squawking birds. 'That's what it means.'

'You know the funny thing is, he is actually English.'

I stop laughing. My throat closes, and I drag in a breath. 'Really? What are the odds of that?'

'I live in Kingswood. Strangely enough, we do get out-of-towners there. I even saw an Indian there once, and I surely don't mean an Apache.'

'Ha, bloody ha!' I lean forward and touch her on her shoulder. She doesn't flinch, so that's good. 'What I meant was, I've kind of got a thing about England at the moment.'

'Of course, you have. You've always had a thing about England, even down to speaking with an English accent. That's always been a laugh, how you can do it perfectly. You've fooled so many people into thinking you're *actually* English.' She stretches and gets up. 'How about a dip, and then we go back to your room and talk, you know, a bit more private?'

I watch as her hips lead her down the steps. I follow and feel the warm water grasp at me, hold me up. This beautiful person with her crooked smile, now languidly swimming down the length of the pool, is someone I finally feel comfortable with. I think I'm happy, though I don't want to jinx it. Under the cabana, we towel ourselves off on fresh towels that Dolores has left hanging over the back of the loungers.

'Come on, we'll take the other bottle and the glasses. Oh, and let's not forget my bag, which has all our special needs in it.' She winks at me, and I'm reminded of Dolores and the limoncello enhanced lemonade. A wink means a secret, a conspiracy of two, but as yet, I don't know what this particular wink might mean.

We encounter no one and tip-toe into my room without being seen, like two members of the French Resistance in an Alpine fortress. Marcie locks the door, opens the second bottle and hands me my glass.

'You know Nick, don't you?' I feel the bubbles tickle up my nose.

'Like a brother. Hell, Cee, if you don't want him anymore, please pass him my way.'

'You want to sleep with my husband? What about the English guy?' I can feel the hairs on the back of my neck rise, and I think I'm living up to being a "green-eyed" girl. I must have a tone to my voice.

She snorts her response. 'Nick wouldn't have me. He's *so* in love with you. I have no idea why, the poor darling, not with your track record.'

I sit cross-legged on the rug, leaning against the wardrobe door. It creaks. 'Tell me about that.'

'You want me to tell you about all your infidelities? Where do I start?'

'Do I sleep with anyone? I mean, do I go to bars and find men or what? I need to know.'

'You're not a slut, Cee, if that's what you're asking, but you sure are bored. As I said earlier, marriage sucks the romance out, and a little spice every so often is good for the soul. At least it was good for my soul.'

'What about Senator Bob Raines?'

'That old dog? He's got his sticky fingers over every

Southern gal from here to Mississippi. I don't think that's serious, but you told me a while ago that it might come in handy.'

'For what?'

'I don't know, maybe something to do with gun laws? I'm not like you, in case you didn't know. I don't live by politics or ambition. I live by spending my husband's money on beautiful things and drinking fine champagne.' She sips, staring at me. She's now slouched against the bed. 'Cassie? How much can you remember?'

I shrug. 'Weird stuff. Stuff that doesn't relate to here and now. What can you tell me, Marcie? Do you know why I was in England?'

'Kinda.' She glances at the door, and her voice lowers. She leans forward. 'You were going to see a man.'

'Who?'

'You never really told me; only hints, though I got the impression that he was a real beast. You told me before the last trip that you'd never had a monster, and you wondered what that would be like.'

'A monster? What the hell would I want a monster for?'

Some part of me knows that I've definitely had monsters, and no amount of hiding under the bed will make them go away.

'For the best sex you'd ever had. You said he was like a panther, wild and beautiful, and you wanted him more than you'd wanted anything in your life.'

'Really? I said that? How did I find him? I mean, is there a website for women looking for monsters to shag?'

'Probably. There's a website for anything you want in this world. I asked you to bring me a photo of him, but you said you couldn't get hold of any without raising suspicions.'

'Raising whose suspicions?'

'Probably his wife.'

'Oh great. Am I having an affair with another woman's husband? I hoped I wouldn't be that sort of person, but hell, it fits with everything else I know about myself.' I bite on my bottom lip. There's an undercurrent of unease building up around me as if the air pressure has changed.

'Hey, Cee? Like you said, you don't know. How about a line? That'll make you feel fine.' Her voice has gone sort of sing-song, and my hair literally stands on end. A line?

From the depths of her bag, she produces a small plastic bag with white powder in it. Out comes a credit card and she clears a space on my sideboard with a practised hand. Two lines are cut and chopped, and measured while I watch. A hundred-dollar bill is rolled into a thin tight tube, and she holds it out to me to be the first...

... Standing at his side of the bed, I stare at his sleeping face. When he's out of it, there's a certain animal beauty about him, and I can see what attracted mum to him, but this illusion is lost the moment he surfaces back to the light. They've been "using" all night. The spoons, lighters, foil and syringes litter the bedside table. If he opens his eyes now, he'll see me with the breadknife in my hand, and he'll most likely kill me with it. Convinced my shuddering breathing will wake him, I raise the knife, but mum stirs and turns over. Her arm flops out, and I see the track marks. If I kill him now, what will become of her? I know she'd say it was her, cover for me. We'll be separated, and as I'm only fourteen, I'll be put in a home. I know what happens there. I know what they do to girls like me. He snorts suddenly, and his eyes flick open. He's staring right at me, except his pupils tell a different story. I run from their room, tripping over all the filthy clothes they've left strewn across the floor, together with the debris from our ruined lives. Will he have an imprint on his eyes of me standing over him with a great big knife aimed at his heart? I want him to feel as afraid as he makes us feel. I want him to wonder if one fine and wondrous day, he'll not wake up. I hope so, even if he beats me senseless for it.

I want to shake my mum until she comes round, though I know that's useless. I've tried that before and shaken her until her teeth clacked together, but when they've taken that much, you could have the telly on full blast, and they won't hear it, lost in their drug-induced dreams. Is that the only time she's happy? How many times has she tried to get off the stuff, but it needs the both of you to help each other, and there's no way that Craig will give up. I pray to a God I don't believe in every night, 'Dear Lord, please make Craig choke on his own vomit and die horribly. Amen.' But he never does…

'Cee? Oh, dear God! Cee! What the hell is the matter?'

I feel like I'm coming back from looking over the edge of a sheer cliff. 'I'm okay. What happened? Did I faint?'

'And then some. Oh man, you really scared me. You said, 'I hope you fucking die, you bastard', and at first, I thought you were talking to me, but it was like you were looking at someone else. You were holding something in your hands–'

'The breadknife. I was going to kill him. I really wanted to, and I didn't care if I went to prison, except I couldn't do it.'

Her voice is small. 'Who did you want to kill?'

'Craig. I was going to ram the breadknife right through his heart.'

'Who is Craig? Is he the man you went to see in England?'

I feel calm in a dazed kind of way. 'He's the man in my head who killed my mother.'

'Cee, you're frightening me now. Your mother is very much alive. I don't understand what you're saying.'

'Nor do I, but Craig is as real as you and I, and he killed her.'

'Do you want me to call your mom? I have her number.'

I look over at the sideboard, but there's no trace of the lines. 'What were we going to have?'

'Coke. It makes us happy, you know? At least it did.'

'It was heroin with my mum. That made her happy. I couldn't help her, Marcie. I tried, but there was nothing I could do.' I smile at her, my best friend, my sister and my confidante. 'I think I love you dearly, but I want you to leave now and never come back. I never want to see or hear from you again.'

'Cee?' She reaches out to me, but I pull away from her. 'What the hell just happened? We always do this, you and me, together.'

'Not anymore. I don't want to die like she did.'

She's shrieking now. 'Your mother is alive and very much kicking and probably buying yet another fancy gun. What the hell has got into you?'

'She's not my mother, not really. She's not the person in my head.'

'You're right, you know. You're fucking crazy, and you really need help.' She gropes for her bag, scoops up her shoes and unlocks the door without taking her eyes from mine. Her hands are shaking, then the door is open, and she's gone, padding feet running down the stairs and the sound of the front door slamming.

Dolores is suddenly in the room. I think she might have been hanging about on purpose.

'Cassie? Are you okay? *Carida?* What happened with Marcie?'

I'm slumped down the side of the bed, and she kneels down beside me. 'I told her I never wanted to see her again.'

'Why?'

'Because we were going to do some coke, and I never, ever want to do drugs. I promised myself years ago I'd never go down that route.'

'That's strange because I got the impression that you always did coke with Marcie. Judging by your behaviour when she was here.'

'I know what's happened to me.' I lean my head on her shoulder. 'You see, I died, either when I had the accident or sometime after. It doesn't matter. What matters is that when they brought me back, I came back with someone else's memories.'

She pushes my sweat-matted hair from my face. 'I know you believe this, but it's not true. Things like that do not happen. You've had a terrible accident, yes, but you've not come back as someone else. These things you see are imaginings, your mind trying to heal itself–'

'No,' I swivel to look at her. 'They're real. The people in my head are real. More real to me than everyone here.'

Dolores peers over her shoulder, and I can see fear in her eyes.

'Cassie, you must promise me not to say these things to your parents. Keep them in until we can figure out what is going on. Do you understand me? If you tell your parents, they will send you for psychiatric assessment, and if you end up in one of those hospitals, you might never come out.'

'They'd send me to a loony bin?'

Her face, close to mine, is etched with concern. 'Many years ago, my aunt was sent to one after being raped by a group of men. She got pregnant and wanted an abortion. They said that was a sin against God. She went to a backstreet abortionist, and when her parents found out, they sent her to an institution for the insane. She tried to convince them that she wasn't mentally ill. That's what they were expecting. She died in there, and at the end, I think she was a little crazy.'

'Dear God, Dolores. Life is really shit, isn't it?'

'Promise me. I don't want you to end up in such a place. You have no rights, and I think you can become victims of whoever works there.'

'You get preyed upon. I know, after my mum died, I got sent to a kid's home, and I was assaulted by one of the staff there. I was there for three weeks before I ran away.'

'This has never happened to you.'

'Yes, it did.' I reach out to touch her cheek. 'Whose memories have I got?'

'There will be a reason for this. We just have to find it.'

'We?'

'Of course "we". I will help you as best I can, but you must not say anything to anyone. Promise me now.'

'I promise.'

I promise on the grave of my dead mother, who doesn't exist...

... I want the clock to turn backward, rewind time by thirty years so I can tell her, beg her to stop smoking. But time travel hasn't been invented yet, and the chemo didn't work that well. All her hair fell out in clumps. I'd find great matted swirls of it in the bath plughole. No matter how many times I fished it out and flushed it down the loo, another mat of it would appear. She never complained.

'Listen, sweetheart, it was the done thing in those days. Even the bloody doctors smoked. You were the odd one out if you didn't. We were told all the benefits, but no one realised the danger, and even if they did, they never told us. It's my fault. I couldn't kick the habit. Can't seem to kick any of them.'

'We'll do more chemo.'

I want to scream. I feel she's given up on life, and if she has, then she's given up on me. I can't take that, not after everything that's happened to the both of us. She may be tired beyond anything that I can ever know, yet I won't accept that as a reason to quit trying.

'Yeah, sure.' She smiles that sweet smile, and I force my teeth closed and clamp my throat shut, so the tears and the sobs stay below inside of me.

Don't die! Don't leave me alone. Please don't die. But she did, and the worst bit was that I never got to say goodbye, never got one final chance to tell her how much I loved her, never held her hand as her last breath slipped out of her. Craig took all that from me.

'One last time with me, babe,' he said.

I push between them. 'Please, no. She's too weak. Mum, don't do this. You don't have to do this.'

But then I see the way he's looking at me, the hungry animal look, and I know she'll do whatever he wants to ensure *he doesn't do it to me.* That's what she'd done all these years, protected me, and now there is nothing I can do to protect her. He's gone by the time I sneak into the bedroom. I know by her stillness and the smell that what is in front of me is just the husk. Craig can't get to me as I'm not his kid, but that's not to say he won't try. Stepfather. Stepfather? The shit who killed my mother. Yeah, he might try for custody, and then I'll kill him, alright. One less bastard in the world. Hoo-bloody-ray! Some part of me doesn't care. All my emotions have trickled out with my tears, and I'm an empty shell.

I bury the husk and carry her memory cocooned in my heart. I'll never let her go. The grave has letters chiselled upon it, though I can't make out the name because it's a dream. I want someone to club me with a large, heavy implement, so I have real pain to cover the pain in my heart.

Why can't I wake from this dream?

21

ESCAPE

The realisation that mum has gone forever comes when I wake up in the room I share with two other girls in the children's home. I find the carer who watches us at night sitting on the side of my bed.

Before I can do anything, he clamps a large calloused hand across my mouth.

'Shh, now. Shh.' He smiles at me, and his teeth are stained brown and crooked. I try to pull away from him, but he shakes his head, still smiling. I can hear by their breathing that the other girls are awake, although they don't move or make any other sound.

'There, there, you're a nice-looking girl, ain't yer. Come on now, don't be mean.' His other hand is hitching up my regulation nightie, hauling it over my hips and up around my waist. I'm not wearing anything else. His fat fingers sidle up my ribs and slide greasily over my left tit. He tweaks at my nipple, and I jump, kicking out, but he takes his hand off my face enough to slap me. It stings, although I've had worse. I can hear the girls' breathing quicken. They must know what's coming next. It's like all my senses suddenly open up. His breath stinks of alcohol, and there's dirt under his unclipped nails. What is he, about thirty or so? He's got a face the texture of an orange, but it's more lemon yellow, and I stare at his great sweating pores, trying to rein in my fear and think of what I can do that won't get me beaten senseless and then raped. My stomach heaves as his other hand creeps down my belly and pokes slowly between my legs.

'Aahh.' It's an animal noise, and I go limp.

'There's a good girl,' he says, and his hand comes off my tit to undo the button on his straining trousers. I know that I have only this moment, so I let my arm flop out the side of the bed, and I grab the small alarm clock that wakes us all up far too early so we can do our chores. It smashes him in the side of his head before he can rip his hand out of his trousers. I swing again and hear the satisfying *crunch* as it shatters against his balding skull. I don't hold back until his mewling stops, and he is lying prone across the bed. His cock flops out. It's purple and thickly veined.

'You piece of crap!' I spit on him and then knee him as hard as I can in his bollocks. 'I should cut it off you and throw it in the bin.'

I can't risk him coming round, so I stuff his mouth with a dirty sock and, pulling his arms behind his back, I tie a scarf as tightly as I can around his wrists. I don't think it will hold him for long.

'What the fuck have you done?' One girl has surfaced from her thin cover and is holding a hand across her mouth. The other has pulled the bedclothes over her head, and I can hear her sobbing.

'I hope I've killed him.' I am aware of the amount of blood that's smeared all over the covers. I rip off the nightie and drag on my clothes, filling a bag with what I can scavenge. I undo the clasp on his watch and shove that into the bag too, then gingerly search his pockets to reveal a wallet stuffed with notes, a driving licence, a boiled sweet and some coins. I leave him the sweet.

'You can't run. They'll catch you easy,' says the girl.

'Watch me.' I pull open the drawer that contains my worldly goods, all I have left of Mum, and then place them carefully in all my pockets so I won't lose them should I be forced to drop the bag.

'Don't scream yet. Please.' I look at the girl, and she nods. How many times has this happened to them? I don't even know their names. Then I'm running. I find the front door key hanging on a hook on the wall behind the desk. He's not supposed to leave it alone for any reason, not even for raping the vulnerable girls in this home. Opening the door doesn't trigger the alarm, so I'm out fast and down the road before I hear her start to scream...

Walking is the only thing that can clear my head of all these dreams. But which way? Down the road that leads to Atlanta? Or the pathway toward the stables and the low rolling slopes beyond, dotted with wooded areas. I head toward the woods, but as I pass the stables, I can hear voices coming from the nearest field. It's not my business, so I should carry on, then I think I recognise Lucy's little throaty chuckle.

Hanging over the fence, I can see Tyreese riding Caesar, and Lucy is thundering along by his side on that white-footed horse. I can hear snatches of what they are calling, but the tone is warm and friendly, yes, definitely friendly. She holds out her hand, and he reaches for it, nearly tipping off Caesar, but they touch fingertips and laugh. They gallop around the paddock and over the enormous fences; although they don't see me, they only see each other. I admire their grace and dexterity, their ability to control these massive living beasts with such ease. White froth gathers in Caesar's mouth, and there is a sheen of sweat on the other horse's flanks. They must have been out for a while, but as I turn to go, I hear Lucy shout: 'Let's go in now. I think they've had enough for today.'

'I haven't,' Tyreese shouts back and races Caesar round again. I shrink back against the stable wall, half-hidden behind a tree trunk growing far too close and already breaking up the ground with great knobbly roots.

'Come on, we're running out of time. We've got to rub the horses down and feed them first.' Lucy beckons to him, and he follows. They dismount and lead their quivering mounts into the stable.

I begin to walk toward the wood where, although the incline is very gentle, I am still huffing and puffing like an invalid before I finally stand beneath the boughs and breathe in the rich scent of pine needles underfoot. Sunlight breaks through in dazzling beams with dust motes dancing in them, lit green and hazy through the branches above. My idyll is broken by the insistent hum of mosquitoes, and there seems to be an enormous ant crawling across my bare arm. I flick it off, but another replaces it. I realise that I could well be standing on an anthill when I look down and see them piling out of a mound of mulch. Most of them are running at speed in all directions, but quite a few have diverted up the leg of my jeans. I bash them off as I hop about. So much for the peace and tranquillity of the countryside. I'm either going to be found as a pile of stripped clean bones at a later date or at least end up looking as if I've got a pox of some sort. I knock off the few determined ants still clinging to my leg, waving their tiny pincers menacingly at me, and then I run down the hill.

Oh, my God! I'm now having visions and I'm still awake. I

can't see the wood around me, so I stumble to a halt and cling to a tree. It's like a film playing inside my head...

... I'm in a courtroom, high up, and I think I'm purposefully hiding from whoever is in the dock. I'm wearing a baseball cap, my eyes shaded by reflective sunglasses. I'm hunched into an old hoodie. This is the Crown Court. It's serious. Since the day he was nicked, he's been in custody but I don't hang over the rail in case he spots me. This is the second court he's been in as the magistrates' court deemed the case too serious for them to deal with and sent him packing up to here.

I can't bear to see his face, but I listen to the words. *He is such a lying bastard!* His defence lawyer is doing him proud. You'd think he was a fucking saint by the way he's going on about him. Hand on the holy book? The only time he ever laid eyes on the bloody holy book was when he threw one at me, which hit me on my cheek and nearly took out my eye. He'd found a small red Gideon edition in a drawer of a bedside cabinet in some cheap hotel on the motorway after we'd got married. I should've known then, shouldn't I? Seen it all before with Craig. Why didn't I learn my lesson? *Stupid bitch!*

I was beyond ecstatic when they told me he'd been nicked again, except that couldn't prepare me for what he's been nicked for. Even I never thought he was that much of an idiot, and I've always known he was dumber than a dead dog.

He was in a cheap suit and had managed to get a bit of a wash-and-brush-up in prison. Looking down on him, he looked neat enough but would that sway the jury of twelve true men and women who were currently frowning at him? He must be off the booze and drugs, but I heard you can get most of what you want in the nick, so who's to know?

It's the prosecution that I'm listening to the most. She's a woman, and I hope it doesn't go against her in this misogynistic world. But her words are hard-hitting. She's not going to let him off without a fight. She knows what kind of man he is. A lying, cheating, knuckles-dragging-on-the-ground, drunken, out-of-it, speed-snorting, God's-gift-to-women Neanderthal, and don't you forget it! She's obviously got a good education, and she can look after herself. I wonder if I'll ever be able to do that, or will he always find me and drag me back by my hair? After everything I've been through, after all Mum taught me, gave up for me, how could I have found another man the same as Craig?

I pray diligently to a God I don't believe in, have never believed in, for him to get sent down forever...

It's like the film judders to a stop. These must be memories, but whose? I cover my face with both hands and close my eyes. When I open them again, I can see the trees, the carpet of leaves and the patches of blue sky through the topmost branches. I know Dolores doesn't believe me, but I know that none of the things I am seeing could ever have happened to Cassie Barber-Davenport. But they happened to someone. Whose memories have I got? Does this other woman have mine? Am I completely mad now? I start to walk but I no longer know where to go.

Something draws me to the stable. Will they still be in there? I hesitate and unlatch the door. By the looks on their faces, you'd have thought I'd just walked in and pointed a Kalashnikov at them. They ping apart like they're two opposing magnets.

'I saw you both earlier when I went for a walk up to the hill over there.' I motion behind me. 'I, er, wanted to say hello.' I stop. 'Sorry, I didn't mean to barge in.' I don't know where to put myself. They'd been in what I think is called "a clinch", lips welded together and hands foraging.

'Mrs Davenport,' Tyreese waves his hands like he's conducting an orchestra. 'I can explain–'

'Mom?' Lucy lays a hand on his arm. She tucks her shirt back in her trousers, and Tyreese has pulled his T-shirt down. His work trousers are filthy jeans splattered with paint and crusted with dirt. 'What are you doing here? We, I mean I, thought Marcie came over.'

'She did, and now she's gone.' I nod repeatedly. 'Yes, she's gone, gone, gone.'

'Mom? Are you okay? Did something happen with Marcie?'

'Yep, I booted her out and told her never to darken my door again.'

'You did what? Why? She's your best friend!'

'Was my best friend. Past tense. Anyway, like I said, I didn't mean to barge in on you. It never occurred to me...' I look at the hay-strewn ground and listen to old Caesar munching in his stall. 'That came out wrong. What I meant was...' What did I mean?

Tyreese shuffles. 'Can we help you, Mrs Davenport?'

'No, I don't think so. I don't think anyone can. Lucy?' I take a deep shuddering breath, 'Am I a racist bigot as well as a homophobic gun-toting nutcase?'

There is such silence and stillness that I think they might have evaporated.

'Um,' says Lucy.

Tyreese says, 'Why do you want to know this?'

'So I know who this person used to be in all her glory.' I touch my chest lightly and look up at them. If I'd been rolled onto barbed wire and then filled with water, I don't think that could encompass the amount of liquid spraying out of me now.

'And now you know?' Lucy reaches out to Tyreese. 'What will you do?'

'Change. I'm not who any of you think I am. I promised Dolores I wouldn't say anything to my parents but–' I clench my fists. 'All this isn't me. None of it. But until I know what I was, I can't be who I am. Does that make sense?'

'You have to show her the letters.' Tyreese pulls Lucy round. 'I think she'd understand then.'

'Mom? What time will Grandma and Grandpa be back?'

'They said they might stay out tonight.'

'It's nearly eight. Even if they are coming back, it's unlikely they'll be back before nine, minimum, right?'

I shrug. 'They left at three, but I wasn't really sure what they were going to buy.' I sniff. 'Marcie said they were probably buying guns. Like we need more.'

'We'll have to be quick,' says Lucy, 'and ensure there's no evidence to suggest we've been in their room.'

'I'll finish off here.' Tyreese pulls Lucy into a hug and kisses her quickly on the lips.

'Can you run?' She holds out her hand and pulls me along. I must be running in slow motion, although eventually we clamber up the stairs, heading into forbidden territory.

22

THE EVIDENCE

My parents' room is up another flight of stairs that leads to their private master suite. I don't get a chance to admire their magnificent furniture before Lucy has whipped a long thin frame off the wall above their bed.

'Read it.'

I angle the frame in the light from the window. It's cumbersome, and I worry that I might drop it. It contains handwritten letters in copperplate script, the ink faded and the paper aged as if they had been dipped in weak tea. The words might have been faint, but their meaning shines brightly.

The first is from a Reverend from South Carolina and dated 1864. I read the words but I'm having trouble with what they are telling me. He seems to be taking umbrage at the thought that, if Lincoln is elected, a man of colour might one day be his equal and could marry one of his daughters. He goes on to tell us that slavery was rampant in the Bible, so therefore it is sanctioned by God...

And on it went.

I close my eyes for a moment and then read the second. This

one and the next again links Christianity and slavery, extolling the virtues of slavery as a means where the rich and poor can live together in a charitable patriarchy, where they can hold fast to the Christian principles of enslaving human beings.

Oh, and the next one. Such hateful sentiments, and now the words are blurring through my tears. Degradation... Ignorant... Barbarian and unable to self-govern. And the final part... not sanctioned to be associated with the white man on any terms... The writer of the last letter would rather see the white men, women and children burn together on one massive pyre than be subjected to the humiliation of equality with the negro race...

I fumble with the disgusting thing as if it were scaly with beady eyes and a forked tongue.

'Have you seen enough?' asks Lucy.

'More than enough, thank you.'

'We've got to get out of here. If Grandma and Grandpa know I've been in here, they'll be furious.' She puts the frame back, smooths the embroidered bedspread and looks around to see if we have left any discernible evidence that could be picked up by forensics.

'What the hell is that?' I point at a thing meant for torture that is hanging on their wall. Most people would have a nice fancy plate or painting, but my parents appear to have a cat o'nine tails.

'That's a beloved relic from the bygone days of slavery. A symbol of their dominance.'

'Do I hold these ideals?' She's tugging me from the room, careful to leave the door the exact distance open it was when we came in.

'You did.' She's still tugging, and I lurch along behind her like a three-legged dog.

'You expected me to be angry when I saw you with Tyreese.'

She turns quickly. 'Shh! Even saying something like that in here could get us into trouble.' We run down the two flights of stairs and dodge into the kitchen. Dolores is conspicuously absent. Lucy unlatches the door that leads out across the decking.

'I have to be ready in case they do come back.' She pours a glass of cola. 'Want one?'

'Yeah.'

She hands it to me. 'I thought you'd go crazy when you saw us. You would have done before. That's what I was trying to get at in the restaurant. You know, one of the quotes that isn't up in that frame is one from a revered clergyman at the time. He said, "Suppose they elevate an abolitionist to the Presidency or one of your escaped slaves? I say, give me pestilence and famine sooner than that." These guys were both black, in case you missed that point.'

'What will happen if your grandpa found out about you and Tyreese?'

'He'd shoot him.'

'Well, that's a fine reason not to tell him then.'

'I think we're all in a bit of a mess.'

'Really? Whatever gave you that idea?' I raise my cold frosted glass. 'I think a toast is needed. Here's to change and enlightenment. Isn't that what you said back at Cardamon Hill?'

'Open minds.' She raises her glass.

'How long have you...'

'About two years.'

'He's a very nice young man. Have you thought of trying to extricate yourself from this family and their abhorrent beliefs?'

'I've got my final year to do at college, and then I think we might consider it. Get as far away from this family as possible. You have to understand that the right use women to target other American women.'

I feel a shiver tickle around my neck and down between my shoulder blades. 'Am I one of them?'

'Yes. When you go on your rallies for the American Gun Association, there is an underlying message in your words.'

'Can this day get any better? I think I need another drink.' I yank open the fridge door. There is an opened bottle of chardonnay, and although I've already drunk four-hundred dollars' worth of champagne, I find a fluted glass and pour a substantial amount into it.

'It's so weird,' says Lucy. 'You've got mom's face, but your expressions aren't the same, nor are your mannerisms. You don't even speak like she does.'

'I thought I was doing pretty well with the accent.'

'And that! The fact you're putting it on. It's not even the accent. It's the words you use, the way you say stuff. I've never heard you speak like this.'

'As George said that first day, "It's so fucked up!" I think I agree with him.'

'What do you think has happened to you? Is this really due to a bang on the head?'

'Do you actually want to know what I think?'

'Yeah, I do.'

'My first theory is I died in the hospital, and I've come back with some other woman's memories. Or the second, which is much more likely, is that I've gone nuts.'

'I don't like either of those options. The first is too freaky to even think about, and the second is too easy. No, there's something we're missing.'

'We've covered that, my darling girl. What's missing is me.'

'We'll sort it out, don't worry.'

I run my finger through my hair. It's tangled. Maybe I haven't brushed it today?

'How did I find out about George?' I ask. 'You know, why did I send him to Jesus Camp?'

'You found him kissing one of the male grooms. I mean, a guy with a guy! It's not like they were kids or anything. You told Grandpa, and that was that. The employee was sent packing with a few cracked ribs, and George was shipped off to be re-educated.'

'He must really hate me.'

'No. I think he just believes you're a product of your own upbringing. But you seem to have changed. That's one we've all got to get our heads around.'

There's a sound, and we look at each other. 'They're back,' I say.

Lucy gulps her cola and washes the glass quickly. 'I'll call you tomorrow.' There's a moment's hesitation, then she leans and kisses me quickly before she's out the door and across the decking. She melts into the darkness and is gone, though I can still feel her lips on my cheek. I close my eyes to savour the feel of it, and then I'm somewhere else, some time else, and I can see it all so clearly...

... He's pleaded "not guilty" to armed robbery. I suppose that he's hoping that his barrister, in his black gown and dirty grey wig, will challenge the prosecution's evidence. Innocent until proven guilty. How can he wiggle out of the fact that he has been identified as being at the scene, his fingerprints are all over the weapon and that they even have him on their CCTV footage? Admittedly, it was blurry, and his barrister said it should not be admissible as evidence, except you can, if you squint, still see it's him.

He's a bloody idiot, and thank God for that! Even I've

watched enough CSI episodes to know to use gloves while you're holding up your local post office or at least wipe the gun clean. And wearing a *Scream* mask from last Halloween where the elastic is old is not a good idea, especially when it snaps and the mask falls off in front of eight witnesses. It may sound funny, and many jurors smirked when they heard about that, yet you can't get away from the fact that he wasn't waving a replica. It was a real gun with real bullets in the chamber.

I'm back at the Crown Court, and we're all waiting for the foreperson to tell us what the jury's verdict is. Between Callum and his silver-tongued barrister, I have a bad feeling. Have they managed to sway the jury? If they fail to agree a unanimous verdict, the judge could allow a majority verdict of ten out of the twelve of them, but what if more than a couple of the younger women in the jury have thought better of locking up such a fine specimen of a man? They don't know him, and it's not come out about the other stuff he does. They're not allowed to know about that in case it influences their decision. What would happen if I shout it all from the gallery?

If you knew what he's done to me, you'd triple the number of years you'd give him! Make sure the bastard never sees the light of day again.

But I lower my head and wait. The prosecution betrays no emotion; she's done the best she can to show what sort of man he is. We both have to rely on the judgement of these fine true men and women, his peers, who sit in judgement of him.

They shuffle in, and the foreman stands and coughs nervously. If I hold my breath for any longer, I'll pass out. He has to be found guilty, or he'll be coming for me. He asked me to give evidence in support of his alibi, but I refused. I could've easily said he was tucked up beside me in bed that night after we'd had our evening cup of hot chocolate and watched the ten o'clock news. But I said I didn't have a clue where he was. I said,

'Have you seen his record? If you think he did something, I'll bet my bottom teeth he did it. Go on, keep him and throw away the key.' That's what I said to the police when they came a-knocking.

The court usher steps to face the foreperson. 'On the count of armed robbery, do you find the defendant guilty or not guilty?'

The foreperson takes a breath, and I hold mine. 'Guilty.'

The usher nods and says, 'And so say all of you?' She looks along the row of jurors.

'And so say all of us.' He sits down, wiping his face with his hand.

My breath whooshes out, and I hang over the rail. I want to see Callum's face. I need to see his face, but I don't think it's sunk in yet. He still has that confident, smug look.

I know that sentencing will be at a later date and that even if he gets put away for years, he'll still get out in my lifetime. I hang onto that word guilty. It's a start at least. It's then he looks up and our eyes lock. 'I'll kill you,' he mouths and points at me.

I duck behind the rail. My prayer has changed. 'Please God, let Callum be knifed in prison as soon as possible. Thanks, amen.'

What the hell is all this? I can see the colour of his eyes, smell the wood polish and hear the snatches of conversation from the seated crowd. Sweat beads my upper lip and I wipe my arm across my face.

I totter up the stairs to bed, narrowly missing bumping into my mom and dad as they head into the family room. I have no spare energy to deal with them and a headache of gigantic proportions is hammering inside my skull. I flop onto the bed, though before I've even managed to close my eyes, the next dream comes...

... I have the key in my hand. The Post Office Box is painted a grungy green. It took me a while to orientate myself and get used to London's frenetic pace after the relative calm of Brighton. I may have lived in London for years, yet it's amazing how fast you forget what it's like, and I mentally nearly froze getting off the train at Victoria. For a moment, I couldn't move. After running from the kids' home, I've not been back to London in more than twenty-two years, but I found the key yesterday. For the first few months, it was at the forefront of my thoughts, although I was kind of occupied by trying not to end up a crack whore. Living on the streets as a fifteen-year-old means you're vulnerable to every dealer and pimp just so you can get a meal and somewhere to sleep. Ripping out the address of the nearest women's refuge changed all that. Craig didn't know where I was, so he couldn't get to me there, and they didn't ask that many questions. I suppose my life was written all over my angry little face. Still, it was the anger that kept me going, anger at how my life had turned out, anger that my mum was diagnosed with lung cancer when I was fourteen and then after chemo and baldness, died of an overdose when she'd been told she was in remission. He just couldn't leave her alone, could he? If I saw him now, here in London, I'd kill him.

Mum always warned me, 'Don't fall into the same trap I did. Find a nice young man, have a good life and die in your bed when you're ninety, surrounded by your kids and grandchildren.'

Then what did I do? I found Callum. Or at least, he found me. So gorgeous, so big and strong, so dangerous. They say the apple doesn't fall far from the tree, and what a bloody stupid thing to say, but they're right. You can't break the bonds that bind you easily. You can't change what you've experienced all your life. You fall naturally toward what you know, even if that means being beaten senseless, being ostracised from the few friends you might have built up and knowing that the man you love is most likely either fucking some girl he met in a club somewhere or else he's in someone's house, robbing them blind. In my defence, it didn't start off like that. I thought it was real love. I thought he cared. At least he's not into crack. Well, there's a blessing.

How brainless am I?

But the key is now in the lock. I'm shaking like I've got some disease. Callum is in prison and not coming out any day soon, and I pray the parole board don't grant leniency next time he comes up before them.

The door swings open, and inside there are bundles of papers. I scoop them out and stuff them in my bag, check I haven't missed anything, and then I'm back on the station platform at Victoria. There and back, I'll be home within three hours. Inside my bag, the papers are calling to me. I desperately want to look at them. Even though I have a seat on the crowded train, I hold back, as whatever is inside might blow my tiny world to bits.

Shutting my front door, I run down the hall to put the kettle on. Whatever this is, it has waited over twenty years, so it can wait until I have a cuppa in front of me. As the kettle boils, I eye the papers now on the table. Is there a massive inheritance in there? Some dead aunt who has bequeathed me millions? The tension breaks, and I laugh loudly. If we'd had any money, we'd have never been where we were. She'd have got us out. So, not money then. I spoon sugar into my mug and reach for the bundle. The papers smell musty, and I worry they might crumble before they give up their secrets.

I wish they had...

I wake, trembling and curled into a ball, hugging myself. What was in those papers? Why can't I remember? Why didn't I want to know?

Fuck!

THE NEWS

'Marcie?' The phone is clamped to my ear. 'It's Cassie... I mean Cee.' I say, not knowing if she'll talk to me. I take a deep breath, and the words tumble out like I've *sicked* them up. 'I'm so sorry, Marcie. I never meant to hurt you. I know I love you loads and loads, and I don't know if you can forgive me. I'm so sorry—'

'Dear God, Cee, you scared the crap out of me—'

'I'm so sorry, I'm so sorry—'

'Hey, there's nothing to forgive. You just gave me quite a fright. Are you back to being *you* now?'

'No idea. I needed to let you know that I don't want you out of my life. I had a really bad moment there.'

'No shit!' There's a pause. 'Listen, what's that old saying? Friends are for life. You can't get rid of me that easily, no matter how weird and pissed you seem.'

'You won't believe how glad I am to hear that. I cried for hours thinking I'd lost you.'

'You'd never lose me, silly. I spoke to your mom, and she said that you're pretty disorientated right now. Maybe you need to get away and stay with me next time. I promise there'll be no surprises.'

'Yeah, I'd like that. What about that man you told me about? Are you going to see him again?'

'Funny you should say that. I'm meeting him tonight at a local bar.'

Something skitters down my backbone. 'I know I'm going to sound superstitious or something, but I wish you wouldn't go. There's something funny about it all. I've got a bad feeling.'

I can hear the line freeze and crackle as she weighs this statement up. 'I hate to say this. You've had a whack on the head that should've killed you. I'm going to meet up with him because I want to meet up with him, and that's nothing to do with you.'

'You said he was dangerous.'

'He's not going to kill me or anything. It's just a little... kinky.'

'Okay, more information than I need right now. Have fun but be careful and call me when it's convenient for me to come over.'

There's a sound blaring at me, though I don't know what it is. I'm groggy from sleep, and it takes seconds for me to recognise the phone ringing. What bloody time is it? My room is dark with shadows and rectangles of ghost grey moonlight angling through the windows. Grabbing the phone, I answer.

'Yeah?'

'Cassie?' She doesn't usually call me Cassie, does she? And there's something in her voice. Just one word, and I know she's in some sort of danger.

I jerk upright in bed. A big switch is thrown, all my senses alive and throbbing. I swear I can see through the walls, across the countryside, past the suburban estates, right through to where she is. I can see her. My hearing stretches out like I'm Superman because I can hear a stereo set of breaths. One is panting hard, but I understand what makes a person pant like that. Panic. The other is less ragged, controlled and deeper. And so close to her. Their breathing mingled.

'Marcie?' I can't ask her if she's okay as I know she's not.

The heavy breath consolidates into words, barely heard. *Tell her*.

'Cassie, he says *you're* next.' The terror breaks from her, a guttural scream of fear bubbles up. Then the phone is dropped. It smashes onto a hard floor, but I can still hear the struggle. Her mouth must be clamped, and the sounds she's making makes my heart shrivel as if it's been tossed into a pan of searing oil. There's scuffling and banging, and I can hear horrible scraping noises as if someone is being held just off the ground, their feet kicking, desperate to find some hold.

'Marcie!' I don't want to hear any more. '*Marcie!*'

Then there's a "thud", a weighty thud and some wet, gurgling, sucking sounds.

'Bye, bye, Marcie,' says the voice and then the phone is dead. And so is Marcie. *Oh God, I know she is!*

I kick the covers off me and fumble for the light switch. I can hear voices outside on the landing.

'Cassie?' Dad is banging on my door as I fling it open.

Mom is wrapping a red dressing gown around her, and I shy from the intensity of the colour. 'Bad dreams, baby-girl?'

'We have to call the police. I think Marcie's been killed.'

'What? Why?'

'Quick, Dad. Phone the police. I don't even know what the number is for them.' I hand my phone to him, and he punches in a number.

'Are you sure? This wasn't a nightmare, was it?'

'*Do it now!*' I don't want to shout at him, but I'm having difficulty holding it all together.

'Here,' he says and hands it back. I slide to the floor, my back braced by the wall.

What's my emergency?

'I think my friend's just been killed.'

What's my name, and where am I?

'I'm Cassie Barber-Davenport, and I'm in Atlanta. Now, did you hear what I said? You're wasting time. My friend Marcie has been attacked. She may still be alive–'

I listen. 'No, I don't know where she is. She said she was going to a bar somewhere in Midtown... no, I don't know exactly, but she's just phoned me, and there was a struggle. There was a man and he–'

The voice continues.

'I know, except she's in terrible trouble, you must find her. Can't you track her phone? What? I don't want to be passed to your colleague–'

I repeat it all to someone else. That voice is also calm, authoritative.

'We'll track her phone and send someone to her home address. There's not a lot we can do after that, Mrs Barber-Davenport. We don't have the resources to trawl every bar in Midtown. Now I don't want you to worry. You don't know what really happened. You were woken and probably disorientated. I'm sure she'll turn up fine tomorrow.'

Except for the fact that *I'm next!*

Coffee is brewed in the kitchen. It's gone three in the morning by now, and all of us are wired. I hit redial on my phone over and over, though all I get is the engaged tone.

'You've called her a hundred times,' says Dad. 'The police will find her.'

'Honey?' says Mom. 'Is there any way you could have misunderstood what was happening?'

'I wish.'

The "Media room" is its official title. It's simply a big room with an even bigger telly, our own little cinema. There's surround sound that means you can hear the killer creeping up behind you and the bombs going off around you. There are also two huge speakers that look like upended boats with smoked glass side panels that reveal the splendour of the workings inside.

We've all slept in late after our interrupted night. There's been no news on Marcie, even though I've called the police twice already, and they sound a little pissed now.

'We *will* contact you when we have any information, Mrs Davenport, so there's no need to call again.'

Recently I've taken up watching the news. I find it fascinating, like I've never seen it before. And today, I need it even more. I need to take my mind off Marcie. I'm hooked on the daily drama that plays out around us in glorious technicolour and in horrifying detail.

At every crime scene, the reporter tells it how it is, and boy, are we afraid.

It's funny, but I remember the news always finishing on a high, where the end result gave you a boost, not suicidal depression. The two-year-old who calls the police after her grandmother has a stroke. The dog that pulls his owner from the lake when they've fallen in, and the neighbour who rescues the family next door from a house fire. Where are these stories? The news feels as if it is endlessly violent, and I can see why we are fearful. The news channels would all have us believe that we live in a scary place. But is this true? I think of the words in the framed letters hanging above my parents' bed, now etched into my mind. Do they believe they must arm themselves with guns because the news reports scare them senseless or is it because it's a deep-held belief from generations past?

'Hey there, baby-girl.' Dad has come to watch the local TV news with me. It loops around and around until another story breaks. The headlines drizzle along the bottom, where every so often, I miss either the beginning or the end of the line and have to wait until it slides past again.

'Still nothing?' He is trying to hide the fact that even he's worried now.

'No.'

'She'll turn up safe and sound. I'm sure.' He sits heavily on the couch beside me.

'Dad? Do the media choose what they cover on the news?' I'm beginning to see a pattern here.

'What do you mean exactly?'

'If they had to choose between covering a wonderful story, with a happy ending or something that's not so nice, which would they cover?'

'A story about the bad guys, of course.'

'But why?'

'I suppose they have to.' He leans back in his seat. 'Because the American people have to be alerted to what is happening under their very noses.'

'But doesn't this colour our perceptions, so we start to fear the world more than we should?'

'Maybe *we should* be scared, judging by what we see in the news.'

'Isn't this just creating a culture of fear, though?'

'Like I said, we should be fearful.' He stands and stretches. 'Coffee? I surely need one.'

'Yeah, great', I nod.

'I'll get Dolores to put one on for us all.' He walks stiffly out. I put my head in my hands and only hear the words as the newscaster tells us yet another tale of woe.

'Early this morning, a woman's body was discovered in a dumpster in Midtown, Atlanta. She was spotted by the early morning crew of a garbage truck. Her family have been notified. She's been identified as Marcie Harper.'

I raise my head slowly, my breath caught in my throat. A recent photo of Marcie is splashed across the screen. If I'd been hoping that it was another Marcie Harper, even for a few seconds, then it is dashed. I stare at her face, her amazing violet eyes and her lovely crooked smile. My hand involuntarily covers my mouth. A reflex. Shock.

The newscaster continues: 'The police are treating this as murder. If anyone has any information, please call the onscreen hotline now.'

The phone number swirls before my eyes, merging with her image as I'm blinded by tears. She's dead. *Oh my God, it was real!* The sound that erupts from my throat is animal, wounded, and then I hear running footsteps, the door banging open and arms encircle me.

'*Carida!* What has happened?'

'Oh, Dolores. Marcie is dead. She's been murdered. Someone's killed Marcie. *Oh, God!* Please tell me that's it's not true? *It can't be true!*' I tangle my fingers in my hair and yank. 'I heard her die. On the phone last night. *I heard her die!*'

Footsteps clump heavily into the room. Dad's voice comes from afar. 'What did she say?'

'Señor. She says that Marcie has been murdered.'

'Oh, Sweet Lord.' He pats at me ineffectually. 'Baby-girl. I truly thought you'd dreamt it all last night. I truly did. Why would anyone hurt that dear sweet girl?'

Dolores is trying to pull my fingers from my hair before I tear out clumps.

'I don't know.' But do I? Sushi? Had her new diet killed her? Was this the Englishman whom she'd hooked up with? What the hell is going on? And the message that I'd be next, is this man going to kill me, too? Why?

I'm sitting across from Dolores in the kitchen. She's made me a stiff coffee with added extras. Mom and Dad are in the media room, alternately on the phone or staring wide-eyed at the TV.

'I want this nightmare to end.' I start to rock, backward and forward, backward and forward.

'It will, *carida*. Do you have any idea who might have done this to Marcie?'

'She had a couple of one-night stands with a random man who fixed her car. She made out he was dangerous.'

'Then you need to call the police with any information you have.'

'What about her husband? How's he going to feel if he finds out she was having casual sex with men she dragged off the street?'

'I think he has enough to occupy him at the moment. They'll be testing for stuff like that, so he probably won't be surprised.'

'No, he'll be devastated.'

'That's as maybe, but the point is, you have knowledge that might catch whoever did this to her.' She reaches for the phone and keys in the numbers.

The police officer who answers passes me to the team dealing with her case.

'You should've called me,' I say, reproach making my voice thick like treacle. 'I found out by seeing it on the news.'

'I'm very sorry for that. This must be a great shock to you, after all you've been through, Mrs Davenport.'

'Yes, it is.'

'We'll find the perpetrator, don't worry.'

'Thank you.' *Is there anyone who doesn't know about me? Is my name that recognisable?*

'We do need you to come in and tell us all you know. Can you come in now? The faster we get information, the faster we can act on it.'

'I'll be there as soon as I can.' I end the call and switch the phone off.

'I still can't see any reason why this man would kill her.' says Dolores, 'It may have been an accident, and then he panicked, tried to cover it up.'

'You mean a sex game that went wrong? When she said he was dangerous, maybe that's what she meant? She did use the word "kinky".' I blow out my cheeks. 'Hell, these last few days have been awful. I feel like I've been put through an old wringer. I'm all flattened and dried out.' I have to trust her. 'Dolores? He told Marcie to tell me I'd be next. Right before he killed her.'

The look on her face is pure shock. 'Do *you know* who this man might be then? Why would he threaten you like that? Marcie must've been playing with fire?'

'I think she was bored senseless with her marriage. I don't think she knew what she was really getting into.'

'Then she got her wish, didn't she?' Dolores isn't being facetious. She looks stricken. 'Are you going to tell the police you might be his next victim?'

'Should I? What else can I say?'

'You can ask for help when you go in today. You must ask for protection.'

'How do I get through all of this? I mean all of it, all the dirty, nasty little secrets?'

'You have to be strong for all of us.' Dolores pulls me into her arms and rubs my back and shoulders, like my mum used to do. 'There's nothing you can do to help Marcie, but there is something you can do for yourself.' She glances over her shoulder and lowers her voice. 'You can distance yourself from your family and their... values. You can show them that you are now someone different, who can think for herself, who is not brainwashed.' She pulls my face up to look me in the eyes. '*Puedes hacer esto?*' (Can you do this?)

'*Sí, puedo hacerlo. Si estás conmigo, puedo hacer cualquier cosa.*' (Yes, I can do it. If you are with me, I can do everything.)

'Where did you learn Spanish, *carida?*'

'From my mother. She was from Puerto Rico and had African heritage. I know that. I know that as clearly as I know that the blonde woman next door is a total stranger to me. My mother was Afro-Latina.'

'Then I think God is having a good old joke over this.' Dolores laughs, great guffaws. 'Think about it. The daughter of the great Señor Davenport, a racist white supremacist, believes her mother is black! How funny is that!'

I go upstairs to shower. *So many bloody questions!* Even the warm water and exotic-smelling shower gel cannot wash away the ignorant, intolerant, bigoted, homophobic and racist beliefs that now swirl around my head and are held by this family.

And what about Marcie? Did she die because of something to do with me? I couldn't live with that. Where are the answers? Do I have to go back to London to find out? Is that it? Or is London now coming to me?

Tyreese drives me to the police station. I tell them what I

heard on the phone. *And no, I say, I have no idea what could have happened, you see I have amnesia. And yes, please do tell me if there are any developments, and yes, I'm happy to answer any questions.*

When I get to the bit where Marcie told me I'd be his next victim, there is a definite roll of their eyes.

'Is there something you're not telling me?' I ask.

'Not at all,' but when I leave, I overhear one of them remark to their colleague: 'She couldn't stay out of the limelight even for the death of a friend. It had to be all about her.' They squirm only a little when they see me staring at them. I run from the room that has no answers for me, only more questions.

24

A CUNNING PLAN

Dolores seems happy. She's driving us both to the lodge in the Aston Martin.

'I could get used to this,' she says, hurtling around a corner.

'I know it's a *Bond* car, but do you have to drive like him?' My feet are wedged against the dashboard. I'm having trouble dislodging Marcie's smiling face from my mind. It's not that I want to forget her. It's just I can't cope right now. Even though I've known her for years, I feel as if I only really met her for the first time a couple of days ago. After my initial outburst, I was desperate to see her again, to bask in the warmth of her friendship, as if I've never felt friendship like that in my life. Guilt, sadness and anger vie for top position, and I'm exhausted. I've cried so much that my eyeballs feel like peeled grapes with salt thrown on them.

Lucy is waiting outside when we arrive in a spurt of burned tyres. She guides me by the elbow as we enter the living room, and I fall onto the sofa. Dolores sits across from us.

'I'm so sorry about Marcie,' says Lucy. 'I can't even imagine how you must be feeling.' She wrestles me into a brief hug and then lets me go, obviously embarrassed at her sudden bout of empathy.

'I don't want to talk about her. I'm here for a reason, remember?' My limbs feel heavy. Maybe I'm coming down with something. A life-threatening dose of miserable-itous.

'Okay.' Lucy rummages beneath the widescreen TV and pulls out a DVD. 'Grandma made it for you for your thirtieth birthday.'

'Is this really necessary?' Dolores rubs her forehead as if a headache is starting. 'On top of everything that has been going on?'

'Mom said she needed to know who she was. This shows who she was.'

The DVD starts with my parents' smiling faces, and they've unfurled a banner with 'Happy Birthday Cassie' in massive gold script across a deep red background. At each end is the Confederate flag.

'We'd like to commemorate your big birthday,' says Mom, looming into view, 'with a little keepsake to show you what you mean to us and to show you how proud we are of you.'

Dad is grinning. 'We hope you like it, baby-girl.' They both blow me a kiss via the TV screen.

There are loads of fireworks and popping noises, and then I see myself on a platform. The camera pans around, and facing me are hundreds of people. I go cold as if someone has opened a window on a winter's night. It homes in on my face, slightly pink, my eyes are glowing, and I smile sweetly at them. Then I begin to talk. The crowd quietens to listen to my words.

'The break-up of the family is destroying our country. When parents break up the marital home, their kids are left vulnerable to all sorts of vices. Parents must stay together for the good of the children, be a stable family unit for their young. If a child has no Christian father figure, he will grow up wild. More and more of our population is violent because of this. Mothers left to be both parents, unable to cope, most on drugs, then our people are murdered in the streets where they've lived for generations, raped and tortured in their own homes by those who have lost their way to God. It's no good looking at the government for help either. They are not the father, and they should not be counted on to solve all our problems. Let's face it, they've done a poor job so far, haven't they?'

A peal of laughter and a few claps follow this statement.

'People who can't take care of themselves should not rely on the government to look after them, as we all know, this means we, the taxpayer, are looking after them.'

The clapping is more vigorous, and there are a few shouts.

'Everyone must stand on their own two feet. You work hard, you obey God, and you will be rewarded. It's wild and dangerous out there, and we have to be prepared for what's coming and what's coming isn't nice. So, I'm telling you now, my friends, the mothers and sisters and daughters of our noble Southern States, that it is your American responsibility to be armed. Every woman now needs to step up and learn to fire a gun. It is our constitutional right to bear arms. We must protect ourselves against the coming of the barbarians. We need controlled force to meet the aggression of our enemies, and we must be prepared now.'

The cheering reaches a crescendo.

I wave them quiet with a practised move. 'We must all stand up and be counted. We must meet this violence with force, our force, backed by our God. We must be strong for the weak, be moral for those who have been led astray and be ruthless to those who stand in our way. We won in San Francisco. Proposition H tried to ban the sale, manufacture and distribution of firearms and ammunition as well as the possession of hand guns within the city limits. Well, we showed them, didn't we? We filed a lawsuit challenging the ban. And what happened?'

The crowd obviously know and start to call out the required response.

'What happened?' I scream again. 'Yes, the court agreed with us! Law-abiding adults cannot be prohibited from possessing handguns. We won, and we'll win everywhere we go against those out to take away our gun rights.'

I wave as the crowd roars its appreciation. I smile smugly at the camera.

'Switch it off.' I drop my head into my hands.

'I'm sorry, but you had to know.' Lucy puts her arm across my shoulders.

'What the hell is going on?' Nick has materialised behind us. I don't think any of us heard him come in.

'How long have you been there?' asks Dolores.

'Long enough.' He walks around, but I don't raise my head. 'I thought we all swore never to watch that video again?'

I don't know how to approach Nick. Not physically, I mean mentally.

'Mom's had a rough few days,' says Lucy. 'You heard about Marcie, didn't you?

'I was very fond of Marcie.' Nick sits down on the opposing chair and starts to chew on the edges of his thumb, ripping the skin, and I know, because this is what I also do when I'm stressed, that he won't stop until there is blood. 'She was the only one of your friends who I did like. She was real.'

'Thanks.' I wipe my eyes. I don't want to cry any more.

'We're in a bit of a fix, Dad.' Lucy plops herself down next to me, and I see his eyes widen. Something has shifted in the family dynamics, although he doesn't know what.

I try to help. 'I've gone stark raving bonkers.' I smile at him. He shifts back in his seat as if I've just coughed out a nasty virus.

Dolores shakes her head. 'I think we have to explain it to Nick in terms that he'll understand.'

'Oh, sorry. I thought that was self-explanatory.'

Lucy blows out the side of her mouth. 'Mom has memories, except they're not the same as ours. Basically, her old belief system has gone up in smoke, and she's now a completely different person.'

'Is that so. Right. Okay.' Nick nods. 'I have no idea what you mean by that.'

'Mom just found me with Tyreese, and she thinks we make a cute couple.'

Nick shoves back even further into the seat, tilts his head and then his eyes crinkle at the edges. 'They make a cute couple?'

'Hell yes,' I say. 'She shouldn't give a young man like that up. Nice young men are hard to come by.'

'He's black,' says Nick. 'You hate blacks, therefore you would condemn their relationship and demand they never see each other again. Or you would threaten them with the wrath of your father and his myriad guns.'

'*Wrong!*' Lucy shouts, 'She recommended that we stay together as a couple, but move away from Grandma and Grandpa.'

'You've got to be kidding me.'

'Did you know,' Lucy pats my knee almost affectionately, 'that she went to visit George in Atlanta and she met his partner, John? No? I thought not. Again, she thought they made a lovely couple. Now, do you believe us?'

'Nick, I'm so sorry,' I say, 'I'm beginning to get the picture about what kind of woman I was before. Cruel, selfish, hypocritical, bigoted, racist, homophobic... Feel free to stop me anytime...' He's staring at me as if I'm a stranger he's never met now sat on his couch. 'I gather that I love that brute of a horse more than I love my family, and I get off on power and politics. Have I missed anything out?'

'No.' His voice has a tremor in it. 'I think you've about covered it all.'

Lucy says, 'Let's not forget how tasteless you are. Not to mention spoilt, arrogant and rude to anyone who isn't important.'

'Thank you, Lucy.' I swallow, but the spit in my throat is dust. 'Now that we've encompassed all my faults, I want to say that although I have been that woman, I never want to be her again. But I don't know how to go about it.'

'There is also one other very strange thing.' Dolores looks over at me. 'Cassie can now speak Spanish. Do either of you know if she was taking lessons?'

'Cassie wouldn't speak Spanish if her life depended on it,' says Nick. 'We all know that.'

'Why wouldn't I?'

'Because,' says Dolores, 'it's not the language of the white Protestants who came over to show the non-whites the way of the Lord.'

'This is getting too much.' I pull off the sofa. 'Have we got anything to drink? I'd kill for a beer.'

'You never drink beer–' says Nick.

'Well, I do now!' Walking into the kitchen, I yank open the silver fridge door. Nestled between a plastic bag of opened bagels and a wedge of really orange cheese is a six-pack of beer. I grab it and plonk it on the table between us.

'Hope you don't mind if I get stuck in.' I rip the card casing off, and before I can take a deep enough breath to scream at the volume that feels necessary in such a situation, Nick has flipped off the cap on my bottle and handed it to me.

'Thanks,' I squeak. Froth bubbles out of the neck of the bottle, and I suck it down.

'Don't mind if I do,' says Lucy, taking a bottle. The cap rolls across the table. Nick hands one to Dolores and opens one for himself.

'*Un brindis por el cambio*' I say and raise my bottle.

'*Sí, al cambio.* To change,' says Dolores. 'I have an idea. If you want to show true change, you cannot do it in the privacy of your living room. For someone like you, as high profile as you, it has to be done on a bigger scale. You have to have an epiphany of some sort. Let it be known to your circle of friends and all your acquaintances that this is a lifelong transformation.'

'Your mom and pa will kill you,' says Nick. 'Is this wise?'

'From what I've experienced so far, I need to let them know that I'm not their little girl anymore.' I swig the last mouthful of the beer. These are tiny bottles, barely a mouthful. 'But how and where do I do it?'

'This area,' says Dolores, 'is socially conservative evangelical protestant, but us "non-whites" still have our foothold here. Come to Tyreese's church and tell the world that you have "seen the light" and will repent of your old ways!' She is waving her hands, and her eyes are rolling. I can feel that religious fervour. 'Tell them you now believe we are all equal and that racial violence will not solve our problems.'

'Yeah, of course.' Lucy sits upright. 'St. Luke's Baptist Church. They're hot on equality and diversity, and they preach non-violent ways to solve problems.'

Dolores clasps her hands together. 'Tyreese's father has been praying there all his life and is a key member of the congregation.'

'What better way,' says Lucy, 'to show you repent your behaviour than to say it there, for all the world to see and to announce that you are leaving the American Gun Association.'

'Lucy!' Nick doesn't look convinced; in fact, he's shaking his head. 'This is dangerous stuff you're saying. Think about who Cassie is. Think about who else is involved and what they are capable of. This shouldn't be done lightly. It's not a joke. What if it backfired and something happened to Cassie?'

'It won't.' Lucy frowns at him.

'How do you know?' says Nick. 'I hate to point this out, but you know squat. You're barely twenty-one, and you're pretty naïve if you think that there will be no backlash.'

'From whom?' I say. I don't know these people either, and I'm in the dark more than Lucy. 'Do you think they'd hire hitmen to get me if I denounce them?'

'You've got to realise the power of the people you will be up against, like Senator Robert Raines, your lover. And let's not forget your own church, with its wonderful white supremacist theology and racist interpretation of Christianity. Do you think they would take your denial of them lying down? And in a predominantly black church?'

'I suppose we need to ask Tyreese what he thinks first,' says Dolores. 'It might be that he won't want such a controversial event happening. As Nick has pointed out, there may be many more repercussions than we first thought.' She finishes her beer. 'Have we got any more? These bottles are far too small.'

I couldn't agree more.

We have to call Tyreese to come and pick us up. 'I think we're drunk,' I slur down the phone.

'We?'

'Me an' Dolores. A bit pickled. Worked our way through the beer and then found the bourbon. Wow, that's good stuff. I think we also polished off the cooking wine, but that might not have been a good idea.'

'No shit!' I can hear Tyreese laughing. 'I'll be there in a bit.'

He's not laughing when we explain our plan.

25

HAVING A LAUGH?

I'm sitting on the sofa in the cramped living room watching *EastEnders*, a mug of tea on my knee, a plate of custard creams on the seat beside me. The phone rings. I hesitate as I rarely get calls. It's the police, and they're telling me something, except now my mind has gone into shock. It's filled with white light that's sparkling at the edges like I'm surrounded by fireworks. The mug of tea falls to the floor.

We advise, they say, we *seriously advise* you get out of there. *You must find somewhere safe to hide or come straight to the police station. Can you do that?* The voice is calm, which is good because I want to scream and scream... He'll be watching the police station, and he'll grab me before I can make it through the door. *Where the fuck can I go?* How much time have I got? Is he already descending the steps outside, putting his key in the lock? Dear God, why didn't I change the locks? Because they told me he was never getting out. Not for years. And now he's escaped while in transit to a higher-security prison. If I wasn't so terrified, I'd laugh.

Shoving magazines off the table, I snatch the phone and my bag. Grabbing my hoodie and cap off the hook by the front door,

I stop and listen. Are those footsteps? Is that a silhouette through the frosted pane of glass? He's stupid enough to try to get to me, even if it means being caught and banged up again. With him, vengeance will always win out over common sense. Pulling the hood over my cap, I twist the lock and open the door an inch. If he were there, he would have punched my face in by now. I run up the steps and stop again. Maybe he's in a car, watching the flat, waiting to see where I go. Where can I go? I don't have any friends. He scared them all off. There won't be any stopping him now. I have to run away. He knows where I'll hide. He'll find me like he always does, and this time there won't just be "hell to pay". I'm on my own...

I've reached the Meeting Place café in Hove, and I'm hiding in the toilets on the seafront. That's when her voicemail comes through.

'It's me. I'm in a taxi. I'll get to your place in a few minutes. See ya later, alligator, C. Kiss kiss.'

I can hear the air kisses. I listen to the message again and again and can't believe it. She'll be there if he comes back to the flat. He'll take one look at her and... I rummage through my bag. I'm staring down at a photo in my hand. It's a photo of a woman with straightened blonde hair. She's smiling as if she hasn't a care in the world, yet when I look at this photo, a searing pain rips through my chest like I'm having a heart attack. I hate this person in the picture, but I love her too.

I punch in her number and wait. It directs me to voicemail. 'Get out of there now. He's escaped, and he's more than likely on his way to rip your lungs out. I know you want him, but you're a fucking stupid idiot if you think he's going to play nice with you. I can't let him hurt you, so run and get as far away from him as you can.'

I creep outside, stamping up and down on the promenade, making growling sounds, and get startled looks from a couple passing by licking at ice cream cones with flakes in. I can hear the waves sluicing up the pebbles on the beach to my right. It's always been a calming sound to me, but not today.

She's probably drinking a glass of wine with her headphones on, completely oblivious to the wave of destruction that will be crashing down about her lovely ears. *I have to warn the stupid bitch.* God! She's going to get us both killed...

It's nearly there. I can feel it. These dreams are so real but when I clutch at them, they slip away. Who do I love and hate so much? And I seem to have woken with yet another hangover. In fact, I can't remember a morning where I haven't woken up feeling like shite. But at least this time, I know I'm in good company as I hear Dolores has called in sick.

'Cassie darling?' says Mom, and there's bitterness to her voice. 'Can I speak to you in the family room?'

We settle on the plump sofa.

'We can't tell you how sorry we are about Marcie,' says Mom. 'We loved her so much. She was like another daughter to us. It's all too horrible to think about. I'm sure they'll find him, and they'll sentence him to the death penalty. I'll tell you, lethal injection would be too good for the likes of him.'

'Thanks, Mom.'

The images in my head are beginning to overtake me, and I'm confused as to which is my reality.

'Will you join me for a drink to toast your recovery? We can only pray that you regain your memories soon. We all need our Cassie back.'

'Yeah, why not?' Hasn't she heard of the word "sarcasm"? But it seems to have slipped over her head. She hates me, doesn't she?

She pours us two bourbons.

I raise mine. 'Actually, I'd like to make a toast to Marcie. May she rest in peace, wherever she is.' I slug it back with gusto and hold out my glass.

Her hand twitches. 'To Marcie. I heard they're looking for an Englishman. Seemed she found him on the street and took him home to do the dirty. I bet poor Phil isn't feeling so high and mighty now, eh?'

'I wouldn't know about that as I've never, ostensibly, met him.' I feel guilt shimmy up from my stomach. I was the one who informed on her about her infidelity.

'And what's all this I hear about her killer threatening *you?*'

'He did.'

'Not another one of your delightful publicity stunts?'

'I don't know what you mean. My best friend is dead–'

'Well, you're never one to miss an opportunity to get your face in the papers, are you? Even if it is by crawling over the corpse of a dear friend.'

'That's disgusting!'

'No, that's you. We've discovered that you can use any situation to your advantage.'

'You say that because I don't know any different right now.' I wave the glass, and she tops it up. Isn't that what the cops said about me? Am I really the sort of woman that'd do that? I can see Marcie's face in my mind, and there's a deep heavy pain in my chest. Maybe before I would.

She raises a white-blond eyebrow. 'Not driving after this, are you? There's only so many favours we can call in for you.'

I ignore the jibe. 'Dad says you and he work for the Langdon Corporation. Who are they again?'

'They're the largest weapons manufacturer in the states. We make missiles to defend our fair country.'

'And do you also sell them to the highest bidders?'

'That's not my business.'

'Oh, I thought the American way of life was to sell sand to the Arabs?'

'That's a rather horrific way of looking at our culture, and the Cassie I know would never advocate such a thought.' She's looking at me with those cold blue eyes.

'I'm not the Cassie you know.'

'Perhaps you've forgotten where all this came from.' She sweeps her hand around.

'What's that supposed to mean?'

'Our shares in the Langdon Corporation? Where do you think this wealth comes from?'

'Peaches and pecans.' I stop.

'Is that what he told you?'

'But not peanuts.'

'Unbelievable. Even he doesn't like to admit it. In the beginning, it did, but your Pa was astute enough to know that there will always be war, and if there's war, then you will have armies, and you need to arm them.'

I feel the ground under my feet begin to shift. The fabric of my world is crumbling.

'Whoever that army is? Even if they end up using arms we sold to them to kill our own people?'

'Hard cash is hard cash.' Her eyes narrow. 'You've never complained about having too much money before.'

'That's not a good prospect for peace then.'

'Not in this family. Peace would mean losing our rather lovely lifestyle.'

'What a truly great family I've woken up into.'

'About that. I know you're not doing so well.' She hands me back another freshly filled glass. I hadn't realised I'd drunk the second glass. That bloody dog must be bald by now. 'You probably don't remember this, but you were spoiled rotten, and it has often made you rotten.'

'And yet you're the one working for an arms manufacturer whose products blow millions of innocent people into tiny pieces every year.'

'Maybe you need to go for a psychiatric assessment? You're really not yourself.'

'Thank God for that.'

'Shall I make an appointment for you? All it needs is all the family signatures, and we can have you, er, hospitalized, for your own good.'

'That's very kind of you, but then I'll make sure it hits all the papers. I'll definitely make sure my face is in the news. That'll be great for the family reputation.'

She finishes her drink. 'It's been lovely talking to you, Cassie.' She walks out, and I'm left wondering if my life has taken a terrible turn for the worse. Who can I turn to? Who might help me?

26

REVELATIONS ALL ROUND

Nick's driving a sleek black car with an insignia I don't recognise. We purr over to the lodge as the light fades in the sky and tiny pinpricks of stars struggle to be seen. The countryside around us morphs as the night sky takes hold.

'I'm glad you called me,' he says.

'I'm sorry to land this on you, but I'm pretty desperate.'

His driving is controlled. 'I've been looking this all up online, the fact that you can suddenly speak Spanish and you're remembering weird stuff. As far as I can ascertain, something like this is impossible.'

'I'm getting sick of people telling me what is possible.'

'I've loved you more than half my life, except recently, it's changed so much. If you're not the Cassie I remember, then in many ways, that can only be for the better.'

'Why don't we get on anymore?'

'You stand for all the things I hate most... How did your family make their money before they decided to invest in weapons of mass destruction and all that?'

'I don't know.'

'You mentioned the peaches. Your family had one of the

greatest plantations here in Georgia, and they also had the culture that went with it, economic dependence on slavery.'

'That makes me sick.'

'Do you know what your great grandpa told his sons?'

'I presume you're going to tell me.'

'He said, "Our future generations will be forced to flee from where they were born and to lose their inheritance of slaves that their forebears worked so hard to acquire, because the alternative is to be reduced to being equal with these slaves. And that would be true horror!" There is a very big picture here, and we are not the only ones in it. It stretches back for more than one hundred and fifty years.' He glances sideways and then stares back at the road winding away from us. 'You're one of the leading advocates for the AGA. I can walk into a gun shop and buy guns and then get my bullets from a local sporting goods store three blocks up, and we wonder why we have so many deaths from shootings in America. It's not rocket science. The statistics tell the story better than any of us can. Guns deaths in other countries barely top four hundred at the very most. Do you know how many gun deaths there are here?'

'A lot more?'

'Well over eleven thousand, and it's embedded deep within our culture. We have to try to stop it.'

'It's funny, but I said the same thing to Mom and Dad at dinner the other day.'

'How did that go down?'

'Like the proverbial lead balloon. They weren't impressed.'

He snorts. 'I'd have liked to see the looks on their faces at that.'

'Nick, why is the AGA so powerful? I heard about what happened in San Francisco. How could they do that against what the actual city wanted?'

'It's the most influential lobbying organisation. You've got to see what's going on here. America can't afford peace. They breed a culture of fear, so we all have a gun under our pillow and expect our military to be bombing the heck out of our evil enemies abroad. But do you know how many countries the US goes into to overthrow their democratically elected leaders because we don't like what they're doing? We put in our own people and usually murder millions of innocents, though that's okay because we're American and we know best.' He bangs the driving wheel, and we swerve for a second.

'Sorry,' he says and smiles. 'Companies like the Langdon Corporation, where your parents work, do sell arms to other countries. Our wonderful government can then invade other countries, and we'll have even more sticky fingers in the pot. Remember Columbine? When Eric Harris and Dillon Klebold murdered all those kids at school?'

'I remember.'

'While I'm not taking away from that, and I would never wish to cause offence, what the news never told us was that on the same day NATO dropped more bombs on Kosovo than they had ever dropped up until that point. Thousands of people died that day, but American TV decided it wasn't important enough as it was happening elsewhere, and most Americans don't care about anywhere but here.'

'You're passionate about all this, aren't you?'

'Hell, yes.'

As we drive up, lights are on in the lodge, and muffled music drifts out. Nick parks, and as the engine dies, he turns to me. 'I could get to like the new you.'

We walk, side by side, stepping from the gloom outside into the living room. As we enter, Lucy stops reading, laying her book so flat, I can hear the spine crack.

'Dad? Mom?'

'I think,' says Nick, ushering me to a soft-looking chair, 'we need to crack open a beer and then see what we can make of this mess.'

I fall into the seat, and Lucy settles herself into the sofa. The fridge door clangs, and Nick returns with frosted bottles.

'I've been seriously thinking about the plan.' He grabs a photo that's on the side. It's one of the whole family, Mom and Dad, Nick and I with our arms around each other, the kids. One big, happy family.

'They're still your family. You've woken up as a stranger. It might seem simple, logical even, because you don't know them and you don't know us. You could walk away from the lot of us if you wanted to, and what would you feel? Sadness? Remorse? But you could walk away. It's the rest of us who'll have to bear the fallout of this and fallout there will be, the likes of which you can't envision.'

'Then what can I do?'

'Just walk away. You said you've got money, so use it and build a better life for yourself somewhere else.'

'Is that what you all want?'

Nick runs his fingers through his hair. 'Maybe we've gone overboard about all this. It's a really drastic action. We should be sure it's right before we blunder into it all.'

'Of course, it's right!' Lucy stands up, her hands out, pleading. 'You know it is. It's the only way we can say that what they stand for is reprehensible. If we walk away, they've won. They go on spreading their lies and filth and corrupting everyone. It should have stopped years ago, except it's stronger now than it ever was.'

'Lucy,' says Nick. 'I know how you feel about it, but look at us. We have to know that what we're doing is for the best for all of us.'

'You're young and impetuous,' I try to smile at her, 'and what Nick said is true. I could walk. I'm not going to, but if anyone got hurt because we were trying to send a message, think how we'd feel.'

'They'll fight back,' says Nick. 'They'll throw our lives back into our faces. They'll let all the world know about George, they'll brand you,' he nods at Lucy, 'a sort of crazy goth punk, and as for us, they'd have a field day.'

'Why?' I lean forward.

'You, because you're sleeping with a right-wing senator and me because I'm head of the Georgia branch of the Families Against Gun Violence. So far, we've managed to keep that out of the news but what a scoop. Our faces will be plastered all over the papers, and we'll make the headline news. Is that what you want?'

'Bollocks!' I say. 'I'm not that photogenic.' But there's another reason I don't want my face in the news, and it's nothing to do with this.

'Let's sleep on it,' says Nick, 'and see how we feel in the morning.' He stands, and I can see he's tired and worn. 'I can give you a lift back, or you can stay here.' He grins. 'There's George's room or the small box room where we leave all our junk. You can get in there, although you may never come out.'

'If it's all right with everyone, I'd like to stay here. I don't think it fair to use George's room without his permission, so the box room sounds great.'

'I'll help you clear it,' says Lucy, holding out her hand. 'Come on, it's a mess, and I'm bushed.'

As I take hold of my daughter's hand, I think this could be home.

27

NOT WHO WE THOUGHT WE WERE

I can see her bag on the edge of the kitchen table, half hanging off. It's open, and her things are spilling out. He's turning. I know I've barely got a second, but I snatch it and run down the long hallway and crash out of the front door. I'm up the steps leading out of our basement in two strides. I'm counting on the fact that I've been running at least three times a week for the last two years up and down the seafront, as I was too broke to go to a gym. He looks like he's been working out while he's been inside, he's much bulkier than I remember, but I pray it'll slow him down. I'll soon know if he manages to get one hand round my throat, as that's all it'll take to snap my neck. I'm round the corner and down the next road before I risk a look behind me. He's not there. Maybe he's so stunned to see me alive he can't react fast enough. I keep on running, my feet thumping on the tarmac, my breath controlled so I can run for longer, dodging past early summer tourists. I clutch her bag under my arm, and I hope nothing has fallen out. Do I hide on the beach? Try to blend in with the sunbathers and the office workers on their lunch breaks? I slow down. He'd wait until there was no one left but me sitting on the pebbles, and then he'd only have to grab me and pull me under the pier. Kill me twice. I know he could do it. Has she got any money in her bag? I speed up, turning up the road that leads to the clock tower and then right. The station is at the top and if I can get on a train to London, I know I'll be all right. I can work out what to do then. I'll go to London. They'll help me, I'm sure of it...

It's only when I hear him grunt that I realise I've kicked Nick hard, and I hear the thud as he lands on the floor.

'Oh shite!' I'm so tangled in the duvet that as I try to get up to help him, I also roll off the bed.

'What the hell?' Lucy has switched on the light, and Nick and I must look like we're in a compromising position, except there's no amusement in her eyes, only fear. 'Mom? Oh my God, are you okay?'

'Why wouldn't I be?'

'You were screaming so loudly, I thought you were being murdered!'

'Dreams. I told you I had bad dreams.' I can hear Nick moaning. 'Nick, I'm so sorry. Which bit did I get?'

'The bit that means that we might only ever have two kids.'

'Oh, bollocks!'

'Precisely.' He levers himself upright. 'What can you remember of the dream?'

'I don't want to remember–'

'Cassie, this is important, think!'

'I'm running, running for my life, and he's behind me. I've got to get to London–' I throw up over the duvet and half over Nick.

'I'll get a cloth,' says Lucy and I hear her feet patter quickly down the hallway.

'Apart from this being utterly gross,' says Nick, 'you understand what this means? Cassie, you say you have bad dreams but do you remember them clearly? They could be the key.' He squints down at the mess splattered over his legs.

'I'm so sorry.' My stomach heaves again.

'Forget it, Cas. Just try to remember your dreams. Focus on them.'

This is so hard for me. 'Some are so clear it's like watching TV, and others are like whispers when I wake up, yet all of them are horrible. I'm always terrified.'

'Who was after you?'

'My husband.'

'*What?*' Nick lurches upright, and I laugh at his Bermuda shorts.

'Not you,' I wipe dribble off my chin onto the duvet. 'My other husband.'

'You're a bigamist?' Nick sits down on the edge of the bed. 'You married some guy in England?'

'I don't know. But I met him when I was not much older than Lucy.'

'That doesn't make sense. You only started to go to England about ten months ago, so you can't have known him for long.'

'Who?' says Lucy as she comes in with a damp towel and a bucket of soapy water.

'Your mother's other husband.' Nick is staring at me.

'What?' Lucy nearly drops the bucket.

'We've covered that bit.'

'He killed her.' I take the towel from Lucy and start to mop up the sick.

Nick says, 'Your husband killed someone?'

'Stop saying that.' Lucy looks so small. 'She's not married to anyone else but Dad.'

'Oh, but I am, and if he ever finds me, he'll kill me too.'

'Cassie, dear God,' says Nick, 'what the hell have you got yourself into?'

'Perhaps I should show you the texts?'

'What texts?'

'The texts from the man who wanted to kill me. They're on my other iPhone, but that's back at the house.'

'Why didn't you tell us earlier?' says Lucy.

'It all got muddled up with the dreams.'

'Then try to remember the dreams,' says Nick, 'the answer must be in the dreams.'

'The dreams leave me with fear, jealousy, anger, resentment, hate. That's what I remember from the dreams.'

'No good ones?' I can hear the sadness in Lucy's voice.

'I remember my mum. She's not Margaret Davenport. I remember she loved me so much, but in the end, she betrayed me.'

They told me afterwards I just fainted face-first into the stinking duvet.

'I'm going to try to talk to them,' I tell everyone at breakfast.

They seem to be struggling with their scrambled eggs and crispy bacon, but mine are slipping down nicely. Since I've showered, I feel kind of "peachy", and I think this has something to do with my decision to postpone ruining the family and trying re-education instead.

'Good luck with that,' says Lucy, moving her breakfast around with a fork. 'It might sway them if their beloved daughter Cassie starts to have doubts. It could work.'

Nick makes a face, and I'm not sure if it's due to the eggs or the statement. 'You think after all these years and the weight of their bloody Southern heritage, they'll suddenly change their minds because their amnesiac daughter has had a change of heart?' He crunches into a slice of slightly burnt toast. 'More likely, she'll be in a psychiatric unit quicker than the blink of an eye.'

'Mom's already offered that as an option.'

'I'd come and visit you.' Lucy looks somewhat bewildered, which is no surprise. No one has really tried to go into what happened last night, least of all me.

'Thanks for that, Lucy,' I smile at her.

'Then,' says Nick, 'that's even more reason to be careful, isn't it?'

'They're ignorant, so they need to learn the truth.' How simple it all sounds in the light of a beautiful summer's morning.

'Hmm,' says Nick. 'They're people with a belief system that has lasted hundreds of years and is inbred and built-in.'

'And let's not forget,' says Lucy, 'that they are people with a huge amount of guns.'

'Quite frankly,' I stand and stretch, 'I've had more than my fill of guns. It stops now.'

'Way to go, Mom.' Lucy claps a few times but then stops when she sees the look Nick is giving her.

'You can but try,' says Nick, 'but don't forget to put on your bulletproof vest, eh?'

'Don't joke,' says Lucy. 'They're not exactly known for their forgiving and compassionate nature. Now could we possibly talk about what happened last night?'

The sun has dodged behind a cloud.

When I return to the house, I search for my mother.

'Mom?' I find her reading in the soft light of the sun room. She seems relaxed, so I hope this is a good time to speak to her.

She pre-empts me. 'Sorry about earlier, darling. We should really try to be more civil toward each other, don't you think?

'Yes, of course.' I clear my throat. 'Mom? Do you know of any reason why I might be remembering things that obviously haven't happened?'

She closes her book with a *snap*.

'The doctor said you could be trying to piece together memories of every bit of your life, including all the books, films, programmes you've seen. That could well account for it, couldn't it?'

'I suppose so, but they're getting worse.'

'Perhaps this is like your mind having one last go at shaking it all up, and then you'll wake up, and it will all be back to normal. We'll laugh about your madness.'

'Yes, madness.' I close my eyes. I have to ask her one last question, but I baulk. Crossing over this line means I can never go back. If she answers how I think she will, I don't know if I can forgive her. Those letters above their bed might be some sick heirloom that is only a "keepsake" from a bygone era, though Lucy is convinced they still adhere to every hateful word.

'Do you remember when you came home, and we were going to talk about everything we stand for? Could you go over that again for me?' I pull up another chair close to hers.

'Like I said, it's strange to have to explain this to you.' She pushes her hair back from her forehead and then looks at me.

'What, as a Southern woman, is your philosophy?'

Mom smiles up at me. Her face is so beautiful; I can barely look at her. 'Why, to keep the black population and the Hispanics where they should be, and that is under us. I believe black people are like children. They are totally incapable of caring for themselves. Slavery was a benevolent institution that kept them fed, clothed and occupied. In my opinion, blacks are inferior to whites.'

'Are you serious?'

'You have forgotten a crucial point in our history, Cassie. The United States Supreme Court in the 1857 Dred Scott Decision ruled that slaves were subhuman property with no rights of citizenship. And so it should have stayed because look at where we are now.'

'Where are we now?'

'They have elected a descendant of a slave to the American presidency. They have stained the blood of the white race so that it has been contaminated for all time.'

'And we fit in where?'

'We ensure our Militia is trained and armed. We ensure the concerned citizens of America fulfil their duties and responsibilities as true Americans.'

'True, white Americans?'

'Exactly. We need to be secure in our land of the free and home of the brave.'

'Hallelujah! Praise be.' I raise my hands in the air. I must be in some reality TV show because this can't be happening.

'Hallelujah,' she responds and pulls me into a hug. 'There she is, our little girl.'

I want to run screaming from the room. This is not my life!

She continues, 'The South's "peculiar institution" was that we could own human beings as our property and that these slaves were deeply embedded in every aspect of our way of life. How could we be expected to give all that up?'

'And you agree with all this?'

'Yes. I believe in the infallibility of the Bible. It is the best way to explain slavery to the masses.'

'God is your key witness for the defence then?'

'It is in the Bible, Cassie.'

'So is throwing the Christians to the lions, although I don't see much of that still going on. The Bible is two thousand years old and is archaic? They might have had slaves then, but that's because they weren't educated and civilised.'

'I don't understand what you're getting at. My view is that the abolition of slavery has plunged us into a race war and contaminated the pure blood of the white race.'

I have to override my inclination to spit at her. 'You don't find anything you've said to me in the slightest bit reprehensible?'

'Of course not. The truth is the truth.'

I don't think re-education is on the cards now. 'And what if you'd been born into slavery, would the truth still be the truth then?'

'I am not black, and my God knows who I am. I find your line of thought disturbing.'

'Not half as disturbing as I find yours. We took innocent people from their homes and treated them worse than we do our animals. Slavery was abolished in this country more than a hundred and fifty years ago, yet it seems to have bypassed this family. We are all equal, but not according to the Davenports!'

'We have fought long and hard, Cassie Davenport, to keep the negro where he should be, and now I hear you undermining our beliefs? Shame on you and shame on who is filling your sweet head with these falsehoods. Who have you been speaking with? You're not seeing Nick again, are you? That's it, isn't it? He's pulled you back into his web of lies and deceit when you are at your most vulnerable. Oh, Cassie, baby. We should have been more vigilant. We'll save you, don't you worry.'

Oh, but I don't want to be saved!

I slip out and go to sit at the far end of the pool from the house. I've already looked it all up, my heritage. My family got rich off the back of the slaves working in our fruit plantations. Nick was right. My family was at the forefront of the South's "peculiar institution", which, to put it in a nutshell, was the right to own human beings as property. Our motto was "All men are not created equal". I remember the tattoo that Lucy has. There are no more tears left to cry. I have only one more thing to experience: church, then there is only action left. I have to make a stand, and I have to do it now.

28

FOR A BOWL OF RED STEW

C hurch. What did I expect? And we're the mainstay of the community. The Davenports. The building is simple, with clean straight lines and no ornate extravagancies. There's no incense billowing, no candles lit for prayers. It all seems pretty low key. The congregation call greetings, shake hands and kiss each other's cheeks. It's nice, friendly, a close-knit, small-town community coming together to worship their God.

Every face is white here. Except for the few of us that have tans, but that's different, isn't it? Blonde and tanned? The American dream. But that tan was paid for, and most of that blonde came out of a bottle. I look around, and I realise that I might be the darkest one amongst us. How funny is that?

We take our usual, allotted places. Front pew, right below the pulpit, ready to be sprayed with fervent spit by God's spokesperson on Earth.

'Welcome, brethren, to our church. I see today before me new faces, and I welcome you into our flock. I also see well-known, beloved faces and one in particular who we have been praying for. Welcome back to us, Cassie Davenport.' His blazing eyes are fixed on me like I'm being skewered on a giant meat hook.

'Thanks,' I squeak and give a little wave. The congregation all clap heartily, and Dad pushes me upright.

'Say how happy you are to be back amongst your own kind.'

The clapping dies down, and I am transfixed by all the eyes that are on me. 'Hi?' I look down at Dad, and he mouths some sort of encouragement. Mom holds my hand.

I try again. 'I'm delighted to be back amongst you all.' I can see that Mom and Dad are pleased. They both sit there smiling at each other, and I wonder if they've forgotten our previous conversations. Maybe they believe that visiting their God in his house will restore order. There is a movement to my other side. And then I can smell his cologne. It may be costly and probably comes from Europe, but it still makes me want to heave my guts out.

'Hello, Cassie. Nice to see you out and about.'

'Senator Raines.' He's combed his hair in a different style today, and I wonder if it's to hide the lumps?

He leans across me to shake hands with my dad and wave a fingered kiss at my mom.

He is the epitome of a Southern gentleman, although I'm beginning to realise that *Southern gentleman* might mean something else entirely in these parts.

I am acutely aware of his presence beside me, his knee resting against my own, his elbow digging into my rib. I start to listen closely, except there's something wrong with the sermon.

'Salvation must be conferred through the absolution of race. Non-Caucasian people can never receive God's favour, as they have no soul! We have always known that. They can never be saved.'

The congregation groans as if they're so upset by his words. 'Never be saved,' they intone.

'They have no soul!' The preacher shouts this from the pulpit.

'They have no soul.' The congregation know the ropes then.

'Only the white Europeans, the literal descendants of the sons or grandsons of Jacob, the ten tribes of the independent Kingdom of Israel, only they are God's chosen people!' He waves his hands like a conjurer at a kid's party.

'Jesus was an Israelite of the tribe of 'Judah,' he points an accusing finger. 'We all know what that means, don't we?'

Yep! Everyone but me.

'Modern Jews are not Israelites or Hebrews, and why is that?'

It's like he's never asked this question before. The congregation are hanging on his words like dogs on a gnawed old bone.

'Yes, we know, don't we? They are descended from people with Turco-Mongol blood. *Tainted blood.*'

'Tainted blood,' wails the congregation.

'*Khazars!*' shrieks the preacher, 'Descendants of the biblical Esau-Edom, the ancient enemy nation of Israel! And what did Esau-Edom do?'

I don't know, so bloody well tell us! What did he do?

His voice lowers to a gravelly whisper. We all strain forward in our seats. 'He traded his birthright for a bowl of red lentil pottage! Did you hear *that*! *He traded his birthright for a bowl of red lentil pottage!*'

...I suddenly realise that I'd have probably traded my birthright, once-upon-a-time, for a bowl of any coloured stew. Have any of them ever been truly hungry? The sort of hunger that twists your gut into knots and makes eating the living room carpet appetising? Have any of them wondered if they would eat that week or if they'd have to scavenge in bins, frightened of rolling drunks with sweaty, bloated faces, foul language along with foul breath and coppers that chased you with long outstretched fingers. Have any of them had to steal from supermarkets, stuffing frozen chickens in prams and sausages up jumpers, frightened that you'll get nicked and separated? I'd go to a kids' home, and mum knew I wouldn't fare well there.

'You're too pretty,' she said. 'They'd have you as quick as look at you.'

I didn't want to be "had", but I nearly was...

I have to get out of here. I stand up. 'Please excuse me. I'm going to be sick.'

It's incredible how fast people can shift out of the way after you've said that. I run down the aisle and hurtle out the door. My insides are roiling around like a toy ship at sea, but I keep my breakfast down for once. I hear the hymns, and I wonder if I would ever know the lyrics or are they all based on Aryan marching anthems? Oh come all ye white-haired, blue-eyed children, Oh come ye, Oh come ye and learn how to be a racist pig... I know it doesn't rhyme, but what the hell.

I dawdle about on the pavement as I haven't a clue where I am, and I know that home is a long way off. I can get lost in a shoebox, so I don't fancy my chances of finding my way home by walking. How do I explain myself this time? They must be getting suspicious by now.

'Cassie?' Dad is looking anxious. 'Are you okay?'

'Came over all wobbly. Listen, I know you've probably been coming here for years–'

'And my pa and his pa before him.'

'Yes, well. But do you really believe that only white people can earn God's favour? And that utter tosh that black people have no soul, I mean, what is that all about?'

I can see by the granite set of his jaw that I might have said something I shouldn't. Yay for that.

'This is the divine truth. *Your* divine truth.' He winces like I've poked him with a sharp stick. 'True blacks cannot earn a place in Heaven, and that is our truth.'

I shake my head. 'Well, maybe they don't want to be in *your* Heaven, maybe they'll be in *their* own with their God.'

'You dare to say such blasphemous things? I'll only take such filth from you once in this lifetime. If you ever say anything like that again, I'll wash your mouth out with carbolic soap for a week. Is that understood?'

'Every word. It's been such a pleasure coming to your church and meeting your God. Now I know.'

'Now you know what?'

'Now I know I'll never be coming back here. Not in this lifetime or any other.'

'What has gotten into you? You're not my little girl anymore.'

'Thank God for that! My eyes have been opened, and I don't like what I see.'

Mom comes up, gliding in that Stepford-Wife way she has. 'What don't you like?'

'As far as I can tell,' says Dad, 'she doesn't like us or our ways.'

'Cassie? What does he mean?'

'That I'm going to get a taxi back.'

'Why?'

'I read what you've got hanging above your bed. I've read those hateful letters, and I can't believe I come from such a disgusting background. You spout on about being "morally superior", and yet you're the lowest of the low and I–'

Senator Robert Raines is suddenly in front of me. 'What are you saying here?' His voice is quiet but full of menace. I recognise that voice.

'Do you know what? I've had enough of being intimidated by men with inferiority complexes. What are you going to do, *Bob*? Are you going to hit me to keep me in my place because I've been there and got the fucking T-shirt, mate!'

I square up to him, and he stumbles backward. People are beginning to slow down and stare, voices are hushed, and I know they're all listening.

'You lot,' I wave around me at all the hungry spectators, 'What do you know? A heritage full of hate? Wake up and smell the coffee! Black people don't hate you. *You* hate black people. They aren't coming for you; you're coming for them. And why? Because they dared to say they didn't want to be your slaves any more. Well, what a fucking eye-opener that is, eh? All they ever wanted was to be able to live in peace, but you couldn't leave them alone, could you.'

Bob slides into my line of vision. 'Shut up now. You keep your dirty mouth closed.' He cannot ever emulate the sheer aggression I've experienced in my life, and I find this hysterically funny.

'Ha! Or what? What will you do, senator?' I think I might be screaming now, and the crowd is rumbling ominously. 'I renounce my so-called Southern heritage. You can all stuff it up your arse!'

'Dear God,' I hear Mom say as I head off probably in the wrong direction, 'she's regressed to being sixteen again.'

'That's it,' says Dad. 'The accident has made her regress. That explains all this strange behaviour. We have to live through her teenage years again.'

'I think I would rather kill myself,' says Mom, and I smile.

29

GHOST IN THE NIGHT

I can see him down by the edge of the lake. The fire is burning brightly, although it's that in-between time when the leaching light of dusk makes it difficult to see clearly.

He's doing some weird dance. I hear him say, 'Goddamn mosquitoes!'

'Hey, Nick?' I stop by the fire and watch him through the flames and smoke as he approaches me.

'Cas?' He stops on the other side of the fire. 'I need to go and get the insect repellent and some citronella candles, or we're going to be eaten alive. It might be a placebo effect, but I wholeheartedly believe I don't get bitten as much.'

'Do I get bitten?'

'Barely. I think they bypass you to get to me. I must have very sweet blood.'

'Like a fine wine.'

'Possibly more beer flavoured. I'll be back in a minute. Keep putting logs on the fire, as this initial bit is crucial. There's beer and chips and marshmallows in the cool box.' He races back up the slope and disappears into the house.

I don't know what I was expecting, whether he'd even see

me like this, alone. I must have wounded him so many times, and he'll have these memories, yet I'm like a blank sheet. I can write afresh.

'Here we are.' He lights three candles with pungent scent and places them around us. There's an old blanket on the ground and a few tatty cushions.

'I've shaken it all out to get rid of any ants.' He pulls open the cool box and rips off two beer cans from their plastic holder. 'There you go.'

I snap the top and slurp the froth off. 'How does it feel to have me here?'

'Weird.' He raises the can. 'Here's to meeting again.'

'Do you think you can? Meet me again?'

'I am meeting you again. If I didn't know better, I would say the accident has changed you into someone else entirely.'

'Talking of which, I think I threw a right old wobbler when I went to church this morning.'

'Wobbler?'

'I mean, I lost it.'

'How come?'

'Well, I managed to disrespect our whole Southern heritage, be really rude to Senator Robert Raines and piss my parents off like you wouldn't believe.'

'I'll drink to that.' He raises his beer, and we clunk. 'How did you manage that?'

'I told them the truth as I now see it. Mom says she's thinking of killing herself as I've regressed to being sixteen.'

'I remember that the first time around. It must have been one helluva show.'

'Is that why you married me? You must have known my background, what I believed in?'

'You were going through a rebellious period. We were very young and pretty naïve, possibly even really stupid. I thought I could change you, and you thought you could change me. And the sex was hot!' He grins at me. 'Don't worry; I'm not expecting any matrimonial duties tonight. That went out the window a long time ago.'

'Was that before or after I started the affair with the senator?'

'That was after I found you were sleeping with George's soccer coach. And let us not forget the guy that came after him, one of your high-class horseback riding pals. There might have been another in between, although I gave up at that point.'

'I'm not like that anymore.'

'In the hospital, you practically screamed when I touched you.'

'I thought you were the other one. He's the one I'm frightened of.'

'None of this makes sense.'

'No, but what does make sense is opening that bag of marshmallows and getting a massive sugar hit.' I open the cool box. 'And what are the chips for?'

'Balance.' He tugs out the bag, and it *pops*. 'The toasting sticks are on the barbecue over there.'

'There's something comforting about toasting marshmallows over an open fire.' I wave my stick and watch as the little white and pink things turn a golden brown.

'Unless it attracts a local grizzly bear and you have to run for your life.'

My stick is now stationary. 'What? Are their grizzlies here?'

'It's okay. You just have to remember your bear law.'

'Which is?'

'Don't run, as he can run much faster than you can. Shout a lot to see if that frightens him. Never climb a tree as they're very adept at that, and if all that fails, point to the weakest member of the group and let him eat them first.'

'You mean me? You're saying you'd let him eat me first?'

'It's called Darwinism. The survival of the fittest. By the way, your mouth is hanging open, and you might accidentally swallow a mosquito.'

'Oh! That's a joke! Ha bloody ha!' I throw a half-cooked marshmallow at him.

'Thanks.' He pops it in his mouth and looks at me. 'Do you think we can start again? I mean,' he leans forward, 'do we have a second chance? Could we make it now, and I don't mean for the sake of the kids? I mean for our sakes.'

I can feel a blush on my cheeks and hope they're prettily pink, not crimson red and blotchy. 'I must admit I do think you're scrumptious.'

'You do? Then that's good enough for me. Like I said, I'm not pushing for anything, and we're not going to be stupid tonight and ruin it all.'

'Oh!' I say.

'I could be persuaded to change my mind.'

'No, you're right. Little steps.'

'Oh!' He takes a deep breath. 'How about a swim in the lake? Are we allowed to do that?'

'As long as there aren't any sharks in there.'

He laughs. 'No sharks.'

'What about giant alligators?'

'Only a few little ones. Just bang them on the nose if they try to have a bite.'

'I'm not going in.'

'That was a joke. We don't have gators here, you know that.'

'No, I don't. Are you sure?'

'Come on.' He drags off his T-shirt and kicks off his shorts. He's in black boxers, holding out his hand. I touch fingers with him and feel a tingle twizzle up my arm, like a tiny electric shock. A nice one. I shimmy out of my top and skirt, feeling bashful, showing myself in my lacy knickers and bra. The momentary euphoria is radically different to the shock I get when I splash into the lake.

'Woo, that's cold.' This is how I remember swimming.

'You've been spoiled with that big pool of yours. Now you're going to have to rough it.'

I'm under the water before he's finished the sentence, and I'm off, heading out to where I can see moonlight dancing on the surface. As I breach the shadows of the trees, I can see the big, fat yellow moon as it crests the hills on the other shore. I know it's an optical illusion, but it's vast and practically golden, and I swear I can feel heat radiating off it. I dip under and push my hair back, squeezing the water out.

'God, you were off so fast I nearly lost you.' Nick is beside me. 'Your poor head. Oh, Cassie, I didn't realise.'

I finger at the stubble that is painfully slow in growing back.

'Cassie?' There's something in his voice, which makes me turn to him. We're paddling about in circles, but as the moonlight glides over his face, I can see fear in his widened eyes.

'What! It's the alligator, isn't it!' I thrash around, but he pulls me close. He's not staring romantically into my eyes; he's staring at the side of my head.

'It'll grow back.'

'What's that scar?'

'That's probably where I head-butted a London taxi. What do you think it is?'

'Not that scar.' He touches a part of my skull. 'This one! I've never seen it before.'

I reach up and touch where he's touching. I know the alligator is right behind me as the fear threatens to drag me down.

'I tried to leave him,' I lose the ability to move; my arms and legs aren't responding. 'He came home while I was packing, and he hit me and kept on hitting me. His ring did that, tore off part of my skin and hair, and he knocked out a tooth. I saw it fly across the room.' The water rises up over my face.

A voice is coming from a distance. I can feel something soft under me but what's under that is a bit lumpy. The smell is familiar, burning wood and smoke, with a hint of lemon. I must be back by the campfire, but how did I get here?

'Cassie?' I can feel Nick's breath on my cheek.

My eyes flutter open like they're mechanised. My sight is a little blurry. I can see firelight reflected in Nick's greeny-gold eyes as if they're on fire. Although I'm concentrating on his face, I see the movement behind his shoulder. Nick jerks sideways, and there is the most awful sound I've ever heard. The sound of a skull being caved in, smashed, shattering. I try to grab hold of Nick, but his body is limp, and I can see dark stuff glistening down his neck and across his shoulders.

'*Nick!*'

A shadow materialises like smoke and coalesces into a man.

'Hello, sugar. Haven't forgotten me, have you?' The man rearing above me grabs me by my hair and starts to drag me toward the water's edge. 'Told you we'd meet up again soon.'

I slap ineffectually at the hand as my hair is ripping from my skull.

'You're hurting me.' Agony focuses my mind.

'That's the idea, sugar.'

'Who the hell are you?' But I know who he is: my nightmares become flesh. I flail and thrash, but I'm like a little baby, and he's built like the proverbial brick-shithouse. 'Get off me.' I don't even stop him for a second. I twist to kick and manage to connect with some part of him, although it doesn't seem to register. Maybe he can't feel pain.

'*Help!*'

A fist punches me in my mouth. I know this. 'Don't scream, sugar. You know that only makes it worse for you.' He shakes my head, and the pain is so excruciating I nearly black out. 'Now you've caused me a great deal of trouble, my little honey-pie.' His voice is deep but raspy, like he's been eating grit. I slowly register that he has an English accent. *Oh, God!* It must be him.

I try to dig my heels into the soft sand, but we're still moving, and now I'm splashing. We must be at the lake's edge. Water is lapping up my back. He keeps on walking, and the waves slosh against my shoulders, break over my legs and creep up my chest. I'm at such an angle that I'll be submerged before he's even chest-deep. His hold on my hair doesn't lessen, and now he's got his arm around my neck.

'Why are you doing this?' I try to scratch at his eyes, but he's kept his face well away from me. I can't even see it. Terror curdles my voice, makes it thick and sludgy. I can't swallow properly as his arm is tight around my throat. My legs are heavy, cold and I don't have the strength to kick anymore.

'Why?' He sounds so normal as if we're merely conversing, but I know he means to kill me, drown me here in the lake. 'Because you ruined my life. Twice. You and the other one. I can't have that now, can I?'

'I don't know who you are. Please don't do this. I've got money if that's what you want?' Oh, God! I'm pleading for my life! *Don't do this! Don't kill me!*

'Money? I don't want your money. I want revenge for what you did to me. Got a bit of that with the slut Marcie. But it wasn't enough.'

'*I don't know what I did!*' I'm screaming now, and I think I might have wet myself. 'Oh God, you killed Marcie. Why? She's nothing to do with you.' Water slaps at my face, blinds me and fills my left ear.

'No, but she was your best friend, wasn't she? Took that away from you. All you had to do was give me an alibi. Could've saved us all a lot of grief. But oh no, you let me go down, didn't you?'

'I don't remember you. I have no idea who you are. Please don't kill me!'

'Don't remember who I am? Well, I'll tell you who I am. I'm your husband. I killed the other one, by mistake like, but then who'd have thought there'd be another you, and now I'm going to kill you. Kill you properly this time.'

Another *me*? What the hell? He's pushing my head downwards. I gulp in a breath before the cold water rushes over my face, but I've never been good at holding my breath. I know, with the fear and panic enveloping me, that I'll let it all out, and then I'll die. I pull at the arm around my throat and kick and roll, except he's like a rock, immovable and solid. I can feel my blood thumping inside my head, heavy beat after beat. How long has it been? How long can I last? My lungs are burning, and white spots dance behind my closed eyelids. I can't hold it in anymore, and as my breath bubbles out, the water gushes back into my mouth, and I suck it up my nose. It's so cold.

I'm going to die, and I don't even know *why*.

There's a muffled resonance through the water I can't identify.

His fingers loosen abruptly. I can see a well of blackness spiralling in front of me. A pinpoint of white light is at its centre, and I start to float toward it, then there's a tug.

Leave me alone.

The tug turns into a shake, and then I feel someone pounding on my chest and blowing air into me. I retch and cough. Water shoots out of my mouth. I roll over and vomit more of the lake water.

'Dad?' It's Lucy's voice, at a distance. 'Dad? Is she okay?'

'She is thanks to you.'

I open my eyes. Nick is straddling me. He has obviously given me CPR.

'You're bleeding,' I say. Red stuff is smeared all over his face and dripping down his chest.

'Well, you were dead.' He clambers off me. 'And we need to call an ambulance and the police.'

'Where is he?' I try to lever myself up, but Nick pushes me down.

'Lucy shot him.'

'What?' I sit upright, then a wave of dizziness threatens, so I lie back on the old blanket.

Lucy kneels by my side, and I can see her small frame shaking. She holds out the rifle, and Nick takes it, lays it by his knees. 'I had to. He was trying to kill you.' She starts to make a sound as if she can't get enough air into her lungs. I know what that feels like.

'It's okay, Lucy,' says Nick, pulling her into his arms. 'It was self-defence.'

'Is he dead?' I turn to look out over the lake. There's nothing to mar its perfect beauty. 'Where the hell is he?'

'I shot him,' says Lucy, 'and he let go of you. I ran to pull you out. Dad was only just coming to, and then by the time I did get you out, he was gone.' She screws up her hands into balls and knuckles at her eyes. 'I thought you were both dead. When I ran down, I saw Dad wasn't moving, and you were... You were...'

'It's alright, Lucy,' I say. 'Come on, love. We're both okay.'

But where is he?' she squeaks and waves toward the lake.

'He must have sunk to the bottom or drifted out,' says Nick, reaching for the rifle.

'Or swum to the shore further up,' I say quietly.

'We don't know if he was badly wounded or what,' Nick peers down at me. 'But the main thing here is, Cassie, why did he try to kill you?'

'He's something to do with my other life. He told me he was my husband.'

'What?' Nick holds out his hands as if pleading. 'What *the fuck* is going on here.'

I shake my head. 'He's the man from my dreams. I do know him from somewhere, although it's like looking into a tarnished mirror. I can't make out details. I can't put things in place. He said...' I close my eyes, 'he said it was my fault because I didn't give him an alibi.'

'What for?' says Nick.

'Haven't a clue.'

'Anything else?'

'Yes, something about killing someone else by mistake.'

'Did he mean Marcie?'

'No. He said he killed her to spite me, but that wasn't enough. This sounded like another person altogether.' I think for a moment, try to delve through the words left in my head, not torn to shreds by fear. 'He said it was another "me".'

'This is too much,' says Nick. 'We need to call the police now.'

The distress in Lucy's voice breaks my heart. 'Have I killed a man?'

'No, Lucy,' I say. 'Even if you had, your dad is right. You were saving my life. I'd be dead now if you hadn't done what you did. Thank you.'

Lucy is as wet as the rest of us, and I can see the tears streaming down her face. 'If he killed Marcie, why would he want to kill you, too? What's he got to do with you? If he's your husband, which of course he can't be, *why* does he want to kill you?'

I turn back to Nick. 'I fainted out on the lake, didn't I?'

'Good job I've got my lifeguard skills honed.' There's a catch in his voice. I realise this is his way of dealing. Play it down, make it funny.

'I think,' I say, tentatively rubbing my jaw, 'you dragged me back by my neck. Mind you, I've had an evening of being dragged around by my neck.'

'Isn't that how you're supposed to save someone from drowning?' I can see his eyes are also wet.

'Nick? Why did I faint?'

'Well,' Nick rocks back on his heels. 'Um.' His fingers worry at the back of his head and come back smeared with blood. How badly has he been hurt?

'Dad?' I feel Lucy creep closer to me on the old blanket by my side. 'I don't understand what's going on.'

'Your mom has a scar that her other husband gave her when he beat her to pulp.'

'That's impossible.' She's shivering but not from the cold. She must be going into shock.

'Then how do you account for this?' He gently pushes my damp hair back further.

I smile at Lucy and poke at an incisor. 'And I lost my tooth. I found it under the bed a couple of weeks later, after I'd been discharged from the hospital. Callum super-glued it back on.'

'He did what?' Lucy pulls me into her arms. 'Callum? That's his name?'

'He said he didn't want any trouble, and it was easier like this. He was really pissed when he did it, so I'm lucky he didn't just glue my mouth together.'

'Mom, none of this can be real.'

'Oh, it is real. He killed her, killed the blonde woman.

That's what he means by the "other one". Killed her dead, and it was supposed to be me. Came back to finish the job.'

'What blonde woman?'

'Why, that'll be me.' For one moment, I understand, can see it and then I've lost it. I look up at Nick. 'You need to get your head seen to.'

'*What* blonde woman?'

'What do you mean, what blonde woman?'

He's staring at me in such a way that I can practically hear his thoughts: *you need to get yours seen to too.*

While we're changing into dry clothes, we align our stories.

'Listen,' says Nick, 'we only tell them that Cassie was attacked by the campfire. We don't say anything about this Callum or about Cassie's so-called other life. Agreed?'

Both Lucy and I nod. After all, what could we say that would make sense to anyone?

The police go over our statements at the local station, and we are told that they have called in experts to search the lake for a body. The rifle is taken as evidence. We admit our guilt but plead that it was in self-defence. The police doctor is called to examine me.

'Mrs Davenport,' he says as he raises my chin and checks my throat and scalp. 'I think you've had a bad time of it recently. I read about your accident in the *Madison News*. I'm going to give you some pain killers that would knock out an elephant. Do you need any tranquillisers?'

'Not me, though my daughter Lucy might need something. She's in shock.'

'The possibility that she has killed another human being rests heavily on the soul. I'll see her after I've seen you.'

Photos are taken.

'What happens now?' I ask the police officer who's been assigned to me.

'I think it all depends on whether they find a body. It looks like he's someone who has either got a grudge against your family or you personally. You think it is the same man who killed Marcie Harper?'

'Yes.'

'Do *you* have any idea why?'

'No, but I told you he said I'd be next. Do you remember that?'

'Yes, we do.' The police officer had the grace to look sheepish. 'But we still need to find a motive. We're putting out an all-points bulletin for his arrest. We have an artist's impression of him, and we have the type of truck he was driving and the fact that he's supposedly English. He can't get far.' He sighed loudly. 'Just wish we knew why. We'll assign someone to keep an eye on you.'

I found out as we drove home that Nick gave them all sorts of reasons why. But not one that was the truth.

Do I pray that they find a body, even if that means that Lucy is tried for involuntary manslaughter? I keep my thoughts hidden even from God.

30

REALITY BITES HARD

W e're going in convoy to St. Luke's. The white, casually dressed, plain-clothed police officer they've assigned to protect me has not been invited, for which he seems eternally grateful and a little perplexed. He looks about sixteen if a day and has only a few chin hairs and a sprinkling of blackheads across his nose. Looks to me like the police are really taking me seriously. Not!

'You're all going to the black church?' He scratches at his nose. 'I mean the *black church*? Really?'

'Things to do, my friend,' says Nick.

'At the black church?' We must be speaking some alien tongue as his brow furrows, but he doesn't insist on coming. Force of numbers, I suppose.

Nick nods and puts both his hands on my shoulders. 'You don't have to go through with this, Cas. There's still time to back out.'

'Hey,' I look down and bite my bottom lip. 'That was some pep talk.'

'I'm not going to cajole you into this. You have to do this freely.'

'Then let's do it.' My legs are shaking, although I don't want them to see how frightened I am. I'm in a pair of black trousers and a white shirt with three-quarter length sleeves. My shoes are flat, all the better for running should the need arise.

Nick is driving George and me, and Dolores is going with Lucy and Tyreese. The drive is pretty through the woods, and as we leave the lake behind, I wonder what else we're all leaving. Atlanta is a beautiful city. On a day like today, with a soft blue sky and fluffy clouds and the sun warming the skin, there couldn't be a better day to change your life.

'Parking is getting tricky,' says Nick. 'We can walk to the church easily from here.' The other car pulls in behind us, and we gaggle together on the pavement.

The church has a steep roof and a curved porch entrance. People are milling about outside, calling greetings and embracing. What are we doing here? I stop walking.

'Cas?' Nick hovers uncertainly at my side. 'Are you okay? Especially after everything that's happened recently?'

We've managed to keep some of the details of the attack out of the news. The police have been circumspect, with no leaks that could hinder the capture of the perpetrator. However, the sensational headline splattered over the local *Madison News* read: *"Cassie Davenport attacked in own homestead. Daughter Lucy defends her with a rifle"*. You can imagine the glee of the American Gun Association aficionados and the pro-gun lobbyists. Not to mention my mom and dad.

'It's certainly been a tough few days,' I say. 'I must admit, I've got the collywobbles.'

'The what?' George sniggers.

'I think she means she's frightened shitless,' says Lucy. 'She's not the only one.'

I start walking again. Once I'm through the door, there's no turning back.

'Dad!' Tyreese trots over to a grizzled man wearing a dark suit and tie. As we approach, his dad grins.

'Never thought I'd live to see this day. Mrs Davenport, I can't say it's a pleasure but welcome to St. Luke's.'

'Dad,' Tyreese is actually blushing. 'Don't be rude.'

'That's not rude, son. That's the truth. Now, if Mrs Davenport does what she says she'll do, then that's a different matter.' He sweeps his hand to show us in. 'We've allocated you the front pew, all the better for everyone to see and hear you.'

'How kind of you,' I say and then stumble. The nerves are kicking in. The church is bathed in white light that streams in through tall, stately glass windows. The walls are painted white, and apart from the ornate podium in front of a raised stage, there doesn't seem to be any other ostentatious flourish that you would typically find inside a church. It's not that different to the last church I was in. Except, I expect, for the doctrine. The pews are long wooden benches, and even the cross in the nave is simply a cross, backlit, so it stands out but not shaped in any way, and there is no Christ nailed to it in agony. I'm thankful for that. The organ pipes sweep out like silver wings on either side. The choir are preparing themselves on the stage, dressed in white robes with deep red bands around their necks and cuffs embroidered with silver crosses.

The large congregation turn to look at us. I have a sneaky suspicion by the way they are staring at me with their mouths open that they know who I am. We are herded toward the front and the *pew of redemption*.

There is a vast space around us as if we've been cordoned off.

'Have we got an invisible force field around us?' George indicates the area that separates us from everyone else.

'Sit down.' Nick pushes us all into our spaces. He seems

worried. He knows better than I do what this all means. 'Have you got your speech ready, Cassie?'

'I've got it here.' I wave the notes I'd made but whether I'll use them is another matter.

The congregation slowly settles, and then the show begins. The reverend is an animated man who can throw his voice to the very back or make you crane forward in your seat to hear his whispered words. He doesn't need a microphone as he has the power of God inside him.

'We have new members in our congregation today, and so I'm going to say a few words of welcome to them. You've heard these words before, but I don't think there has been a day when they are so apt.'

The assembled group start to hum.

'We started our church in a boxcar, sent to us by our brethren in Chattanooga in 1862 before the Civil war. That first boxcar, used for education as well as worship, was the start of what became Atlanta University. Now look at where we are, in this most beautiful of churches.' He's looking down at us. 'And here we are, inside St. Luke's, bathed in God's light. I welcome old friends,' he nods at the rest of the congregation, 'and new friends,' he smiles at us. 'Here we honour God's word. We are a family of faith. Hallelujah!'

'Hallelujah!' shout the congregation.

'That the name of Christ be exalted is our fervent prayer and that all may know that our Lord Jesus Christ is our liberator.' He steps from behind the podium. 'Today we have someone very special who has asked to say a few words, here, inside St. Luke's.' His hand is reaching down for me. 'We have with us today someone who I think most of you will know. Mrs Cassandra Barber- Davenport.'

I stand, and then my legs are moving of their own volition because the rest of me wants to be sprinting for the door.

'I believe there is something you wish to express to us?' His eyes are gentle and he has an encouraging look on his face.

I cough. 'Um, yes.' There is a prolonged silence as I try not to focus on the few hundred or so faces out in front of me. Maybe some are merely curious, some might well be angry that I dare step foot here in their sacred place, except all of them are waiting to hear what I have to say. My family join me on the stage.

'I've spoken in front of twice this many people before, and the words have come easily to me, but these are not the words I have to say to you today.' I swallow loudly and feel heat flaring up my neck and burning my cheeks. 'My name is Cassie Davenport, and for all my life, I have spread words of hate and fear, I have even encouraged the culture of fear in this country, and I have done it with energy and gusto. I have stated that all of America should be armed, but most importantly, against you. This was my upbringing. This is what I believed until now.'

'Get out. We don't want you here!' The voice comes from somewhere in the middle.

Brows are furrowed as well they might be, and I can hear rumblings like a pack of angry dogs.

The reverend steps forward and raises his hands. 'Let her speak. You will be surprised.'

I plough on. 'So what has changed, you might say? A few weeks ago I had a terrible accident, and when I woke up, I was lucky to be alive, except I couldn't remember a thing about my life. Not a thing, and so I had to relearn, like a tiny child, who I was, and as each part of the puzzle that was Cassie Davenport fell into place–' I stop and clutch at my chest.

'Cassie?' Nick holds me by the elbow. 'We're with you. You're doing fine.'

I nod and then shout out across the church. 'The woman that I found myself to be was loathsome. Imagine waking up to find that every aspect of your personality is reprehensible. That you disagree with every statement made about you, that they have to show you evidence of what you were for you to believe it and then when you see it's all true, what can you do?'

The room is silent. No bums are wiggling on the hard benches, no movement whatsoever, no coughs or clearing of throats, no babies crying or children whispering.

'I'm here with my family, my husband, my daughter and son. And with special friends.' I look at Dolores, who nods and mouths something at me. I continue. 'We're all here to say that we can't wipe out hundreds of years of the pain and misery that our family has inflicted on yours. We can only say that it stops here with us.' I hold out my hands to my family. 'It stops with us now.'

Lucy takes my right hand, and George takes hers. Nick is on their other side as Dolores steps to take my left. 'We will undertake to use our energies, resources and facilities to help our black community in any way we can.'

A single person who starts to clap very slowly breaks the long silence. A beat builds up, and then another joins in until the applause is thunderous.

The reverend waves them quiet. 'The vision of our church is to become a church full of the Spirit of Christ, attracting all people and striving to expand. I know it must have been the hardest thing that our sister Cassie has ever had to do, to stand up in front of all the people that have been wronged by her family and to say, "I'm sorry." As she said, she cannot take back the wrongs, but now she can start to make it right.' He lays an arm across my shoulders. 'I applaud her for her strength in coming forward. I applaud her for her moral fortitude. Cassie Davenport, you are indeed welcome in our church.'

Tyreese has joined us at the foot of the stage. He holds his arms wide. 'I also have to do something, and I need you all to keep it down. I don't want to miss the answer.'

A few startled whispers follow but others *shhh* them.

'Lucy Barber-Davenport,' Tyreese lowers himself onto one knee and holds out a small black box. 'Will you do me the honour of becoming my wife?'

I feel her hand clench in mine, and there's a mass intake of breath from those who are watching, but most of all from me. I don't like surprises. When I've seen stuff like this on TV, all I've ever felt is mortification for the poor sod whose intended turns on her heel and runs away. Oh, please let her say "yes".

Time, that funny old thing seems to be stretching before Lucy finally squeaks, 'Yes, yes, yes!' She's in his arms, and I've come over all maternal and teary. Nick is congratulating them both, and everyone is whoop-whooping and calling out.

Dolores is still holding my hand. 'You did it. Well done, Cassie.'

I watch as Tyreese places a small glittery ring on Lucy's finger. It's not the size of a golf ball as I would expect a Davenport to wear, but it's got love in every molecule.

The reverend is speaking, but I barely hear his words apart from "momentous day". Yes, it is. It is indeed. I am filled with joy, and as the choir starts up, belting out a traditional gospel anthem, a group of dancers climb the stage and start to dance, worshipping their God through movement. I am swept along with the rhythms and the ecstasy. I stand, wave my arms, and dance like I'm on drugs because that is how this feels. We are all expressing our love, and I am enveloped in this strange and wonderful feeling that I think might be called *happiness*. I'm not entirely sure, as I don't think I've ever felt it before.

'We have to have the reception at the lodge,' says George as we're driving back toward the lake. 'And I'd like to volunteer as the wedding planner. I've always wanted to be one, and I know I'll make a good job of it.'

'Of course, you will,' says Lucy, sitting in the back with him. 'You have a great eye for such things.'

'We have to tell Grandma and Grandpa before they find out via the newspapers,' says Nick.

'Oh hell!' I snort. 'I've forgotten about them. I'll break it to them this afternoon. I'm sure they'll be fine about it.'

'I presume you've got your fingers crossed behind your back, Mom?' Lucy hangs over the back of my seat. 'Tyreese will be lucky if he just loses his job. I think it's best if we get everything he owns out before they torch it all and then tell them from a great distance.' She pauses. 'Like Canada.'

'I'm with Lucy on this,' says George. 'We've got to get Dolores out as well. Your parents are vicious and cruel, but they're not stupid. They'll know she's got something to do with it too, and we know what they can do.'

'Yep, Canada is great this time of year,' says Nick.

'You mustn't forget to find that other phone,' says Lucy and my world comes crashing down. I'd forgotten about that too.

31

BETRAYAL

'This doesn't look good,' says Nick after we'd dropped everyone else off at the lodge to change cars. Lucy will drive Tyreese and Dolores up the back lane, so they can get their stuff, hopefully without being spotted while Nick and I go in the front way. We didn't enlighten the police boy of our intentions, leaving him drinking cola out by the edge of the lake, flipping stones and staring intently at the water. Maybe I shouldn't mention alligators...

The drive is too short. Dad is waiting out on the porch, and the word "livid" springs to mind. The others had better be quick.

'Someone's got to them ahead of us. Damn,' says Nick, 'I wanted more time. We're going to have to tough it out.'

We've barely climbed out of the car before he is down the steps. 'What have you done? I get a phone call from our local paper saying that you've been in the black church and told them all you're sorry for what our family has done to them. Is this true? I told that man he was truly mistaken because no child of mine would ever do such a thing.'

'Oh, it's true,' I say and then duck as his hand lashes out, so he misses. 'I've had my fill of that, and if you ever try to lay a hand on me again,' I lunge at him, 'I'll break your fucking arm.'

'Don't you speak to me like that. Don't you *ever speak to me like that!*'

'Or what? What will you do? Shoot me? I'm going in to get what's mine, and then we'll be off.'

'What part have you played in all this?' He turns to Nick. 'How have you stabbed this family in the back?'

'With a great big knife, I would presume.' Nick raises an eyebrow. 'Don't worry. We won't be staying—'

There then comes a cry so high and piercing that it feels like we have been physically cut with a razor blade.

'Margaret?' Dad is practically snarling. 'What now?'

Mom comes to the door and clings to the frame. 'How could you?' She's sobbing, and fat tears are rolling down her cheeks like two tiny waterfalls. 'You've sullied the family, brought shame and degradation to our door. Oh, sweet Jesus! Lucy has said she'll marry Tyreese!' She slumps onto the porch.

'Sorry if we've messed up your make-up, Mom.' I push past her, and she really starts to wail.

'*She's what?*' Dad comes at me, but again I dodge. 'What is happening here? This can't be true. Tell me it's not true!' He clenches his hands together. '*Tell me!*'

'All right,' says Nick. 'We'll spell it out for you. Your granddaughter is going to marry a black boy.'

'I'll kill you for this!' His spit showers me.

'Get in line!'

I'm through the door and pounding up the stairs. There's only one thing I really want from my room. I tug the small drawer in the writing bureau open and tweak out the locket. I know I don't have time, but I prise it open. Inside are two cut out faces. I recognise them from the photo downstairs, the one where Nick is looking at me. Closing my eyes for only a second,

I kiss the locket and tuck it deep into my trouser pocket. Then I find my other phone. I hold it like it might bite me. But I also stuff my new clothes into a hold-all, and then I'm back down the stairs where I find Mom and Dad screaming at Nick. Their combined rage has left the both of them nigh on incoherent. Which is probably a blessing.

Nick says nothing, although his face is beetroot red.

Dad finally finds his voice. 'Betrayer! God will judge you, and you will be sent to the fiery pits of hell!'

'You brought all this on yourselves,' Nick steps forward until his face is level with Dad's. 'You do not take the moral high ground with me. All this wealth has come from the misery of others, and yet you believe that God sanctioned this? Do you really think any loving God would want this? And what if you'd been born black all those years ago, then it's alright for someone to enslave you and destroy your life?'

'You blaspheme! I would never have been born black.'

I butt in, although I'm careful to keep my distance. 'That's convenient, except you'd soon change your tune if you had been.' I wave at Nick. 'Come on, time to go.'

'You'll pay for this, you little bitch!' My mom has finally shown her true colours. She's still kneeling like she's praying, but I don't think it's for forgiveness, more like vengeance.

'I already have,' I shout back, and we leave them in a spurt of dust and a honk of the horn.

They have all read the texts. I can't bear to look at them again.

'There's a recent voicemail from you,' says Lucy. 'Look, it's your number.' She hands the phone back to me.

'Really?' I take it from her. 'Oh yeah, I phoned it before Dad gave it back to me.'

'You think his name is Callum?' George rests his chin on his hand. 'This man who's after you?'

'Yes. I should've known better after Craig.'

'Who is Craig?'

'My stepfather.'

'Of course, he is,' says George. 'Stupid me. He's obviously a wicked stepfather, or he wouldn't be in this tale–'

'Oy, this isn't a fairy tale with the wicked witch and the evil whoever. It's bloody real, and those texts bear me out.'

'Yes,' says Nick, 'but how does this all fit together unless you've been living two completely separate lives. All the stuff you've told us bears no relation to what we know you were doing at the same time.'

'I don't know either.'

'I've got an idea,' says George. 'Where are your diaries? You've written a diary every day of your life as far as I know so surely, you'd have written about what was going on in England? Even if it's only a few lines?'

'That's brilliant, George,' says Nick. 'It would have been even better if you'd mentioned them before we went over there the last time?'

'Only just thought of them. Sorry.'

'Do we have any idea where they are?'

'Ah!' George sucks on his teeth, and I resist the need to slap him. 'Houston, I think we might have a problem.'

'Where are they?'

'Dolores said that you keep them under a loose floorboard in your study.'

'Back at Mom and Dad's?'

'Where else?'

'Bollocks! That means I have to get in, and I'll probably be done for trespassing.'

'Or shot at.' George nods. 'You know how good a shot Grandpa is.'

'Thanks for that, George. That's a weight off my mind!' I poke at him with my foot. 'That's called sarcasm in case you missed it.'

'I'll go with you.' Nick gets up. 'After I've had another cup of coffee.'

'What? We're going now?'

'They're disorientated, so it'll be better sooner rather than later when their troops will be rallying.'

'Troops? They have an army?'

'Come on, Cassie. They're an integral part of right-wing American society, which has just had its butt kicked and lost a daughter's support, and their church has lost a member to a rival church.'

'Put like that, I can see where you're coming from. Let's go.' It's then that I notice the texts are no longer seven; they're eight. I turn from Nick and scroll down to read the new one.

It's dated the day that Marcie was killed.

You'll be next. X

There's no 'C', but I feel like things are piling up too fast, and I'm losing track. I haven't made a mistake and missed this one when I read them before, have I? But no, the date bears me out. It's the heavy breather who was on the line and didn't answer. It must be him. It must be Callum. I was next, wasn't I? But he didn't complete the job. My world is disintegrating around me, cracking into myriad facets and falling sharply to earth. I believe I will eventually get speared by a piece.

In the car, we have to decide on our strategy.

Nick says, 'Do we ring the bell and go in through the front door or shin up the drainpipe onto the balcony?'

'I vote for the drainpipe.'

'We'll park up the lane and hide the car in the woods and come via the stables. We can see what's going on then.'

Nick wasn't wrong when he said they would call in the troops. Cars are working their way up the driveway and parking at angles, their occupants piling out in stiff and prickly poses. Anger exudes from them.

'My God, we're going to have to be careful here.' Nick points at a group standing to attention like they've got broom handles down their trousers. 'You've got two senators and the leader of the Atlanta American Gun Association in that group, not to mention a few congressmen, and there's even the Governor of Georgia.'

'Not good then? Should we come back later? Like in a decade or two?'

'Do you want to find out the truth or not? All that over there is immaterial compared to what you're going through. Listen Cas, you are entitled to those diaries.'

'And you know that Dad has the police in his pocket.'

'He's so proud of that. Money can get you anything.'

'Well, if he calls the police, we don't stand a chance.'

He leans over me and whispers, 'Have you got a police record in England then?'

'Ha, bloody ha!' I look around. 'Maybe I have. How the hell should I know? Anyway, there's a bit of a lull in bodies. If we're going to do it, it should be now.'

We hunker down and dodge from bush to bush. Most of the activity is on the other side of the house. There is a wisteria the size of a tree growing up around the struts of the porch. It's not as hard as it looks, as there are many gnarly branches to grab hold of. We're soon over the rail and crouching low. It's quiet, so we creep around to my study window, but it's either been locked, or it's jammed.

'If we bang too hard,' Nick's voice is in my ear, 'they'll all come running.'

Whichever it is, we can't get in. I'm loath to try my bedroom, yet there's no other way. We push our way in and close the shutters. Listening at the door reveals nothing, but then the doors are thick. It could be that all of them are waiting on the other side, ready to pounce on us when we emerge like blind moles into the light.

I twist the handle, and it makes a tiny squeaking sound. I stop, my hand shaking.

'Go on,' he mouths.

I pull the handle down and open the door a crack. Outraged voices can be heard mumbling from below. We slink out and into the study next door, closing it behind us and then barring it with a tilted chair.

Dolores had told us the approximate whereabouts of the floorboard, so it's easy to find it. Lifting it, I delve around and find a shoebox. I prise it out of its hole. There's another one below it and another below that.

'There's no way we can try to sneak out of here with this many boxes,' says Nick. 'We'll have to try and look at them as fast as we can and pick the most recent.'

Dust gets up my nose, and I cough. Nick clamps a hand over my mouth.

'Shh!'

We daren't risk the light, so we prise the shuttered window open and search through the diaries by the crack of sunshine they allow in. There are years' worth of journals here. But where do I start? Much as I long to read about my life right from the beginning, I know we have to find the most recent. I pull them all out in a cascade, and they land about my legs like flapping fish taking their last breath. The early diaries are easy to identify, with stickers and Disney characters and childish handwriting. They morph from diaries to journals. The writing gets more adult as well as the content. Nick is flicking through them; we are both feverish until I find two that have heart-shaped locks on the front with tiny keyholes. They are dated from the year before. Where have I hidden the keys? Do I really have time to search?

'These two?'

He nods. 'Out the window?'

But there are now voices outside on the balcony. One is Senator Raines, and the other is my father.

'I can't believe this has happened, Bob.'

'You think any of us can?' There is the scraping of leather soles on the wooden decking and the sound of sitting down. I can picture the green chaise longue and the small table and chairs outside my bedroom. If they turn and look to their left, will they spy the open window of the study? Something clinks, and I realise that drinks are being poured.

'Betrayed by our own child,' says Dad. 'I never thought this would come from Cassie. She was far too indoctrinated. And she loved her life.'

'How's Margaret holding up?'

'She brought that girl up as her own, Bob. You know she could never have her own children. She always said that if she had to pretend she was her mother, then by God, she'd be her mother. That was the pact, remember?'

'I remember. She'd have sole autonomy as to how she was brought up so she could make her into the daughter she'd always longed for. I also remember the day you brought her home. A tiny, squalling thing with lungs the size of an ox.'

'My baby-girl.' There's a terrible catch in his voice, and even now, I want to throw open the shutters and shout that *I'm sorry!* But what did he mean about my mom? That she brought me up as her own? Nick is trying to shake me off. I'm holding his hand so tightly; I might have broken some tiny bones.

'If you could have seen her mom. Oh man, forbidden fruit tastes so good, Bob. Well, you already know that don't you.'

'Do you know if she's still alive?'

'Hell, I cut off all ties with her. Just promised I'd give the child a good home, and I fulfilled my side of the bargain. Cassie couldn't have got a better life than the one we gave her, and now she repays us with this.'

'It's in the blood, and she's passed that on to her own child.'

'Margaret put all her efforts into raising Cassie. It was the challenge of turning a child from a feral background into a Southern lady. The challenge and the winning are all with Margaret.'

'I think they're calling us back down into the mêlée,' says Bob. 'Come on, William, it's time to go and face the music.'

We hear them walk off, but neither of us can move. Our ears must be bright red and burning from what we've heard.

'Nick?' I whisper.

'I'm still here.'

'I've got the diaries, and I think we'd better go.'

'You think?' He pushes the shutter, and it swings open. If anyone had been standing on the other side, I think they would have met with Nick's fist first. He helps me over the rail back on to the wisteria, and then we're off like rabbits into the wood. Any second I expect to hear the baying of the hounds and the cry of the hunting horn, but all remains quiet. Except for the frantic beating of my heart. Finding the car, we hurtle up the lane.

'Did you understand what they just said out there?' I eye Nick quickly, but I don't want to distract him as he's driving. His jaw is clamped so tightly that I don't think you could prise it open with a crowbar.

It takes a few moments for him to speak. 'I need a moment or two to digest what they said. I'll get back to you.'

'Okay, I'm not going anywhere.'

Lucy's car is parked out front of the lodge, so hopefully, it's been a successful mission.

Tyreese and Dolores are sitting in the living room, bundles of their belongings strewn across the floor, though everyone stops when we walk in.

'How did it go?' Lucy looks to Nick and then to me. She jerks her head imperceptibly toward the kitchen.

'Oh fine,' says Nick, dropping like a dead weight into a spare chair. 'Officer?' He waits while the young man ambles in. 'Couldn't give us a bit of breathing space, could you?'

The young officer looks a little discomforted. 'I'm supposed to stay with Mrs Davenport at all times, Sir.'

'Listen, son,' says Nick in his best Southern drawl. 'No one is going to threaten her while we're all around her. What d'ya say?'

'Okay. I'll be outside on the deck then.'

We all watch as he sidles out. There is silence until we see him well out of earshot.

'So what really happened?' says Lucy.

Nick rubs his face. 'We've just found out that Cassie's mother isn't Margaret Davenport.'

'You've got to be kidding.' George turns to me. 'Mom's got a different mother?'

Dolores stands up, her hand fluttering over her mouth. 'Was her mother a woman of colour by any chance?'

'How the hell did you know that?' says Nick. 'How could you know that when we've only just heard it from her own father's lips?'

'Cassie told me a few days ago she believed her mother was Afro-Latina.'

'Who told you that?' Nick is now hovering.

'No one, she's the woman in my head. Any chance of a cup

of tea?'

'Your British accent has come back,' says George. 'What the hell is going on?'

'Well, I'm not making the tea, especially as I don't drink it,' says Lucy, 'I don't want to miss a word of this.' She stretches. 'Any chance we can have a coffee instead?'

I'll go,' says Dolores. 'I might as well make myself useful here as I'm currently out of a job.'

'You're not the maid!' I can hear the anger in my voice. 'I'll make the bloody coffee, and then I'm going to read those bloody diaries, and if there's nothing in them, then I'll scream the place down.' I stamp into the small galley kitchen. 'If nobody minds, that is.'

'No, no.' There's a chorus.

The coffee must have percolated a while ago, as the pot is full. When Nick comes in, presumably to find out when I'm coming back, he takes hold of my hand. 'We're waiting for the rest of the story.' He grabs a handful of mugs and the pot and I trail behind him in a daze. 'I think we should give Cassie some space,' says Nick. He smiles at me, and the corners of his eyes crinkle. 'We'll be by the campfire when you're ready.' My family, coffee mugs in hand, file outside.

I sit cross-legged on the sofa. The two books are in front of me. I pick the one that has the earliest date on it. Is this Pandora's box? It's ironic because I've wanted to know what happened for so long, except now I might have the answer in my hand I hesitate. Oh, and let's not forget the bloody great lock on the soft leather front. A part of me wonders if the diary is bound in human skin, judging by the image I've built up of my former self. Obviously a screwdriver is called for before I lose one of my nails scrabbling to break in. I use a teaspoon instead, and the lock *pings* off and shoots across the room. My fingers are trembling so much I can hardly open the front cover.

32

THE DIARIES OF CASSIE BARBER-DAVENPORT

The Diary of Cassie Barber-Davenport.

I read through the first few pages, but it's all about Caesar. It seems I write utter drivel. After numerous entries detailing a lot of horseback riding, shooting and gun rallies, I start to flick, then one entry catches my eye. It's dated about eighteen months ago.

> *I can't believe I just got that through the post. What a way to let someone know something like this. A letter. Do I believe it? This is insane. I'll have to go check it out. I should tell Papa, but I know he'll go nuts about this. He'll say it's someone hitching a ride on the gravy train, and then he'll make sure they meet some of his "associates". But I can't let that happen, so I've booked a flight, and I'm going on the "red eye" tomorrow. I've told Mom and Papa some bullshit story, so they won't ask. Why should they? It can't be true, but if it is, what should I do?*

The following entry is dated two days later.

I've met her. There's no denying it. What a fucking life! Holy shit! She tells me stuff, but I don't want to listen to her. It has no bearing on my life now. But what am I to do about her? It's a fucking fiasco, no doubt about that. I can't bear to even look at her, see the desperation in her face. Oh my God, her face. My face. It's just too horrible. To think it could have been me! God chose well that day.

I can feel my hair start to rise as if I've been gently electrocuted. Her face? My face?

The next day reads...

She's telling me about her husband, how he's such a bad man. How she made such a dreadful mistake, followed in her mother's footsteps and married the same, brutish man as her stepfather. Can I help her? The bastard is in prison, so what more does she want? To get away from him? She told me she'd tried that, but he dragged her back by her hair. If that'd been me, I'd have blown his fucking head off! She wants a new life, and she's asking me what I'm going to do about it. She wants to be me, and I'm not having that. I'm not up for sharing. I never have been. I know what her mom asked, but she's not my mom. She's not.

Who's not her mum? I see the doodle on the Post-it note. I feel like someone is stood behind me, although I can't see them. I can hear their breathing, though.

Her wallet was open, and I couldn't help just sneaking a peek. If I expected a photo of him to be the first thing I see, then I was wrong. It's a photo of her mother. I looked at it, but it was like looking at a stranger. There's nothing there, and there never will be. But I want to see what he looks like. From all accounts, he sounds like Vin Diesel or maybe that gorgeous hunk from Avatar, Sam somebody. I wouldn't kick either of them out of bed for dropping cookie crumbs. It's now my mission. I have to find out what he looks like. This could be fun. For me, I don't mean her now, do I? She wants what I've got, so I'll reciprocate in kind. I think I'll have a bit of what she's got.

There are weeks of meaningless entries until I find the next one.

Come to Mama! Hell, the boy is beautiful, like a panther or an alligator. The photo was there all along, on the wall, but I hadn't seen it. I'd like to wear his pelt for a while. She wants to know what I can do. Will I return? My flight is tonight. Although I don't think I'll come back for her, I'll definitely return for him. I've been so bored recently, so what a laugh this all is.

There are sparkles of light going off in my head. A picture on the wall... Someone in the kitchen? It takes another diary, but the teaspoon is on hand. The cold envelops me like I've slid my body into a freezer pack. There's more drivel, and then I find it.

It was so easy. They were so accommodating. I put on my red dress that shows my cleavage, my high heels, and I've dyed my hair dark, so I look like her. My perfume was expensive, too expensive for him. I looked beautiful, and he sure wasn't expecting that, not after her. She's a dowdy little mouse compared to me. I kept my eyes lowered until I heard him sit down behind that glass partition. When I looked up, he's everything I expected. Such a pretty "bad boy". I know I made his blood boil, and then I knew I had him. They all stared all right. Hadn't seen a woman like me for an age, I'll bet. I played him. I caught him. And I could do that British accent like it was truly mine. He's a monster, and I've never had a monster. What'll it be like to ride a beast like him? Maybe I'll find out one day. They can't keep him locked up forever. Poor little Joni.

Joni?

I start to shake. A letter falls out. It was tucked at the back of the diary. It's pretty crumpled, so it's either been read a few hundred times, or it's been scrunched up. As I open it, I know I must read it, yet something stays my hand. The handwriting is so familiar that it feels like there's the weight of a body across my chest. I flatten it out...

If you are reading this letter, then it must mean that something has happened to me, and Joni has sent this to you as I asked her to.

This is the second-hardest thing I will ever have to do, and I hope that it is for the right reasons. I don't know if this is a selfish act, an attempt at redemption, or forgiveness, but this is to tell you that I am your true birth mother. I can never know what your father William has told you. I will have to assume that you don't know anything of my existence or that of your twin sister Joni. The time I spent with your father was the most magical of my life, but when I became pregnant, he left me. It was only then that he told me of his connections in America, who he was and what he stood for. He called me his "brown sugar", his illicit love, and he let me know that there could be nothing more between us. He must have relented because he returned one day and demanded his child. I had you in my arms. He told me he could give you a better life than the one that lay with me. He took you, and I gave you up, not willingly because I loved you, but it was because I loved you that I let him take you. I didn't let him know about your twin sister Joni. I wanted one of you for myself.

Something drips onto the paper, and the words begin to smudge and meld.

It was fate that day. Another moment and it could have been Joni in my arms, and you asleep and silent in the bedroom. I'm asking you now, if you have a good life, then share it with your twin, as once you did inside of me. Joni has known only deprivation and misery. That life could have been yours. All I ask is that you can show compassion and mercy, even after so many years.

I leave it with you, my beloved daughter, and I truly believe that although you may never be able to forgive me, you will do the right thing by Joni.

I am, forever, your loving mother, Alicia x

The dam breaks and the memories flood over me until I drown. Alicia! *My mother, Alicia!* I scream.

'Mom? Mom?' Lucy's voice is near. I can feel her hands trying to find a pulse on my throat. There's panic twisting at the edge of her voice. 'Are you okay? Mom? What happened?'

'I'm not your mum.' I say to Lucy. I realise I'm still sat on the sofa but it feels like a million years have passed by in between.

'What?' There's a waver in her voice.

'I'm not your mum, Lucy.' I open my eyes and drag myself to a sitting position. 'I'm your aunt.'

'I don't understand what you're saying.'

'I'm your Aunt Joni. I'm Cassie's sister. Twin sister if you haven't worked it out yet.'

'What the hell are you talking about. Of course, you're my mom!'

'Read the bloody diary. Oh my God. He killed her.' Hot tears are splashing down my cheeks. 'I remember everything. I remember it all.'

'What are you saying? I don't understand.' Hysteria is now in Lucy's voice, and who can blame her?

'I knew this wasn't my life.' I stumble to my feet, but they're made from lead and won't follow even the most basic instructions. I fall sideways near the sofa, pulling off a seat cushion which I hug to me.

'Fuck me, none of this is my life!'

The others are running in.

'Cassie! What's wrong?' Nick turns and sees Lucy, now sobbing at the other end of the sofa. 'Lucy?'

'Mom's gone mad!' Lucy makes the sound that I associate with wounded animals. Yes, I've wounded her, although I'm beginning to realise that it's not entirely my fault.

'No, I'm finally sane. Shut the door, and I'll tell you everything.'

'Mom's dead?' I don't want to look into Lucy's eyes. 'Callum killed her?'

'I'm sorry to say this,' says Dolores, 'from all accounts, she brought it on herself.' Dolores has her arm tightly about my shoulders. 'This wasn't Cassie... I mean Joni's fault.'

Nick has the same look as Carrie when she has the bucket of blood thrown over her at the school prom. 'I can't believe she's dead.'

'What,' says Lucy, 'did your mom just toss a coin and give one of you to Grandpa and then she got to keep the other?'

'Looks that way,' I say. 'How strange. I wanted her life badly, all the money she had and the lifestyle, but I could never envision what that actually meant. She made it out to be so glamorous, and I was so jealous. And then she wanted what I had, and all I had was misery.'

'She got a little taste of that, didn't she?' Nick shakes his head, disbelief in his eyes, and I hear him sob.

What have I brought to this family? 'Why did I post the letter that was in the Post Office Box? I set all this in motion.'

George says quietly, 'Because your mom asked you too.'

'I should have read it first and then burned it.'

'It's fate.' Lucy wipes her eyes, and black smudges cover her cheeks like a Halloween figure. 'Mom could have helped you, but she didn't. She was always greedy and never wanted to share, even with her own twin...'

'Lucy!' says Nick.

'*It's true and you know it!*' Lucy grabs hold of her hair and yanks. Tyreese pulls her into his arms but says nothing.

'She's dead and buried as someone else,' says Nick. 'We can never say goodbye properly and give ourselves closure. I can never say goodbye.'

'God,' says Lucy, 'I said awful, hateful things to her, but I never meant anything bad to happen to Mom.'

'Of course, you didn't,' says Tyreese. 'Lucy, we all say stuff in the heat of the moment.'

George wipes his nose on his shirt sleeve. 'None of us did.'

'So,' Lucy is hesitant, 'the man who tried to kill you really is Callum?'

'Looks that way. God knows how he got here, but he always said he had dodgy connections.'

'Maybe,' says Nick, 'he managed to get a fake passport? Get through customs without being recognised. I can't believe that they'd let a known British criminal who is on the run just waltz into the States.'

Lucy dabs at her eyes. 'And he also killed Marcie to get back at you?'

'Lucy!' Nick pulls roughly on her shoulder. 'Don't you lay that at your mo... at Joni's door. That's not fair. None of this is her fault.'

'She's right though,' I say, 'Both Cassie and Marcie are dead because of me. I have to live with that for the rest of my life.'

Dolores shakes her head. 'This is not because of you. Cassie chose her pathway, as did Marcie. Neither one of them was forced into dealing with this man the way they did. You can't be blamed for their actions.'

'But I led them to him.'

'But they walked to him of their own accord.'

'What are we going to do about Callum?' Nick looks at each of us in turn. 'If we let the police know about him, then we have to admit that Cassie isn't Cassie. William will disown her as fast as anything.'

'I'm not bothered about the money.' I say, and Nick shakes his head.

'You should be,' he says, 'it's just as much yours as it was Cassie's. After what you've had to endure, it's only right you finally get some payback.'

'I can't think about that now.'

'I hate to point this out,' says Tyreese, 'but he's still out there, isn't he? I don't think it's about the money. It's more about whether he's going to try again.'

'He's got to be stopped,' says Dolores, 'but the police already have all the information we can give them. If we tell them who he is, will that make it any easier to find him?'

'He sounds,' says George, 'like he's able to disappear without a trace. I think it's us that should be careful until they catch the bastard.'

I try to stand, albeit I am a bit wobbly, and grab hold of the sofa. 'I think I should get out of here. I don't belong, and you need time to grieve. I'm so sorry that I've done this to you all.'

'You're not my mom,' says Lucy, and I cringe away from her words as I've only just begun to believe that I was. 'But,' she hesitates, 'you could be the best auntie in the world.' She pulls me back to the floor, slips down by my side and hugs me, sobs racking her thin frame. I encircle her with my arms.

'Dad?' says George. 'What about you? Are you going to give her up?'

'I loved Cassie with all my heart, even all her flaws. I need time. I feel like I've already betrayed her by falling in love with her over again, and now?' He rubs his fingers through his hair and tilts his head to look at me. 'Now I find I've fallen in love with someone else.'

'I have time,' I say. 'I've never had a real family. If you give me a chance, I'll be the best at whatever you want me to be.' I look at Lucy and George in turn, but I lower my eyes, so I don't look at Nick.

I see movement out of the corner of my eye. Nick is heading out the door. 'I think I need to get my head around all of this.'

Dolores pulls me back onto the sofa and kisses the top of my head. 'Like he said, he just needs time too, *carida*.'

33

THE IMPOSTOR

I'm doubly plastered; I have a short, squat glass of bourbon in my hand, and the bottle is now more than half empty. My toothy smile and flowing blonde locks are all over the news. Again. I'm a celebrity, and I would dearly like to get out of here! Lucy and Tyreese have driven over to Atlanta to meet up with George and John. The boys have packed what they need and are booked on a flight to New York tomorrow evening. They are staying in a hotel in Atlanta for the night to get away, as Nick knows that the media circus will be camping outside all our doors very soon. Lucy and Tyreese will be joining them on a later flight. We don't want to see any of them vilified and hurt.

Cable TV shows amateur footage shot on a smartphone in St. Luke's of my speech in the church. On the radio, local shock jocks claim I'm "throwing my heritage away", discarding my "values and morals" and shacking up with the enemy. Other media networks claim I am a heroine, standing up for modern Democratic America. and express their delight at my daughter's impending marriage.

'Yeah,' I shout at the TV, 'aren't we the modern family? What with the Southern Belle getting hitched to a man of colour, the gun-toting, racist mom and her equally charming parents, the anti-gun dad and the very gay son and his cute boyfriend. We could have our own show. Whoopedy-doo-dah!' I wave the glass around and shriek, '*Up yours!*'

The local newspapers scream the headline *"Betrayal!"* and there are shots of Mom and Dad, stony-faced and grim, with their avowal of 'no comment.'

The American Gun Association don't hold back, and "vitriolic" barely covers it. I obviously never realised the fundamental part that Cassie played, how many young people she taught to use weapons, how many women she persuaded to take up arms and how many lives she'd changed through her tireless campaigning. What a woman!

'You have to take into account,' says Senator Raines, 'that Mrs Davenport has experienced a massive head trauma. She doesn't know what she is saying, and in these circumstances, all she says should be taken with a large pinch of salt.' Damage control.

But it's now a bush fire that is sweeping across the land from south to north. Lucy has told me that there are hundreds of tweets about me online, although she warned me not to read them. 'Some of them are pretty graphic,' she says.

I upend my glass and nearly choke as the fiery liquid gushes down my throat.

I hear Nick walk into the room.

'Have you seen all this?' I say. 'Holy shit!'

'Ditto. Well, it has proverbially hit the fan.'

'I never thought it would get this big.'

'I did warn you, except even I couldn't envision this.'

'Didn't we say that Canada is nice this time of year?'

'We can't hide. Not now. We have to front this out, and you have to stop drinking.'

'It's what I do.'

'Not any more it isn't. Pull yourself together, Cassie... I mean Joni. Be the woman we know you are. Dear God, if you can survive all that in England, this must be a damn walk in the park!'

'Can you at least let me finish the bottle?'

He picks it up and walks into the kitchen. I hear the *glug-glugging* as it is drained down the sink.

The young police officer has asked to be re-assigned. He feels that possibly he's not up to the job. It's getting too hot around us with the flames of racial hatred being fanned, the baring of teeth by the American Gun Association, the weirdness of family members, and the imminent threat of a psycho stalker. Dear God, why the hell did he join the bloody police force then? We've had no replacement, and they're probably still seeing who has drawn the short straw. Lucky us.

***

I hear the car as it skids to a stop outside the lodge. My "father" is getting out, and he looks mad. My "mom" is unfurling from the back seat.

'What do you want?' I can't bring myself to call him "Dad". Not any more. He may be my biological father and the one I wanted to be my real dad more than anybody, but he's not mine. He never was.

'What's this?' There's something in his eyes that makes me take a step back from him. He's holding out a Post-it note, and there's a scribble on it.

'A note?'

'Don't be facetious. Who is this?' He waves it under my nose, and I remember being in my study and drawing a face...

'Who do you think it is?'

His breathing is laboured as he shakes his head. 'You tell me.'

'It's just a face.'

'How can you have drawn this? She's not yours to remember.'

'You know who she is?'

'Where's Cassie? Where's my baby-girl?'

'I'm stood in front of you.'

My "mom" steps up to me. Her eyes are nearly closed, and there's a rigidness to every moment that screams rage. 'You're not Cassie. You've got her face and her body, but you're not her. You use strange words, you don't speak like her, and you don't believe like we do.'

'What? Have I stolen her from somewhere? Listen to yourself. I've had a message from God, like Saul on the road to Damascus. I've had my eyes opened, and I follow a new path. That's why you're having trouble accepting all this.' I turn to Dad. 'That's why I'm not your little girl anymore.'

Dad waves that scrap of paper. I can see her face. 'I could believe that if it wasn't for this.' Even in the end, she'll betray me. Alicia.

'That's only a doodle. A face I saw on TV. So what?'

'For a start, your drawing skills have never been any greater than a five-year-old kid. Where did you acquire a skill like this?'

'I've been practising.'

'This is not some face you saw on TV. It's her. I know it's her.'

'Who is she then?'

My "mom" reaches out to me, but I stumble from her.

'You know who she is, don't you? I've been told about your... racial background. I can't believe you've repaid our kindness with betrayal. It's in your genes. You can't help it. I understand that. It's what we preach every day. You can't be trusted.'

'You're an arrogant, ignorant bitch, *Mom*.'

'There's more than just this,' says Dad. He looks like he's trying not to cry. Again, some part of me wants to stop, tell him I'm sorry and beg for forgiveness, then I remember that he walked away with Cassie and left mum and me in the dirt.

He points a shaking finger at me. 'Why is your hair dark now? You used to love being the blonde bombshell. And more importantly, why can't you ride any more. You used to ride like you were one creature, not two, and then I see you ride like you're a sack of potatoes strapped to the saddle. There's something wrong here. Very wrong, and I will get to the bottom of it. Mark my words, you'll not get away with this.'

I have to risk it. 'You think I'm an impostor? Have I had plastic surgery to make me look like Cassie? Is that what you think?'

'I think you've murdered my little girl, and you've taken her place. I will find out, and I will deal with you.'

'Come away, William.' My "mom" pulls on my dad's shirt and leads him like a child to the car. He stops and turns to me. 'God will judge you and find you wanting.'

I shout, 'You're bonkers.'

'There will be retribution for what you've done.' Dad's walking away from me, and his shoulders are set hard and stiff.

'And who will believe you?'

***

It's all there, crystal bright; the "why", the "where" and most importantly, the "who" of all my visions, the puzzle pieces fitting together and what a picture it makes...

After that call from the police, panic overrides every sense. It's as if my mind has been encased in bubble wrap and I can't hear or see anything and there's only a searing light. Callum has escaped? Which means he will be coming for me. That calm voice on the phone telling me to run and hide makes me feel like he is already outside my door. What did he say that day in the courtroom? *I'll kill you!* I have to get out of there, but where can I go? Where will I be safe? I have no friends to speak of, as they've all been scared off by Callum. So I run. Hove seafront toilets? Seriously? But then I get that message from Cassie and I know she will be going to my flat, walking blithely into the jaws of the beast. And he'll be waiting for her and she'll look like me and he'll do to her what he wants to do to me. And she won't stand a chance. Yeah, I am insanely jealous of her, sometimes I hate her beyond endurance for the way things have turned out, but she is my sister, my twin, and I have to try to save her. Don't I?

As she doesn't pick up the voicemails and the police will take time, I know I have to run back to her. She'll get us both killed, *the stupid bitch.* And I haven't had a life yet. Terror and love vie against each other. My breath comes in stutters and my legs hardly hold me up. By the time I race up my street, my hands are shaking so badly that I can barely get the key in the lock. Opening the front door a crack, I peer in. Is she here? *Is he here?* Leaving the door open, I creep along the hall toward the kitchen. I hear a sound and my heart nearly stops beating. Was that a gunshot? I stop, my heart pounding, willing my feet to move. As I step forward, I see her. She's lying twisted on the floor by the side of the table and I can see red stuff spattered over the kitchen units and pooling across the floor. Light glints off her wristwatch. There is no movement. Cassie? Dead? *Is my sister dead?* Has Callum shot her? I have to tear my gaze from her as *he is* on the other side of the table, his back to me, washing his hands in the sink. Washing off Cassie's blood. Washing off the blood he thinks is mine. Had he held her as she died? Or simply checked to make sure she was dead? I spot her open bag.

I grab it unthinkingly at the same moment he turns. Callum's eyes widen and he holds out his dripping, blooded hands to me. It's as if we're both frozen in time, for a second that lasts for an eternity. I fall into his gaze and fear I can never get out. He will end me here. But then the moment is broken.

'Joni?' He stares at the shattered woman in front of us. '*What the fuck?*'

'Surprise!' I croak.

He makes an animal noise, a sound of rage, and I know what that means. He wants to kill me twice. I bolt up the hall, slamming the door behind me and kick a potted plant off the wall into his path. Will that be enough to slow him down? I have her bag. I might escape him if I can get to London, then get to... my biological father in the USA. Running to the point where each breath burns, barging past people in my way, I glimpse Brighton station ahead. I cast one quick glance over my shoulder. I don't see him. For once, there is no queue, but with my trembling, clumsy fingers, it still takes time to pull the money from my sister's designer purse and pay for the ticket. The train to Victoria is in ten minutes. I hide in the public toilets and come out a minute before the train departs. In the cubicle, I have time to think. She's lying twisted and alone in my kitchen and there is nothing I can do to save her. The grief I feel for Cassie must wait, or I will be overwhelmed. Creeping out, I scan around. Has he seen me? I long to scream. The sobs bubble up but I have to thrust them back down, deep inside of me. I can't lose control or draw attention to myself. He'll be watching for that.

Although I've looked up the hotel where she stays a million times online and imagined myself swanning through the doors to be waited on hand and foot, I am disorientated when I exit the station. Clutching her keys, I realise too late that I'm on the wrong side of the road. But I can see the doorman has recognised me, or at least Cassie. Is Callum behind me? Will he stop me even now?

The shriek erupts from me. '*Help me!*' And then I'm running, running towards my salvation, still shrieking, but there's something wrong and although I can't hear what the doorman is shouting, I know it's a warning. Has he seen Callum behind me, gun raised? I turn my head and see the horrified look on the taxi driver's face as if it's been magnified. I see the fear in his eyes, the rictus of his mouth as he yells unheard. The force of the taxi hitting me spins me. I can't believe it. I'm going to be killed by a London black taxi. What a joke! I see the key fall from my open hand.

Fuck you, God! Will you never give me a break?

But maybe, for once, God did right by me. The hotel verifies that I am Casandra Barber-Davenport. I have her passport and her hotel key, her wallet and bag. Who else could I possibly be? I am whisked back to Atlanta, to be safe in the bosom of my dear family. Except no one knows, least of all me, who I really am.

———

'Were you listening?' I walk up the steps and see Nick standing in the doorway.

'Can he prove anything? I mean, surely your DNA is the same?'

'Do you think he'd go so far as to have me tested?'

'He knows there's something that's not right here. He'll ferret it out if it's the last thing he does.'

'I'm still his daughter, whichever way you look at it.'

'You're not Cassie.'

'When I had the accident, they told me they picked me up outside the hotel she was staying in. I had her bag, with her passport and all her stuff in it. They didn't think twice that I wasn't Cassie Davenport. She'd even dyed her hair this last time to make her look like me. So she could fool Callum.'

'Yeah, well, look where that got her.'

'I still feel sorry for her, for what happened.'

'I know. We all do.'

'I wouldn't have wanted that for her, even though I was so angry and jealous that she got this life, and I got mine. I feel guilty. I think I wished her dead so I could have this.'

'You didn't really mean it.'

'Didn't I? You don't know how much I longed to get out, to be free. Did I inadvertently do this? Did God finally answer one of my prayers?'

'Don't be ridiculous! This isn't your fault. What about that picture you drew? Could that link you to your old life?'

'Mum's dead and buried in a graveyard in Hackney. I think it'd take a lot of searching to find her, and then what? I fled to Brighton after running from the kids' home and changed my name, so there's no link there. The only way he'd find out the truth is if he paraded me in front of Callum.'

'There's the link.' Nick pulls me into the living room and switches on the laptop that's sitting on the table. He types in a question. 'Look, there's a small article on a murder in Brighton.'

"A woman named Joni Stevenson was found murdered in her flat in Kemptown in Brighton. Her husband Callum Stevenson is being sought for questioning about her murder. He had escaped in transit to a high-security jail a few days before she was killed."

'He hasn't been caught,' Nick says. 'He won't be caught because they're looking for him in the wrong country.' Nick grimaces. 'Hey, they're warning about approaching him as he's possibly armed and dangerous. No shit!' He fingers at the photo of Callum. 'You're right. He does look like a beast.'

I'm not sure if I can detect a hint of jealousy in his voice. I hope so.

'Dad won't make this connection,' I say. 'The only name he had was Craig, and God knows where he ended up, but I hope it was horrible. No, I don't think he can prove a thing.'

'We'll have to work out what to tell the police if they catch Callum. He'll tell them about Cassie, won't he?'

'We'll say he killed Joni, and I walked in on it, saw him do it. Which I did. We'll say he wanted to kill me as I was a witness. How does that sound?'

'Like a plan.' Nick glances out of the window. 'I hope your pa doesn't do anything stupid.' Nick slips his arm over my shoulder. 'Come on, let's go get some dinner on, as Tyreese and Lucy will be back soon. All this fear and trepidation has made me hungry.'

'Have we got any falafel? I'm sick of cow.' I stop. I have to say it out loud, as it's going round and round my head like it's on a loop. 'They haven't found Callum's body.'

'I know.'

'Which means he's still out there.'

'I know.'

'Which means he'll probably have another go.' I dodge behind a pillar in the kitchen.

'If he does, we won't be caught off-guard like last time.' He points out a side window. 'You can still be seen through that. Listen, we can't just hide through abject fear.'

'Speak for yourself.' I pull the fridge door open and lurk behind it, pretending to search for something to cook. 'He's a fucking nutter. You can't reason with, and you can't fight nutters. Their own belief system makes them invulnerable.' I find myself holding some unidentifiable, slightly slimy root vegetable that looks like it's been at the back of the fridge since the dawn of man. I toss it back in and wipe my hands down my jeans.

'I may be the head of the Families Against Gun Violence but I can still shoot a gun as well as any ol' Southern boy.'

'Are you saying that, even though you're against the gun culture of this country, you're going to be armed?'

'Looks that way. I know what you're going to say. Hypocritical, blah, blah. But what else can we do? Wait until the bastard turns up and finishes the job or defend ourselves?'

'As "finishing the job" is not an option I'd like, then we use all the resources we have, and if that means guns, then so be it.'

We're delving through the rest of the contents of the fridge and cupboards when Lucy and Tyreese walk in.

Nick glances at me and then indicates the laptop. 'There's something you should read.'

Lucy is quietly sobbing. Little whimpers escape. I see Tyreese has his arm around her. 'She's really dead, isn't she? I still can't believe it.'

'I'm so sorry,' I say.

'Why didn't you leave him?' I can hear the outrage and scorn in Lucy's voice. 'I would have done if a man had treated me like that.'

'It's easy to say that. You must think I'm a really weak woman.'

'No. Dear God,' Lucy shakes her head, 'I never meant that.'

'It's slow, Lucy. Totally insidious. When I met him, I was struggling to survive. It wasn't only his looks. He was kind, thoughtful and he treated me well. Then it started. It was little things, and at first, you think it's because they care for you. It's only when you can no longer escape that you realise that he's a total control freak, except it's too late by then. Men like Callum ostracise you very slowly from your friends, stop you using Facebook, read all your texts without asking permission, follow you places, so you're cut off. They threaten you and hurt you, and then bit by bit, take every ounce of self-esteem until there's barely anything left of you.'

Tyreese stirs. 'Did you ever try to get away?'

'When I realised at the start what was going on, I knew I had to get as far from him as I could. You remember this scar?' I point at my head. 'He half scalped me and beat me so badly that I was hospitalised.'

Lucy clings onto Tyreese. 'Why didn't you get the police onto him?'

'He threatened to gut me.' I look at her. 'And I believed him. Would you risk that?'

Nick says, 'He obviously had the capability. Look what he did to Cassie.'

I continue. 'And Marcie.' I rub at my eyes. 'The only relief I ever had was when he was banged up for being a thieving shit. This last time, I was going to get away. I'd got my qualifications, and I was planning my escape. I'd got a job in a design studio in Manchester, but that was when I got the call from Cassie. By posting the letter that my mum wrote, my whole life changed.'

Nick interrupts. 'We also need to talk about that. We can't call you Joni, or your father will work it out. We have to carry on calling you Cassie. How do you feel about that?'

'I don't like who Cassie was, but I've heard you call me Cas. I prefer that.'

'Yeah, Cas,' says Nick, 'That'd work.'

'Lucy? Maybe we could say that you're old enough to call me by my name now. I think "auntie" might be a bit of a giveaway?'

'Okay. It'll be weird, but after the last couple of weeks, it's par for the course. I'm going to New York tomorrow to be with George. We can't grieve for Mom in public, though we still have to grieve.'

'Later we'll arrange a trip to England, for us all to say goodbye as a family,' says Nick. 'We need to do that for Cassie.'

***

I've been sitting outside on a rickety wicker chair for nearly an hour, watching the sun go down over the lake. The windows are open, and the telly is blaring. They're all inside, still poring over the varying news reports, talking quietly. I also need time to grieve, to try to compartmentalise each experience so I can handle it all.

My bum is going numb, and at the exact moment that I stand up, I hear the sound of a gunshot. There is the feeling that someone has hit me on the elbow with a cricket bat. I'm spun about like a rag dolly in a kiddie's hand, and then I'm falling onto the deck. Looking down, I can see blood pumping out of the wound. I know I'm going into shock. It feels like someone has poured sulphuric acid over the ragged hole in my arm. This isn't an accident unless the shooter is blind and has no sense of direction. Whoever has shot at me is probably going to shoot me again. I crawl toward the door and roll sideways as a second shot rings out, like in the movies. I see a puff of dust rise in the air as the bullet pierces the wood floor right by my side. An inch or so to the left, and it would've gone through my ribcage.

I can hear footsteps and the door being flung open.

'Cas!' Nick has grabbed hold of my other arm and is dragging me out of the way. Lucy is screaming.

'*Get down!*' Nick shouts, shoving Lucy to the floor. He pulls me behind the sofa. I hear his footsteps run back out. I want to warn him that someone is shooting at us, but the words don't come out.

'That really hurts,' I say, and then it goes dark.

34

GET OUT OF THIS ONE

Been there, done that and got the T-shirt. I can't believe I'm back in the hospital, yet the squeaky footfalls of the orange-hued doctor are welcome this time. It must mean I'm still alive.

'Cassie?'

I focus on him. 'Hiya?'

'Good, you're coming out from the anaesthesia, so you might feel groggy for a while.'

'Have I still got my arm?'

I know I'm mumbling, but any fool can understand what I'm asking.

'It was a bad injury, and yes, we've saved your arm. You'll have a nasty scar, although plastic surgery will be able to minimise that in time.'

'Is Nick here?'

'He's been here for the last day while we operated on you. I believe he's just gone to the cafeteria for a coffee. I think it's the only thing keeping him upright. He'll be back in a minute.'

'Was I shot?'

'I think you must be attempting a world record for the number of different ways to die.'

'I think I'll concede defeat gracefully if you don't mind.' I shy away from the bandage around my arm and try to ignore the faint smell of disinfectant that tickles at my nostrils. 'Do we know who shot at me?'

'I only know what's being reported in the media.'

'And what is that?'

'That you were shot.' He raises an eyebrow. 'Talking of which, there's an armed guard outside your room, just in case there are any more, er, incidents.'

'Is he older than sixteen?'

'I believe so.'

'That's nice to know.'

'I'll be back in a while.' The doctor pats my good hand. 'Try to get some more rest.'

I must've dozed for a moment, then I hear soft footsteps on the lino. Not so squeaky this time, and I groggily wonder if the doctor has changed his shoes? Except when I open my eyes, it's not the doctor who is leaning over me with a smile on his face.

'Hello, sugar.'

'Oh shit!'

I should've had more forethought and screamed the bloody hospital down before he clamped a meaty hand over my mouth, but I'm still groggy from the medication.

'Your little bitch girl got me good. Nearly bought it out there in the lake.' His hand is squeezing my nose closed. I thrash against him. His weight is bearing down on me, and I'm hooked up to things all over the place.

Kill me twice? Kill me three times.

Maybe I'll get in The Guinness Book of Records after all.

My mind freezes like it's been dunked in liquid nitrogen. I

can feel ice crystals crackling and growing out of my brain. He pulls a syringe from a white coat that he must've nicked somewhere in the hospital. He hums a little tune, just a refrain, and I remember it. It's what he does when he's happy. I don't want to see him push that syringe into me, but I can't wrench my eyes from him. He's beautiful, like a tiger or a cobra, their animal magnetism raw and wild, though you don't want either one of them near you without a three-inch pane of glass between you. Where the hell is the guard with the big gun?

I try to shake my head, make noises that mean something, *mnn, mnn.* Try to make him see the words in my head through my eyes, but tears are sliding down my cheeks, wetting his hand, and I know I'm done for as he hates women who cry. *Cry-baby bitches.*

'Thought I was dead, did you?' His breath huffs in my face. It smells of stale beer and heavy meat like he's chewed on a cow without bothering to cook it first. The syringe is hovering over my face, getting closer to my left eye. I twitch, and my body jerks involuntarily. 'Don't do that.' He leans down on me harder, and I glimpse a splash of rusty red across his shirt. How badly has he been hurt? Not badly enough, although it might give me the edge if I can focus through the cotton wool fluffing up and filling my skull.

'There, there, sweetheart. Don't fret so. It'll all be over soon.'

He leans down and kisses me on my forehead. His lips are dry. 'That's for the good times, sugar.' He lowers the syringe to my throat. The point pricks the surface and breaks the skin. I jump, and he slaps my face.

'Now, now. Like I said, don't be like that, Joni.' He pushes the syringe in deeper, its sting travelling down my throat. *Holy shit, what's in it?* 'And this is for the bad.' His smile is slow and tender, just like I remember.

And that's what saved me. The fact that he wanted to savour my dying. See every little bit of fear and suffering. When Nick came through the door, the syringe was barely in.

'*Jesus Christ!*' Nick slams into Callum, knocking the syringe out of his hand. I see it crack against the floor and roll under one of the chairs.

I gulp in air and then scream. Where is the bloody armed guard? I scream again and again until my voice catches. The two men grapple, thumping against walls, upending chairs and the small swing table, tangled together, grunting and snarling. Two wild dogs in a cage, but only one will come out. I don't think the odds are in Nick's favour. I try to wrestle free from the drip in my arm and fight through the covers until I stand, weak and wobbling. I fall to my knees. The bedside cabinet crashes across the floor and knocks heavily into my injured arm. I yowl like a thrashed dog. Crawling to the edge of the room, I tweak out the syringe from under the chair. Callum throws Nick across the bed and smashes a large vase over his head. Roses cascade around him like he's finished a performance at Covent Garden and the audience is ecstatic.

'*Nick!*' I struggle to stand, to stamp on the vial, but Callum's on me quicker than a viper.

'What does it take to kill you, you fucking bitch!'

I'm still holding the syringe in my good arm, but he grabs my hand, covering it entirely with his and is levering it upward. I crane my head away, but I'm losing the last bit of strength I have left.

'What's in this?'

His grin is a frightening snarl ripping across his face. 'Wouldn't you like to know?'

A memory coalesces in my mind. 'Snake venom.'

His eyes betray him. He's always wanted to see what poison

does to a human, leered at the description of the symptoms as if he were drooling at a topless female glamour model.

The door opens, and a shaft of neon light spears us. I twist and look up. The world continues outside that door. There is movement and concerned voices.

'What the–' A man in a dark uniform raises his gun and fires. I register the look of shock on his face. He may be trained, but that's different from actually shooting a real, live person. Callum is blasted off me, his body flopping sideways and blood fountaining across my face. The needle of the syringe hangs from my throat. I can feel its bite. I drop back onto the floor, hearing Nick groan from the bed above me.

'Nick?' I can't swallow. 'Nick, I love you.' Is this it? Is this how I'll die?

'Holy crap!' says the guard. I peer upward and see him, gun still held high, approach Callum.

'Watch out,' I whisper. 'He doesn't die easily.' I'd dearly like to bash his brains out with whatever comes to hand. *He's fucking killed me,* just when I really thought I'd got away. Just when I thought I might have a life. With Nick. What a laugh, eh? When did I ever get a break?

'Nor,' says the orange doctor pushing in through the door, 'do you.' He kneels beside me and very gently pulls the syringe out. I don't want to know, although I keep my eyes open. The vial is empty. *Fuck!*

'We need to get this tested as fast as possible. We'll keep you under observation until we know what we're dealing with.'

I nod at Callum, who is at such an angle that I can't see his face. 'Try snake venom. He... said something about venomous reptiles.'

'Good,' says the doctor, 'that means we can hopefully narrow it down fast.' He glances over to the corner of the room.

'Is he dead?' I need to see his face. I need to see his dead, *really dead* face.

The guard lowers his gun slowly. The muzzle is shaking. 'Sure is.' His face is a wet yellow in the light, his eyes wide and unblinking. He turns to me and licks his lips like a shamed dog. 'I am so sorry, Mrs Davenport. I have no excuse except I had a Thai curry last night with extra chillies, and I just had to go, if you get my meaning.'

'Right,' I say. *Chillies?* Is my life worth a Thai curry? Or a fucking shit? 'And Nick?' Pain tugs at me. My neck feels like it's on fire.

The guard helps Nick to stand, but he looks nearly as out of it as me.

'Is she alright?' Nick staggers toward me, and I'm worried that he'll fall on me.

'The main contents of the syringe were injected, and we need to test the liquid and Mrs Davenport quickly. Guard? Could you call for a gurney for the deceased?'

'Yeah, of course.' The guard rushes from the room, and I finally register the word: deceased.

'Is he dead?' They don't seem to understand how urgent this is for me. I need to know.

'If he isn't,' said Nick, 'he'll wish he was.'

The doctor sniffs loudly. 'We also need to get you checked out, Mr Barber. I gather this is not the first bump on the head in the last few days?'

The doctor glances up at Nick, who seems to have turned a nasty green colour. He's staring at the figure lying prone on the floor.

'I'm trying to get a matching set of scars.' Nick turns to me. His face is slack, impassive. This is too much for him. I've brought all this to his door. How could he love me, ever? Not after what's happened. I must be like a firework that's gone off in his hand and blown his fingers to shreds.

There is a clanking sound outside, and a gurney is pushed into the room by two burly men. 'I don't think Mrs Davenport should see this.' The doctor indicates one of the men. 'Could you fetch a screen, please? And you,' he motions at the other, 'can you help me get Mrs Davenport back into bed.'

The screen of dark blue material is erected around me, yet I can hear the grunts of the orderlies as they haul Callum's body onto the bed of the gurney. The wheels squeal as they roll him out. Nick is on the outside. Not with me.

'Stop,' I tug at the screen. 'I'm sorry, doctor. I want to see him. He's tried to kill me a couple of times, and I need to really know he's not coming back again.'

'Are you sure? It's not a pretty sight.'

I nod, transfixed, as the doctor pulls the cover from Callum's face. A small hole going through his temple, but his head has lolled sideways, and I can see the ragged crater the size of a tennis ball where it exploded out the back. I resist the urge to nudge him to see if he's faking it. The guard had done what they generally tell you not to do in case you missed. A head shot. It's a mess, but there's only a cold kernel deep inside of me. No remorse, no revulsion, although that might come at a later time. I let that image nestle inside of me, so I can recall it at will.

'He's not coming back.' I marvel at how steady my voice is. I touch my neck as the pain is building.

'No, he's not,' says the doctor. 'Now, I need you to tell me what you're feeling.' There's no discernible difference in his expression, except I know he's worried.

'It hurts. A lot. There's a weird tingling sensation like I've trapped a nerve.'

'Do you know what it could be?' says Nick. Now *he* can't hide that he's worried. Hasn't mastered the muscles in his face.

Wears his heart on his sleeve, and I love him all the more for it. Maybe we still have a chance?

'We're going to test for snake venom first as the perpetrator said as much to Mrs Davenport.'

'And if he misled her on purpose?' says Nick.

I know as well as he does that I'm on a time limit. If they don't find out what it is, then it may be too late for me. I'll be dead, dead, dead!

'If that doesn't come up trumps, then we'll search down all the avenues until we find it.' The doctor smiles, and I find it quite chilling. The more he smiles, the worse I feel.

Nick reaches for my hand. 'Are you okay?'

I look at Nick. The drip is back in my arm, and the wound throbs like a bastard. More blood has been taken to be tested. There's a puncture in my neck that might or might not have a totally life-threatening and poisonous substance in it. Strangely, all of that pales into insignificance. *Callum is dead.* It's like I've shed half my body weight of fear and anger. I'm so ephemeral that I could float to the ceiling and just dissipate out the air vents.

'I'm fine,' I say. 'How about you?' Wadding is taped to the side of his face. Being bashed on the head with a vase has left a nasty cut, which they clipped together with butterfly stitches. 'Didn't the doc say you'll have some scars?'

'Oh, I think it'll add to my allure. Make me a man of mystery.' He smiles, but that obviously hurts as he grimaces. 'Anyway, I've still got a way to go to catch up with you.'

It's so different to that last time. His face is still dark shadowed, and his eyes as red, but I hold out my good arm. He sits carefully on the edge of the bed and gently brushes my hair away from my face, and then I pull him to me.

'Ouch,' he says.

I squint closely at him. 'Why have you got a black eye? I don't remember Callum hitting you in the eye.'

'That might be something to do with your stepmom, Margaret hitting me in the face with the butt of her gun. Yesterday seems an awfully long time ago.'

I take a moment to digest this bit of news. Yesterday? 'So "mom" shot me? Not Callum?'

'I'm so sorry to have to say this, but yes, your own beloved mom shot you.'

'She missed.'

'Not really.'

'I stood up just as she fired. She was aiming to kill me. I think I might have pushed her too far.'

'She's in prison in Atlanta. The media's all over this. We've told them that she went mad because her daughter threw back in her family's face all she held dear. She's countered by saying that you're a charlatan who has stolen her daughter's identity.'

'What do they make of that idea?'

'They think she's lost it.'

'You shouldn't have gone after her. She could've shot you too, and not missed. I might be a widow now.' I clear my throat. 'If we'd been married, I mean.'

'The gun has only two cartridges in it. I planned on getting to her before she could reload.'

'What if it had been an assault rifle with the endless capability to shoot you dead?'

'I recognised the sound of it. Cassie Barber, I might be against gun violence, but as I told you, I am still a Southern boy, brought up with all the guns that you were. I mean, Cassie was.' He shakes his head. 'I know what gun that was.'

'Did you also know who was on the end of it?'

'After your meeting with your dad and stepmom, I was aware one of them might flip, though I never for a second thought Margaret would do something like this.'

'What the hell are we going to do about this mess?'

'Say he was a stalker, say you can't remember ever meeting him, but maybe you slighted him or something.'

'They'll identify him, and then that'll link back to England and me. I mean the real me.'

'Not necessarily. If he's come over illegally and they can't find any identification, we might get away with it. If not, we'll hurdle that when we get to it. It's amazing what amnesia might cover. Oh, and moving to Canada.'

'Okay,' I say. 'Or like we said before, we say he murdered Joni and then came across the fact that she had a twin here, in the States. He went berserk and tried to kill me too? We don't have to say that I saw him kill Cassie, I mean Joni, as he's not around to contradict it.'

'It might work, but we need to plan a bit more than that.'

I grimace. 'Let's hope the doc comes back with good news for me.' A wave of nausea washes over me, and I vomit over the bed cover. Oh, this can't be good.

'Doc!' Nick runs from the room, and I hear his voice calling for help from anyone, *anyone, please...*

'Hey,' Nick sits carefully on the bed again.

'Hey yourself.'

'You know,' he says, 'I think we'll have to roll you up in bubble wrap. You can't have that many lives left.'

'Maybe I will get in The Guinness Book of Records. At least

I didn't make the Darwin Awards. I think I made a good run at it, though.'

'You know, if you wrote a book, no one would believe you.'

'If they made the film, I'd like Charlize Theron to play me.'

'And who'd play me?'

'Hmm,' I scratch at my nose. 'Robert Pattinson?'

'Or maybe Scott Eastwood? I like that. Yeah, Scott it is.'

―――――――

The police have interviewed us, and we hopefully managed to match our stories. They gave me a little leeway, as they, and I, have been informed the syringe contained the poison of an Eastern diamondback rattlesnake. I am lucky as they ascertained what it was in time to give me the anti-venom. A few hours longer, and my heart would've failed. Lucky for me, the scaly little devil is a native around here, and they had some anti-venom in cold storage. Any other toxic reptile and I'd be deader than a dodo. How Callum managed to pick some up is incredible. Maybe he wasn't dumber than a dead dog after all.

'Feeling better?' Nick takes hold of my good hand and kisses it. We seem to be able to touch each other a little more.

'I haven't thrown up for a while, but then I can't have anything left to throw up. I must admit, I'm hungry enough to eat a horse.' I stop, and a malicious thought pops into my head. 'I might start with old Caesar.'

'I might join you for that.'

'And the kids? Are they all safe in New York?' I pretend that there's something really interesting to look at in the corner of the room.

'They're outside now. Is it alright to let them in?'

I nod. My eyes are now blurred with tears.

HILLY BARMBY

'I don't know how you feel about this, Cas, but they'd prefer to carry on calling you "mom". If you don't mind, that is?'

The air has disappeared again, and I struggle to pull in some breaths.

The door swishes open, then my nearly-children are in my arms; heads against my all-encompassing motherly breast and my blue gown is wet with their tears.

'This is so fucked up,' says George.

'Right royally fucked up,' says Lucy.

How the world has turned.

THE END

ACKNOWLEDGEMENTS

I would like to thank my publishers, Bloodhound Books and their dedicated team, for believing in me and my work.

So, thanks to Betsy, Fred and Tara, and thanks to my hard-working editor, Caroline, who has steered me straight through choppy waters.

Thanks also to Cornerstones Literary Consultancy, who have critiqued my work and taught me invaluable lessons along the way.

My thanks are extended to Pam Newman, who has read all my work and is perhaps my Number One Fan (but not in an Annie Wilkes sort of way.)

Thanks also to Fi Primarolo for being brave enough to suggest revisions.

Thanks to my partner Malk, who also lives and works in his own box (he's a musician), while I live and work in my own. We meet for coffee in the garden.

And last but by no means least, thanks to my mum and dad (who have now both passed on), as they never wanted me to let go of my dreams and told me to do whatever I wanted with my life. I did, but I wish they were here to see it.

So again, thanks to everyone who has helped me on my journey here.

A NOTE FROM THE PUBLISHER

Thank you for reading this book. If you enjoyed it please do consider leaving a review on Amazon to help others find it too.

We hate typos. All of our books have been rigorously edited and proofread, but sometimes mistakes do slip through. If you have spotted a typo, please do let us know and we can get it amended within hours.

info@bloodhoundbooks.com